STRANGE MUSIC

The Dower House Trilogy by Malcolm Macdonald

THE DOWER HOUSE ★
STRANGE MUSIC ★
PROMISES TO KEEP ★

★ *available from Severn House*

STRANGE MUSIC

Malcolm Macdonald

This first world edition published 2012
in Great Britain and in the USA by
SEVERN HOUSE PUBLISHERS LTD of
9–15 High Street, Sutton, Surrey, England, SM1 1DF.

British Library Cataloguing in Publication Data

Macdonald, Malcolm, 1932–
  Strange music.
  1. Communal living--England--Hertfordshire--Fiction.
  2. Holocaust survivors--Fiction.
  I. Title
  823.9'14-dc23

ISBN-13: 978-0-7278-8129-8 (cased)

All Severn House titles are printed on acid-free paper.

Severn House Publishers support The Forest Stewardship Council [FSC],
the leading international forest certification organisation. All our titles that
are printed on Greenpeace-approved FSC-certified paper carry the FSC logo.

Typeset by Palimpsest Book Production Ltd.,
Falkirk, Stirlingshire, Scotland.
Printed and bound in Great Britain by
MPG Books Ltd., Bodmin, Cornwall.

for Richard
all of whose dials go up to 1011

On truth and memory:

But my dear Bosie, it is so vulgar to remember events exactly as they happened, especially as most of them happen by accident. In recounting them we must often (I would say always and quite literally) *re*-count. You say we were eight on that evening? Yet you can name only six! So of what possible value were Tomniddy and Tomnoddy? Re-*counting*, however, is but the beginning of our enterprise. Your remarks on the sublimity of the brushstrokes in the handkerchief of that Velázquez portrait, delivered that same evening when you were still sober, are not worthy of record when set against your exquisite analysis of the man's countenance – which, alas, you confided to me a full month later (and more than full of that excellent Château d'Yquem). So I shall demote the handkerchief to some other occasion and instead show in my little memoir how you soared like Icarus before he fell. (The presentiment will not be lost upon our readers.)

And thus it shall be with every facet of that memorable evening on the lake in particular and our exquisite lives in general: the dullness of what–actually–happened shall be buffed away to reveal the sublimely glistening jewel of our lives as they *are* (when the pestilential detail that dulls them is no more).

Eric Brandon – private communication dated 30 August 1968 (in a parody of Oscar Wilde)

Who lives where
in April 1949?

A: Head Lad's Cottage: Felix Breit, 37 (German-born leading European sculptor; survivor of Mauthausen concentration camp), Angela, 29 (German-born electronic recording expert with the BBC, survivor of Ravensbrück camp) and newborn daughter Pippin; also Faith Bullen–ffitch, 34 (publishing executive at Manutius Press and Felix's ex-lover). They later buy and convert the Tithe Barn – the ecclesiastical-looking building in the foreground.

B: Tudor-style Victorian annexe: Adam and Sally Wilson (34, 35 – architects and co-founders of the Dower House community; partners of Tony Palmer – below), Theo, 2, and Rachel, <1.

C: Upper floor of genuine Tudor remnant of original manor house: Todd Ferguson (British Rail transport manager) and Gracie (his wife, both in their thirties), Betty, 8, Charley, 5, and Samantha, 1.

D: Main House ground floor front and ground floor of Tudor remnant: Eric Brandon, 25 (children's author), Isabella, 27 (Vogue editor), and Calley, 1.

E: Main House first floor front: Arthur Prentice (BBC TV cameraman), May (his wife, both in their thirties), Sam, 6, Hannah, 4, and Frederick, 1.

F: Entire attic floor: Willard A Johnson, 39 (American-born, high-flying London architect), Marianne, 25 (Swedish-born architect of aristocratic lineage), Siri, 2, and Virgil <1.

G: Ground and first floor back: Tony Palmer, 32 (architect, co-founder of the community and partner of Adam and Sally – above), Nicole, 29, his French-born wife, and Andrew, 2.

H: (In the gate-lodge at the end of the drive – not shown): Terence Lanyon, 34 (economist at LSE), Hilary, 30, his wife, and Maynard, 1.

Monday, 25 April 1949

'Sam! Charley! Get down off that wall!' Angela pegged out the last of the nappies in what had been the wall-fruit garden of the Dower House. 'Not that way!' she added. 'Can't you see all those rusty nails? Go along to the old air-raid shelter and slide down there. If your mothers come out and catch you, I wouldn't like to be in your shoes – which are disgusting, by the way!'

The wall-fruit garden, long since denuded of the cordons and espaliers for which it was named, had been the Dower House community's nappy-drying area since 1948, when Isabella Brandon had complained about nappies being hung on shrubbery and trees all over the garden. The mothers replied that nappies *had* to dry and air in the sun and so eight lines were duly stretched wall-to-wall in the old fruit garden. Isabella conceded with ill grace until, later that year, she gave birth to Calley and then accepted the arrangement gladly. On the first occasion she used her line, Eric hung up a washable condom beside their nappies, with a note: *Useless item going cheap – one penny*.

By April 1949, when Pippin was born to Angela and Felix (the community's first baby to be born under the brand-new National Health Service), they were already calling the collective of children The Tribe, which now numbered fourteen if you included Tommy Marshall, the son of Lena, a local girl who had been left pregnant by a GI who never made it up Omaha Beach; she lived in with the Palmers and helped with the house-keeping. Tommy was going on six.

The Tribe had powers that even Betty Ferguson, the eldest, did not possess on her own. When one of the tyres on the old Armstrong-Siddeley chassis went flat, they stood around in engrossed silence, watching three of the fathers try and fail to dismount the wheel so that it could be brought to the Dormer Green Garage for Jim Churchill to repair. It took The Tribe three days to succeed where the men had failed.

The Tribe was a tidal swarm of children who, on a typical

day, invaded the Johnsons' top-floor apartment for drawing sessions (otherwise called scribbling) on the floor, the coffee table, and Willard's drawing board if he was away at the Curzon Street office . . . then swept onward to the Breits to make sculptures in modelling clay of beasts unidentifiable to adults . . . then descended on the Brandons for dressing-ups and impromptu dramas that involved cowboys, Injuns, South American slave plantations, Flash Gordon, and Tarzan and Jane – all with a fair helping of well-simulated violence . . . and then, with the smallest break for lunch, on to dens in the coppice for stalking polar bears and tigers . . . or – well, you imagine it and they did it.

The Tribe was a self-disciplining boot camp, as their far more liberal parents were amazed to discover. Anyone who got 'out of line,' as Willard put it, would be thrust outside the group, ignored, allowed to share nothing, until the crime was expiated. Children who would howl at the lightest ticking-off from their parents took their punishment from their peers in stoic silence. They knew very well what worked – and what didn't.

'Isn't it the sort of thing we talked about that night we spun off the Autobahn on the way to Bielefeld?' Adam said to Willard one evening in May – the first warm evening of what had been a rather dreary spring.

They had brought out an assortment of war-surplus camp chairs and folding tables and spread them under the weeping ash in the backyard. One by one, as the daytime cowboys and squaws were bathed, powdered, pyjama-ed, read to, sung to, and generally lulled to sleep, half-exhausted parents sauntered out to join the grown-up Tribe – or tribal elders – to rebuild something of their shattered adulthood.

'This isn't that different from America,' Willard replied. 'We were always in and out of everybody's home in a housing lot of – maybe – twenty . . . twenty-five units. Except, I guess . . .'

'Yes?'

'Except people were a whole lot more mobile. By the time I was ten almost all those homes were owned by people who hadn't been there when I was just two. So this is probably better.'

'We won't be able to *afford* to move away from here,' May said, quickly adding, 'even if we wanted to. The rent!'

'The low rent we pay here should help you save the deposit on a house,' Eric pointed out.

'Is that what *you're* doing?' Nicole asked.

'Nope.'

Sally turned to Willard. 'So you couldn't really have formed a Tribe in America – not like our children. I mean, it wouldn't have had the sort of permanence our kids have.'

'*Beh-eh-eh-eh* . . .' Eric bleated.

Sally rounded on him. 'I say *kids*, OK? My father said *kiddiwinks* and I say *kids*.'

Isabella, who had the same aversion to *kids* as Eric, was annoyed at being unable to take a contrary viewpoint, so instead she observed, 'That wasn't anything *like* a goat.'

'I was imitating a rare breed of Swiss mountain goat,' he explained. '*Ibex helvetica*. Found only in Calabria.'

'Calabria is not in Switzerland.'

'Bloody biologists, eh!' he said.

'Eric!' Marianne snapped.

'Sorry. Someone – I feel sure – was about to make the point that having to discipline our two-year-olds makes even our four- and five-year-olds more responsible than is usual for *children* of that age. But it's amazing how they forget it all as soon as the younger ones go in for their nap.'

'How would *you* know when they're taking a nap?' Isabella asked.

'Because that's when Sam and Charley start running races along the tops of the walled-garden walls, which they never do if the younger ones are around.'

'Can we forget the children for an hour or two?' Gracie asked wearily.

'Don't you care if Charley falls and breaks his neck?' May asked (thinking only of Sam, of course).

'Charley has fallen out of every tree for miles around. Listen, I don't like pulling rank here—'

'But someone has to,' Eric assured her.

'Quite! With the first child you worry if they stop breathing for more than five seconds. With the second you worry if the crying goes on for more than . . . two minutes. With the third one you only *start* to worry if you notice that bits of it are missing.'

Felix joined them, having followed the conversation through his open studio window. 'If we're into grown-up talk, then,' he said, 'I wanted to let people know that the Baker Street Classic is holding late-night showings of *Ehe im Schatten* – Marriage in the Shadows. It's a really good post-war German film based on the life of the actor Joachim Gottschalk and his wife, Meta Wolff, who was Jewish.'

'We saw it at the BBC staff film club,' Angela added. 'If people want to go up to town, they'll miss the last train but they're welcome to stay at our place in Robert Street. And we can babysit for them here. Dilys Powell said it's the best flick on in London at the moment.'

There were no takers.

'Willard?' Marianne said.

He pulled a face. 'What is it about? Persecution . . . concentration camps . . . death?'

'It's persecution,' Felix agreed, 'but that's not what follows. I won't tell you how it ends.'

'Not on a yellow-brick road,' Eric put in. 'Please not that! Once is enough.'

Still Willard was reluctant. 'It's not as if we don't *know* what happened back then. Some of us were in at the . . . I mean, we were there when it all got opened up.' He turned to Eric. 'Some of us.'

'Oh, I go there in my dreams,' Eric assured him. 'And where are *you* then, Willard? Just when I need you?'

Willard tried not to laugh.

'I think I would like to go,' Marianne said. 'Nicole?'

'Yes!' She looked defiantly at Tony and added, 'I can also get that Sanderson's wallpaper at Heal's.'

Tony raised both hands in surrender and said, 'Georgian stripes!'

Isabella told him that would be very fashionable, to which he answered, 'Quite! It's also about ten times more expensive than Walpamur.'

Above their heads, unnoticed in her bedroom window, Betty Ferguson watched and listened through the half-open sash. She didn't always understand what they said but she had a better grasp of why they said it. Marianne was often alone because Willard was always practising. All architects spend their days *practising* architecture. But Willard was also practising to fly with his architecture – and to fly very high. He usually spent his days flying high over London but he never brought his aeroplane to Panshanger airfield, where lots of local flyers had aircraft. They would often fly over the Dower House, especially in summer, when they flew very low, because Marianne liked to sunbathe without clothes on, up there on their little balcony at the top of the bow windows on the south side of the house, above the memorial to 'Winnie a Faithful Dog.' Swedish people like her lived where there was no sun for half the year so they needed to soak it in when they could – all over their bodies, so it wasn't sinful for them. But Willard got angry and took the Atco out onto the big lawn and cut a naughty message into the grass, starting with F and ending with OFF, but they paid no attention. So that must be why he never flew his aeroplane to Panshanger. And Mum said if that sort of behaviour continued, they'd leave the community and find somewhere to live in Dormer Green because the school was excellent. (If she meant it seriously, then someone ought to tell her that lots of children there used that word so there would be no point.) Anyway, Marianne wished Willard would spend more time practising at home and less flying high in London. Luckily she herself could still do lots of practising architecture here at the Dower House.

All the other children called their parents by their Christian names because it was no good standing howling in the yard and calling out 'Mummy!' because all eight mummies would leave it to the other seven to go first. All the children at school thought it sounded very naughty and it made them giggle but it was amazing how normal it seemed inside the community. And after all Sally was Sally and Nicole was Nicole years before they became 'Mummy.'

Nicole's baby, Andrew, was looked after by Lena-such-a-sad-case. Her son Tommy got left with her by a GI who was killed in France. He was born on 1 April 1944 and Lena said he was her April Fool's joke. Mummy wasn't really happy with that situation, either. Nor with Felix, who was married to Angela but also lived with Faith. Daddy said Faith was just a lodger and it was perfectly all right and anyway she lived in the annexe to Angela's cottage. Mummy said it stopped being the annexe the moment they knocked a doorway through the dividing wall.

Faith came out of her annexe at that moment and entered the backyard, stretching and rubbing her eyes with the knuckles of her left hand. 'Finished,' she said, handing a proof copy of a book to Angela. 'God, but it's bleak.' She turned to Nicole. 'You're going to hate it. I don't see how anyone can have a shred of belief left in communism after this.'

Communism was what Daddy had believed in once – all about having libraries and parks and schools and doctors for everyone, without needing to pay.

'When's it out?' Willard asked. 'Put me down for half a dozen, if it's that good.'

'Next month. We're not doing it. We don't handle fiction. I got it from a friend at Secker. Orwell had better watch his back. That's all I can say.'

Betty, who heard 'wash his back,' realized this was one of those moments when the grown-up world dissolved into utter incomprehensibility. And it was quite late. And she had sixty hooks and tails to do for her writing homework . . . and . . . *yawn* . . . She left the outside world to its own enigmas.

'Willard!' Adam walked out from his and Sally's wing of the house. 'Is it true?'

'Is what true?'

'You got part of the Festival carve-up?'

Willard levelled a finger at him. 'Stop right there! If you value your life, stop right there.'

Tony laughed. 'So it is true!'

'You'd have done the same. Don't say you wouldn't.'

'What . . . what?' came from several directions.

Reluctantly Willard obliged, after saying, 'I'll get you for this. OK, what happened was I put in for some design work on this Festival of Britain extravaganza that—'

'Your Tory friends won't like that!' Nicole taunted.

'They'll understand when they hear the full of it. I didn't expect to make it at all – now it can be revealed. So I was very happy to meet with the Disbursements Panel yesterday, even though I was last on the list. So I go in, and they're all grinning their heads off – which should have alerted me, I allow – and

they say, "Sorry, old bean, but there's only the public lavatories
left." So I turn on my heel – without a word – and head for
the door. And I've just got my hand on the door handle when
Basil Spence calls out, "It's worth nearly a quarter of a million,
Willard!" And this is me.' He already had his hand on the
imaginary door handle so he dropped it as if poleaxed. Ditto
his jaw. He spun about and sought wildly for something to
steady himself upon, saying, 'Did someone say a quarter-million
or was that my greed and wounded pride talking? And then
Gerald Barry chuckled, like he does, and said, "Pull up a pew
and let's go through it." And here I am.' He bowed with a
Georgian flourish. 'Purveyor of one-, two-, and three-holers
– what am I saying? Purveyor of ten-, twenty-, and *thirty*-holers
to the Festival of Britain – if it ever comes to pass, that is.'

Everybody laughed – except Marianne. Felix was watching
her and saw that this news was news to her, too. She caught
his eye and grimaced.

After that, people broke into smaller groups, some remaining
beneath the ash, others wandering among the beds of newly
planted shrubs and perennials.

Angela put her proof copy onto the umbrella stand just
inside the cottage door and walked off arm-in-arm with Nicole.
'Good news today,' she said. 'One more has gone – Erich
Neumann, you remember? Goering's little darling who wanted
his skilled Jews to be spared until they'd finished work on the
V-rockets? He's been held by the British since 'forty-five but
they let him go last month because of ill-health and I've just
heard he's died.'

'So that's Heydrich, Kritzinger, Freisler, Luther, Meyer,
Bühler, Schöngarth, Lange – and now Neumann!' Nicole did
a little victory dance on the spot. 'Nine.'

'Nine down. Six to go.'

Marianne, seeing them wander off up the short drive, was
about to join them when Felix took her arm. 'She's breaking
the good news that Neumann has died.'

'When?'

'I don't know. Very recently.'

'So they're still keeping count.'

'Angela has the benefit of friends in the World Service and
the monitoring units.'

'The full horror of the *Vernichtung,*' Marianne said, 'has hardly even begun to penetrate in Britain. Yet.'

'Well, the country's been very good to us.'

'I know. I know. I'm not really grumbling.'

'Not about the *British,* anyway!'

'Right!' She leaned her head briefly on his shoulder. 'Why is he so secretive? I *knew* he was in for a piece of the Festival cake. He told me. Does he think I'm not all that concerned? It baffles me, honestly.' After a pause, she added, 'And you can bet your bottom dollar *I'm* going to be doing half the bloody drawings. He's not going to let this little bit of socialist mega-lomania – as he sees it – stand in the way of the latest Willard Johnson multi-storey! Oh, let's talk about something else. Dying Nazis and Willard's wheels-within-wheels are enough for one fucking day.'

Felix turned sharply round to glance behind them.

'What?' she asked.

'Gracie Ferguson. It's all right. She can't have heard. She thinks our language and our morals are not quite *comme-il-faut.*'

'And who's *she*? Her father had a market stall somewhere down in Whitechapel. I ask you!'

Felix laughed. 'You're getting more English than the English.'

'If she doesn't like our ways, she can go. I don't see why *we* should change . . . and look over our shoulders all the time. Anyway, she'd wreck young Betty's life if they upped sticks and went – she's the tribal matriarch.'

'W-e-l-l—'

'Well what?'

'Someone said – back there round the tree – they couldn't afford to leave, and—'

'May. She said that.'

'That's right. Anyway, I was watching Gracie and she had a very superior smile – a smirk, in fact – on her face, so I'm sure—'

'How could you see that from such a distance?'

'With binoculars. I stand back in the room and watch through binoculars. Often. You see people's faces large but with the simplification of distance. I do lots of drawings that way . . .' Her horrified stare halted him. 'So if you were plot-ting a murder,' he concluded, 'do it round the south side of the house.'

She laughed awkwardly. 'It's not *that* bad between Willard and me.'

And that perturbed him, for he had meant it as a fantasy with no actual reference to the real Marianne and the real Willard.

Wednesday, 8 June 1949

As yet only four children attended the local school in Dormer Green – Betty, Charley, Sam, and Tommy, son of Lena-such-a-sad-case. Their way led down through the coppice and up across the fields, emerging onto the road at the edge of the village – the only bit of highway straight enough for their parents to feel comfortable about letting them walk on tarmacadam. The rest of it, having been designed when 'the rolling English drunkard made the rolling English road,' was far too dangerous for pedestrians, even though only one or two vehicles would use it during the average daytime hour. Sooner or later a child would be turning the wrong corner at the *wrong* hour. So, rain or shine, they put on their wellies and oilskins or carried them in bags, and set off before eight thirty for a long mile across the fields.

Usually their mothers, Lena, Gracie Ferguson and May Prentice, took it in turn to accompany them there in the morning and bring them home each weekday afternoon; occasionally one of the other elders – needing something from the shops, taking something to the post, or simply in want of an hour in the fresh air – would give them a break. On this particular morning Gracie had already set off and was just past the deserted pigsties when Eric caught up with her and offered to take over. 'Absolute disaster at Brandon Towers,' he explained breathlessly. 'We ran out of fags.'

'But you don't smoke,' Gracie pointed out.

'Not actively, no, but the light of my life and captain of my soul makes sure I get my share. So you're relieved.'

'Not really. Go on you lot – we'll catch you up. I feel the need of a little walk myself. We can go together.'

'I wish I could have walked to school like this every day,' Eric said as they set off in pursuit of the children. 'A coppice is such a strange form of woodland, don't you think? Not a tree trunk in sight – just half-a-dozen saplings on each single root. You expect the rabbits to have multiple legs and the birds to have four sets of wings to match.'

'You would in one of *your* books,' Gracie agreed – and then giggled. 'Betty loves *The Chocolate Soldier*. I thought he was going to escape by melting . . . but making the warder *eat* him and then him turning into the warder. Oh, my!' She shook her head and then added morosely: 'Me, I grew up in Whitechapel. My school was just two streets away. I was always late.'

'I lived in a village so I trudged along high-walled lanes through a mixture of modern suburban and medieval and all very discreet and withdrawn. There were monsters and monstrous delights concealed behind every wall and hedge.'

'Such as?'

'Oh . . . gryphons and wyverns and manticoras . . . and . . . nudist camps. We must have had at least thirty nudist camps in one street alone, with hedges that would stop a bullet.'

'Boys! Is Charley already imagining things like that?' She raised her voice. 'Charley! Sam! Not that way today. They haven't put a new log over the ditch yet. We'll go the old way.'

'We can jump!' Charley shouted.

And jump he did – as a pheasant took to flight right beside him – but not over the waterlogged ditch.

'It wasn't prurience,' Eric went on as the two boys turned disconsolately toward the old crossing point. 'It was fascination with the grotesque. Like the church organist, whom my father called Praisegod Barebones because even on a good day he looked like those people in Belsen . . . we thought if he was stark naked, it would be a sight worth fighting through an acre of thorns to see.'

'Were you at the liberation of Belsen – like Arthur?' Gracie asked. 'In fact, I've often wondered – what did you do in the war? I can't imagine you as a typical Poor Bloody Infantryman. Pardon my French.'

'I was only fifteen when the war began, and I stayed on at school to take distinction papers, so I didn't join until just after D-Day. They put me in the Intelligence Corps. I had what they call "a bloody good war." You?'

'Todd and I got married in 'thirty-eight, just after I turned twenty-one. I was a dispatcher in the fire service. I should've lost the job then because that was the rule: get a husband, get the sack. But everyone knew the war was coming, so they let me stay on. And I still did it part-time even after Betty came along. Betty!' she called out. 'Help Sam, there's a duck.' She grinned at Eric. 'He's never yet made it all the way to school without his shoelaces coming undone.'

Until recently, Eric, being still in his twenties, had considered women in their thirties to belong to his mother's generation – not exactly out of bounds but more useful as people to talk with rather than as girls to pursue. But now, looking dispassionately at Gracie, with her clear skin, bright eyes, warm smile, and lustrous hair, he began to feel that he had, perhaps, been a mite *too* discriminating. Not that he would *do* anything about it, but to live in a world peopled by many more attractive females than he had been aware of before now . . . well, it could only be an enhancement.

However, that was a distraction from his main purpose in joining Gracie on the school walk on this particular morning. Time to get down to it. 'In five years from now,' he said, 'there'll be fourteen taking this path to school. And that's not counting the ones not yet born. Could be sixteen . . . eighteen. One parent isn't going to manage that.'

Gracie remained silent, as he thought she might.

'Not even a mother with all the experience *you'll* have by then,' he added, not taking his eyes off her.

She stopped dead and stared at him, a baffled smile on her lips. She knew what he was getting at. 'You take the biscuit, Eric, honestly you do. I don't believe Isabella's out of fags at all. I've half a mind to go back and ask her; leave you to take them up the field.'

'I only lied slightly. She *will* have run out by midday.'

'Come on,' she said wearily, pushing him ahead of her. 'You might as well tell me what's on your mind now, because I'll badger it out of you by the time we get to the school. Who told you? Or how did you find out?'

'I don't know what you're on about.' He grinned.

'Did Betty say anything? I'll kill her if she did.'

Eric gave in with a sigh. 'You dropped a piece of paper the

other day. With a phone number. I rang them. I wasn't expecting
it to be an estate agent so I had to pretend I was looking for a
property in Dormer Green. And it turns out there's only one
house there with that estate agent's *For Sale* sign outside. Are
you really thinking of leaving the community?'

'We'll talk about it on the way back. Betty's already overheard
more than she should.'

They left the children at the school gate and went next door
to the village shop, where Gracie bought a jar of Virol and Eric
chose a packet of Capstan Full Strength.

'Is that what Isabella is smoking these days?' Gracie asked. 'I
thought she was on Balkan Sobranie. Her and Faith.'

'It's what she's going to be smoking these *next few* days,
anyway,' he replied.

'They're lethal. She won't thank you.'

'Oh, that'll make a change!' He laughed. 'I'll tell her that's
all they had.'

They flattened themselves against the hedge to let a tractor
and trailer-load of dung go by. Gracie fanned her nose in distaste.

'He takes a load through the village every day,' Eric warned.
'Including Sundays. Are you still thinking of moving?'

She sighed. 'It's not that we're unhappy at the Dower House.
But that lovely little cottage, right on the green – it's only five
hundred and fifty quid and we could put twenty per cent down
and get tax relief on the mortgage, and all that. We're accumu-
lating nothing at the Dower House, but bricks and mortar is
bricks and mortar.'

'Or wattle and daub in your case.'

'Go on, it's not that old.' After a pause she added, 'Is it?'

'Get Tony or Adam to do a survey. Or they'd know someone
who would.'

'Then the cat *would* be out of the bag.'

'It's probably out anyway, bonny lass. Someone in Dormer
Green will have seen you going in there. They'll remark on it
to someone who'll pass it on to someone else . . . and pretty
soon it'll be blurted out to one of us.'

She slumped and slowed to a snail's pace. 'We should tell
everyone, I suppose.'

He gave her arm a squeeze. 'It's not a confession, pet. Adam
is the most evangelical. He'll probably be disappointed, but the

rest of us will understand. And I'm sure you won't be the only family to leave, as the years go by.'

'Thanks.' She brightened up. 'And I'm grateful, even though I suspect this cigarettes-for-Isabella story was just a ruse to . . . to—'

'Help you face facts. You joined us. You liked us – still do, I hope. We liked you – still do, I know. You want to move on . . . place of your own. What's wrong with that?'

She almost shed a tear but, with one good blow of her nose, avoided it.

They walked on down the hill, keeping to the hedge, in an easy silence. After a while Gracie said, 'You know you mentioned Belsen back there – is that where Felix was? I often wanted to ask but you don't like to, do you. He did once say he was in a Car Elle. But I didn't know then that was German for concentration camp.'

'*Koncentrations* . . . *lager*. Kay . . . el to us, *ka* . . . *el* to them. I don't think he'd mind. He neither hides it nor wears it on his sleeve. Though, come to think of it, he does wear it *under* his sleeve. Amazing, really. He wasn't in Belsen but another one – there were more than a thousand of those camps, you know. He was in one in Austria called Mauthausen. You know he met Tony and Adam and Willard there on the day it was liberated?'

'Yeah. That's what Tony told Todd. Hard to credit. And here we all are!'

'Here we all are, pet! Angela was another concentration camp victim – I suppose you know that, too?'

'Is that where they met? There was an Eyetie prisoner of war camp over Wheathamstead way. They used to go out with lots of local girls – after Italy surrendered and they opened the camps and let the Eyeties out to work. Some of them got married and settled here.'

'No, Felix met Angela over here, in London, after the war – just a month or two before you first came here. Funny, isn't it, how we all live in the same house – except Felix and Angela – and Faith – and they're only just ten steps away across the yard – and yet there's so much we don't know about one another. I don't really think this is an experiment in communal living at all. We're just flat dwellers who share a garden and three electricity meters. Do you think we'll ever sort that out?'

'Communal meetings!' she said. 'That's one thing I *won't* miss.' After a pause she asked, 'Are you really going to make poor Isabella smoke those awful cigarettes? Don't take offence now but I can't make you two out at all, and I hear more of you than most – mainly through our lounge floor.'

'Isabella is very good in bed, you know.'

She gave a little gasp and turned away. 'That's not . . . I wasn't . . . All right, I give up.'

'If we didn't keep repelling each other verbally, she and I, we'd be at it like rabbits. When people say it takes all sorts to make a world, it's Isabella and me they have in mind. Usually without knowing it.'

By now they were back in the coppice. Halfway up the rise, leading to the pigsties, he stopped. 'When we were just here – on our way up to the school – you asked me if Betty had told me anything about your moving on. In fact, she did, but entirely without knowing it. I was looking out of my study window one evening last week, about the time when The Tribe was being called in for tea or bath time et cetera, and they all went running indoors – all except Betty. She just stood there, watching all the others vanishing indoors. You had to call her twice.'

'Oh yes, I remember that.'

'Well, did you see the look on her face?'

'No. I mean, what look?'

'As soon as I saw it I thought, *I know that look. Where have I seen it before?* And then it came back to me. Remember I said I had a bloody good war? Well, I wasn't the only one. But I didn't mind it coming to an end. I knew I was returning to something exciting – the publication of my first book and my first step toward becoming the Grand Old Man of English Literature. But for most of them the outlook was pretty bleak. Paradise Lost. They wanted the comradeship and irresponsibility of military life to go on. It had a lot in common with the life of the Dower House Tribe. But one by one their demob papers came through – and *that's* when I saw that same look in their eyes.'

Saturday, 20 August 1949

Tony checked himself in the hall mirror just as they were about to leave. 'Maybe I should wear a tie?' he murmured.

'Did Adam say to wear a tie?' Nicole asked.

'No.'

'Then don't bother. Did you get the wine from our cellar?'

He lifted it out of the umbrella stand. '*Château Curé Bon la Madeleine*. We must bring back more of this next year.'

Lena-such-a-sad-case came out of their kitchen. 'Enjoy the meal,' she said.

'I doubt it,' Tony replied. 'You've not yet had the pleasure of Sally's cooking. Don't wait up. And' – he turned on Fifi and Xupé, their two dogs – 'you behave yourselves!'

It was one of those summer evenings when the overcast sky is so low and the air so warm and still that 'outdoors' feels more like a large room than truly open air. 'I was picking up lightning flashes on long wave,' he said as they crossed the brief expanse of lawn that separated them from the Wilsons.

Just as Adam – wearing a tie – opened the door to them they heard the first distant rumble of thunder. 'Did Bob solder the strap of the lightning conductor back on that rod?' he asked them.

Tony replied: 'He said he did but I haven't had time to check yet. Oh, hang on, I forgot something.'

He ran back and put on a tie but when he returned to the Wilsons he found that Adam had removed his. 'It's too muggy tonight,' he said. 'Take off your jacket, too.' He handed Tony a tankard of McMullen's, the local brew.

Sally joined them, dressed with casual elegance – a New Look dress, made from a Liberty print, and a stole to match. 'Gee and tee for me,' she said. And then, seeing Nicole's surprise, added, 'You'll be delighted to hear I've hired two students from the catering course at Hatfield to manage tonight's meal. We have much to discuss.'

'We do?' Tony asked.

Sally turned to her husband. 'You haven't told them?'

'I was waiting for you. But in any case, I think we should eat first and get down to it over coffee.'

Tony smiled. 'I think I know what it's about, anyway. I was going to bring it up if you didn't.'

Adam frowned. 'Has Willard been speaking to you?'

'No. Gracie told me herself.'

'Gracie? What—?'

'The Fergusons are going to buy that cottage on the green in Dormer Green. Isn't that what you want to discuss – who's going to get their flat here?'

Adam sat down, stunned, then stood again, realizing he had poured only half his wife's cocktail. 'I've heard nothing of this.'

'I thought we might ask Chris Riley-Potter. He'll get his Slade diploma this summer and will be looking for somewhere cheap. The Fergusons want to stay on until Michaelmas.'

'But what's wrong . . . I mean . . . Good Lord – the *Fergusons*? Have they fallen out with anyone? Can't we persuade them to think again?'

Sally almost had to prise the glass from his fingers. There was a distant flash of lightning, somewhere above the clouds. Automatically she began counting the seconds.

'They've put down the deposit,' Nicole said.

'I think Chris would fit in very well here,' Tony added.

'Did you know about this, Sally?' Adam asked.

'. . . eight, nine, ten.' There was a barely perceptible rumble of thunder. 'Two miles,' she said. 'No, I didn't know – though it explains why Betty has been a bit mopey lately.'

'Dormer Green's not that far off,' Tony said. 'Surely she can come back and play whenever she wants?'

Nicole and Sally exchanged glances, each thinking what the other was thinking.

'Gracie,' Nicole said.

'She thinks our language and our manners are just a little too free,' Sally explained. 'Eric says the Fergusons are working class on their way up *to* respectability and we are middle class on our way down *from* it.'

'Well!' Adam sat down heavily. 'It's a bit of a blow, all right.'

Nicole said, 'I think it will be wrong if everybody in the first wave should stay. It would mean we are . . . *amorphe*.'

'Amorphous,' Tony said. 'Yes, we stand for something and if the Fergusons feel they can't join in wholeheartedly . . . well then, it's best to part amicably. So what about Chris Riley-Potter? He'd certainly be right with us from day one.'

Sally said she didn't know him.

'You do,' Tony assured her. 'He was the bloke who climbed up the copper beech at last year's midsummer party and sang . . . well, yes, Gracie Ferguson certainly wouldn't have liked *that* song!'

'As long as he doesn't complain incessantly about the smell of onions from our kitchen,' Sally said.

One of the catering students came in and laid the table in the dining end of the room, which was large enough to serve as a sitting room, too. 'This is a smashing place,' she said cheerily. 'They should do this with all these big country houses. Kick Lord Salisbury out of Hatfield House and let us students move in. He could have my place. I call it a *place* − it's a rat-hole.'

'How's the meal coming on?' Sally asked.

'Pretty good. You must have been saving up ration points for weeks. You all going to drink wine, are you? The white and the red? Only we'll have to wash up the glasses in between − there's only six.'

'Don't you know there's a war on?' Sally asked.

'Yeah − it still feels like that sometimes, dunnit!' She raised her eyes to the ceiling.

There was another, slightly less remote flash of lightning; this time Sally counted to seven.

Nicole said, 'Willard has started on designs for the Festival *pissoirs*. But it's a joke from the RIBA, no? And from all those left-wing people in power who he has insulted? Can't he see that?'

Sally replied, 'I don't think an American *could* see it. Too understated.'

'Too subtle,' Adam said.

'No. I mean understated. Americans can be subtle, too, but in a different way.'

'He's going about telling everyone who mentions it that they're going to be "the best goddam brick shithouses in the world." Subtle, huh?'

'That's not fair. Americans are *never* subtle about their own careers or achievements. You can't expect it of Willard.'

'Any Englishman who got given that contract,' Tony put in, 'would have gone about saying something like, "At least they knew what I'm good for – *and* they gave me the chance to show it." *That's* subtle.'

Nicole stage-whispered to Sally, 'If that's subtle, I can play, too.' Then, raising her voice: 'Englishmen *are* marvellous.'

When the meal petered out in port and cigars, or Gaulloises for Sally and Nicole, Adam said, 'Well, it's pretty obvious we didn't invite you to dinner to discuss a replacement for the Fergusons. In fact—'

'You will think about Chris Riley-Potter?' Tony urged.

'I said I would. But what do you think about this? The "inspiration phase" part of the Greater London Plan is over. The strategy is complete, and you and I have had a hell of a time working on it. But now it's pretty obvious – to me at any rate, and to Sally – that the implementation calls for a different kind of architect. Men like Wally Edwards, Jim Partridge, Harry Doyle. We did all that in AMGOT, and bloody good fun it was, too. But I don't want to go back to that. And Hull has turned down the Abercrombie-Lutyens plan. And we all agree that Plymouth is going to be abso-bloody-lutely awful—'

'Well, you surely don't want to follow Willard?' Tony asked. 'I know he's transforming parts of London, but—'

'No! I'm glad you mentioned Willard and the work he's turning out because that's exactly what I don't want to do—'

'And exactly what *I* don't want to do, either,' Sally put in. 'Even though Willard was right – damn him – about the Greater London Plan.'

'What?' Tony and Adam were in scandalized unison.

'Well, he was! Commerce has beaten the bureaucrats hands down. Willard's tower blocks are the proletariat's homes for the foreseeable future. The Churchill Gardens Estate is the only bit of Abercrombie that will ever be built.'

'Leave that aside,' Adam said impatiently. 'Let's talk about *us*. What *we* want to do – Sally and me – is the sort of architecture we thought we were going to do when we started our studies at the Bartlett before the war: individual houses for individual clients . . . a small estate for the local council or a private builder . . . half-a-dozen houses in a landscape . . . a sensitive extension to a period house . . . that sort of thing. We'll never be millionaires but we'll never be poor, either.'

'So we wondered if you'd like to join us,' Sally concluded. 'Both of you.'

'*Moi?*' Nicole exclaimed.

'We will need an office manager – someone to look after the correspondence, keep the day-to-day accounts, answer the tele-phone, organize the diary, remind people of deadlines well in advance . . . a myriad things. We'd split the profits equally – four ways, and we'd need to—'

'Two ways, surely?' Adam said.

'Four ways,' Sally insisted. 'And we'd need to be sure we could survive six months with very little coming in. Preferably nine months.'

'You needn't answer now. Talk it over and let us know what you think of the idea. Or are you absolutely set against it now in principle?'

'No!' the Palmers answered in unison.

Out in the grounds a streak of lightning struck the copper beech; the following morning they found its bark all peeled into strips and laid out around it like the spokes of a wheel.

Thursday, 27 October 1949

When Felix arrived in London, penniless, in 1947, it was Wolf Fogel, boss of the Manutius Press, who had thrown him the first lifeline – a consultancy on a series of books on modern art. It included a commission to provide a sculpture to be photographed in different ways as an introductory image to each section in each book. Felix started with an egg, only partly carved out of its marble, but in each subsequent book and section a fraction more of the egg was liberated. In its final appearance at the end of the last volume it would be smashed to bits, as if to say 'Art is now free and mature' (though, in fact, this was

Felix's way of preventing Fogel from acquiring a valuable Felix Breit sculpture for peanuts).

One day, when the final volume was in production, he called on the Manutius series editor, Peter Murdoch, dropped a portfolio on the man's desk and tweaked one of the ribbons. 'Have a gander at this,' he said. 'A slight change of plan.'

Murdoch tweaked the other two ribbons and opened the covers. 'Slight?' he cried.

Felix explained: 'It always worried me that we just smashed the egg and found that it contained nothing . . . as if the egg were some kind of climax in its own right. When we started out it was meant to symbolize the art *process* not art itself. But that's how critics and reviewers have interpreted it in the earlier volumes.'

'But . . . *this!*' Murdoch gestured at the sketches. 'These . . . *things* . . . what are they?'

'Grotesques . . . chimeras . . . a Dipsas, a Manticora, a Wyvern, a Simurgh . . .'

Murdoch gave a baffled laugh. 'Where do you dig up stuff like this?'

'Not me, actually. A bloke who lives at the Dower House – Eric Brandon. He's persuaded me that from this generation onward all pictorial art will be pastiche . . . *can only be* pastiche.'

'Then he's mad.'

'Think about it. What is Sutherland doing that Bacon hasn't already done? What is Bacon doing that Sutherland hasn't done? Or Colquhoun and MacBride? What's Ruskin-Spear doing that Sickert didn't? Isn't Ben Nicholson just painting tasteful variations of Léger? And Barbara is surely just giving us a native version of Arp and Brancusi. That's the whole point. The work we've been covering in these six volumes was the last great explosion of revolutionary originality in the visual arts.'

'And you?'

'I'm not doing anything that Epstein didn't. Or Gill. And even they hardly pushed the boundaries beyond Rodin and Maillol.'

Murdoch scratched his head. 'There has to be the possibility of further revolution. A genius – another Picasso – will arise. Maybe he's leaving the Royal College this summer. He'll break out of the pastiche straitjacket and show us whole new worlds to explore.'

Felix sat down and played the ace. 'So we delay publication until then?'

'Christ, no! We just assume it will happen because it always has happened. Raphael and Leonardo take art up to the heights of the sublime – and then along comes Caravaggio and El Greco. Ingres and Leighton push realism as far as it will go and – hey presto! Along come Cézanne and Monet.'

'But you're making *my* point. There have now been so many reactions and revolutions that everything an artist can possibly do has been done. There's a painter – so-called – in America, born in the same year as me, 1912, and he has given up any attempt to *paint* his pictures. Instead he buys cans of liquid paint and pops a hole in the bottom and swings can after can back and forth over his canvases, which he lays on the studio floor. And he lets them dry and he sells them as "paintings!" Really they're just a record of the conspiracy between gravity and the laws of reciprocal motion. If *that's* the sort of genius you think is going to come up with the next great revolution, then I believe that my grotesques being hatched out of our shattered egg are very appropriate – no?' After a pause he added, 'Shall we just run this past Fogel?'

Faith, Fogel's right hand (and Felix's first lover in England, before he had met and married Angela) breezed in at that moment. 'How's it going? What d'you think, Peter?'

'You know all about this idea?'

'Hasn't anyone told you? I used to be Felix's bit of stuff. Now I'm just his lodger, and the drone from him and Eric Brandon – despite being muffled by two stout walls – has been lulling me to sleep for weeks.'

Murdoch hid his embarrassment well. 'So you disagree?'

'No! I happen to agree, but isn't that slightly beside the point?'

'How?'

'It'll certainly set the cat among the pigeons – accusing all the London galleries and dealers of handling nothing but pastiche . . . telling William Corvo and Grigson and Herbert Read and all the other scribblers that they're wasting their sensibilities on second-hand goods. It'll be a scandal – and I never yet heard of a book whose sales weren't helped along by a whiff of scandal.'

Murdoch's face was a study. He was at heart a lover of the arts, especially of painting and sculpture; and he was an ardent admirer of Felix, especially of the commissions the man had carried out since settling in England, for it seemed to him that Breit was at last able to work at his full potential. In just three years he had fulfilled half-a-dozen public commissions on a monumental scale and several more modestly proportioned works for private clients. So how could he claim that *everything,* including what he himself was doing, was nothing but pastiche? Or, at best, homage to some past genius?

But he didn't want to put that question directly to Felix because he suspected the man had an unpalatable answer. He was, however, a commercial publisher, too. He knew what sells well and what gets remaindered. And Faith was right. 'I suppose we leave it to Fogel to decide, then,' he said wearily.

'Fogel will accept whatever Felix wants,' Faith said. 'Partly because it will create a scandal, which will be good. But mainly because' – she turned to Felix – 'he wants you to be the overall design consultant on a new series of books he's planning with Julian Huxley and James Fisher. That's what I—'

'How long have you known this?' Felix asked.

She grinned and levelled a finger at him. 'You see! If you hadn't married that woman – if my head and yours still lay on the same soft pillow – you'd learn all these things a lot earlier.'

Felix laughed. 'If I hadn't married "that woman," you'd have no one to—'

Her eyes flashed alarms as she thought he might be about to give away her ambitions toward television.

'. . . look after your horse when you and Fogel go across the channel to bamboozle Larousse and Hachette and Ullstein into parting with their shekels.'

'Well, that's getting harder than ever now they've withdrawn the foreign travel allowance yet again. Did you read about that poor Englishman who had to sell his silk shirts in Zurich because none of the banks would touch his sterling? Anyway, I came in here to say Fogel wants to take you to lunch at the White Tower. Both of you.'

The White Tower menu was so mouth-watering they had a hard time ordering a meal totalling less than five shillings a head, above which price they would have been obliged to surrender ration coupons. Despite these limitations there was hardly an empty table in the room; here you could believe that Austerity was being challenged not just in sybaritic meals at less than five bob a head but in the plans being discussed, the intelligence being exchanged, the deals being hammered out while the food and wine went down.

'The biggest gap in the market now,' Fogel said, 'is in learning books for children. We have van Loon – *The Story of Man* . . . Arthur Mee . . . such things. But all pre-war. And they *look* pre-war, too. Black and white, cheap gravure. It's a big chance for Manutius – the way we can do things.'

'What particular subjects?' Felix asked.

'All the experiences we had in the war – making informations easy to grasp. Using colour logically, not just for prettiness. Integrating pictures and diagrams into the same page with the text. Dividing the total subject into smaller units and making each one into a self-contained two-page spread. All this we now can use in information books for young people.'

'What sort of age range?' Felix tried to ask.

'And Huxley and Fisher will see all the texts so we can put their names on the jacket – *Under the editorial supervision of Julian Huxley and James Fisher*. It's good, yes?'

'I saw T. S. Eliot on the Tube this morning,' Felix said. 'Nobody recognized him – or, if they did, they gave no sign of it. Like me. But I thought if you saw Sartre or Camus on the Métro, people would crowd round . . . talk to him . . . argue. So maybe you're just importing European attitudes to celebrity and assuming they work in England?'

Fogel stared at him, young eyes in an old face. 'Ask Murdoch.'

'It's excellent, Fogel,' Murdoch said. 'We may not pester celebrities on the Tube but we'll buy the books they recommend. However, I presume they're just lending their names and making the odd comment?'

'Certainly not supplying actual text,' Faith put in. 'And text is our bottleneck right now.'

'Is there nobody in-house?' Felix asked.

Fogel shook his head. 'I want new ideas. Everybody is . . .' Lacking the precise words he put up his hands like a horse's blinkers. 'Too focused on the "Modern Art" series. Wonderful. Wonderful work. But not for this. It will be simpler, not too subtle – you understand?'

'You want me to design a grid? Make a few samples?' Felix asked.

Fogel glanced at Faith, who said, 'What about Eric Brandon? D'you think he could organize an outline? First a general series outline and then a detailed breakdown, spread by spread, of each volume. Sixty-four pages each. Forty per cent pictorial, sixty per cent text. Ten volumes in all.'

'Is this that guy who thinks all art is pastiche?' Murdoch asked.

'It doesn't stop him painting,' Faith said.

'Good-good,' Fogel cut in. 'Copyright is our big problem. The British Museum wants us to pay for images. The Science Museum . . . ditto, even if we pay the photographer. So we can make a *painting* of a photo. The artist will cost three pounds compared with the Science Museum copyright fee of five pounds. A hundred illustrations . . . two hundred pounds saved!'

Faith turned to Felix. 'It's an advantage that you, me, and Eric live so close. Together you and he could work out the whole series, right down to what goes in each individual spread. Eric understands how young people's minds work, and—'

'Oh!' Murdoch interrupted. 'Is he the same Eric Brandon who writes and illustrates children's books? He's good.'

'You know him?' Fogel asked.

'Not personally but Macdonald published a couple of his early books before Gollancz poached him. Did very well.'

'His wife, Isabella, is a fashion dictator,' Faith added. 'She was on *Good Housekeeping*. Now she's on *Vogue*.'

'Eric,' Felix put in, 'is trying to persuade the Oxford Dictionary people that *fashion* and *fascist* have the same root.'

'To get back to the point,' Fogel said.

'Yes.' Felix was brisk. 'Why ask Eric to outline all ten books? Why not go to an expert in each?'

'Because they give you an outline – each – for a thousand-page encyclopedia. Sixty-four pages? Impossible, they say. No. We give them an outline for sixty-four pages and say, "Comments please."'

'Have you a list of subjects?'

Fogel looked at Faith, who drew a single sheet of folded paper from her handbag. Felix read:

```
Machines
Ancient Egypt
Explorers
Astronomy
Dinosaurs
The American West
Navigation
Flight
Fashion
War
```

'There's no thread,' Fogel said as Felix drew breath to comment. 'These books will all sell very well as singletons. We have to make some money now for a very *big* project that comes next . . . nineteen fifty-one . . . fifty-two.'

'And why should Julian Huxley and James Fisher want their names on the cover of a book on fashion?' Felix asked.

Fogel grinned. 'Trust me,' he said. 'Ve are all prostitoots now.'

Tuesday, 8 November 1949

'We can easily boil them all down to just sixty-four pages each,' Eric told Felix and Faith. 'Except for the volume on fashion. My consultant on that subject tells me it will need at least six hundred.'

They had gathered in Eric's studio after a few jars at The Plume of Feathers, from which they had returned, singing, across the fields.

'Get a new consultant,' Faith retorted.

'It's easy for you to say that – you don't have to live with the consequences. Much less sleep with them.'

'When you say you can easily boil them down . . . does that mean you've already done it and it *was* easy or just that you've thought about it and it *looks* easy?'

Eric, assuming the air of a magician, rose to his feet to reveal that he had been sitting on a blue marbled folder whose cover was loosely held by diagonal elastics at the corners.

'Impressively fat,' Faith commented.

'All six hundred and forty pages outlined.'

Faith scanned the titles for the 'Junior Knowledge' series: *Men and Machines, Men and Gods of the Nile, Man Discovers the World, Man Discovers the Universe* . . . each had a title that included the word *Man* or *Men* – except one, which was stamped *Top Secret*. She held it up and raised an eyebrow. 'Fashion?'

He nodded. 'For God's sake, don't let it fall into the hands of The Enemy. I don't know what to call it. The best I can come up with is *Man Hides the Fat*. All the top couturiers are men and they all show their designs on slender mannequins for sale to women who simply aren't. Slender, that is. Nor are they mannequins, come to think of it.'

Faye speed-read the typescript, speaking as her eyes quartered the pages. 'This must all come from Isabella. You can't possibly know all this. Why d'you do it, Eric?'

'Do what?'

'Talk and behave as if you and she are permanently teetering on the edge of divorce?'

'Me? Do I do that? But she is the light of my life and captain of my soul. I am devoted to her. But don't quote me. I shall deny it.'

'Ho hum.' She handed the folder to Felix and picked up *Man Conquers the Air*. Very soon she was shaking her head the way people do when they see something impossible yet cannot deny the evidence of their eyes. 'What was Willy Messerschmitt's greatest contribution to . . .' she began.

'I haven't the foggiest,' he admitted.

'But you've put it down here – as a heading.'

'You should have asked me . . .' He rolled his eyes dramatically. '. . . a week ago last Wednesday. On that day I was the London Library's greatest expert on the history of aviation.'

'Is that how it works?'

'It's the *only* way it works, Faith. Can I invoice for the remainder of the fee?'

She flipped rapidly through a couple of other folders and then smiled at him. 'I'm sure you can . . . pending—'

But before she could mention whatever was 'pending,' he snatched up a paper dart from his desk and threw it at her. On top of one of the aerofoils was written the word *Invoice* and on the other some smudged ink from a rubber stamp, reading: 'Brandon and Son – High Class Butchers since 1820 – *Prompt settlement would oblige.*

'Family heirloom,' he explained. 'What next?'

'Next,' she replied, not looking at Felix, 'we try to persuade our illustrious designer-consultant to give us his final layout grid. Then we do a few sample pages for each book and then Fogel and I set off for New York, Paris, Hamburg, Florence . . . and try and sign up Doubleday . . . Larousse . . . Springer . . . Sansoni . . . to join us in a co-edition. Money upfront. We call it positive cash flow. Aren't you glad you asked?'

'Very! Especially the bit about "positive cash flow." For instance – how much would you pay me to write a couple of these volumes myself? Positively upfront, of course.'

Monday, 5 December 1949

For the second time that evening Terence Lanyon had to call the community meeting to order. 'We're getting absolutely nowhere with all this,' he said.

'Don't be too hard on us,' Eric pleaded. 'We're just so happy not to be arguing about electricity for once.'

'Thank you, Eric,' Terence said wearily. 'Helpful as always. Unless someone can tell us the actual words that Betty used, this whole discussion is pretty futile. So far we've had everything from "Nigger" to a pretty straightforward statement of the undeniable fact that Lena and Tommy are not leaseholders here at the Dower House.'

'Betty is desperately lonely,' Nicole said. 'The poor girl is heartbroken at having to leave The Tribe. She just lashed out at Tommy because he only half-belongs here. Because his mother works for us.'

'All of which might very well excuse whatever she said,' Terence insisted. 'But until we know *what* she said, we can't know what it is we're excusing – *if*, that is—'

'Nothing can excuse the word Nigger,' Willard said.

'That may be true in America,' Sally told him. 'It's probably very insulting over there. But that's not so here. My parents have a dog called Nigger.'

'And,' Isabella put in, 'the top autumn colour next year is Nigger Brown. You'd better get used to the word, Willard, because it's going to be in every magazine and every shop window.'

'What d'you call them in America, honey?' Marianne asked. 'In Sweden we say *Neger*.'

'In French it's *nègre* . . . *négresse*,' Nicole said. 'Accent grave on one, accent *aigu* on the other. That was always a trap in our dictatings.'

'Dictations.'

Willard grabbed up fistfuls of hair. 'Can we just cut out the linguistics and get to the logistics?'

'What are they?' several asked.

'Let me put it this way. Maybe we have *no* right to be discussing whatever it was that Betty said to Tommy at the school gate. Maybe we have *every* right to discuss it. To me it's irrelevant because I think it's really up to The Tribe. We've all seen—'

Angela interrupted him: 'But they're just children.'

Willard continued: 'Another way of putting that is to say they are Betty's peers. And we've all seen – in fact, we've all remarked on – the amazing way they discipline one another. If any of us tells one of the kids off (wince away, Eric) it's just water off a duck's back. But if The Tribe censures one of them, boy-oh-boy does he fall back in line!'

'You're suggesting we leave it to them?' Tony asked.

'I'm suggesting we put it to them – ask them if they want to handle it . . . or will they leave it to us?'

'Really it means asking our Sam and our Hannah,' Arthur Prentice pointed out. 'They're the leaders since Betty and Charley moved to Dormer Green. The others are much too young to understand.'

'How has Tommy taken it, incidentally?' Hilary Lanyon asked.

'There's no way of knowing,' Tony said. 'He just laughs, of course, but you'll never know what's going on inside. If he was sent to the guillotine, his head would still be laughing half an hour later.'

'So!' Terence reasserted his authority. 'Do we generally agree to give Willard's idea of a trial — leave it, in the first instance, to The Tribe?'

There were murmurs of guarded assent.

'Will you put it to them, then?' He looked at Arthur and May.

'They're asleep now,' May objected. 'And breakfast time — in our place — is hardly the appropriate—'

'Ask them on the walk to school,' Nicole put in. 'It's your turn tomorrow.'

May looked at Eric. 'Sorry, chum! I didn't know this was going to come up.' Then, to the others: 'I have to go up to town with Arthur tomorrow. Eric has to go into the village to collect their car. It fitted nicely.'

'Don't worry,' Eric assured them. 'I shall put all sides of the case with such forensic clarity that they will have no possible way of reaching the correct conclusion. But it will be fun!'

'So!' Isabella said. 'You'll just have to find your gardening shoes before tomorrow. You're not going in those.'

'If I were an animal,' Eric said as he set off through the coppice with Sam, Hannah, and Tommy, 'what animal would I be?'

'A human!' Sam told him. 'All humans are animals.'

'Not me,' Hannah assured him.

'It's true.'

''Tisn't!'

''Tis!'

'Stoppit you two! I mean any animal *other* than a human. Would I be a fish? Or a bird?'

'A pig,' Tommy said. 'Look at your shoes already.'

'Oh, shhh . . . sugar! I was supposed to change. Never mind. You, Tommy, would be an eagle, because you've got the sharpest eyes.'

'What would I be?' Hannah asked.

'You tell me.'

'A peacock. Because I'd have all those gorgeous colours.'

'No, this isn't a wishing game. You might *want* to be a peacock but I think you'd actually be a squirrel, because you're very good at hiding things.'

Hannah laughed. 'How d'you know?'

'Because,' Eric said, 'I see all the games you play out of my studio window. And when you all play Hot or Cold, you always pick the best places to hide what's Hot.'

Condensed mist fell from every branch; sodden twigs refused to snap but broke with a dull crackle among the no-longer-colourful leaf mould. A pheasant startled them, rising from almost underfoot with a harsh clatter of feathery alarm. It flew high, swiftly breaking clear of the leafless canopy and heading south beneath the leaden sky.

'A wild pheasant,' Tommy said.

'How d'you know?' Eric asked.

'They always fly high, the wild ones. The ones they rear for shooting don't. A beater told me that at the last shoot.'

'You'd be an elephant, Tommy, because elephants never forget.'

They crossed the waterlogged ditch by the 'new bridge' – a couple of felled trees, trimmed of branches and laid side by side. 'Let's play the same game only with fruit,' Tommy suggested. 'What sort of fruit would I be?'

'Sort of like that!' Sam mimed a dumb-bell shape in the air. ''Cos you've got a big head and a big bum!'

'Oh, yeah? Well, you'd be the same only gone rotten 'cos you've got a smelly bum!'

They dissolved in fits of giggles, chanting, 'Smelly bum! Smelly bum!' at each other and glancing slyly at Eric in hope of a reprimand. Hannah looked at him with weary sympathy.

'You'd be an apple at the top of a tree,' he told her.

'Why?'

'Because you're a good girl – one of the best, and that's where all the best apples are. But it gets pretty lonely up there because the boys are all lazy and they find it easier to pick the apples on the ground – the windfalls. But it pays to wait for the boys who only want to climb to the top; they're the cream.'

'I climb to the top of the apple trees,' Tommy assured them.

Sam put his face right up close and said, 'And all the apples cry out "Smelly bum! Smelly bum!" and then they all faint!' He flung himself backward among the autumn stubble with a force that would have dislocated an adult spine and raised all four limbs in the air – the way they drew dead dogs and cats in the *Dandy*.

'Oh, just look at you!' his sister yelled. 'How d'you expect to go into Miss Dooley's class like that?'

'Easy.' He sprang to his feet and mimed the opening of a door and shutting it behind him; then he raced ahead of them with a Chaplin-esque gait, feet at right angles, head in the air.

'Would Betty be an apple at the top of the tree?' Hannah asked Eric.

'Why Betty?' he replied.

'I miss her.'

'Oh, *do* you? What about you, Tommy? D'you miss Betty?'

He stared ahead for three or four paces, eyes fixed on the stile between this ploughed field and the road, where Sam now sat, wearing an assumed air of boredom. 'She was good when they lived at the Dower House,' he said.

'But not since then?'

'Todd and Gracie won't let her come back and play with us.'

'Nor Charley,' Tommy put in. 'I miss Charley.'

'I believe that. Racing all alone on the top of the walled-garden wall isn't much cop, is it! So d'you want someone to talk to Todd and Gracie and try to change their minds?'

'Yes!' they both said.

'And,' he asked Hannah, 'd'you think Betty should apologize to Tommy before she's allowed back, because she said . . .'

'Yes,' Hannah said.

'No,' Tommy said.

'Well, that's something you youngsters will have to sort out among yourselves − as usual.'

They had arrived at the stile.

'Smelly bum!' Sam taunted.

The other two, feeling almost grown-up by now, looked at him with a disdain that was a far more effective silencer than annoyance or disgust would have been.

'Can you take us to school *every* day?' Tommy asked as they set out along the short stretch of road.

'D'you know how to catch a pink elephant?' Eric asked them.

'No!' they chorused, laughing.

'D'you know how to catch a *black* elephant?'

'No!' The laughter was louder, wilder.

'Using binoculars, a matchbox, a pair of tweezers, and a telephone directory − you don't know that?'

'No!' Louder yet and wilder.

'Dear-oh-dear! Don't they teach you *anything* useful at that school? Oh! I see it has turned into *this* school – we've arrived. No time left to tell you how to catch a black elephant. I can see I shall have to collect you this afternoon and tell you the secret. Now I must go and get my car and I think I'll just call on Gracie and see if I can clean these elegant shoes up a bit.'

That afternoon, Eric and Gracie (whom he had invited back to the Dower House for tea) led five children out of the coppice.

'Remember,' he warned them for the umpteenth time, 'this is how to catch a *pink* elephant. Not a *black* elephant – because . . .'

'. . . *everybody* knows how to catch a black elephant,' the other six parroted with weary exasperation – and for the umpteenth time, too.

'So, on the laaaast day, you tie the piece of rope round your very laaaast plum cake and let it float down the river and round the bend. And you hear the cry, "Oh! Goody-goody-goody – plum cake, plum cake!" and so you know the pink elephant has taken the bait. So you start hauling in on the rope as fast as you can, and the pink elephant comes charging upstream after it. Only this time you haul it *right round the bend*. And so, when the pink elephant comes after it, he sees you! For the first time, he *sees* you! And then he realizes you've been playing tricks with him all those other times. And what does he do? Why, he turns *black* with rage, of course. And everybody . . .?'

'. . . KNOWS HOW TO CATCH A BLACK ELEPHANT! Do-o-o-h.'

They mimed weary collapse, the way people always do after a shaggy-dog story.

Then: 'Again! Tell us again! Pleeeeease!'

Betty and Tommy were hand-in-hand.

Thursday, 8 December 1949

Chris Riley-Potter was due to move into the Fergusons' old flat shortly before that Christmas of 1949; but long before then he had made it unrecognizable to anyone who had known it originally. The first time he saw the place, shortly after Todd and

Gracie had moved out at Michaelmas, he said, 'I'm sure they are perfectly wonderful people – and but for them I'd be having to paint portraits of Oswald Moseley – but I really cannot breathe surrounded by this wallpaper.'

He had studied art for three years at Maidstone until 1939, when he volunteered for the Army Service Corps and trained as a 'Don-R' – a dispatch rider, in which capacity he had served throughout the war, refusing all promotions above corporal because he had become addicted to motorbikes. Being among the first in at the start of the war, he was among the first out when it ended. He had then followed a three-year painting course at the Slade, culminating in the much-coveted diploma in that same summer. Unfortunately his ex-serviceman's grant had run out a month or two earlier, forcing him to rely on his girlfriend, Nina – half-Danish, half-Egyptian – who did 'some sort of work' around the Danish Embassy.

'*At* the embassy?' people sometimes asked.

'Connected with it,' she would reply.

Whatever it was, it obviously paid well.

'Have you *seen* her!' Felix asked Eric the first time the couple came out to strip the wallpaper in their flat.

'No one has ever seen *her*,' Eric claimed, and it was true that she did wear an astonishing amount and variety of make-up.

Their decorative scheme for the flat could not have been simpler: paint everything black except the floor. When, some weekends later, they finished the sitting room, they realized that it did look ever so slightly stark and depressing. Eric, in his ground-floor studio immediately below, was the first to become aware that they had found a solution. It began with a scream, followed by a heavy thump on his ceiling, followed by laughter.

He dashed upstairs to apply first aid, only to discover the pair of them – naked – lying in helpless laughter in the middle of the empty sitting-room floor.

'No, no! Come in!' Chris called out as he saw Eric trying to tiptoe away. 'Tell us what you think.'

Gingerly Eric sidled into the room.

A cheerful fire burned in the hearth, illuminating a bucket full of bright orange distemper. There were bright orange spills here and there upon the floorboards. Nina's feet and legs, halfway up to her knees, were bright orange. And a trail of bright orange footprints – hers, obviously – traced a path up the wall and halfway across the ceiling.

'I couldn't hold her up any longer,' Chris explained. 'Still, the way they finish halfway across the ceiling adds a sort of sense of mystery. What d'you think?'

'We haven't finished,' Nina added.

'I was going to say,' Eric replied. 'It needs more.'

'Like what?'

'What was the original idea, with the black?'

'A new start. From nothing – blackness – sort of like the womb.'

'Long time since I was there,' Eric confessed. 'Take your word for it.' Then, quite suddenly, he caught himself entering into the spirit of the thing. 'Try two orange caryatids,' he suggested. 'One each side of the fireplace.'

'Paint them?' Chris was doubtful.

'No. In body prints. Just like the footprints. Paint each other's bodies and press yourselves against the wall.' The idea took hold and he added, 'Your front sides beside the fireplace and your backsides on the opposite wall. So the opposing images are sort of frozen points on a timeline of your trajectory in space, penetrating the womb of this room. Have you enough gas for the bathroom geyser? Oh, never mind – you can have a shower in our place. Come down when you're done.'

'No, no, mate. It's your idea. You've got to paint us. There's a big distemper brush on the window sill.'

And so Eric found himself standing a mere two feet before naked and voluptuous Nina, painting anything that jutted out enough to print itself bright orange on the wall. Her Nefertiti lips curled in a knowing smile; her dark, Queen of Sheba eyes sparkled with feminine certainties. 'You have a delicate touch, dear Eric,' she murmured.

All he dared do was clear his throat.

'God, you've silenced the bugger!' Chris said admiringly.

Eric found his voice then. 'I'm coming to you in a minute, mate.'

'Enough!' Nina wafted him aside and approached the wall. 'Here?'

'As close to the fireplace as you can get.' Eric-the-director reasserted himself. 'Arms above your head as if you're holding something up – like a real caryatid.'

'Print me, then! Come on!' she said. 'Hard as you can.'

The two men pressed every tangible portion of her to the wall, while she guessed whose hand it might be: 'Eric . . . Chris . . . Chris again . . . Eric . . . Eric? Chris – *you* should be pressing that bit.'

The result was extraordinary – Indian erotic art (the breasts and torso) reinterpreted by someone who had supped on all the horrors of the war (the skeletal limbs and severed ankles of a Giacometti).

'Christ!' Nina murmured as they stared at the result in awe. This *jeu d'ésprit* was going somewhere.

Eric tried to rekindle the horseplay when it came to painting Chris's front, lingering suggestively over his nipples and penis; but all he proved was that cold, wet distemper, no matter how brightly orange, has no aphrodisiac qualities to speak of. When they had printed him on the wall on the other side of the fireplace, the awe-inducing effect of the iconography was more than doubled.

'Fucking fantastic, mate!' Chris said. 'We could be on to a new *Guernica* here, d'you realize? A post-war *Guernica!*'

They completed the 'timeline' by printing their head-to-heel backsides on the opposite wall and then they joined the two by planting orange footprints across the floorboards between their images – except that Chris's footprints linked Nina's two body-prints and hers linked his – 'to symbolize the crossing of our paths in life,' Chris explained.

While the two of them took the promised shower in the Brandons' bathroom – and incidentally discovered that the orange pigment must have contained some chemical that caused it to dye human skin – Eric went around the other flats telling everyone they simply had to come and see what the Fergusons' old place looked like now.

Faith Bullen-ffitch was the only strong dissenter. On their way back across the yard, she said, 'I know Tony thinks the world of Chris and I'm sure he's a most talented painter, and Adam thinks that what with all the babies everybody's been having, we're all getting a bit bourgeois and need stirring up, but I do wonder if the sort of stirring Chris Riley-Potter and Nina what's-her-name are going to wreak upon the community is quite what he has in mind?' Then, turning to Angela: 'Why did you say you liked it? I can't see anything to like. They've made a terrible mess of the floorboards.'

Angela just shrugged, and put the kettle on the range. 'Tea, anyone?'

There was a knock at the cottage door. Eric opened it and came in without waiting for an answer. 'Mind if I hide out here for a while?' he asked. 'Mrs Brandon is being terribly sweet and encouraging to Chris and Nina and I can't take any more of it.'

'Well,' Faith answered him. 'We had just decided not to say another word on the subject of Chris and Nina. I think they'll prove disruptive – which may, in turn, prove to be the grit in the oyster. Or just grit, of course. Angela is . . . what, darling? Lukewarm to indifferent? And Felix is worried.'

'Me?' Felix protested. 'Don't be absurd. Why d'you say that?'

'Because you're opening a tin of baked beans – and that's what you always do when you're worried.'

Felix started to protest but Angela cut in: 'My God, she's right! I never noticed that, or never made the connection – but that's what you always do. And d'you know what I do? When I'm in a state? I straighten up all the notes on my pinboard and start to check that all the papers in the files are in their correct order – until I *realize* what I'm doing and force myself to stop. Oh, Felix! Will we ever . . .' The thought petered out.

'Survival behaviour!' Eric murmured.

'I just like baked beans,' Felix said as he took up a well-used wooden spoon and stirred the saucepan on the stove. 'If you want to be *useful*, Eric, you could cut a few slices of bread and pop them in the toaster.' After a short silence he added, 'But you could be right, Faith. I am . . . "worried" isn't quite the word. What would you call the feeling when an unexpected parcel arrives and it might contain a kilo of the finest beluga caviar or just a pile of shit – which actually happened to a Jewish couple I knew in Paris – the shit, not the caviar. What's the word for that?'

'A paradigm,' Eric said. 'It's a paradigm for life in general.'

'Trepidation,' Faith told him.

'OK, I feel trepidation about Chris coming to join the community. He's a powerful painter, a man with vision—'

Eric interrupted him. 'You mean it's like someone saying, "Oh but you absolutely *must* read this book – it could have been written *for* you." And you know the bugger's right but you still don't want to borrow it or read it or have anything to do with it. Well . . . you're not the only one, mate.' He explained why he had run up to the flat and how he'd been inveigled into collaborating over the body prints.

'God in heaven!' Angela said. 'You mean the inspiration was yours?'

'No! Precisely the opposite. I thought, *What is the most ridiculous suggestion I can make?* But it also had to be something they'd swallow hook, line, and sinker. So, seeing the footprints they'd already made, I suggested the whole body prints. But even as I put it into words, I felt it was actually an exciting idea as well. Mind you, that may just have been at the prospect of painting Nina, naked, all over, with orange distemper.'

'*You* did that?' Angela and Faith asked almost in unison. Felix laughed.

'Yeah, I wasn't going to say – until I realized that Nina isn't going to keep her trap shut. So what the hell! It was fun. They tried to embarrass me and discovered I'm made of sterner stuff.' After a ruminative silence he concluded, 'All the same, I don't think the life is going to trundle along in the same old way once Chris Riley-Potter and Nina move in.'

Wednesday, 14 December 1949

Faith waited until she saw the light go on over Eric's drawing board. Then, coffee in hand – so as to look sort-of casual – she crossed the yard, tapped on his window, and mimed at him, *Can we talk?* She let herself into the Brandons' flat and was about to call out 'Only me!' when she heard Isabella and Eric at their favourite pastime. She hesitated outside Eric's studio door.

'How can you live in all this dust?' Isabella asked.

'Well, in the first place, it isn't *all this* dust, it is *a very fine film* that most people wouldn't even notice. But as to your question – "How do I *live* in it" – I confess I only have the haziest—'

'If I let our sitting room get like this we'd both die of hay fever.'

'Would it be as simple as that?'

'What d'you mean?'

'Well, since I can clearly tolerate a fine film of dust like this, whereas you, or so you claim, would die of—'

'Oh, ha ha. What I came in here to ask was why did you leave the lid off the toothpowder tin?'

'Oh, dear. That's a real tough one. Especially at this time in the morning. I could lie and say I simply forgot but we both know enough Freud to realize that things are never so simple. My subconscious must have been struggling very hard to express—'

'Just don't do it again.'

'Hang on. Don't go. I must write that down word-for-word . . . Don't . . .? What was it?'

But Isabella had already left the room. On seeing Faith waiting not six feet from the door, she said, 'Did you hear him?' And as she passed by she added, 'You are *so* lucky!'

And finally, at the top of the short flight of stairs that led up to the rest of their flat: 'See if you can talk some sense into him.'

'D'you think you'll manage it?' Eric asked as she entered his studio.

'She must be psychic,' Faith replied. 'Actually, it's not so much to talk sense as to see whether we agree on certain basic ground rules – if you're going to write two of these volumes for Manutius.'

'You've brought a contract? Pull up a pew.'

She nodded. 'It's over in my room. We can sign it this morning if we can agree certain ground rules.' She sat down after he had ostentatiously wiped that invisible coating of dust from the seat. 'The only writing of yours I know is your children's books and the thing I notice is that you never come out with anything straight . . .'

Without turning round, Eric reached behind him and plucked a book at random from his shelves. He opened it and read: '"In a cellar in Threadneedle Street, in the heart of the City of London, lived a family of mice and all their relations." Not straight, eh? Would you have preferred it to go—'

'No, I don't mean in places like that. But later on, when Titchy Mouse sees his brother climbing the rope to go on board the ship . . .'

Eric gawped at her. 'You've actually *read* this tale?'

'I've read just about everything you've written, Eric.' She held out her hand for the Titchy Mouse book. 'Yes,' she went on after flipping a couple of pages. 'This is the sort of thing: "Little Sammy's lip trembled. There was a stinging feeling behind his eyelids and soon the tears began to fall." Why didn't you just say: "Poor little Sammy was very sad and soon began to cry"?'

Eric spoke patiently: 'Because my readers for that book are about eight years old. They are Jung and easily Freudened.'

'I beg your pardon?'

'Granted. Go and get the contract.'

'No! I meant . . . what did that mean − Jung and easily Freudened?'

'Lips trembling, prickling eyelids, tears falling . . . these are *sensations*. They speak directly to my little readers' own experiences. They've all been there. But: "Sammy was sad and began to cry" is just a report. It has to be teased apart and reassembled into an eight-year-old's raw sensations. Actually, it's no different from stories for grown-ups. If I write, "Isabella was furious as she turned her car into the driveway of their home," I'm writing a report that the reader has to reassemble into . . . what? The grim set of Isabella's jaw . . . the way she grinds her teeth . . . her white knuckles on the steering wheel . . . the way she jams on the brakes and then slams the door as she steps out . . . the way she yells "*Eric!*" before she's even through the front door. So why write reports when you can be so wonderfully graphic? Why *tell* when you can *show*, instead?' He smiled mischievously and, turning toward the door, called out, 'Come in, darling. Faith won't mind.'

'I just thought you might like some coffee,' his wife said wearily as she came in, bearing a tray with three Denby stoneware coffee mugs, a matching coffee pot, sugar bowl, cream jug, and a plate holding three shortbread fingers.

Faith docked her own coffee cup on the window sill.

'You'll find this coffee much tastier than that stuff Felix and Angela serve,' Isabella assured her. 'The Austrians understand coffee but the Germans haven't the first idea.'

'It's the same with television,' Eric continued, as if there had been no interruption at all. 'It's all *tell* even though they're actually *showing* it, too. I've been watching it lately, up in the Johnsons': factual programmes, like the one the other night on London's markets. There were super pictures of Covent Garden, Billingsgate, Smithfield, Petticoat Lane, et cetera, and the commentary, I'll swear, was lifted straight out of some tourist guidebook. I think what they do is write a script and then go out and film pictures to go with it. That seat has half an inch of dust on it, darling – do be *terribly* careful, knowing how susceptible you are. And then they don't change a word of the script once they've got the film – even if the pictures make the same point. Or even much better ones. And they speak in that Bah-Bee-Cee voice which could turn a rainbow grey. It's very sad when you think what "the telly" *could* be like. Darling! You have some astounding insight to contribute, I'm sure. I know when you get that creative look in your eye and the birds all start singing in minor keys.'

'Not about "the telly,"' Isabella said. 'I couldn't care less about "the telly." I've just had Selincourt on the phone about their spring collection. They're willing to pay us fifty quid to use the Dower House as a location for a photo shoot – mainly the front steps, the ballroom, the lawn, our drawing room with the Adam fireplace . . . I told them it was Adam—'

'And, of course, Chris and Nina's womb-of-time,' Eric added. 'By "us" you mean the communal fund?'

'Of course.'

'And Felix's studio?' Faith asked. 'He's working on a quarter-size maquette for the bronze globe for BOAC in Buckingham Palace Road. It's impressive.'

'If there's no problem with copyright – yes. Super. I don't think we'll need a communal meeting, do you – not if I speak to people individually? It'll be next weekend, Saturday and Sunday. One problem is they want to bring two borzois.'

'Ballet dancers!' Eric was surprised.

Isabella ignored him. 'I'll have to warn Nicole about Fifi and Xupé.'

'And Adam,' Eric said. 'No. On second thoughts, better to warn the mannequins about *him.*' When Isabella had gone, he turned to Faith. 'Funny name – mannequins . . . mannikins . . . little dwarfs? Anyway, what did you really pop over here for? A chat about storytelling techniques? *Everything* is storytelling, Faith. A bus timetable tells a story. "How to repair a puncture" is a story. Will Heathcliff get Cathy – a story—'

'. . . and a half!'

'Exactly! Each kind of story has its appropriate technique – and I am master of them all. So you'd better nail me down on the Rock of Manutius, PDQ as Willard says, or someone else will poach me. I'll give you ten minutes.'

Her eyes narrowed. 'Have you been talking to other publishers?'

'OK, make that ten years. But that's my final offer.'

With a sigh, Faith picked up her own coffee cup, and went to fetch the contract.

When it was signed – all three copies – she said, 'I was interested in what you were saying earlier, about TV documentaries . . .'

'You disagree?'

'No. Quite the contrary. Listen, Angela has brought some film back from the Bah-Bee-Cee, as you call it. And a projector – sixteen mil. I don't know what it's about but, considering its source, it probably has all those faults you savaged just now. Would you like to put some flesh on those brave words of yours – that you are master of all storytelling techniques – and write your own commentary?'

'What are you paying?'

'Nothing. But' – her raised finger stemmed his refusal – 'I've been thinking of switching from publishing to television for a couple of years, as I'm sure you know – and I think the time has come. But there'll be an interview at the BBC, of course, and I don't want to . . . I mean, it would be impressive if I could sit there with an actual example of the sort of change I'd like to influence, if I had the chance. I'll pay whatever actor we can get to read your script and I'll meet all the recording and dubbing costs. All that will be on spec. That'll be my contribution. If you write the script on spec, that'll be your contribution. And if I get the job, I'll dig a hole and pull you through. So are you in or out?'

Wednesday, 14 December 1949

That same evening Faith met Eric at the cottage door. 'This documentary of Angela's isn't what I thought,' she said. 'Not a BBC documentary. Something from the military. But it's not a big reel, so the most we'll risk wasting is twenty minutes. Are you still on?'

'Military? What's it about?' he asked as he shook the rain off his umbrella and stamped his feet. 'Twenty yards and I'm soaked.'

'I don't want to say – in case I'm wrong – but it's something I've heard her talk about a time or two.' She led him into Felix's studio. 'Angela? Eric wants to watch, too. You don't mind, I hope?'

'The more the merrier.' Angela waved her hand toward the couch at one end of the studio. 'Just make sure you can see the screen.' She was slightly breathless and her voice was more high-pitched than usual; the 'screen' was a white sheet pinned to the crimson curtains that were normally drawn across the studio window after dark.

'Where's Felix?' Eric asked. The quarter-size maquette for his BOAC sculpture was pushed over against the wall – a random lacework of bird wings forming a pierced sphere.

Faith nudged him and shook her head.

'Sulking,' Angela said airily. 'Eric, dear, can you reach that switch?'

The room was plunged into darkness. Simultaneously the projector clattered into life, projecting a countdown – 10 . . . 9 . . . 8 . . . At five it started to show a clock-style timer, sweeping toward zero.

Then, as the hand reached two – darkness.

Then an institutional sort of room with bare floorboards, a dark gray wall up to waist height, and light gray above. The camera pans right toward the door. It opens to reveal two female sergeants in the Corps of Royal Military Police. A caption fades in: *Hamelin – former* SS-*Oberaufseherin Elisabeth Völkenrath – Ravensbrück Concentration Camp, 13 December 1945*. It fades out as the woman herself comes into view – a thin, haggard female in prison drab, handcuffed behind, and shuffling in cloth slippers.

'Bitch!' Angela shouted at the screen. 'This is for Milena! This is for Margarete! This is for *me!*'

'Dear God!' Eric whispered; Faith reached out and squeezed his wrist.

A German padre mouths words but the condemned woman waves him away.

'"*Gott mitt uns!*"' Angela sneered. '*Das war ja eine L-ü-ge!*'

The camera pans left to follow the execution party and, when they shuffle to a halt, pans down to show she is standing in the centre of a trapdoor, painted white. The hangman stands at the far side; behind him are grouped a number of British officers and a couple of civilians, one in the wig of a court official.

'That's Albert Pierrepoint,' Angela told them. 'The hangman. I went to his pub up in Hollinwood but he's not allowed to talk about being a hangman.'

'Where's Hollinwood?' Faith asked.

'Near Manchester.' She went up to the screen and shouted again: 'That's the sheet on which Felix Breit, late of Mauthausen and Angela Wirth, late of Ravensbrück, made their baby. Here we live! Here you die!' Her laughter was warm and melodious, as if she had just told the sort of joke you can tell to children.

One sergeant cuffs the condemned woman's ankles while the other places a black cloth hood over her head. The rope is lowered. Albert Pierrepoint takes one step forward, to the edge of the trapdoor and slips the noose around her head, tightening it slightly to one side at the back of her neck; in the same movement he pulls a lever. The white trapdoor turns suddenly black and the condemned woman falls with astonishing speed into the void. Three frames and she's gone. Pierrepoint steadies the taut rope – or is he feeling for twitchings of life? He stares down through the open door, gives a little nod of satisfaction. Nobody appears to speak. Nobody smiles.

Smiling, Angela froze the projector and walked up to the screen. 'They took longer than that to die when you were in charge!' she shouted into the image of the open trapdoor. 'Butcher!'

Then followed the almost identical execution – again conducted by Albert Pierrepoint but in a different execution chamber – of ss-*Hauptsturmführer Johann Schwarzhüber* – *Deputy Commandant, Ravensbrück Concentration Camp* – *3 May 1947*.

'This next group were tried and sentenced at the Curiohaus in Hamburg at almost exactly the same time as Willard was back there looking for Marianne,' Angela said. 'Think! Their world ending – ours just beginning. Marianne should be here to enjoy it.'

'Who was this Schwarzhüber johnny?' Eric asked.

'Deputy commandant – like it said just now. He was in charge of the big gas chambers at Auschwitz, so when the ss knew they were going to lose the war and Ravensbrück had to start killing prisoners much more quickly than just slave labour and starvation was managing, he was the man who built the gas chamber there. The Swedish Red Cross was actually in the camp while it was working – that's how well disguised it was and how desperate they were. Who's next?'

Faith stood up. 'I don't think this is quite my cup of tea,' she said. 'Sorry, Angela, darling, but . . . well . . .'

'I don't mind,' Angela assured her cheerfully. 'I was all set to enjoy the feast alone. Eric?'

'It's not exactly what I watch as a rule, either,' he replied. 'But what are rules if we can't break them, eh?' He dry-soaped his hands. 'I'll stay if it's all the same to you?'

There followed the execution rituals of fourteen more former ss warders, wardresses, doctors, and officers, all hanged with gravity (and by it) at the hand of Albert Pierrepoint. Angela gave Eric a brief biography of each: this one pulled teeth containing gold from living prisoners and kept the proceeds . . . that one let a vicious dog loose on prisoners, at random, whenever she got bored, and if you resisted the dog, she shot you . . . another ran a lethal regime in the solitary confinement cells in the infamous punishment *Bunker* . . . another did medical experiments on children, making friends of them because if they were afraid, the experiments wouldn't work. In between, Angela whooped for joy and shouted curses at each pathetic prisoner as he or she underwent the sentence of the court.

When the reel ran out – going flip-flip-flip in the take-up

reel – she let out a great sigh of satisfaction and turned to Eric. 'D'you know a story by Franz Kafka called – in English – *In the Penal Settlement*?' she asked.

He nodded. 'A friend lent it me – round about the time Belsen was liberated.'

'You remember the punishment machine in it? With needles that pricked the skin, writing the prisoners' crimes in blood, all over their bodies, from head to toe? And the companion needles that puffed a little squirt of acid into each pinprick? Well, if such a machine existed, I would gladly operate it myself on each and every one of those criminals.'

'Does it annoy you . . . oh, would you like a whisky, by the way?' He went through to the kitchen – to his raincoat – and extracted a half-bottle of Haig.

'Use the glasses on the second shelf of the dresser,' she called out to him.

'They're rather large.'

She laughed. 'That's why I picked them. No water in mine.'

She swallowed a good slug and gasped at the fire and the afterburn. 'Does what annoy me?'

'Oh. These hangings – these deaths. They're all so unheroic. They just shuffle in like zombies and let it happen. D'you think they learned how to die from watching you prisoners dying?'

Angela drew breath, sharply, and opened her mouth to protest . . . but no words came.

'Mmm?' he prompted.

'Damn you,' she said quietly.

'Not really an answer.'

'They took away everything from us. Everything . . . except . . .'

'What?'

'Our ability to respond. They could enforce an *outward* response – eyes down . . . passive . . . but they could never know what was going on behind those eyes. That was our ultimate victory. And now . . .' She gestured toward the projector. 'The same with them.'

'So there is no ultimate victory. You'll just have to settle for their deaths. Cut your coat according to your cloth – they must have taught you that lesson, too.' He grinned. 'The other thing I was going to ask – do you resent it that Felix won't share in this *Schadenfreudefest*? Is he annoyed that you didn't get film of Pierrepoint at work on the butchers of Mauthausen?'

She took another, calmer, slug and gazed evenly at him. 'That's actually none of your business, Eric.'

'What a very bourgeois reason for not answering. I thought you communists were—'

'I'm not a communist. I'm a Marxist.'

'Ah! That explains it. Few of the great men of the nineteenth century were more bourgeois than the Old Karl. I'm sorry. I wouldn't have asked if I'd realized. Cheers!'

'Double damn you!' She laughed and accepted the toast. 'Cheers! Felix has not yet . . . what would the word be . . . assimilated? digested? . . . his time in Mauthausen. He was plucked from the staircase of death by a communist who knew of his pre-war support of workers' rights in Paris. He was taught carving – a masonry sort of carving – by a Nazi who knew he was a fine artist and thought that was more important than being a quarter-Jew. And he was taken from there to the diet experiment by another Nazi who wanted to save Felix for the same reasons, even though he was an ss doctor. Artist Felix thinks those actions were his by right, but human Felix cannot accept that he had any right to be saved when so many good friends were murdered, especially as he was so indifferent to the fate of the Jews before the Gestapo told him he was one himself. He just says, "We survived. They didn't. It's over. Look forward. Get on with it." That's Felix.'

'And what's so wrong with that?'

'What's wrong is that he doesn't know which life to get on with – the life of nineteen thirty-six or the life of nineteen *forty*-six. And if you want to know something that *really* is none of your business – he's thinking of becoming a practising Jew.' She slumped. 'Damn! This was going to be such a jolly evening!'

Upstairs, Pippin began to cry.

Faith knew exactly where to find Felix – up in the Johnsons' at the top of the house. Even when he and she had been lovers, he had always gone to Marianne for 'an impartial opinion,' as he called it. Willard called it 'touching base with Europe.' She didn't think there was any sort of sexual, or even romantic, element in their relationship; in a way, it was too deep for either sort of involvement – more like kinship than desire.

She paused at the first-floor landing, outside the door to Chris Riley-Potter's and Nina's. Here the choice was to go directly up the new flight of stairs to the Johnsons' or take the old way, which led through the Palmers'.

She chose the Palmers', with some vague hope of buttonholing Nicole on the way up. Standing there in the passage, irresolute, she heard Nicole singing that lullaby Willard had taught the whole community: *Don't wander away love* . . . She stood outside the nursery door, entranced, for Nicole had a strangely compelling singing voice, with all the femininity of Josephine Baker but edged with the stridency of Edith Piaf.

Nicole was jealous of life – her own life. She never lingered to gaze fondly at her little darling if her singing had already sent him – and young Tommy – to sleep; instead, as now, she backed away toward the door, singing the final line again and again until she was out on the landing.

'Oh!' she cried out in surprise, catching Faith on the threshold.

'That was just so beautiful,' Faith told her. 'Actually, I was on my way up to see if Felix was with the Johnsons, but I wanted first—'

'He's with Marianne, I think. Willard's in town, closing some big deal, Marianne says.'

'But I wanted to ask you first about . . . well, what sort of mood he's in – Felix, that is. He didn't want to watch these films of Angela's – and having seen them, I can quite understand—'

'You *saw* them?' Nicole was aghast.

'I saw two – and that was more than enough. Eric's still there, in case . . . you know?' She wound an imaginary handle beside her head. 'I just wonder if you saw Felix on the way up . . . and whether he said anything?'

Nicole shrugged. 'I've been bathing Andrew and Tommy and putting them to bed. Lena's gone to the village – her mother's not well.'

'But Felix . . .?'

'I should think Felix is livid.'

'D'you think he has a *right* to be livid?' Faith asked.

Nicole stared blankly at her for a moment and then said, 'Come downstairs and have a glass of wine – *vin ordinaire,* nothing special.'

When they were seated – before a roaring log fire that cast massive shadows in that huge drawing room – Nicole said, 'Why would he need a *right* to be angry with Angela? He thinks what she's doing is self-destructive. So do I. And I'll bet Marianne does, too.'

'It's just this,' Faith replied. 'You risked your life in the war. You must have woken up on many mornings wondering if today was the day when you'd be betrayed and then shot. The same was true of Marianne. Maybe you and she still have those night-mares – and please, I don't want to know, I'm not poking my nose in there, but the point is: you don't *seem to*. You both have new lives and you both get on with them, whatever nightmare memories—'

'I think I know one reason why he might be angry, or not want to take part this evening,' Nicole said. 'I joined the resistance, so did Angela. So did Marianne. And we all know why Felix couldn't possibly do the same – why it was far better for him to try to carry the news to America . . . with his reputation. He knows it, too, but there's still something in there' – she tapped her skull – 'that wishes it could have been different.'

'Has he talked to you about it?'

'Sometimes. Not often. But yes, he has talked about it. I tell him I hardly ever think of it now. When I do, it seems like it happened to another person . . . or a previous existence. Like now I only do maths *en français*. I dream in English.' She laughed. 'I even discuss French novels in English, with a French couple we know in Welwyn Garden City. She lends me French books and I am happier discussing them in English. French is too vague, too abstract. English is concrete. Sorry! I only wish to show—'

'Exactly. I think Marianne would generally feel the same, and she, too, risked her life, day in and day out, during the war, as you said. But she has also built a new life and put all that behind her. I think – in fact, I know – that Felix believes Angela should be able to do the same. She has gone back to a wonderful job, with a crêche for Pippin, and no loss of seniority. But there's this *bloody* man at the BBC who somehow has access to the war-crimes archives . . . oh, I don't know. This is super wine.'

'Have some more.' Nicole held out the bottle.

'No, thanks all the same. I'd better go up and see how Felix
. . . If he's simmered down.'

Casually, carefully busying herself with returning the bottle
to the tray beside her, Nicole said, 'Do you still carry a torch
for him – just a little bit?'

'Yes,' Faith admitted, rising to go back upstairs. 'But in a
motherly sort of way. Felix is like a lot of artists, and I've met
quite a few – there's an eternal child within him.'

'Dangerous people,' Nicole commented. 'For any woman with
a motherly streak!'

Faith hesitated, laughed, and went on up the stairs. She had
reached the top of the flight before she said, 'Actually, that lets
me out.'

'It must be over by now.' Faith spoke while crossing the threshold
into the Johnsons' drawing room, which had been their workshop when they first moved in. Now it was the Scandinavian
showpiece Marianne and Willard had intended to build from
the start – the room whose functional elegance and superb
craftsmanship (actually, more crafts*woman*ship in this case) would
seduce all inquirers and waverers into the blessed state of client-
hood. Unfortunately, for Marianne that seduction now tended
to happen at the Garrick Club, the Lansdowne Club, and the
Royal Automobile Club, all of which august institutions had
strict rules against the transaction of any business on their prem-
ises, even though their very existence was designed for no other
purpose than to ensure that good chaps gave preferment to other
good chaps whom they knew and trusted. It was an ambiguity
Willard might have been born in order to exploit. He was
certainly one of the *good chaps* these days – 'our starchitect,' as
Eric had started calling him after that business with the Festival
of Britain lavatories.

Felix was sitting on the sofa, staring into the fire; Marianne
was squatting on the floor by his left leg but hunched forward
over a magazine, turning the pages as if searching for a particular
image. '*Hej* Faith!' she said. 'The coffee's still hot. Help
yourself.'

'You didn't stay to the end?' Felix asked.

'I endured two of them and then fled. But I stopped by
Nicole's on the way.'

'*That's* what you should have in your studio!' Marianne held up the magazine. 'We call it *kakelugn* – I don't know the English. A ceramic stove?'

'*Kachelofen*,' Felix said.

'What would it be in English?' Marianne passed the magazine to Faith as she sat down on the far side of Felix.

It was a photograph of an elegant – eighteenth-century? – drawing room, clearly Swedish, with a tall, highly decorated pillar of porcelain tiles.

'It's an oven,' Marianne explained. 'Or stove. The fire door is outside the room – in the passage on the other side of the wall. The servants fill it from there and there's about a kilometre of flue inside the pillar . . . well, ten metres, anyway. And if you take the wood we use just for *kindling* a fire here and light it in that, it will burn out in fifteen minutes and stay warm all night.'

Faith looked at the caption to the illustration. It was all in Swedish but among the sea of incomprehensibility she saw . . . *slosset har ägts av von Ritters sedan 1652* . . . 'Your family home?' she guessed, flipping the pages and admiring something like a domestic version of Versailles.

'Yes,' Marianne said impatiently. 'What would you call it?'

'Words almost fail me, but you're obviously slumming it here in the Dower House.'

Felix laughed but Marianne was not amused. 'The ceramic stove!' she insisted.

'Oh. Yes, well . . . ceramic stove . . . porcelain stove. We don't have them in England but if they ever caught on, I suppose we'd annexe the foreign word and plant the Union Jack on it. What's the German word for schadenfreude – which is what I came up here hoping to discuss?'

Felix's expression darkened at once; Marianne reached behind him and wagged a finger out of his sight.

But Faith was undeterred. 'You can't just run away like this, Felix. That's your *wife* who's flirting with . . . with . . . with *mental breakdown* over there.'

'I tried to stop her,' he said in a voice suddenly hoarse and unsteady; tears were forming, too. (*Good!* Faith thought. His turn-the-other-cheek brand of stoicism was out of place here.) 'The first time we ever met – or, rather, got talking – we went for a walk in Regent's Park and she told me how the BBC was full of Secret Service people and she said one of them thought he'd be able to get copies of those films for her. It was probably just bait to get her to sleep with him but he obviously had no idea what she's like once she sinks her teeth into something. Anyway, he has – at long last – delivered.'

The obvious question hung in the air: *Is* that *why he's 'livid'?*

Faith saw that a big change of tack – and tact – was needed. 'Well, that's the *history* bit,' she said. 'What about the psychology? She's risking some kind of crisis with that film over there and—'

'I don't think so,' he said. 'You're too melodramatic.'

'Oh, really? You should have been there to see it . . .' And she went on to describe how Angela had screamed at the flickering ghosts on that bedsheet – and that *particular* bedsheet, no less. 'I don't know if she's doing the right thing,' she went on. 'I do know it's risky but if it helps her . . . I mean, I cannot even begin to imagine (and believe me, I have tried) but I cannot have the first idea what it was like to survive in those camps, one day at a time . . . Camps? My God, the very *word* is an insult. Scouts have camps. Those places were . . . gaping *wounds* opened into hell itself. But you do, Felix. You *know*! You were there, too. So if it helps her cope with the aftermath, you should be there to celebrate. And if it doesn't . . . well . . . she's your wife.'

Felix sprang to his feet, spilling Marianne's coffee as he ran to the door and vanished. He muttered something that might have been 'sorry' but outside they heard him give a cry – a howl – that sounded barely human. Then his feet on the stairs. Then . . . silence.

'God in heaven,' Faith murmured. 'Have I done the right thing? Have I even the *right* to do the right thing?'

She sought for reassurance in Marianne's eyes but there was none. Nor was there any censure, either.

'Perhaps I should be there, too?' Marianne said, little above a whisper. 'Me and Nicole.'

'No!' Faith was quite firm. 'That was two hours ago. Now it's different. Now it's for Felix and Angela.' After a pause she added, 'And, oddly enough, Eric.'

Marianne looked up sharply. 'Eric?'

'Yes. I know we all think he's just flippant and tries to make a joke of *everything* – which shows he's got no deep feelings about *anything* . . . but . . . I'm not so sure. I've got to know him a lot better since he started writing for us. I think he had even less stomach than me for Angela's picture show but he knew she shouldn't be alone.'

'But to choose the same sheet where she and Felix conceived Pippin and then show those . . .' Marianne shook her head. '*Herrrrre Gud!*'

The rain had stopped, leaving a noisy memory of itself among the bare branches of the weeping ash in the centre of the court-yard. Felix hesitated before the cottage door; the fire that Faith's words had lighted within him expired somewhere on the three flights down to the ground, as the enormity of his wife's symbolic use of their bedsheet sank more deeply home. He lifted the latch silently and silently let himself in.

'Mine certainly isn't a fraud,' Angela was saying. 'If any marriage in this community is a fraud, it's yours and Isabella's. From the moment you came here – even before you got out of the car – you were arguing with each other even then. And so it has been ever since.'

Eric laughed. 'How do you know? You weren't even here then.'

'Nicole told me – but that wasn't all. She said she caught the pair of you looking at each other when you thought no one could see you, and it made her quite jealous. So there!'

'I can't imagine why,' Eric said loftily and, Felix thought, slightly uncomfortably, too.

'Because of the love she saw between you. You can't fool Nicole in things like that.'

'Well . . . love can lead us into strange, dark places. We must all learn to forgive it if we possibly can.'

'Ha ha. that's just the whisky talking. And look – you've drunk it all! Never mind, there's another bottle on the top shelf in the larder.'

Eric rose, and was pointing out that *his* glass still held half the portion he had first poured into it when Felix appeared, holding the bottle Angela had mentioned.

'Hey, Felix!' Eric called out. 'Jewish joke for you: never serve calamari at a bris! Good, eh?'

Felix almost dropped the bottle. Fumbling to retain it, he stared from Eric to Angela and back to Eric again. 'You told him!' he accused her.

Eric resumed his walk toward the kitchen, now intent on leaving the house. 'Time for the truth all round, old chum,' he said. Then, gripping Felix by the arm: 'Rewind the film and watch it. I was surprised how quickly I grew accustomed to repetitive sudden deaths but I suppose that won't surprise you at all, eh?'

Angela lay in his arms and they watched the rerun of the film in stillness and in silence. When the last pathetic body dropped into oblivion – ss-*Aufseherin Gertrud Schreiter, 20 Sept 1948* – Angela closed her eyes and whispered ecstatically, 'It's over, *Liebling*. I never want to see this film again.'

Felix rose without replying, jerked the plug from its socket, went to the curtains, unpinned the bedsheet, turned off the lights, and came back to the couch. Wordless, he spread the sheet on the air, slipped beneath it, let it fall to shroud them both. There they squirmed out of their clothes and made slow, uncomfortable, ecstatic love.

When they awoke in their bed next morning, still beneath that same sheet, she said, as if no time at all had intervened, 'But it's not the same for you. It's still not over for you.'

Felix sighed but offered no argument.

'Maybe,' she went on in that same speculative tone, 'it would be better if you never resolved it? I think each time you start a new sculpture something in you says, *This is it! This is where I finally get out from under that* . . . whatever it is that's overhanging your life. Not a cloud. Something heavier, darker, more active than that. Like a devil riding the cloud and throwing down bolts of lightning. Is that right?'

These images were so alien to her that Felix knew immediately where they came from and what sort of conversation she and Eric must have had before he burst in upon them. 'I used to joke that Art saved me from death for her own inscrutable reasons,' he said. 'If you're right, then I got it precisely the wrong way round. Art had nothing to do with the preservation of my life back then but it has everything to do with the preservation of my sanity now. Well, you could be right. In which case, why not leave well alone. Remove the devil from the thundercloud and what becomes of me? A sculptor who is no longer *driven*. A sculptor who can turn out nothing but kitsch versions of his former glorious works.' He gave a sudden, delighted laugh. 'By God, that's exactly what's happened to old Picasso! That's why he's just turning out kitsch these days!' He calmed down and added, 'But you didn't need to tell him I'm interested in Judaism, all the same.'

'Are you afraid he'll tell everyone? He won't even tell Isabella – honestly. If you think anything else, you don't know him at all.'

He chuckled glumly. 'Oh, I know him only too well. He'll try and argue me out of it – that's what I'm afraid of. Help a lame dog over a stile.'

'What's that mean?'

'It's an old English saying. Eric once told me that English people are so good at helping lame dogs over stiles that they'll often not only build the stile in order to prove it – they'll bloody well lame the dog, too! And he has such an abiding distrust of all religions, he'll be unable to resist the chance to try and convert me. What's a "bris," by the way? Some sort of Jewish festival, I'm sure. And he could tell I didn't understand it, so he'll think he starts off with a good chance. Oy-veh!'

Friday, 15 December 1949 – January 1950

Eric knocked at the cottage door and opened it without waiting for Angela's 'Come in!' 'Only me!' he cried.

She tripped silently downstairs with her finger to her lips. 'I've just got her off to sleep.' She spoke more normally when the kitchen door was closed behind them. 'If you've come looking for blood on the carpets, you're going to be disappointed. Coffee?'

'Please. I'm glad to hear it. I felt a bit guilty going back across the yard last night.'

'Oh, sure!' She measured the grounds into the cafetière and

filled it with not-quite-boiling water from the kettle that sang on the Aga, which she and Felix had just had installed. 'I know you and Isabella like to boil it to death in a percolator but this is *real* coffee, European style.'

'Did Faith explain why she wanted to see your movie show last night – and why she wanted me to be there, too?'

'Something about writing a new soundtrack to it?' She jiggled the filter to make the floating grounds fall.

'Yes, but for what reason? Did she explain that? She thinks that what passes for documentary on television is just too bland.'

Angela laughed as she pressed down the filter disc.

'Yes,' Eric agreed. 'Albert Pierrepoint would be a slight case of *overkill,* as our nuclear warriors say. But she would like to produce a documentary with more bite. More substance.'

Angela paused. Then she set the cafetière down. 'You can finish filling this cup,' she said. 'I think I've got something for you. It's an illegal transcript I made during the war – the thing they sent me to Ravensbrück for. It's a transcript of a conference in January 'forty-two in Wannsee at which the ss told the rest of the Nazi hierarchy how they were going to murder up to ten thousand Jews a day. The final solution to the Jewish problem, they called it.'

Eric did not return to the cottage until after lunch.

'I can't stop long,' Angela warned him. 'I'm on a special night shift. We're migrating a whole studio.'

'OK,' he said, laying the English translation of her Wannsee transcript down. 'This is genuine? It says you were the recording engineer? And this is exactly what you recorded?'

'Word for word.'

'Jesus flaming Christ! And that's why they sent you to that concentration camp? Why didn't you ever say? I'd have cheered along with you last night. Who did the translation, if I may ask?'

'Felix and me, if you're worried about copyright. D'you suppose you and Faith could make something of it? For tv – a sort of half-drama-semi-documentary?'

Eric sat down. 'What have you done with it so far? Who've you shown it to? I mean, you didn't originally do it for radio or television, I suppose. In fact, why *did* you translate it at all?'

Rather than answer him, she explained how it all came about . . . how she, a lowly recording engineer in the ss, recorded the Wannsee Conference, which determined 'the Final Solution of the Jewish Question' . . . was so appalled that she made a transcript and a carbon copy . . . met Marianne (then working as an apprentice architect under Albert Speer, at the behest of her father, a Swedish steel baron) . . . and passed the transcript to her to convey to the neutral Swedish embassy.

'And the carbon?' Eric asked.

'I hid it. Then gave it to the British after the war. British army intelligence – who said they lost it. Felix and I got the top copy back from Hermann Treite, the chauffeur at the Swedish Embassy, after the war – that time we went to Hamburg.'

Eric returned to his question: why had they translated it?

She shrugged. 'Felix got too busy with commissions . . . and then we started Pippin and . . . you know. D'you and Faith want to take it up?'

He nodded. 'How can we not? But I need to know more. How did British army intelligence lose it?'

'They *say* they lost it. And then they found a *supposed* protocol of the conference, which we – Felix and I and some friends in Germany – think was a deliberately watered-down version planted in the archives near the end of the war, probably by Eichmann, to deceive the allies. The covering letter was in poor German but not poor enough for the allies to notice. And that has now become the officially accepted protocol. I don't suppose anything will change that now. Too many reputations are at stake. So . . . one-up to Eichmann, if he's still out there somewhere. Listen – oh God! – I should be halfway to Welwyn North by now!'

'Fear not! I'll drive you up to town and I can collect Faith from Manutius, and we can discuss the idea on the way back. I don't think it would be fair to ask her to read it without some preparation!'

On the way into town he asked about Felix.

She bridled. 'What about him?'

'The translation is half his, I suppose.'

'Oh, that!'

'No, Angela, you know I'm not really talking about "oh, that." I'm talking about letting it go. About Felix letting it go. Flirting with Judaism isn't going to help.'

'Maybe he just has to go through with it. I don't know.'

'There's no guarantee he'd come out the other side. And his art would suffer. It would degenerate into sentimental lechery.'

'How can you be sure of that? You can't know.'

'Marc Chagall? Jules Pascin? How many more do you need? When is Felix's birthday?'

'The fifteenth of January – next month.'

'Perhaps I'll buy him a decent copy of the Old Testament. He can read all about the *Vernichtung* of the Hittites and Amorites and Canaanites, et cetera – "as the Lord God commanded." Did you ever read it? Your Wannsee transcript is just milk and water by comparison with the arrangements God had in mind. And they were all Semites, too! Hitler wasn't the first with the darkness.'

When it came to making a documentary drama out of the Wannsee transcript, the strategy also changed: no longer would Faith go into her interview with a ready-made demonstration film, which would probably have been considered too pushy, in any case. As Eric pointed out: 'I can just hear one of those plummy voices saying, "We already have enough male Napoleons in television; the last thing we want is a female Napoleon to add to them, thank you very much!"'

So now the plan was for Eric to submit Angela's transcript (suitably edited and adapted for a radio play) to the Home Service drama department. Its broadcast would undoubtedly be a sensation, especially if the actors were told to use normal English accents rather than music-hall-comic German – and Eric would insist on that. And then, when Faith went for her interview, it would be the talk of everyone in the business, so she could say, 'That's *exactly* the sort of thing television drama should be doing – hard-hitting realism with a social purpose. Stop just doing extracts from West End productions. Forget Priestley and Rattigan. Television is a window on the *world*!' et cetera.

It didn't work like that.

The Home Service turned it down flat, with a standard printed rejection slip saying they had considered it carefully but could not envisage a space for it in their present schedule. But one producer did leave a note a few pages into the script, saying, *Try the Third – this is more their territory than ours.*

Harold Byron, who commissioned enigmatic but ground-breaking scripts for the Third Programme, wrote:

> We think we could possibly see our way to commissioning a work based on this script but we do feel several rather drastic changes will be necessary. Large parts of it strike one as being in very poor taste.
>
> (1)   Many Roman Catholics will find parts of it gratuitously insulting to Pope Pius XII, who is, after all, still in office.
>
> (2)   The bestial nature of the Nazi regime has been copiously documented – rather too copiously, some might say (personally I like Jews and have many Jewish friends but as a political force they are becoming rather strident) – so the more gruesome contributions of some participants at this supposed conference (we assume it is fictional, by the way?) will appear unnecessarily distasteful to the average Third Programme listener. We think in particular of your Herr Lange and his crass contributions to the discussion. Somewhere in the script you refer to him as 'Doktor,' but, whether medical or academic, would a man with a doctorate speak so vulgarly?
>
> (3)   The rather pedestrian recital of the Jewish populations of the various countries of Europe by the character you name Eichmann is tediously repetitive but we could handle that with judicious fadings in and out.
>
> (4)   If there is a basis of historical fact behind this script, and if these participants are genuine members of the ss and the Nazi bureaucracy, their names are virtually unknown and it seems strange that they would be invited to take part in a conference which, if genuine, was pivotal in the campaign of extermination. However, mention is also made of Mr Felix Breit who is, indeed, a very well-known artist, now living in England. It will be necessary to gain clearance from him before we can use his name in the way you intend.

'There's more in the same vein,' Eric told Faith. 'But you get the drift. Are you sure you want to work for this shower?'

'More than ever!' was her response. 'But TV not radio.'

They were walking in aimless circles round the big lawn, kicking snow, and dodging miniature snowballs from toddlers who had to walk right up to them in order to score.

'So let's forget radio and let's forget high drama.' He folded the letter away.

'And?'

'In three weeks' time Selincourt is coming back to the Dower House to do another fashion shoot. The summer collection this time – they waited for the snow, of course, because that's the way *everyone* in the fashion industry's mind works. Anyway (speak of the Devil) my own darling Isabella is willing to sweet-talk them into letting us make a documentary of the event – to have a go at it, I mean. The outfits will be sumptuous. The lighting will be at least equal to the best the BBC can do. The girls will be gorgeous in their stately, snooty way. There will be tension, tantrums, and triumphs – I say! There's our title: *Tensions, Tantrums, and Triumphs!* What I'm suggesting is that we make the documentary ourselves and simply offer it to BBC television – as if we're a small independent. They already buy a load of crap from America – have you seen *The Cisco Kid*? – so why not from us?'

'And if they don't buy it?'

'That doesn't really matter. It's a sprat to catch a mackerel. Someone in Wardour Street will snap it up – to go in that *Look at Life* slot between the supporting film and the main feature, which is only there to pad out the time until they've sold enough ice cream.'

Faith stopped dead and hoicked some snow out from inside her collar – a lucky throw from Theo Wilson who, now rising four, was slightly more accurate than the others. 'Go away, you little beast!' she shouted with enough menace to send him off with screams that turned to laughter. Then, to Eric: 'Sometimes you frighten me, you really do.'

'The point is, you'd be going in there to sell a documentary, not to tell them how much cleverer you are than they will ever be. Why, the very idea of applying for a position at Ally Pally hasn't even entered your mind . . . though now they come to suggest it (and here comes the mackerel) . . . well . . . yes, you're certainly *interested*. What are they offering? Only you have to know quite quickly because negotiations with *Look at Life Productions* in Wardour Street are already approaching the stage where binding commitments are looming. I think that's the way to play it. Why do I frighten you?'

'What happened to all that missionary zeal about Angela's Wannsee transcript?'

'Its time will come. Don't worry. We'll find a way one day.'

She laughed and said, 'I rest my case.'

And then they turned to swoop upon The Tribe like angry raptors, flapping their overcoats and roaring while the children darted in all directions, screaming, laughing, scooping up snow and throwing it in comet-tails of powder.

The following evening Eric went over to Faith's little flat in the cottage and said, 'I could frighten you even more.'

She shrugged resignedly. 'Go on, then.'

'You've been approaching this entirely the wrong way—'

'*I* have!'

'OK – *we* have. We're missing the fundamental point, which is that we – or you, with whatever assistance you think I might be able to give – want to do something *new* with TV. That's the important word – *new*. New TV. Not old TV. As soon as you have a new *anything* you also have an old *something*, too.'

'Yes . . . and the war is over and grass is green and what else?'

'It's *so* obvious we've overlooked it. You have to make them think they represent old TV. That there's some vague, shadowy new TV waiting to come flooding in and leave them all washed up in some old backwater. We've been thrashing around for a single new programme when what we want is a whole new order.'

Faith swallowed audibly. 'Right! It's my fault – I misled you. I misled myself. I thought the way we sell books to other publishers . . . I sort of assumed I could sell a TV idea that way, too. But I like this much better.' After a moment's thought she added: 'What we must do next, obviously, is make a list of all the things we consider to be old TV, like putting a camera in one of the boxes at Sadler's Wells and showing a ballet from there—'

'Instead of commissioning a new ballet and producing it themselves.'

'*Ourselves!*'

'Right! We're already the new broom, OK?' He rubbed his hands. 'This is going to be *fun!*'

Within an hour they had compiled two lists.

Old TV
- Live broadcasts from West End theatres
- The Potter's Wheel
- London to Brighton in Four Minutes
- Sports coverage using a single camera
- News you could mostly watch with closed eyes, because it's just read out by a man at a desk
- Magazine programmes in the 'Look at Life' style with hackneyed voice-over commentaries. (Example: 'And from the beauties of the deep to beauties of another kind; for here in the calm of this charming garden an ancient craft is being carried on in a noble tradition . . .' etc. ad nauseam)
- Commissioned dramas that look more like stage plays than movies (because they're mostly stage plays that were rejected?)
- Critics' Choice programmes that have a 'Last Supper' style of seating and no visual references to whatever they're discussing
- All programmes in which doctors, scientists, historians and other academics, lawyers, etc. are so afraid of their colleagues' contempt for their 'popularizing' of their specialities that they talk far above their viewers' heads
- Programmes in which politicians are allowed to make statements without being challenged, except occasionally by other politicians

(Enough to be going on with . . .)

New TV
- Television is not cinema (a mass experience), it is domestic (a family experience). The people who appear on it are guests in our homes.

- The cinema can show us the orator addressing thousands. Television must also show his face filling the screen and talking to <u>us</u>. We want to see his eyes, how his lips move – is he sweating?
- Commissioned television dramas can throw the conventions of acts and scenes away. They cannot match the resources of Denham or Pinewood but the judicious intercutting of filmed sequences can take us where the theatre cannot and with an intimacy denied to the movie.
- In live sports coverage we must develop telescope cameras that can catch the agony on the oarsman's face, the triumph in the batsman's grin as he hits a six, the blood streaming from a cut above the boxer's eye.
- There is not enough <u>fun</u> on television. We must devise new parlour games, or adapt old ones, to suit a weekly half-hour period – charades, dumb-crambos, hangman, word games . . . all could be adapted in this way with, say, three or four well-known faces doing the guessing or performing the forfeits. These games would be the sprat to catch the mackerel of an enlarged audience for a more serious programme to follow.
- The BBC must scour the universities for trustworthy academics who are not afraid to popularize their subjects. And instead of standing at a lectern in the studio they could, for instance, walk through Hampton Court, talking about some relevant point in the life of Cardinal Wolsey or Henry the Eighth – all to be shown on film, of course. And why not Pisa, for Galileo's gravity experiments . . . St Peter's for Michelangelo's art . . . the Cavendish for a talk on the atom . . . the Mount of Olives for a Good Friday meditation?
- And the BBC must stand up to the other estates of the realm – indeed, take its place among them as an equal, especially when handling politics. There is a Home Service programme from Bristol which is only heard in the West Country at the moment, called *Any Questions* in which a 'question master' (Freddy Grisewood) puts questions from the audience to three backbenchers in Parliament (one from each main party) plus a common-sense layman like Russell Braddon or Arthur Street. It

would transfer admirably to television where, at the moment, serious political questions of the day are never aired. And the convention whereby all mention of politics vanishes from the BBC as soon as an election gets under way really must be overturned. And we must be able to discuss matters that come before Parliament up to, during, and after the debate in the House; this fourteen-day rule is monstrous.

(Enough to be going on with — we only want to scare them witless, not to death.)

Tuesday, 14 February 1950

Chris Riley-Potter waited through minutes that weighed like hours while Felix examined 'The New Guernica.' Actually, it could no longer be called by that name because, although Picasso's masterpiece was the inspiration for starting a mural on the same grand scale, the painting had evolved in quite a different direction – inspired by Nina's original bright orange footprints. Now the entire wall was one heaving, seething mass of footprints – herds and shoals and skeins and flocks of footprints . . . footprints of every colour available in Rowney's, Winsor and Newton's, the Universal Drawing Office, and Cornellisen's (and Jewson's, the builders' merchants in Hertford) . . . cheeky urchins' feet . . . tired waiters' feet . . . streetwalkers' . . . policemen's . . . newborn babies' . . . Winston Churchill's . . . Mahatma Ghandi's . . . and the foot of the one-legged flute player in Oxford Street ('Forty Years' Service and not a Penny Pension') . . . think of them and they were there. Somewhere.

At last Felix spoke: 'It is everything I hate about modern art,' he said. 'And yet I have to admit it is one of the most powerful and dramatic paintings that I, personally, have seen since *Les demoiselles d'Avignon.*' He looked directly at Chris for the first time. 'And I hated that, too. God, how I resisted that one! But it got me in the end. And now, I suppose, I'm going to have to do the same all over again with this!'

Chris let out a quantity of breath that even he had not been aware of holding back. 'Yippee-kyoh!' he whooped. And with a hop and a skip to the window he flung up the bottom sash and laid a hand to a bottle of champagne kept cold on the outside sill. But then he withdrew and closed the window again. 'Better wait for Anna,' he said. 'She won't be long now.'

'Anna?'

'Yeah.' He grinned. 'Nina and I . . . we sort of . . . she's gone, anyway. You must be the last to know.'

'I've been in town the last two days. Who's Anna?'

'She's still at the Slade. She'll be here soon.' He walked up to his mural, near the doorway into the kitchen. 'I wasn't too sure about this bit. You see how the feet sort of organize themselves into groups, except—'

Felix interrupted. 'When you say she'll be here soon—'

'Quite soon. This is the group you see first. Or are supposed to see first—'

'Does she have a car?'

'Who?'

'This Anna.'

'Oh. No. She walks from the station. But no sooner does your eye—'

'Three miles? In this snow? It's not safe.'

'She's Danish. She's a lot more used to snow than you or me. Well, than me, anyway. What I'm trying to explain is—'

'But the roads . . . cars . . . skidding . . . they're treacherous. And it'll be dark soon.'

'She walks over the fields. It's only two and a half miles. She's done it every day so far. She says she loves it – tramping through the snow, even in the dark. It reminds her of home. Wait till you clap eyes her, man. She – is – *the* – most beautiful girl you've ever seen. Heads turn in the street, I tell you. Anyway,' he turned back to the painting, 'can you see any sort of a group in this shower of feet near the door?'

They were still discussing the painting an hour later when Willard entered the flat without knocking and said, 'You'd better come up to our place, Chris. There's been a spot of trouble.'

'What d'you think?' Chris asked, waving at his painting.

'Later, man. I love it. I wanna talk to you about a commission, but right now this is more important.'

'Me, too?' Felix asked.

'Sure. Everyone should hear this.' Leading the way back upstairs, he added, 'And *do* something about it.'

They heard Anna before they saw her – talking voluble, excited Danish to Marianne, who was trying to calm her in quiet, soothing Swedish. Though the two languages sounded quite different, the women seemed to understand each other.

And Chris had not exaggerated, Felix realized, the moment he set eyes on her. Small, petite, honey-blonde with the most intensely radiant blue eyes imaginable, she glowed with the innocent sexiness of all pretty blonde children, but heightened, because of her near-maturity, to a degree that caught his breath.

The moment she saw Chris she flung herself into his arms. 'Did I kill him? I don't think so.' She spoke to him as if he must have understood what she had been saying earlier.

'What? Who? *Kill?*'

'Someone followed her across the fields,' Marianne explained. 'And when she reached the stile into the churchyard—'

'Yes!' Anna, still hugged tight by Chris, took up her story. 'He grabbed me and said the more you struggle, such more will it hurt. But with a torch I shone it in his eyes and ran and he fell over a . . . a stone . . .'

'Gravestone,' Marianne said.

'Yes. And I sprang on him—'

'Jumped on him.'

'Yes.' She slipped out of Chris's arms and made the old floor-boards tremble with her demonstration.

'Where?' Willard asked.

Tony and Nicole joined the crowd. 'We heard,' Tony said. 'Adam's coming up, too.'

'Where?' Willard repeated.

'Still in the churchyard,' Anna said, slightly bewildered.

'No. On him. Where did you jump on him? Whereabouts on his body?'

She shrugged. 'All over.'

'Head? Neck? Spine? Stomach?'

Every man was thinking, *balls*? This time she just shrugged.

There was a moment of awed silence as they pictured this beautiful, doll-like young girl stomping 'all over' a supine man and then leaving him in such a state that she could not be sure he was still alive.

'Did he cry out? Try to get up?'

'Steady on, old boy!' Chris complained.

''Fraid not,' Willard replied. 'If she did kill him, or even leave him seriously injured – well, we've got to work things out here. The cops will turn up soon enough.'

'Maybe no one saw her,' Chris objected. 'Did anyone see you, darling?'

She shook her head.

'There's snow all around. Footprints . . .'

'She made them yesterday. Felix gave her a lift today, right, Felix?'

'I would have if you hadn't—'

Willard cut in again. 'There was fresh snow last night. There'll be only one set of prints between the churchyard and here.'

'We'll say she made them this morning on her way *to* the station.'

'Walking backward for three miles? Butt out, Chris – you're not helping.'

Adam joined them at that moment. 'No one was killed,' he said. 'I rang Bob Ambrose to see if he'd heard anything. The only excitement he knows of is that someone called an ambulance to the council houses and it took Con Christie to Hertford Hospital. He's the one who broke into The Bull last Saturday night. They think a car knocked him over and didn't stop.'

When Eric arrived Adam's retelling was even more terse: 'Someone called Con Christie tried to attack Anna in the churchyard and the ambulance has just taken him to hospital.'

Eric reached out and shook her hand. 'You're a real daughter of Waldemar!' he said. 'Denmark would be proud of you, Princess!'

The smile almost split her face. 'Yes!' And she laughed for the first time. 'And my second name is Margaret, indeed!'

'Queen of Denmark, Norway, *and* Sweden,' Marianne explained to the others. 'Daughter of King Waldemar.'

'Trust bloody Eric!' Tony murmured. 'So, is the panic over?'

'Not by a mile!' Willard insisted. 'We've got to make sure this Christie guy doesn't try to take it out on Anna. Or anyone else here at the Dower House. We've gotta make it so he turns back and walks down some side street if he sees even the smallest, youngest kid from this place. And *we* don't want to come out one morning and find paint stripper over our cars . . . tires slashed . . . pigs let into the walled garden . . . stuff like that. I *know* guys like this. Scum. We should strike while the iron is hot. How can we find out when they turn him loose?'

'Who's his doctor?' Marianne asked. 'Probably Doc Wallace in Old Welwyn. Who knows him socially?'

Nobody volunteered. At length Adam said, 'He's asked us to design a detached surgery in his garden. I could try.'

'There's another phone in the bedroom,' Marianne told him.

'Here's a silly question,' Eric said when Adam had gone. 'Why the vigilante stuff, Willard? Why are we not simply driving Anna to the police station in Hertford – or asking them to send someone out here?'

'Because this piece of excrement knows the police will need *evidence* to arrest him for revenge acts like that, and he'll be careful not to leave it. But we only need *suspicion* before we pay him back. And we'll make sure he knows it, too. Come on, people! We can't leave our kids vulnerable to a bit of pond-life like that. They walk across those fields twice a day.'

It was a telling point but Eric persisted: 'It's illegal, Willard – and he will know that, too. He'll say it wasn't him in the churchyard. He was knocked down by a car that failed to stop. And then we all turned up out of the blue, headed him off at the pass, circled our horses around him, pulled out our six-shooters, burned a fiery cross on his lawn, and told him to head down the arroyo for Mexico if he knew what was good for him. Then *we're* in the hoosegow, man!'

Willard looked as if he were going to hit him. 'Oh! Typical of you to turn it into a joke, Eric. Your county police are just about the most useless bunch you could think of. While Anna was being attacked, they were probably hiding in the ditch on the B1000, catching drivers doing five miles per hour over the limit!'

'Which is what happened to Willard last week,' Marianne added helpfully.

The laughter defused the situation somewhat, but Willard remained unpersuaded. 'You guys do what you like – protect your kids in your own way. But I'm going to make it clear to this guy that he's sitting in the Last Chance Saloon.'

Adam returned. 'Doc Wilson says they're keeping him in overnight. He has a couple of broken ribs and some extensive bruising but they think he'll be OK to discharge tomorrow morning.'

'I don't wish to speak to the police,' Anna said suddenly. 'I think Mister Johnson has right. Make him fear.'

'Well, there's nothing we can do until tomorrow night, anyway—' Willard began.

'Oh, but there is!' Eric interrupted.

All eyes turned to him.

'Six concerned friends who turn up at the hospital, wanting to wish him well . . . bring him a box of chocolates . . . Of course, they won't let all six crowd around the bed, but two could go forward and give him a message of good cheer while the rest smile and wave in the doorway to the ward. Cheers mate! Thumbs up! Meanwhile, we all know exactly what message those two are murmuring in his ear. And there'd be a host of impeccable witnesses to the fact that nobody shouted, no one shook a fist in his face, no one carried a pick handle or a meat cleaver. You could do that, Willard. You must be quite used to smiling at people you'd much rather strangle.'

They all laughed, of course, but they also saw it was quite feasible . . . and extremely cunning. And when Eric added: 'A very *small* box of chocolates, of course,' the suggestion hardened into an actual operations order.

But, as frequently happened with Eric's plans, it didn't quite work out like that.

No one had reckoned that a detective from the despised Hertfordshire Constabulary – DC Warren, by name – might just be leaving the 'victim's' bedside, having taken a statement about the 'unfortunate hit-and-run accident.' Nor that he would form the rather obvious suspicion that one of these 'concerned friends and neighbours' had, in fact, been the hit-and-run driver.

Fortunately, his mind was still full of the cock-and-bull story he had just compiled into a statement and he was wondering which of the many holes it contained would offer the most leverage for a demolition job, so he did not arrive at this fresh suspicion until he was back in the hospital car park. And by the time he returned to the ward, Willard and Adam had given Con Christie both the chocolates and the message, and were leaving him adequately terrified and ready to protect even the Dower House pet animals with his life if need be.

Detective Constable Warren began with the obvious question: 'May I ask how many of you gentlemen are owners of cars or other vehicular transport – and I don't mean bicycles, by the way?'

Willard started to say something about calling his attorney but Eric stepped in: 'We all own cars, officer, and fortunately—'

'I'm not an officer,' Warren said.

'. . . and fortunately for you, we all live in the same house – the Dower House – so may I suggest that you allow me to drive you there? We came in two cars, so my friends can all go back in Willard's. And then you can satisfy yourself that none of them – the cars, I mean – is contaminated with Mister Christie's blood, or whatever sort of slime takes the place of blood in that man's veins. Shall we go?'

The man looked from face to face, chewed his lip, and at last accepted the suggestion, though with little show of eagerness. 'So you're not exactly friends of his?' he asked as they drew near Eric's car, the Bentley-engined Lagonda, which he could see was undamaged by any recent collision.

'All will be revealed,' Eric promised as he held open the door.

When they arrived at the Dower House, Eric shouted a jocular, 'Stand by your cars!' and then, parodying a company sergeant-major conducting an OC's kit inspection, took Warren round from car to car. It was pretty clear to everyone that Warren's suspicions had been laid to rest during the brief journey with Eric and this inspection was quite perfunctory. They finished up in front of the house, where the Wilsons' Jowett van was parked. In fact, with no snow beneath it and one axle up on a stand, there was no need to inspect it at all. Warren looked up at the house and said, 'So how do you lot all live here, then?'

Eric invited him in to see for himself; the others followed, turning the affair into an impromptu party. They were still there a couple of hours later when a sober Eric returned from having driven a slightly less sober DC Warren back to the hospital to collect his bicycle and wobble home. The only sticky moment had been when Willard had tackled him on the futility of speed traps on a perfectly safe, perfectly straight portion of road late at night. 'The moral of that,' Warren had told him, 'is *don't go speeding in the last fortnight of a quarter*! We've got our quotas, see, and the way to fill them without wasting too much police time is to "shoot fish in a barrel," as you call it.'

'What did you do? What did you say to him?' they all asked when Eric came back indoors.

'I learned he has a fourteen-year-old daughter,' Eric explained. 'So I put a completely hypothetical situation to him and he agreed – stressing that his answer was also completely hypothetical – that certain ways of resolving the situation without damage to his daughter's reputation or psyche would at least be contemplated, especially if the totally hypothetical perpetrator of the outrage was well known for his slipperiness, vindictiveness, and general flouting of all legal constraints. And we agreed that the great strength of Britain's constabulary was the enormous flexibility of its operational procedures at the day-to-day level. And then, just now, on the way back into Hertford, he commented that we – all of us here – were a real community. And I have to confess that I agreed with him. I said, "It's the way we can all rally round and act with unity of purpose when the need arises that makes life here worth so much more than it would be if we just lived on some housing estate." And actually, I think there's possibly a grain of truth in that – no?'

Tuesday, 18 April 1950

When Faith went to Paris with Fogel they always stayed either at the Ritz or the Bristol, but when she went on her own – even though still on business for Manutius – she preferred a small hotel on the west side of the Place du Tertre in Montmartre, just a few streets away from the Cathedral of Sacré Coeur. The views over Paris were spectacular, summer or winter, and the nightlife was bohemian and joyful.

Her errand, on this occasion, was delicate. Fogel, flying back from a deal with Sansoni in Florence, had been forced down in Paris by severe turbulence. The following day he had taken the chance to conclude another deal. this time for a French co-edition of the 'Junior Knowledge' series, with the Paris house of Hachette, signed and sealed over lunch. At dinner that evening, however, who should walk into the Grillon but Pierre Lavayssière of Larousse. The temptation was too great for Fogel. He took the dummies from his briefcase, showed them to Lavayssière, boasted about the wonders of the entire series, and ended up concluding a verbal deal in direct conflict with the one he had signed just eight hours earlier.

True, this new deal was merely verbal – to be cemented in writing after Lavayssière had visited Manutius and seen the operation for himself – but it was worth significantly more than that morning's deal with Hachette. Moreover, there was a good chance that Lavayssière would then sign a further deal for a series of adult illustrated books on philosophy, mathematics, contemporary history, and psychology that Fogel was planning. So there was no chance that Manutius would honour the original deal with Hachette. All Faith had to do was talk them out of it.

But how? Fogel left such trivial details to her discretion.

Perhaps one of the authors had turned *in* some wonderful text – which, *hélas!* turned *out* to be plagiarized from a Dutch book on the same subject? All deadlines were scrapped while checks were made on the remaining texts from the same author; so Manutius would quite understand if Hachette now wished to withdraw?

No.

Or maybe Fogel had had some kind of brainstorm because he had sold the series to Larousse on his way *to* Florence – and completely forgotten it when forced down in Paris – and then woke up convinced that his intention, all along, had been to sell the series to Hachette?

No.

Or two of the authors already had contractual obligations to Larousse . . . no.

At last she had it: the deal in Florence had been for a picture archive owned by Sansoni; Fogel had bought up the rights to exploit the archive in the world book markets. But, on looking at the contract more closely, Manutius's legal advisors were worried by one particular clause, which could be construed to provide for a rising royalty for each publisher who joined in any co-edition; so Fogel had sent her round the partners to ask if they were willing to pay their share of that rising royalty; if not (and she was pretty sure Hachette would not) he would allow them to drop out of the project.

It worked. Albert Faure of Hachette declined to pay the 'surcharge,' especially when Faith added a sweetener: 'You may remember our outstandingly successful "Modern Art" series? Well, we are planning to rearrange that material in small-format, board-covered books on single subjects – *Les Fauves, Der Blaue Reiter, Cubism, Abstract Expressionism* . . . and so forth . . .'

Faure interrupted eagerly to say he would be far more

interested in such a series; there was a greater hunger in France for books on art than for those on more general knowledge (a conclusion Faith had already reached at the Louvre bookstall that same morning).

On her last evening in Paris she spent a delicious hour between the crème brûlée and the last Armagnac, sketching an outline for the 'cannibalization' of the 'Modern Art' series in twelve slim, small-format hardbacks; it would be her parting gift to Fogel – though she still had no clear plan for her move to a position of power and authority in BBC television. Another minor detail that could be left to the last minute?

All while she juggled with titles, themes, and contents she became aware of another hotel guest who seemed to be paying unusual attention to her. Only twice did she catch him looking directly at her, but on several other occasions when she glanced his way, she felt sure he had only just taken his eyes off her a split-second earlier. At last he gave a rueful sort of 'caught-me' smile, raised his hands a defensive inch or two, and rose to his feet. He managed it with athletic ease, suggesting a greater strength than he had actually exerted. He walked across the floor to her, skirting the intervening tables with equal finesse.

'I must seem awfully rude,' he said as he drew near. 'Do forgive me but I feel sure we've met before.'

Her spirit sagged and she was about to tell him that he was not the first person ever to try that old chestnut when he added, 'Tell me – d'you ever hunt with the Beaufort?'

'Aha!' With her foot she pushed out the chair facing her and wafted her free hand toward it. 'Now you're talking!'

'Alexander Findlater.' He offered her his hand before sitting down.

'Faith Bullen-ffitch.'

'Right! Your father's the master—'

'Joint master.'

'Of course.'

'D'you live in their country?' she asked.

'Cigarette?' He offered his case.

She was about to take one when she realized they were all Gauloises. 'Think I'll stick to Balkan Sobranie,' she said. 'But thanks all the same. I was asking if you lived in the Beaufort's country?'

'I'd love to, but no – I'm friends with the Stutchberrys, near Tormarton. Go down there every chance I get, in the season. Well, I say that, but I've been in India for the past five years and my last leave was two years ago. I was down then, and that's when I'm sure I saw you. You flew a hedge and a ditch that had baffled five gentlemen riders – or alleged riders. You were on a magnificent chestnut gelding – once seen, never forgotten.'

'Golly!' Faith laughed. 'I'm afraid to interrupt. Pray continue, Mister Findlater!'

'Well . . . I'm thinking of going down this weekend and I did sort of wonder whether – not to say "hoped" – you'd be riding to hounds, too?'

She considered him: well preserved . . . mid–thirties, tanned (India, no doubt – what had he been doing there?), well spoken . . . air of command . . . definitely interesting. 'I don't really have time. I hunt more with the West Herts these days. The country isn't a patch on the Beaufort's, of course, but the foxes are well preserved.' Then this was the test question: 'Would you like a day out with *us* this Saturday? The cap's quite modest and I could get you a good mount for free.' She was thinking of Copenhagen, Sally's horse, who hadn't been out hunting for a month.

He compressed his lips into a sardonic smile and gave a little nod. 'It would be churlish to refuse such an amiable invitation. I'd be delighted. Have you finished your work for tonight? I usually take a little toddle around the square before turning in. Perhaps you might care to join me?'

'I'm not sure I know *how* to toddle,' she said, packing up her papers. 'But you can teach me. I'll just slip upstairs and put these away . . . fetch my coat.'

She did more. She refreshed her lipstick and powder, dabbed fresh perfume behind her earlobes, and – not as an afterthought – slipped in her dutch cap. It had been a long time.

'D'you happen to know the Stutchberrys?' he asked as they set off. He had donned a British warm, a bowler, and fine pigskin gloves.

How odd, she thought, to escape to Paris only to find myself reunited with my old tribe! 'I was at school with Gwen,' she told him.

'Ah, yes,' he murmured. 'Gwen.'

The night had turned cool – more like winter than spring. Paris in capricious mood. The lights hanging among the trees and the music that drifted out from the cafés and bars suggested that the pavements should be more populated than they were.

'Are you here on business?' she asked.

'Ha! I was about to ask the same of you. I've just finished a five-year secondment with All India Radio and now I'm on my way back to a spot of leave before resuming my place with dear old Auntie.'

'The BBC?' He had been interesting enough before, but this . . .

'You've heard of us!' he exclaimed.

She laughed. 'Just about. I hope you have nothing to do with television because I could bore for Gloucestershire on the short-comings and disappointments of *that* branch – or limb, I suppose – of "dear old Auntie."'

'Alas, I'm at the opposite end of the spectrum – Bush House – the Overseas Service. Now that we're letting go of our empire, bit by bit, our overseas broadcasts are considered evermore vital. But bore away if you like – you won't bore *me* – and I'm sure to bump into someone I can pass it on to.'

There was an odd note of eagerness in his voice – at odds, that is, with the rather laconic tone he had adopted earlier.

So she let him have both barrels – a twice-round-the-square recital of everything she and Eric had compiled together. At first he tried to answer her criticisms but his responses grew increasingly half-hearted and eventually petered out altogether.

'Now I *am* boring you,' she said. 'You just can't wait for it to be over so that we can drop into that bar on the corner and dance to that divine accordion.'

'Oh, what a dilemma! I do, of course, long for that – now that you mention it – but I can't deny I'm eager to hear *all* you have to say. I started answering back at first because I thought you were just firing off piecemeal objections. But I soon realized that they are part of a whole – a coherent whole . . . a philosophy of television. And that *is* interesting. Very! Why don't you apply for a post there?'

'Oh, they'd just hate me!'

'Of course they would, but that's no reason to shrink from it. But forgive me – you're probably already in some highly satisfying and rewarding profession?'

'Publishing.'

'Oh, really?'

'Yes . . . but not in the glamorous, three-hour-luncheons-with-T. S. Eliot end of the trade. We're in "integrated illustrated non-fiction," where careers and lives hang on the success of a single volume.'

'It sounds like a natural kindergarten for a life in television. They don't give too many chances there.'

The suggestion that there was a place where the knives were sharper and the claws longer than in 'her end' of the publishing trade stirred something visceral in her. 'Exactly what will you be doing at Bush House?' she asked. 'Actually, you can tell me while we dance.'

The accordionist and his violinist companion were about to take a break but when two hundred new francs appeared as if by magic between Findlater's finger and thumb, they took up their instruments again and began a rumba. They played with that peculiar upbeat melancholy that only French musicians seem able to achieve with any conviction – the sort of music that fills each moment with a ready-made nostalgia, telling you that these pleasures will not last, that the dawn will break cold, and the water carts will soak the streets, and the dogs of Paris, a breed unique, will commandeer all public spaces and hold them until the humans come out, all bleary eyed, and take over.

'Bush House?' she reminded him as they took to the floor.

As she expected, he danced with a delightful ease – with more than mere ease, in fact: with a grace and a firmness that was a joy to follow. He turned the little eight-by-eight dance floor into a ballroom.

'I'm at the sort of level now,' he said, 'where more than half my job will be whatever I decide it will be – which is only natural, because I will probably know more about the Far East – not just India – than anyone else there.'

'Really?'

'Are you surprised? As I said, I've been five years in India, during which I travelled to most other countries in the region.'

'Oh, yes, I'm not doubting *you* but I'd have thought the place was crawling with Secret Service people, some of whom would be pretty genned up about . . . well, *every* part of the world.'

He stiffened and his next few steps were ungainly. Then, in

a light, inconsequential sort of tone, he asked, 'What on earth makes you think that?'

'Schmidt's is just round the corner from where I work. I meet a lot of folk from Broadcasting House there. They say it's riddled with bods from the Secret Service. And anyway, it would be a very incompetent sort of government that let a powerful broadcaster like Auntie run the show completely unsupervised – home or abroad. Don't you think?'

He seemed to lose interest then. 'I've been thinking about your offer of a mount and an outing with the West Herts . . .'

'And?'

'And the more I think about it, and the more I discover about you, the more attractive it becomes. How do I get there – to where the horse is stabled? I will have the loan of my brother's car for a few weeks.'

So she told him about the Dower House, and then she had to tell him about the Dower House community.

They danced and sipped iced Pernod until shortly before two, when the café closed. During those hours she learned that he had lost his wife (to cancer) the previous year, leaving a year-old daughter – now almost two – who was presently with his parents in Bournemouth. Her name was Jasmine. For his part, he learned that she was still single, and highly attached to her career.

As they rose to leave, she realized she had never felt so sober after drinking so much; there was something about Findlater . . . his manner . . . his air of power kept under perfect control . . . which compelled her to retain that grip on each fleeting moment which alcohol usually relaxes.

They walked back arm-in-arm to the hotel. 'Can you recommend a good hostelry near this Dower House of yours?' he asked. 'I thought, since I have the car, we might drive down to the Cotswolds on Sunday, take luncheon at Castle Combe, and go for a stroll. D'you know the little stream there – the By Brook? It's very pretty.' After a pause he added, 'I might have some word for you then about careers and openings in television.'

'Oh!' She gave an embarrassed laugh. 'I was just being a barroom expert. I've never thought of leaving publishing.'

Why am I lying like this? she wondered.

'Of course you haven't,' he said. 'But there's a rung on every career ladder where you'll hurt yourself if you crash to the ground – and that's the rung where you start to look at nearby ladders and ask, "Could I make it from here?" And I'm guessing you're already standing on that rung of your present ladder.'

'Well . . . Alex? Alexander? . . .'

'Alex. Anything but Al!'

'Well, Alex, there's certainly a spare bed for you at the Dower House. And I'm flattered that you should think my gripes about television add up to a philosophy, so of course I'll take anything you tell me about it very seriously, indeed. Oh – and I adore Castle Combe.'

'Well . . . Faith . . .' They were outside her bedroom door by now. 'I have every reason – more reasons than I can count – to look forward to this coming weekend.'

He kissed her hand lightly but the glint in his eye made it clear this was a surrogate for one that could wait.

Lying in bed, in the time for waking dreams, she felt so glad the night had not descended toward the ending she would originally have welcomed – which was when she remembered to remove the dutch cap.

Saturday, 22 April 1950

There was no frost. A fitful north-east wind blew a dampness over the country, threatening rain that never quite fell.

'There'll be scent enough today,' Faith said as she and Alex set off for the meet at Dormer Green. She was on Jubilee, of course, and he, as promised, was riding Sally's Copenhagen, who was champing at the bit and frothing with excitement. 'We'll have to put some manners on this lad,' he said, 'or he'll overrun the hounds.'

It was a big field, more than forty riders, all as certain as Faith that the scent would burn today. Their excited babble and their laughter carried far – the cacophony that ruined many a good hunt. Her spirits sank.

Stirrup cups downed, the cap for Alex paid, the master – Sir

George Fenby, a City banker – lifted the hounds and set off in the direction of Queen Hoo.

'D'you know a ride where we could put this fellow over a couple of jumps?' Alex asked. 'I doubt I could hold him if we find early.'

She led him at a good trot through the country lanes, by Bramfield and Tattle Hill, through Thieves Lane to Hertingfordbury. There they turned west, into the grounds of Panshanger, which stretched up the Maran valley for a couple of miles. It was unkempt park and pheasant covert and partridge manor all the way.

'Ready?' she called. 'Hold tight.'

He increased his grip.

'Now!'

The two horses had been waiting for it. They went at once from walk to gallop. Faith felt the blood begin to race. She knew the ground well, of course, and led the way unhesitatingly through a maze of rides, some broad and straight, some narrow and zigzag. The clouds had passed and now a brilliant sun shone through the trees. The dry leaves crackled underhoof. And from somewhere came drifting the lazy smell of woodsmoke. All the fears and stresses of London and her delicate mission in Paris deserted her on that gallop. Here and there the way opened into glades, in one of which the woodsmen had left the trunk of a once-mighty beech.

To his astonishment Alex saw Jubilee fly at it as if to clear it in one bound – which was impossible, surely. Then he began to feel anxious, for he could sense that Copenhagen was getting set to make the same impossible leap. In fact, he was on the point of reining in when he saw that Faith had come to rest on the top of the trunk; she stood there, poised like a trick rider in a circus.

Very well, he thought, determined not to be outclassed by her. *On you go!* And he touched Copenhagen forward as soon as she had jumped down the other side.

He leaned over the crupper, ready for the jump, but at the last minute his courage failed. The height of the trunk, which had before seemed merely daunting, now looked terrifying. No horse could do it, not even this great-muscled giant. But they were both committed and had to go forward. For a moment he thought it shared his doubts; he did his best to gather it but there was a hint of a fumble as it doubled its hind legs under for the leap.

'Haaaa!' he yelled at the top of his voice, which frightened it into the supreme effort that carried it up, soaring and stretching, reaching beyond any achievement it knew of, until, by a hair's breadth, it gained the crest of the fallen trunk. It did not need the tug of his rein to stop; every ounce of its ability had gone into that puissance leap. There was no momentum left to be checked. Their coming to rest seemed both magic and effortless.

'Heigh!' He gave a cry of relief – not to say delight – and turned to Faith . . . only to see that she was as pale as the bleached wood on which he was now perched.

'Magnificent!' She merely breathed the word, shaking her head in disbelief. 'But mad!'

'Why?' He laughed. '*You* did it.'

'Would you just look behind you.'

He obeyed. 'Oh!'

A ridge, perhaps the foundations of an ancient wall, crossed the glade at an angle to the trunk, running beneath it. Faith had made her impressive leap from the top of it, but he had made his from fully three feet lower. 'That was stupid,' he said, feeling slightly hollow at the thought of what he had done. 'But I say – what a hunter!' He patted Copenhagen's mane.

'No one's going to believe me,' she said, looking around. 'Did anyone see?'

'I hope not! But at least this chap has quietened down. Shall we rejoin the hunt? I think we're safe enough now.'

It went badly. Sir George, the master, was his own huntsman that day; they found him drawing a covert in such a slipshod way he was more likely to send the fox to earth for the rest of the day than to put him up. He asked them to hold up the southern edge of the covert and scare the fox away westwards if he broke.

They made their way cautiously along its downhill fringes. There was a rider standing ten yards out in the fallow.

'You'll head him if he breaks here,' she shouted.

He looked at her scornfully. 'They won't *find* in that!' he said.

But just at that moment came a hound's opening challenge,

quickly taken up by two others. The rider spurred for the edge of the covert, immediately in front of Faith, arriving there only just before the fox broke. There was a great deal of crashing behind.

The stranger gave the fox no chance to get well away. As soon as it entered the fallow he began an excited scream of 'View halloa, halloa!' and flapped his arms.

'No!' Faith and Alex shouted in unison, but he paid no heed. She could have shot him.

Of course, the fox turned at once and went back into the covert, about ten yards from the point where he broke. All the activity around his earth, and the fact that there were a mere three hounds, had combined to make him think the open country might be safer today; now they'd given him proof that it wasn't. He'd go to earth and stay there till dark.

To be milling around in clouds of cigar smoke while the crowd caught up on the week's gossip and the servants dug Charley out was not her idea of fun. She almost suggested to Alex that they turn for home then. But the day was now blessed with such perfect weather that, even if they could not get a fox away, the most incompetent hunt in England couldn't fail to make something of it.

'I'm sorry,' she said. 'They're not usually this daft.'

'He won't do it at the next find,' Alex promised – with a strange air of certainty.

They went back to the overgrown ride where they had left Sir George. He was just remounting as she reined in. 'Gone back to earth,' he said.

'See that small bit of sticks there?' he asked them when they reached the edge again. 'In the hollow, two fields away? I'm going to draw that next. From the upwind side – I don't want to surprise the fox and have the hounds chop him. As I'm short of a huntsman, might I ask you two very kindly to go down-wind and watch him away? You seem to know what you're doing.'

'Something bloody odd here,' Faith said as soon as they were out of the master's hearing.

'His reputation in the City is none too savoury,' Alex said.

'You know him?'

'No. But when you told me the name of the hunt, I looked

him up and . . . asked around. He made his fortune in the war.'
After a brief pause he added, 'And you're right – something
pretty odd *is* going on here.'

For the next draw they chose a place to the south of the
covert, where they could stand unseen in a gateway, their silhou-
ettes lost against a spreading hornbeam at their back. There they
waited for the hounds to open and challenge.

Sir George gave one crack of his whip as a signal to his pack
to begin drawing the covert. The fox needed nothing more to
start him from his kennel. As soon as the hounds entered at the
farther side he slipped from the edge nearest Faith and Alex.
Only they could see him, a gash of red streaking over the pasture.
They let him pass, fifty yards to the east; the temptation to shout
was strong but they waited until he was at the farther hedge.
Then 'View halloa! halloa!' they yelled, making sure that the
pack had started to chase before spurring toward the point in
the hedge where Charley Fox had vanished.

But then the fox's behaviour went somehow wrong. He ran
a great circle almost passing through the covert where they'd
started him.

'A ringer!' people shouted.

Then he ran a short foil along part of his original track and
broke abruptly northward, almost dead straight. Through
Perrywood he led them, and Watkins Hall, between Datchworth
and Broom Hall, over the Stevenage road, through the park at
Frogmore Hall and on up the valley of the Beane.

All the while a dark suspicion was growing in Faith's mind:
a ringer that broke and then ran dead straight for so many miles?
Something was amiss. It was not Charley, not in such country
as this.

Then there was the slovenly, almost token, way they had
drawn the first covert. And then that other rider had *deliberately*
headed the fox back to earth. Everything about this chase was
wrong.

'Are you thinking what I'm thinking?' Alex asked.

'A bagman?'

'Just so! I think we now know why he's short of a huntsman
today – the fellow is now lying low in that covert clutching an
empty sack that smells strongly of Charley Fox.'

She was mortified. 'Oh . . . Alex! I'm so sorry. I promised

you some *sport* – not this. I've no stomach left for it, have you? Shall we pop these two in the trailer and see if there's anything doing with the *East* Herts? They're near Ware today. We could be there in twenty minutes.'

'Frankly, old darling, I'd as soon ride around the park by the Dower House. There are some fallen trees we could jump – more reasonable than that giant you put me over.'

'On one condition,' she said. 'That you never call me "old darling" again. *My* darling – fine. *Old* darling – you're dead.'

His eyes dwelled in hers for a long moment. 'I'd be happy to comply with that,' he said.

They were two fields away before Alex spoke again. 'We ought to report this,' he said. 'I was always taught that putting up a bagman was the biggest crime in the hunting calendar.'

'But we won't,' Faith replied. 'His money is all that's keeping this hunt alive. Most of the others are what my grandfather would have called "distressed gentlefolk." Oh, Alex! What is happening to our world – when the MFH of a respectable hunt can behave like that . . . and tradesmen earn more than bank clerks, and middle-class children have to sit *exams* to get a good education? And if they fail, they're condemned to be hod-carriers and nameless faces in the typing pool. Don't jump that hedge – the farmer measures every hoof print and comes cap-in-hand for compensation. We'll go round.'

'I think the answer lies in what's happening at your Dower House. Before the war it was home to one retired colonel, his wife, and seven servants. Now, seven families and no servants. Would you prefer the world as it was?'

She sighed. 'Not in that way. But I'd hate it if the sort of despicable behaviour we've suffered this morning became the norm.'

'You never cut corners in publishing?'

'All the time.' She looked back at him in surprise. 'But that's business – different traditions. But fox hunting . . . I *mean* . . .'

'It's just business to Sir George Fenby. He probably promised some splendid kills to some bigwig in industry – that fellow whose clothes smelled of mothballs, I'll bet – and the bagman was to ensure a good start. If hunting can only be sustained by money from business, it'll have to adapt. And that's a paradigm for everything else in this post-war world.'

She looked at him in a new light. 'You suspected him from the beginning! Even before you drove down from town?'

He chuckled. 'Hardly that early. But when he cursed the hounds for finding at that first covert I was pretty certain he *wanted* to draw blank there. And then, when he put us on the blind side of the second covert . . . I was in no doubt at all. Why such a rueful face?'

'Because *I* didn't suspect we had a bagman until Charley Fox did a reconnaissance circuit and then made a beeline for home. And I like to think of myself as pretty astute.'

'You're more astute than the rest of the field. I don't think any of them suspected a thing. Also, I had the advantage of looking up his record in the City.'

'Yes! How do you *do* that?'

'Oh,' he said airily, 'you just need to know the right people.'

'This will be your room, Mister Findlater,' Marianne said. 'The farthest bedroom from the nursery!'

'Alex, please,' he insisted. 'Faith tells me your maiden name was von Ritter?'

'The bathroom is along there – turn right and it's the first . . . in fact, the *only* door on your left. Our bedroom is at the end of that same passage.'

He waited.

'I broke off all connection with my parents in nineteen forty-four . . . Alex. Did Faith explain that we'd love to have you and her to dinner tonight – and two other friends from the community? They live on the ground floor.'

'Eric and Isabella Brandon – yes. I'm looking forward to it very much. You are all very kind. I hope that soon, when I'm fully settled back in England, I'll have the chance to repay your hospitality?'

Marianne glanced over his shoulder, back down the corridor and, lowering her voice, said, 'You can do that right now, if you wish – by doing what you can to help Faith make the move into television. We think she's absolutely made for it.' Then, seeing a flicker of doubt in his eye, she explained: 'We have the best TV reception in the house, so she often comes up here to watch. So we hear the comments she makes and, believe me, she doesn't miss a thing.'

He nodded. 'I agree. You are pushing at an open door here
. . . Marianne? May I?'

'Please do.'

'But I want to help in such a way that she won't feel beholden
to me. Will we hear when she comes upstairs?'

'Yes.'

'I have already spoken to . . . certain people . . . presently
in television . . . and they are very eager to meet her. But that
puts me in a quandary, you see. May I trust you with a secret?'

'Me? Why me?'

'Because you are her friend and I want to ask your advice
– after I have told you.'

'Very well. You may trust me, for her sake. And I hope it *is*
for her sake.'

'It is this: the moment I saw her I knew – I became utterly
convinced that she was the woman I wanted to marry. It knocked
me for six because I'm simply not the sort of person who makes
decisions like that. I'm a cold fish. I observe. I inquire. I deliberate – all before reaching the most tentative conclusion. But
there it was – a sudden and absolute and quite unshakeable
conviction that we were meant for each other.' He laughed.
'Even as I say it – knowing it's true – I can feel the absurdity
of it all.'

'This was in Paris last Tuesday? She told me about meeting
you there.'

He shook his head. 'Two or three years ago – out hunting
in Gloucestershire. I took one look at her, and . . . I just *knew*.
It upset me so much that I cut short my leave and went back
to India – because, you see, I was already married to a lovely
woman, whom I also loved, but not in the passionate, over-
whelming way that I'd been smitten by Faith Bullen-ffitch. I
was sure that a passion which had ignited so swiftly would also
subside with equal speed. And so it seemed. So it seemed.'

He gazed over her shoulder, out through the window, where
he caught sight of Faith, hanging up some washing in the wall-
fruit orchard. His stomach hollowed as his eyes possessed her.
'But,' he continued, 'it was simply being masked . . . obscured
by my concern for Wendy, my wife, who was . . . fighting . . .
and losing, to . . . the cancer that eventually killed her.'

'Did she know about Faith?'

'No!' He was shocked.

'I don't mean "did you tell her"! But did she sense it anyway?'

'Oh, God, I hope not. No. I'm sure she didn't.'

'Did she – when she knew she was dying – did she urge you to marry again?'

'Yes, but only for the sake of Jasmine, our daughter.'

'So your meeting in Paris was no accident!'

His grimace was a rueful admission.

'But how did you know she was there?'

He waved his hand vaguely and said, 'Inquiries.'

'Well,' she said in a tone that signified an end to their conversation, 'I'll answer the one question you have not asked – perhaps have not dared to ask. And I'll tell you this: I don't believe I will need to carry your secret for very many weeks . . . in fact, the secrecy itself may become pointless within a matter of days.'

Isabella plonked her elbows hard on the table and, even more demonstratively, pulled them off it, staring balefully at her husband throughout. Eric went on expounding his 'Chinese Whispers' theory of history: 'For instance, what Samuel Adams *actually* said to Paul Revere and the Sons of Liberty was . . .' and his voice rose and fell, emphasising certain words, seemingly at random: '"Down by *Boston harbour* on *December the sixteenth* I'm *throwing* a *tea party* – fancy dress, of course, on the theme of *Mohawks* – and we'll maybe drink a few ironic toasts to *show the British what we think of this absurd new tax*." But all that survived when his words had finished doing the rounds was "Boston harbour . . . throw . . . tea party . . . December the sixteenth . . . disguised as Mohawks . . . show the British what we think of this absurd new tax!" A combination of high winds, slovenly Yankee speech, and root beer laced with moonshine that changed the course of history.'

The laughter gave Isabella covering fire, so to speak, to repeat her demonstration.

Eric, elbows firmly planted, leaned forward to hear Willard's response: 'OK. A dollar to a nickel that what Henry Five actually cried was "*God* – if only there was a fair wind *for England*, then by *Harry* I'd be down at the Crown *and St George*, drinking with my old pal Falstaff!"'

'Not bad! Not bad!' people cried, as Isabella made a third attempt to convey her message to her husband.

'Or,' Faith said, 'what Queen Elizabeth actually said was, "I may have the body of a frail and feeble woman but, by heaven, I have the heart and stomach of a king!"'

They stared at her in bewilderment. Isabella said, 'But isn't that exactly what she *did* say?'

'Precisely, darling! You see! When a woman *speaks* her mind – outright just like that – men do actually listen, take note, and record her words correctly. That's because conversation among men is all verbal duelling – they don't listen to each other closely because they're too busy honing the next barb.'

'Ah.' Isabella appeared to see the light. 'In that case, I've often wondered why we say "half *past* eight" when the Germans say "half nine."'

'The same in Swedish,' Marianne said. '*Halv nio.*'

The rest looked bemused. 'What has this to do with Chinese Whispers?' Eric asked.

'Nothing,' Isabella said. 'Why should it? Anyway, *you* wouldn't take your elbows off the table.'

'Oh, stupid me! I really should have remembered that keeping elbows on tables automatically leads to a change of subject. But, actually, it *is* quite a fascinating question: why do the Germans and – we now learn – the Swedes look forward while we Anglo-Saxons look back?'

Willard said, 'In America you can say "a quarter of eight" – meaning "quarter to."'

'You can say it here, too, pal,' Eric said magnanimously. 'I think we can all agree to allow that, eh?' He looked round the table. 'Carried *nem con*! The port is with you, Alex.'

As the decanter made its round, Eric continued: 'What do we all think of Felix becoming a Jew, eh?'

Marianne looked at him sharply. 'I don't think we should discuss it at all. It's entirely a private matter.'

'Not since he spilled the beans to me, it isn't,' he responded. 'I thought it was a cry for help, as a matter of fact – considering, you know, Felix and beans.'

'What do the French say?' Isabella asked. 'Eight *less* a quarter and we say quarter *to* eight!'

'I advised him to take a holiday in Israel,' Eric continued.

'The light would be pretty good, I'd imagine. And those wind-scoured Crusader castles would suggest lots of themes to a sculptor.'

'Isn't he already Jewish?' Willard asked. 'Otherwise why did they put him—'

'Half Jewish,' Eric said. 'Or quarter, actually. What the Nazis called a *Mischling*. Though mind you – anatomically he's an *entire* gentile, which will be fun for him when the mohel reaches for the broken bottle.'

'Is there anything you take seriously, Eric?' Alex asked.

'Humour. I take that very seriously. Kierkegaard said it is morality's stoutest shield.'

'I've only met Felix once, briefly, this afternoon, but I don't imagine wind-scoured Crusader castles would lure him all the way to Israel.'

'Well, I may also have mentioned the side-attraction of meeting Jews in the top-dog position, no longer outcast and persecuted. He should experience that before he takes the plunge.'

'And do you think that might change his mind?'

'From half-informed to fully-informed? Yes.'

'I was thinking more on the lines of "from half-inclined to not on your life."'

Eric smiled. 'It's one of many possibilities. But you can blame my public school for the suggestion. We fourth-formers were flogged and abused without mercy by boys just three years older than us, and we often resolved that we'd behave *sooo* differently when we were top dogs. But we didn't, of course. It's something in human nature.'

'*Boys'* nature,' his wife said.

'I beg to differ,' Faith put in, remembering the days before she was expelled from Cheltenham.

The door opened and Terence Lanyon stuck his head inside. 'Hilary? No Hilary.'

'She came earlier,' Marianne told him, 'about collecting for a new piano for the school. She's probably with the Palmers. Join us – have a coffee. Or a glass of port.'

He accepted the invitation and she introduced him to Alex.

'Is that your DB2 in the yard?' Terence asked eagerly.

'My brother's, actually. You're at LSE? Just across the road from me – I'm at Bush House.'

'Oh! Well then, we must meet . . . compare canteens.'

'We certainly must. You've just been appointed to the new Economic Advisory Council, I think?' He suddenly caught himself and looked around with a grimace. 'Sorry all! Shop! Not good.' He turned again to Terence, who was open-mouthed. 'Yes, it's the new Aston Martin, with the Lagonda engine. Pretty soon now they'll walk away with the Le Mans twenty-four hour – I'm sure of it.'

Willard said, 'Felix is thinking of converting one hundred per cent to—'

'I heard,' Terence said. 'Is that what you were discussing?'

Faith said, 'Eric has advised him to go to Israel first and nobody can tell whether it's one of his jokey jokes or one of his serious ones. But Felix is taking it seriously.'

'You've been out there recently, haven't you?' Marianne asked.

Terence nodded. 'Going again, too. Maybe we can travel together.'

'What's he going to find?' Willard asked.

Terence stared around with a haunted, where-to-begin sort of expression. 'He'll find a land that, within living memory, was ruled as one caliphate by the Ottoman Turks. Ruled with fairly tolerant inefficiency, which suited most people. In the First World War, the Ottomans sought alliance with us but short-sightedly we turned them down. So they put a clothes peg on their noses and sided with the Germans – which, of course, was their undoing . . . just as I think it will now be ours. Because we did precisely what nobody who lived there wanted us to do. Their former colony of Syria wanted to stay as one unit – in fact, that's what Lawrence promised the Arabs to make sure they fought on our side. But once we no longer needed them we reneged and handed it to the French, who thought only of protecting the Maronite Christians. So, naturally, they split it into *four*: Transjordan, Palestine, Lebanon, and rump Syria. The tribes farther east *wanted* to split into three areas – one friendly with Persia, another friendly with Arabia, and the third wanting to form the nucleus of a Kurdish nation. So what did we do? And by the way, Willard, the "we" here includes Uncle Sam. Or it did until Woodrow Wilson got tired of it all and washed his hands of the lot. What did we do there? We rammed the three of them into one artificial state under the

ancient name of Iraq. That was all of twenty . . . thirty years
ago. Meanwhile the Zionists had been slowly buying up land
in Palestine. That started back in Queen Victoria's time under
the Rothschilds. Up until nineteen forty-five something close to
half a million acres of Arab Palestine had been bought from
them, at a fair and amicable price, by Zionist Jews – just short
of eight hundred square miles, which is about a tenth of the
present area of Israel.

'But then, after this latest war – full of guilt at how we'd
refused sanctuary to more than a few token Jews in Europe –
we said, "You don't need to buy the Arabs' land any more. Just
march in and take it." The thinking seems to be that three
mutually hostile people living in Iraq will exhaust themselves
squabbling with each other in the usual Arab fashion. And next
door, the once-mighty Syria is drawn and quartered, and those
quarters will also do the usual Arab thing and squabble with
each other, leaving the Zionists to go quietly about their business. So that's "the sick man of Europe" – the old Ottoman
caliphate – taken care of. And we'll have a European bridgehead
of liberal, intelligent, educated, hard-working people right in
the heart of it. Turning the desert into a garden. The odd thing
is I still meet people in our Foreign Office who believe it'll
happen!'

Alex said, 'And you think it won't?'

'Of course it won't. This isn't politics – it's faith. A Battle of
the Books. One book promises the land to the Jews and the bit
by Joshua tells them precisely how to go about it with God's
blessing. And the other book says that *no* other religion has any
right whatever to exist on the sacred soil of Islam. It is a blas-
phemy deserving of death. And we fondly imagine that modern
democratic politics will sort it out and the two will eventually
coexist in the one land.'

Alex was still curious. 'May I ask what's your particular interest
out there?'

'What every economist is interested in – oil. And here's the
supreme irony. Almost all of *our* oil – the commodity without
which we will not be able to live for at least the next hundred
years – lies under this land that we have shattered and rendered
totally dysfunctional. God help us when, one – they wake up
to the power it gives them and, two – they realize what

unforgivable things we have done to them. How did I start on all this . . . oh, yes! Felix. Well, I hope he takes up your suggestion, Eric. It'll be interesting to see what he makes of it all.'

Sunday, 23 April 1950

Faith had both driven and ridden in expensive cars as far back as she could remember, everything from her uncle Artie's Phantom 2 right up to Mick Brackenbury's sporty little 30HP Allard, but the Aston Martin DB2 was like a step into an undreamed-of future. Cars that 'devoured the road' or 'ate up the miles' were ten-a-penny in the advertisements and the puffs in the trade magazines, but here at last was one that truly lived up to those fancies. It was unnerving at first to take corners at speeds that would have sent almost every other vehicle sliding off the tarmac, and to feel that mighty thrust at her back whenever they came to a straight bit of road and Alex put his foot down. But once they were through St Albans and scorching toward Watford she was able to relax and stretch as near-horizontal as her seat allowed, and enjoy the day and all that it promised.

'Want to find some music on that thing?' He pointed to the radio. 'The Light Programme's on the second button.'

She just smiled at him and shook her head.

'Not going too fast, am I?'

'I thought so for the first few miles but not now. This is heavenly. And d'you know what I enjoy most?'

'What?'

'When we met in Paris you just mentioned that you had the loan of your brother's car. No other man that I've ever known could have resisted adding in a modest sort of undertone – "an Aston Martin DB2, actually." But you didn't even sound as if you *half*-thought of saying it. I wouldn't be surprised if you didn't turn out to be the *real* controller of the BBC.'

He laughed. 'Tread softly because you tread upon my dreams!'

She sat up a little straighter. 'Why? What would you do if you were?'

'All the things you spoke about last week in Paris, for a start. Especially TV news! It's absurd not to have *visual* news on television. And it's ridiculous to have to shut down between six and seven each evening so that mothers can put their toddlers to bed. And documentaries – everything from a year in the life of a Welsh hill farmer to—'

'A year in the life of the Queen?'

His jaw dropped, and then he gave a bark of a laugh. 'Indeed! Why not!' He glanced at her. 'You've got to apply, you know. I wish I could do more to help. But Auntie needs you down at Lime Grove.'

She gave an abstracted sort of nod. 'D'you know what I was thinking the other night, watching them broadcast an excerpt from some play that's on in the West End? I mean, the screen is only twelve inches high, so the people were just little Tom Thumbs and you could hardly make out their expressions. And I kept wishing they'd just cut from close-up to close-up so we could see their bloody faces. Television isn't just a tiny cinema screen, it's like a window in our drawing rooms. We watch it from eight feet away so we want to see faces just as they would be if the people were right there – eight feet away. And not only in dramas but in everything. Television is using the . . . can one talk of visual *grammar*?'

'You can now.'

'It's *mis*using the grammar of the movies.'

'If this weren't a Sunday,' he said, 'I'd turn round right now and drive directly to Lime Grove.' He sighed and added, 'But we'd only find the workers there.'

They threaded their way through the southern Chilterns – Watford, Rickmansworth, Denham, and Slough – to reach the A4 as soon as possible. There, at last on that great east-west artery between London and Bath, Alex could floor the throttle and really show off the paces of the DB2. He could push the beast from thirty to ninety in just a couple of seconds.

Between Maidenhead and Reading he floored it again and the speedo touched a ton. 'D'you mind?' he asked. 'I'll slow down if you'd prefer it.'

She shook her head and said, dreamily, 'It doesn't seem fast at all. I mean, it feels right. Natural.' Settling deep into her seat she added, 'It's one of those moments when you realize that the war really is over. We've lived so long in its . . . I mean it's been tailing off and—'

'We still have rationing. And a government that insists it knows best.'

There were few other cars on the road – mostly lorries making for an early opening of the London markets on Monday; their drivers flashed a thumbs-up, meaning 'no police ahead.' But a series of thumbs-down encounters warned them of a trap at Calcot Row on the far side of Reading; they negotiated it successfully and then it was their turn to flash and to thumbs-down the oncoming drivers.

'During the war this would have felt vaguely unpatriotic,' Alex said as he exchanged a comradely wave with a driver who got the message. 'The police were on our side then. Now, if they don't watch out, they'll turn into an army of occupation.'

Just before Newbury the last of the clouds dissolved and a bright spring sun gave the landscape the eye-aching clarity of a Dutch master, picking out cows, knee-deep in pasture, and newly scalped sheep a mile away. At Savernake Forest they stopped for a pee, she to the right of the path, he to the left.

'I think it's quite possible I was conceived here,' she said as she rejoined him near the car. 'My father occasionally mentions that they stopped off here on their way home after the wedding in London, and there's always that glint in his eye. And a certain anxious look in my mother's.'

He cleared his throat but ventured nothing. In the silence, the pinging of the exhaust manifold as it cooled was intrusive.

'I've embarrassed you,' she said.

He laughed as he held the door open for her. 'Not in what you said, only that I can't think of any bright sort of an answer. Except, *wherever* it happened, thank God it did!'

Between there and Chippenham she fed him and herself from their packed lunch, alternating bite-for-bite from the same sandwich. The gleam of his teeth, unsheathing themselves from his finely moulded lips to take a predatory bite, just fractions of an inch from her long, slender, manicured fingers was powerfully erotic to her. He must have sensed it for he shot her several glances, half uneasy, half hopeful.

'We could go for dinner at the Cross Hands,' she suggested.

He swallowed audibly. 'I was wondering about that. It would mean getting back around midnight. What time d'you have to be at work tomorrow?'

'Whenever I like. I told Fogel I was taking work home – writing a prospectus for this new art series – and I'd probably be at it until Tuesday.' She gave his arm a little pinch. 'But I didn't say *what* I'd be at.'

'And instead you've been wasting all that precious working time with me.'

'Oh, but I've finished the prospectus already. So what about it – the Cross Hands?'

After a silence in which she could almost hear his brain whirring, he said, 'We're both *known* in this part of the world. You more so than me.'

'Oh, yes – we'd have to *book* separate rooms.'

They left it at that for the moment.

When they were a quarter-mile or so short of Castle Combe, where the road and the By Brook run side by side, she asked him to stop just there.

'You don't want to go into the village itself?'

She shook her head. 'I know it well enough . . . and I'll only go all nostalgic and it makes me feel my age. I'd start saying things like, "That's where the blacksmith used to be . . . and you used to be able to get ginger pop there for a penny." But this part here is different altogether.'

They parked the car and climbed over a half-hearted wall into a long, straggly, tree-mottled pasture of a riverbank, where she led him southward, farther still from the village. 'I haven't been along here since we were children,' she told him.

'You and your brother.'

She glanced at him sharply. 'How d'you know I've got a brother?'

'Reverend Michael Bullen-ffitch? It's not quite as anonymous as the Reverend Michael Smith. Especially if he's also an OB.'

It stopped her. 'You were at Bedford, too?'

He pulled out his cigarette case, which now contained Balkan Sobranies as well as Gauloises. 'I was just about leaving Upper School when he joined the Inky, so we wouldn't have met.' He lit her cigarette. The smoke drifted away at a snail's pace, barely rising. 'But I see him mentioned in *The Ousel* from time to time. Runs a mission school in Kenya? He's district vice-president for the OBs out there. The Old Boys' Network has its tentacles everywhere.'

She nodded. 'Don't I know it!'

'Have you seen him lately?'

'He came home at Christmas – brown as a white hunter – speaks with a colonial accent. He cannot believe I'm not just Fogel's typist.'

'Ah, yes! That's the old school indoctrination for you. "Bedford laid her hands on each thick skull with this prophetic blessing: Be thou dull!"' He exhaled a long, thin cloud. 'We make bloody good colonial administrators, though – blueprint in one hand, pistol in the other, and a curse on our tongues. Also soldiers. D'you know, eight out of the ten on Monty's staff were OBs.'

She resumed their stroll along the bank. He could have mentioned the Bedford connection last Tuesday in Paris; it must have crossed his mind. Yet he chose not to. It seemed, then, that he gave out information about himself – about anything – only when he thought it necessary. For whom? Necessary for him.

'We used to come here for picnics,' she said. 'We cycled all the way here and back, too. Had very sore bums all next day.' She stopped again. 'Good heavens! It can't be the same one!'

'What can't?'

'See that waterlogged stick there? Lying on the bottom. I must have been just three or four and we had a picnic here and I saw a waterlogged stick lying on the river bed, just about there. And I yelled out that I'd found a stick that wouldn't float. And I heard my grandmother say to my mother that it was very clever of me to realize that it *was* a stick, particularly as it didn't float. And my mother said – very sarcastically – "Oh yes, she's another little nonesuch!" And poor Granny looked so crestfallen I went up to her and whispered, "You're right and Mummy's wrong." And they all laughed when she repeated it. But that can't be the same stick, can it? Not after . . . well, thirty-odd years?'

'No,' he agreed. 'That must be the place where all Pooh-sticks come to die.'

'Oh! Pooh-sticks! We *must* play Pooh-sticks when we get back to the road.'

Then, as if it were the easiest and most natural thing in the world, she took his hand and led him still farther up the meadow.

'That Eric Brandon . . .' he said.

'Ye–es?'

'Interesting fellow.'

'He can be,' she said guardedly. 'He can also be bloody infuriating. No. That's unfair. What I mean is that he has a strong moral sense but if he feels moral outrage about . . . I don't know . . . anything . . . he disguises it as a—'

'Like the concentration camps?'

She dropped his hand and turned to face him. 'What *is* this?'

He was unperturbed. 'I was talking to his wife last night. Isabella? Before dinner. Charming woman. She told me he sent in a play to Harold Byron – for the Third Programme. So I rang Harold this morning. He says it was pretty strong meat. But not a drama at all – no dramatic structure – more like the verbatim minutes of a genuine conference. She showed me some of his books for children. I couldn't see how both could come from the same mind.'

She took his hand again and they resumed their stroll. 'What are you fishing for, Alex?' she asked.

'Hardly "fishing" – just curious. Byron said that the script mentioned Felix and he questioned that, but Brandon never replied to say Felix was a friend. In fact, he never replied at all.'

'Oh, damn you!' She gave a laugh that was half hollow, half genuine. Isabella, in all innocence, must have said even more than Alex had chosen to reveal; pregnancy must be softening all her sharper instincts. Also – the thought lingered pleasantly at the back of her mind – Alex might be wondering if there was anything more intimate going on between her and Eric. 'It was a plan that Eric and I concocted between us.' And she went on to explain the entire history of their abortive attempts to intrude a Trojan Horse inside the BBC. 'I just wanted to go into an interview with something objective, something concrete, something *out there* – and apparently nothing to do with me. So that I could say, "There! *That's* the sort of thing I'm talking about. *That's* what I think television should be doing." It would make it so much easier.'

'And what have you done since?' he asked.

'Nothing.'

'That doesn't sound like you.'

'Well . . .' She sighed. 'The thing is . . . the thing is . . . this detailed prospectus I'm handing over on Tuesday . . . it was supposed to be my farewell gift to Fogel, before I made a really serious move toward a new career in television.'

'But?' He smiled. 'I can hear a "but" coming?'

'Well, I described it to Fogel the day after I got back from Paris and he's been on the phone all week and the excitement for it is very hot. Especially in America, which is a market we've never really cracked. He wants me to go over there and "firm up" their interest.'

'So? Bye-bye television?' The words were spoken casually but she could feel the tension in his grip.

'Not at all,' she said. 'You're going to think me horribly Machiavellian, but it set the brain cogs whirring. If I come back from New York and say to the editorial people, "Saint Martin's Press wants this" or "Random House wants that" – or whoever signs up with the best offer – then that's what will get done. "Ve are all prostitoots now." The editors may have their own pet ideas but it will be *me as the sales person* who'll have the veto. And so I did just wonder if something like that might not be true for the BBC as well? Have I been "barking up the wrong chimæra," as Eric says – thinking only of programme *making*? What about programme *selling* – overseas sales?'

He shook his head. 'They're far too small a tail to wag the programme-making dog – as Eric might say.'

'For now – yes. But, Alex, things have changed since the war. People who base their careers on *now* tend to have now-only careers.'

He whistled.

'Come on!' She dug him with her elbow. 'Don't tell me part of you hasn't rehearsed the arguments for jumping ship when commercial television is allowed!'

His silence told her she might just be wrong. 'The Tories are bound to get back sometime,' she pointed out. 'There's the smell of death about this lot. And the Tories will end Auntie's monopoly – toot sweep! Oh, and can we stop talking about Eric Brandon? I'd much rather talk about us.'

That tension in his grip again. 'Us?'

'Yes. You and me. I'm no longer some little eighteen-year-old girl just expelled from Cheltenham. And you're the easiest, most exciting, most intriguing, most relaxing man I've ever known. And when I remembered about us in Montmartre just now, I thought, "was it *only* last Tuesday?" It's still a shock. Because it feels as if we've been friends for years. Don't you feel that?'

He laughed. 'I *have* felt it for years – in fantasy, anyway. Remember the hunt I spoke about? When we met in Paris? God help me but from that moment on I knew I had married the wrong woman. Not that I didn't *love* Wendy but it was a very comfortable, friendly sort of love. But *you*! You were . . . altogether different. We only spoke a couple of times at that hunt – casual remarks one says to strangers out in the field – but even then the air around you was . . . somehow . . . electric . . . precious . . .'

'I'm not sure I'm altogether happy with the past tense here, Alex.' She laughed and now she linked arms with him.

'Oh God, Faith – it's still true. Even when we're not arm-in-arm, the side of me that's nearest you is twice as alive, twice as warm as the other. You are . . . magical! When I set sail for India the following week . . . as I watched dear old Blighty vanish over the horizon . . . well, that was the bleakest moment ever. Knowing you were there . . . imagining all the fascinating men you were going to meet. That and the guilt.'

'Guilt?'

'Well, I already knew Wendy was dying. The doctor had warned me, though we kept it from her until it was just too obvious. And all the while I was thinking when-when-when? And thinking of you. And almost the last thing she said to me was "Marry again, Alex – don't let Jasmine grow up mother-less." And I couldn't tell her how that was decided long ago – at a hunt in Gloucestershire. I hope you never know guilt like that.'

She twisted round to face him and pulled his face down to hers. Their kiss – the one they both knew they had post-poned in Paris – was a blissful fusion, a nervous melting of the softness of their lips and the padded hardness of their cheeks. When at last they broke, he said, 'It's like . . .' But she pulled his head to hers and silenced him with yet another kiss. And another.

And then, suddenly, it began to rain – from a single pale cloud in an otherwise clear sky.

By the time they reached the car they were too wet for Pooh-sticks; instead they drove as fast as the winding Cotswold roads allowed to the Cross Hands, to steam themselves dry in front of a baronial-scale log fire. On the way they passed that field where the farmer disguises one of his hayricks as a small house, making it slightly different each year. This time he had furnished it with an ivy-covered porch and leaded-light window panes.

'It's a kind of lying, isn't it?' Faith remarked. 'The sort of lie we all conspire to accept, like fancy-dress parties, stage plays . . . even novels. We have to go along with the lie, pretending to accept it as true, even though, underneath it all, we go on knowing it's not true at all. It's a voluntary conspiracy between the pretender and the audience. Or the reader.'

'Whereas in your type of publishing . . .?' he prompted. 'I mean, how "non" is the non-fiction?'

While she considered her response he went on: 'It's Pontius Pilate's question. It sometimes seems to me that *everything* that goes into the making of a civilization . . . or a culture . . . is actually a fiction. All those rock-solid truths we were taught at school about the blessings of empire, and especially the British Empire . . . and just about everything you could lump together as "Victorian values" . . . it's all going up in smoke now.'

'It's certainly making Victorian furniture remarkably cheap. Felix and Angela have bought some superb pieces from that old warehouse on Bull Plain in Hertford, and all for an absolute song. Last week they got a great refectory table – one solid piece of mahogany two and a half inches thick for thirty quid!'

'I saw it. Very good.'

'The architects among us turn up their noses, of course, even as they drown in a sea of Scandinavian bent laminate stuff.'

'. . . while the Breits drown in Victorian gothic! They'll soon need an annexe, surely? I never saw a place so crowded – except in my grandparents' photograph albums.'

When at last they stood, slightly steaming, before the vast open fire at the Cross Hands, Alex returned to the subject of the Breits: 'Angela and Felix . . .' He let the words hang.

'What about them?'

'They're both concentration camp survivors.'

'Yes. Different camps, of course.'

'Of course.'

'Is that all?'

He sighed. 'I don't wish to pry. I mean, I know they're friends of yours. But do you think they were taking an awful risk, marrying each other?'

'No.'

Her abruptness shook him. 'You're very positive. I've met quite a few survivors since 'forty-five. It's amazing how normal they seem in casual contact, but there must be deep scars from such an unimaginably awful experience.'

Her laughter shocked him.

'I'm sorry,' she said. 'It's just that when Felix gets agitated, he opens a tin of baked beans. Or in summer he'll eat raw peas.' She explained the significance. 'And when I pointed it out to him, he saw the funny side, too. So now he does it consciously – he *uses* it as a sort of signal: *if you go on nagging, I'll open a tin of beans* sort of thing.'

'And Angela? I know about her work at the BBC. She learned her trade as a recording engineer for the ss, I gather?'

Faith turned to look at him. He was staring into the fire as if the dance of the flames were far more important than all this chit-chat. The flickering light bronzed his skin and sharpened every detail. It shocked her to realize – quite suddenly – that she was actually falling in love with him. This was the start of something more than a blissful affair with a man who was handsome, charming, not short of a shilling or two, and powerful in ways that could be of use to her. Much more.

She had never been one to want, much less to seek, a man who could stand in a protective role toward her. She had felt herself on that old slippery slope when she first met Felix, that afternoon at the V&A. He was so . . . *European*. He knew Picasso, Derain, Sartre and de Beauvoir, and André Breton . . . oh, so many people who were already part of European legend. And Thomas Mann. They were his friends. The Curator of Prints had almost venerated him. It had been what Willard called 'a close call' but, by bringing him into *her* world, taking charge of his career as far as he'd let her, and joining him in bed, she had put that danger behind them. Hadn't she?

Not really. Even as the comforting gloss occurred to her, she remembered how the sight of Angela had brought him to a halt as he crossed the dining room at Schmidts – and how he had lingered behind that doorway, watching her, unaware that she, Faith, could see him reflected in one of the windowpanes. She had known then, far better than Felix himself, where his heart now lay.

'No. She learned her trade at UFA,' she said, 'where her father was some sort of recording engineer genius.'

She knew he was fishing for information – *and* that he'd never say why – but, curiously, it did not annoy her. This . . . what could one call it? This *penchant* for secrecy became him. He would be less interesting – in a way, less of a man – if he were otherwise. At any moment in her life up until this weekend she would have said she'd never be able to love a man fully unless she knew all about him. She wouldn't have felt *safe* enough to let herself fall in love. But now that seemed absurd, as if to say that love would begin when all the exciting bits were over. How could she have been so stupid?

'If you do go to America . . .' he said.

'Oh!' She laughed. 'D'you know – I was just about to start a train of thought that began: *if I do go to America . . .* Go on.'

He grinned. 'Far be it from me to interrupt.'

She drew a deep breath and stopped smiling. 'I want to say this before I have even the smallest sip of sherry inside me. Or a G&T, actually . . . pink.'

He turned and asked the receptionist for two pink gins and a brace of tonic splits.

'When I go to America,' she said, 'though actually it's just New York, I'll be counting every minute – every second – until I can be with you again. There!'

'Oh, Faith!' He closed his eyes, pressing the lids down tight until a hefty pair of crow's feet spread across his temples.

She blinked, several times, rapidly – and was surprised to feel small tears slithering down her cheeks. 'Steady the Buffs!' she said, embarrassed. 'This is verging on the Continental. We ought to have done this in Paris.'

'Ha! D'you think I didn't want to?' He glanced at her. 'Didn't you?'

'No . . .' She spoke as if it now surprised her. 'For me it happened . . .' But she couldn't pin it down to an actual occasion. The epiphany that overtook her a few moments ago had merely been a conscious realization of something that had actually happened . . . when? 'Perhaps it did happen then,' she admitted. 'When a caterpillar turns into a butterfly – that moment when she first spreads her wings in the sun to dry – does she suddenly realize she's actually been a butterfly for quite a few hours already?'

Sunday, 21 May 1950

There was a hesitant knock at the cottage door and then came Marianne's voice: 'Felix? Angela? Is everything all right?'

She entered the kitchen just as Felix called back: 'Come in!'

She halted in the doorway. 'What have you done?'

'Stubbed my firkin toe. What's it look like?'

'It looks like you're running hot water over it, which certainly won't help. D'you want me to have a look?'

He plucked his foot from the sink and turned off the tap – rather than expose himself, for he was still in his old-fashioned nightshirt. 'It's all right. It's fine.'

Angela appeared at that moment, also in her nightdress. 'What happened? I never heard such a racket.'

'He stubbed his firkin toe.'

'I stubbed my toe.'

'I was on my way to lunge Jubilee. I thought the roof had fallen in or something.'

Angela's expression hardened. 'Stubbed his toe? Well . . . don't expect much sympathy from *me*. We'll be stacking the furniture vertically if we go on much longer.'

Marianne looked around the kitchen and had to agree. 'Two Welsh dressers, one almost bare, must be a great temptation.'

'But it's beautiful!' Felix hobbled painfully across the kitchen, skirting the table, a free-standing butcher's block, and a Victorian wine rack, while ducking under a four-row laundry hoist from which hung two socks and several hundred dried and drying herbs. 'Just feel that!' He ran his hand over the wood. 'There's a century of tender loving care in that surface.'

'Ha!' Angela barked. 'There are thousands of years of tender loving care in all these lovely antiques, but it didn't stop them breaking your toes. I hope you *have* broken your toes. I don't know what else will bring this madness to a halt.' She appealed to Marianne. 'It's a one-man campaign to save *everything* the Victorians ever made in wood . . .'

'Not everything.' He started speaking over her. 'We've seen hundreds of pieces I'd gladly burn myself. Or give to Chris to desecrate. But these are all hand carved. These are made by *sculptors* – even if they're not named as that.'

'. . . from the furnace.'

'Look at the petals on this rose. That one there. It was carved with a single *wrrusssh* of a hollow chisel. Grinling Gibbons couldn't have done it better.'

'Then we should buy that old tithe barn and store them there' – she jerked a thumb toward the back window – 'if it's *that* important.'

Marianne's ears pricked up at that. She said, 'May I make a modest suggestion?'

'You can make a pot of coffee.' Angela threaded her way to the dresser – the one that was laden with collectible earthenware and porcelain.

'That barn out the back . . .' Marianne said when they were finally seated, their hands clutched for warmth round tall, steaming mugs. 'Is it for sale?'

Angela's eyes narrowed. 'Are you thinking of buying it?'

She shook her head. 'I didn't know it might be available. The thing is – don't tell this to Willard, and don't let Sally know you know, not yet, anyway – but the thing is, she and I are thinking of going into partnership. I'm tired of being what Willard calls his troubleshooter . . . and she's—'

'His *what?*'

'Troubleshooter.'

'Ha! Americans! Who else would think that the way to get out of trouble is to start shooting! Go on.'

'Well . . .' Marianne was now transfixed between two strands of thought; the more powerful won. 'Believe me, I never want to be involved with the design of another public lavatory as long as I live! Willard has these giant office blocks to finish so he's long ago forgotten about the Festival of Britain. He comes to the odd site meeting but that's all. The rest is all on my plate now. Anyway! I want to go freelance and Sally doesn't think she's being fully stretched in *their* partnership, so we're exploring – no more than that, just exploring – the possibilities of setting up in a practice together.'

'Exciting!' Angela's eyes sparkled.

'And that's the danger. It *is* exciting. But is it practical? No – is it practic*able*?'

'Do-able,' Felix suggested.

'Yes – do-able. So nothing's decided yet. One of the questions is where would we work? Another is we want to start off with a commission that would create a stir. And the conversion of a listed sixteenth-century tithe barn with medieval traces – grade two-starred – would surely do that if we got it right.'

The other two exchanged a thoughtful glance. 'Conversion to what?' Felix asked.

Marianne stared at him as if she thought he must be joking. 'A place to live in, of course. A dwelling. A home. Somewhere for all this . . . er . . . these antiques, where you wouldn't have to bathe your toes in *cold* water every morning.'

'For us,' Angela began, 'bathing in ice-cold water every morning . . .'

'I know what it means, pet,' Marianne cut in. 'To you and to him. But it's the only proper treatment for bruised toes. That's all.'

'A dwelling,' Felix said thoughtfully.

Marianne looked at Angela. 'Isn't that what you hinted at?'

She nodded. 'But the minute I said it, I thought of Faith. This new man in her life – Alex – seems a lot more serious than any of her previous . . . ah . . .' She cleared her throat tendentiously and grinned at Felix. 'Anyway, I thought what if we could suggest to Faith that *she* buy it – or she and Alex together then—'

'So it *is* for sale?' Marianne pressed the point.

'Officially? I don't know. I just asked John Gordon what the gravel company was hoping to do with it – he was moaning in the usual way about having to repair the roof with genuine seventeenth-century tiles – and he said he didn't know what *they* were hoping but *he* was hoping to get them to sell it off. They're never going to get permission to demolish the Dower

House, not now it's been listed grade-two star as well. So he wants to sell off both properties, with a clause to prevent us from lodging any objections to gravel extraction out in the parkland. But Faith and Alex could live there and still be part of the community, and we'd get two more rooms for' – she waved all around them – '*this!*'

'What sort of conversion would you propose over there?' Felix asked quietly.

Angela drew breath to speak and then, catching his eye, fell silent.

'Lord! The very possibility has only just arisen. But, in very general terms, for them, Faith and Alex, it would be living space and a garage . . . and for *you,* living space and a studio. For them, something fairly conventional but of superb quality. For you' – she licked her lower lip, slowly, teasing them – 'something *astounding!* Think it over, anyway. I must go and lunge Jubilee.'

At the door, over their protests, Marianne added, 'Ta muchly for the coffee.'

Sometime later, on her way back from lungeing Faith's horse, Marianne called in again at the cottage. 'I simply must tell you this,' she said. 'Something that happened at the Festival site yesterday. Willard came down for a site conference . . . this is the sort of thing that drives him absolutely *mad* about the English. He came down to sort out some problems with one of our public lavatory contracts, which is right next door to one of the cafés. And the café is being decorated by a Cornish painter called John Tunnard.'

And she went on to explain that Tunnard had to get a union card before he could start work, and then he couldn't start because he needed to melt the special plastic paints he was using and the power point was loose, and the whole site almost went on strike when he tried to screw it in firmly, and it took the electrician a day to come, and he said it was too close to a water pipe so send for the plumber, and the plumber took another day and when he came he said it was a cold-water pipe and he was only a *hot*-water plumber so the cold-water plumber took another day, and so a whole week went by before he could begin – all for the want of three turns of a screwdriver. 'And best of all,' she concluded, 'they thought they were doing him a *favour*! Allowing him to skive for a week. They've got this government by the balls!'

As she turned to go, Felix said, 'That old Tithe Barn.'

She spun round eagerly. 'Yes?'

'We both went out and had a quick look at it. What would one be able to do with a place like that?'

Angela added, 'It's all doors on one side and all windows on the other.'

'Yes. The windows were added in the nineteenth century, at a guess. The ones in the nearer end wall even later – possibly in the First World War. Mrs Tawney says the Red Cross used it for dressing wounds of the walking wounded, when the Dower House was a convalescent home for officers. Anyway, when a house gets listed, it has to be listed exactly as it is. If there's a corrugated-iron patch in the roof, that's part of the listing and you have to apply for consent to replace it with proper tiles. Hence poor old John Gordon's frustration.'

'The question was—' Felix said.

'Yes, I know – I'm just explaining the constraints. I think we could do you a conversion that wouldn't touch the existing fabric at any point, so it would just fly through the planning process.'

'Build a separate house *inside it*?' Angela asked, not sounding too happy about it.

'Not quite.' Marianne grinned. 'Build a *sculpture* of bright-aluminium scaffolding and cedarwood boxes just a few inches smaller than the interior, all round – a sculpture you could very happily live *inside.*'

Angela looked blank but Marianne could see that Felix was taking the bait. 'I oughtn't to say any more,' she added, turning to go in earnest this time. 'Not until after I've spoken to Sally to see if she agrees that this would be the best project on which to launch our partnership.'

When she had gone, Felix turned to Angela. 'I guess Israel's off for a while – unless we just take a quick fortnight or so there this summer?'

'I'd say it's off for quite a while!' Angela agreed.

Wednesday, 7 June 1950

Aboard the Queen Mary

My darling Alex,

This is absurd, of course. The swiftest vessel for carrying this letter is the one that is already doing so. I shall post it on arrival in Southampton even though you will be there in person to meet me, and the postman will deliver it a couple of days later, by which time I will already have said everything I could possibly write here, maybe many times over. So why bother?

Because, darling, darling, I'm just bursting with so many things to say that if I don't write them now and give myself the illusion of communicating with you, I shall truly burst. But when we dock I don't want it to compete with me in person. Who dares to say women are not logical?

First and if I manage to write nothing else, this is the most important – I love you, I love you, I love you to distraction. You know that. But it's such a novel experience for me – <u>true</u> love. I mean, I've had joyful affairs, comfortable affairs, passionate affairs, often with unwise partners, but they were just affairs and this is real, really, really real. I ache for your touch and I never did that before. I can think of you in any mood. I can think of you and be calm, and be drowsy, and be stirred beyond endurance almost, and be wild with impatience that so many hours still separate us, and be dreamy, and be foolish. ~~I can think of you~~ You are with me on my mind waking and sleeping.

I wish you could've seen me with the editorial board at Doubleday. I felt you there, strong, silent, and approving all the time. When I was with the people at Simon and Schuster and again at Random House I know I did a good job of presenting my 'Junior Art' series but even so I kept feeling something was missing. Then with Doubleday I suddenly knew what it was. The missing element was <u>Manutius!</u> I should be selling <u>us</u> as well as our products. They all knew Fogel of course – everybody in the whole publishing world knows him or knows of him, but

Manutius is the missing dimension to his character, a shadow to most of them. And you know how you can tell how a group of people are gripped by what you're saying — I couldn't describe it in so many words but I'm sure you know the difference between that and mere casual interest. I tell ya — dese guys was <u>gripped!</u>

So I sold the series like a charm, all on the back of first selling Manutius. The BBC will never have that problem (well, maybe in Yoknapatawpha County but not many other places) and, possibly, it was while imagining myself doing this same sort of thing with recordings of radio and TV programmes that I realized that Manutius and Auntie are two very different stables. Anyway, Doubleday bought it! No ifs, ands or buts — they signed heads of agreement on the spot and they're so gung-ho (enthusiastic) that they've sent a senior editor called Norman Crowley back with me to look at the original material and stay on as editorial advisor to the series — and, they hint, to cooperate in other joint ventures. That has to be their true purpose — scout around, get the feel of things, and make an offer to get into bed with us. Manutius might yet end up as Doubleday's Trojan Horse in London — that is, in the British book market, which spans the globe from Canada right round again to Canada, and it's where the Yanks can't sell so much as a shilling life. I know Fogel would just love to have such an admiring sugar daddy with such a bottomless purse. We have big-big ideas and big-big books waiting for Russell (philosophy), Huxley (evolution), Fisher (birds), Hogben (maths), Priestley (England — or Time, he's got a thing about Time), and dear Felix (sculpture). Oh, and more. Jung (psychology). I needn't go on. All they lack is the seed corn of money, more money than Manutius can scrape up yet. But with Doubleday's treasury to dip into and all those million-horsepower names to dazzle even those Manhattan sophisticates . . . the sky is our oyster, as Eric would say.

But back to Norman Crowley. Between you and me I have already renamed him <u>Ab</u>norman Crowley. The man is seriously weird and I'm wondering if they're not just sending him away to be rid of him. He's a pretty good editor. He knows his mind and how to keep focused (the editorial disease is to 'masturbate over text until it's sodden.' Don't be shocked though, it's what I accuse our editors at Manutius of doing in order to shock them into releasing text to the typesetter and give us some faint chance *of meeting a deadline). And he knows the market. There are a lot of good things going for dear Abnorman, so I do not under-estimate him. But when, for example, you ask him a simple question like, 'These are sixty-four pagers but we could save on printing costs by printing 128 pages back-to-back on a bigger press. It would need a bigger print run to justify it, so what are you thinking in terms of the American print run?'*

And he looks at your left eye and he looks at your right eye and he turns his head three-quarters away and looks at you askance and he chews a knuckle and he throws down his pencil, spilling it off the flat of his hand onto the table, and he says, 'Faith — did I ever tell you 'bout mah Uncle Stu?' Well, his Uncle Stu, it turns out, was a chicken farmer, so any quantities like the print run get turned into quantities like weekly off-farm egg shipments, at the end of which he abandons me in the middle of the Oklahoma dustbowl to translate all this into an allegory about the uncertainty involved in forecasting markets.

What? Markets are uncertain? Can that possibly be true?

The thing is, if he said it all plain and straight, everyone would see it's nothing more than a simpleton's guide to uncertainty, but the allegory thing promotes him into some kind of seer who speaks in parables. Except not with me. After a couple of days of this sort of obfuscation I can perceive a sharp and rapacious mind at work. If he advises Doubleday it will be safe to play Daddy Bigbucks with Manutius, he'll make it conditional on taking over <u>my</u> position as Fogel's right brain! Fogel will see through him at once, of course, but if Abnorman is the only key to unlock those Doubleday vaults, he'll shamelessly demote me, on paper, anyway, and make dear Abnorman the titular Number Two (which, in another sense of those words, he already is to me), secretly giving me the task of seeing that the man doesn't do too much damage. (Sorry Fogel, if that's your plan, my letter of resignation is already written and waiting.)

The best news is I won't have to escort him to London from Southampton! This morning at breakfast I asked him if 'a Manhattan sophisticate like you' could manage alone in London, having first ascertained that his New York club has reciprocal rights with the Chelsea Arts, so he won't be pounding the streets, and of course he declined my offer of guided tours to the Tower,

Madame Tussauds, etc. (Actually, in all the years I've lived in London I've never visited the Tower, so I wouldn't have minded that.) So our little weekend tryst in the New Forest is definitely on. Or will have been on and is now over by the time you read this. How was it for you? I adored every minute of it.

What else? Oh, yes. The Q Mary is far superior in the second class than in the first. She's a beautiful old tub but her grandeur is just a wee bit threadbare at the edges, and the people in the first class all have the air of decayed gentlefolk – the sort of people my mother used to visit in homes for distressed gentry, bringing them dainty soaps and small bottles of inexpensive perfume and machine-monogrammed hankies with their initials on. (She had a huge stock and so could always find the apposite initial. Dear Mummy!)

But here in the second class one can sit down and work without the decayed gentlefolk turning up their noses. There's a professor of history who'd be a natural on TV – he can talk the hind leg off a thoroughbred horse, without notes and without the slightest sense that he might be wrong in even the smallest particular. And an economist whose views on the Israel–Palestine conflict are the precise opposite of those we heard from Terence Lanyon that night in the Johnsons' flat. That would be a good old ding-dong – aphorisms at dawn and fire at three paces! And there's a young man from Sotheby's who was an art student and studied under Victor Passmore at Camberwell. He told me that Passmore tells a wonderful story against himself. It wasn't clear when this happened, maybe before the war, but anyway it was when Passmore was on the committee of the New English Art Club and he was deputed to greet Picasso at Victoria and bring him to Whitcomb St. So when he spied Picasso getting off the boat train he went up to him and said, in schoolboy French, 'Je . . . suis . . . Passmore . . . er . . . je suis . . . peintre!' And Picasso looked at him with those great solemn eyes and said, 'Teins! Moi aussi! Je suis peintre!' He tells a good story. (Don't worry – I have all their names, and the purser kindly left a list of addresses in plain view, where I could see them.)

So goodnight, my dearest. Felix once told me that when he heard that line in The Merchant of Venice *where Troilus sighs his soul toward the Grecian tents where Cressid lay that night, he said he knew he was in love with Angela because sighing his soul*

*was exactly how it felt whenever he thought of her. I felt awfully
superior not to be suffering any such malady. But, oh, how are
the superior fallen! Sighing my soul toward you is precisely how
it feels. If this letter is a bit tatty when you get it, it's because
I'm now going to put it under my pillow all night.*

All my love and then some,

Faith

Sunday, 9 July 1950

Eric, Terence, and Hilary carried the last raked pile of yew
clippings to the old, dried-up water fountain at the foot of the
big lawn just as Nicole and May came out, May with a tray of
flapjacks and fly-cemetery buns, Nicole with a large jug of iced
'bolonade' – a fruit drink of her own invention which The
Tribe had voted The Bestest Drink in the World.

'Tea for the serfs!' May called.

'Raaah!' The Tribe – Betty, Sam, Charley, Siri, Andrew,
Samantha, and Theo – all of whom had been 'helping' Willard
and Marianne re-glaze the outhouse they had named 'Rosy
Primrose,' came running round to the big lawn as soon as they
saw Nicole with the jug of bolonade.

'Betty and Sam,' she said, intercepting them. 'There's another
jug and a tray with plastic cups for The Tribe on my kitchen
table. Charley, there's another rug inside the front door for
you lot.'

Chris Riley-Potter raised his head out of the long grass down
by the haha.

'I had no idea *he* was there,' Hilary said.

'Just as well,' Eric told her. 'Some of the things he and Anna
got up to were not for the Jung and easily Freudened.'

Terence commented airily, 'We serfs cannot imagine the
stresses and strains of the creative life.'

'And,' Eric added, 'with the likes of them around we don't
need to imagine the stresses and strains of the *pro*creative life.'

'Jealous, darling?' Isabella asked sweetly as she laid her own
contribution upon the adults' rug – a plate of petits fours from

Fortnum. She was wearing a fisherman's smock and blue jeans that had never been within a hundred yards of a decorator's paintbrush or a net-mender's bodkin. And gold sandals.

'Oh, my runaway tongue!' Eric hung his head in shame.

'We should have had a midsummer party this year,' Terence said as he flopped down at the edge of the rug, smoothing a space for Hilary beside him – she being then in her second trimester and almost into her third.

'Our careers no longer need it,' Eric said. 'And even the village no longer believes this is some sort of free-love community.'

'All the same, we should have one next year,' Hilary said, 'if only to avoid having to contribute to the village's Festival of Britain celebrations.'

'What would be wrong with that?' Isabella asked. 'There are some perfectly sweet people there.'

'But we don't really *belong,* do we? We get on well enough but we don't *mix.'*

'Well, Eric and I are on the Village Hall Committee at Barwick Green.'

Eric added his gloss: 'Thanks to Bob Ambrose, who tricked us into attending the AGM. He just wanted allies to help him bait Mrs Millicent Tawney, which is the local sport among the peasantry these days. So I suppose you could say we, at least, do mix.'

'Mrs Tawney has very *good* motions,' Isabella protested.

Everyone looked at Eric, expecting him to make something of this ambiguity. But, with obvious reluctance, he declined. 'I agree, my darling. And, like her, we almost always pass them, but we have our little bit of fun along the way. It's all part of village life.'

Chris and Anna, bleary eyed and hand-in-hand, walked up the brick path beside the yew hedge. 'Looks grand,' he said. 'You've done a really good job.'

Terence rose and tugged a forelock. 'Us loikes to keep th'ole place lookin all shipshape 'n Bristow fashun fer the young master, Master,' he said.

'Call me next time,' Chris responded with a grin as he and Anna strolled on by. 'You've hardly made a dent in that hedge yet.'

'Are we going to have a bonfire before Mummy and Daddy come to collect us?' Betty asked.

'Are we going to burn it all?' Hilary asked Eric, who made a dubious face. 'I suppose bonfire night is a bit too far away?'

'We could prune back the other two sides for that,' Terence said.

'And Faith and Sally are worried about their horses eating it,' May put in.

'I've seen them eating the yew hedge itself,' Isabella said.

'Apparently, eating the live yew isn't all that dangerous,' May said. 'But even after just twenty minutes of being cut, it's lethal. I think you should burn it.'

'Raah!' The Tribe cried; several of them rose and started a Redskin war dance, as demonstrated on all the best cinema screens every Saturday morning.

Nicole turned to Terence. 'You and Hilary shouldn't need to come up here and work in this garden. You've got enough to look after by yourselves down there at the gate.'

Hilary bridled at that. 'We are part of this community – even if we don't take part in your quaint attachment to shared electricity meters.'

Eric stepped in. 'I'm sure Nicole was thinking of the effort you two put into this place compared with . . . er . . . certain nameless others.'

'Shall I go and get some matches?' Sam asked.

Charley added, 'And there's a bottle of paraffin in the smaller garages.'

'Which will stay there!' Eric said firmly. 'We shall light the fire in the traditional way by rubbing two boy scouts together. Cub scouts will do just as well.'

Terence stuffed the tail end of a flapjack into his mouth and, rising, said indistinctly, 'We'd better start now or it'll still be burning after midnight.'

Nicole went off with Betty and Sam to get potatoes, for baking in the ashes once the fire started to die down. May took Hannah and Frederick, her youngest, to bring round the garden hose and attach it to the tap by the ballroom steps.

There was hardly any wind and what there was came from the west, so the first people to get the smoke would be almost a mile away. Eric gathered The Tribe around. 'Now this stuff would probably burn if we just struck a match and chucked it in anywhere. But here's how you can make a fire with even wet wood.'

He began with a cluster of dried grass, then minute twigs, bigger twigs, even bigger twigs . . . snaps of branches – always bridging any gaps with bunches of yew leaves, which crackled and spat like miniature volcanic fumaroles. Sam and Charley inhaled the smoke until they coughed and reeled like drunkards; seeing them the younger ones had to be restrained . . . until, at length, the heat of the fire drove the smoke up, up, way over their heads.

'I think we can all be quite proud of Fire,' Eric said. 'It's one of our great inventions. But now we must all dance around it just to make sure it knows we are its masters and, of all the animals that ever lived, we alone are not afraid of it. Or not enough, anyway.'

The Tribe started the dance they had rehearsed earlier, but soon everyone joined in – including Marianne and Willard, who laid down their glazing brads and putty knives in Rosy Primrose and ran to join them.

After twenty minutes or so, the fire settled into a comfortable middle age and became approachable enough to rake out some embers to cover the potatoes. 'If you children all go off and have your baths now,' Nicole said, 'and come back in your pyjamas, those spuds will be just about roasted by then. Quick-quick!'

The women went off with them and the three men sat on the ground and gazed into the red heart of the fire. Moments later Marianne shouted, 'Hi!' from their balcony, overlooking the big lawn, and lowered a basket full of Tuborg straight from the fridge – church key and all.

'You have her well trained,' Terence remarked, popping the cap on his bottle.

'Well trained?' Eric asked, taking a swig and belching back the foam. 'Well trained? Have you ever been to Sweden?'

He shook his head.

'Well, you should. Everything we think we have to fight for, or invent for ourselves, they've already got. It's this guy here who needs the training.' He jerked a thumb at Willard.

Willard paid no heed. He emptied the bottle in four jerky

gulps and, wiping his lips on his bare forearm, let out one long sigh. 'Dreamed 'bout that aaaall day.' He reached for another. 'Drink up – we got half the fridge full up there.'

There was a ruminative, staring-into-the-fire sort of silence before he spoke again. 'Felix is being very non-committal about his trip to Israel. Were you with him all the time?',

'Mostly,' Terence said. 'Every evening, anyway, though we went our different ways on most days. It was interesting watching him change.'

'From pro all things Zionist to anti?' Eric asked.

'He certainly started very pro, but I wouldn't say he ended up anti. More like thoughtful . . . watchful. The Zionist Jews are very scornful and unfriendly to the German Jews. They keep saying "You brought it on yourselves. You should have come to Israel before the war." But what none of them realizes is that they're all victims of American policy – keeping the quota, even after the war. Hundreds of thousands of Jews escaped extermination but America still refused them entry – and even America's Jews agreed. "Send them to Israel!" That was the answer. The Zionists were happy enough, of course. Their aim was, is, and always will be to colonize the whole of Palestine.'

Willard said, 'You don't think the Arab countries all around have enough room to take in all the Palestinians – their own people, after all?'

'Of course they do, in the same way that the English-speaking world would have enough room for all the Americans if some Martians invaded and kicked them out. We're from the same stock, after all. Sorry, we've strayed a bit far from Felix. I must say, he was a bit shaken when he saw an Israeli passport – "valid in all countries except Germany" stamped on the cover!'

'I take your point,' Willard said, 'about displacing whole people. But is there nothing good in the current set up? You were pretty anti before you went. Nothing changed your mind?'

Terence shook his head. 'I suppose I moved slightly more toward the thoughtful-watchful part of the spectrum, too. I mean, the Israelis are doing amazing things. Grant them that. The Arabs have been there centuries and did little more than grow olives and herd goats – and in the south they were . . . just Bedouin. But the Israelis move in and the desert blooms. Lush vegetables . . . citrus orchards . . . it's like a biblical miracle.

But those four words – the Israelis move in – are still . . . wrong. Just wrong. It's true that tens of thousands of Middle Eastern Jews were killed – and by the Arabs – but it still doesn't make it right to tell *another* Arab whose family lived there for generations, "You have till sunset – then we start with the bulldozers." We saw dozens of Arabs in Jerusalem – everywhere – with keys hanging from chains round their necks. Not dozens. Hundreds. Everywhere. And then a friend told us those were keys to houses they were kicked out of by Israeli settlers. There are thousands of them now employed as labourers on land they once owned. It's so short-sighted. Those Arabs are never going to just throw away those keys. They'll be handed down as heirlooms, together with the imperative that goes along with them.'

'Is that what changed Felix's mind?' Eric asked.

'Well, he had to agree it was wrong but he also said we had to understand what forces were driving them. The *Vernichtung,* as he calls it, made them realize that unless they have a *Heimat* – a homeland – what the French call a *patrie,* they will be forever vulnerable to that sort of treatment, and they'll have nowhere to go. Which is true, but it doesn't alter the fundamentals. You can't steal your *Heimat* from others and call it your own. But you could agree a price and buy it.'

'Historical precedent favours the first course,' Eric pointed out.

'At what price?'

'Oh, war, of course. In human history peace is never more than an interlude, when we catch our breath and smell the flowers.'

'We'd better stir those potatoes a bit,' Willard said, taking the unburned end of a branch and raking among the ashes. 'So Felix is left in a kind of limbo?' he added.

'Oh, no – I think he's backed right off the idea of converting. That happened when he went to a synagogue, almost at the end of our visit. I wish I'd gone too, just to see it. The rabbi was an American, a new immigrant. A real zealot. He preached every quotation from the Bible where Jahweh promises this land to the Israelites, and he finished with Joshua at Jericho – how the Israelites were commanded by Jahweh to kill everything that moved after the walls fell, except the spies who had betrayed the city to Joshua. So the Israelites killed not just the men but also the women, the children, the oxen, the sheep, the asses . . . everything. And they took the gold and silver, of course. And this man preached this disgusting story as some kind of allegory of what God now wants the modern Israelites – the Israelis – to do with the latter-day unbelievers – the Palestinian Arabs. I really felt so sorry for Felix. He can't possibly have come across that sort of triumphalist Zionism in Mauthausen.' He leaned forward and gingerly tested the firmness of one of the baked potatoes.

'Fundamentally,' Terence said, 'Felix is a loner, not a joiner. He never joined the resistance when he was on the run. He mentioned that a couple of times. Still, he's come back with a nice, juicy commission from Ben Gurion.'

Eric added, '*And* an invitation for Fogel to go out there and talk over some publishing collaborations. That will please Doubleday. And so the world goes on turning, no matter what Joshua may have thought in the Valley of Ajalon. Time passes so slowly when you're on a killing spree for your beliefs. Of course Felix would know all about *that.*'

'Eric?' Willard said. 'Can it, huh?'

'*Pas devant les enfants?* Speak of the devils – here they come. Time for us all to catch our breath and smell the flowers.'

Saturday, 19 August 1950

'But if the Tithe Barn had been part of the *original* renting,' Angela pointed out, 'and Tony says it jolly nearly was – but if it had been part of the *original* lease to the community—'

'. . . I'd have taken it like a shot, rather than this cottage,' Felix said. 'I know. And I'm not arguing that I wouldn't have.'

'So!'

'So, nothing. It *wasn't* part of the original community. Now it's just an afterthought. A postscript. Something we're thinking of tacking on. And I just can't *feel* . . .'

'Come on, *Liebling!* This community is little more than four years old. It's already lost and gained people. Nothing's really fixed here. If we move to the Tithe Barn now, d'you think that when it's four*teen* years old anyone will remember that it *wasn't* part of the original—'

'But we will *own* that land – three quarters of an acre. Nobody else here will own anything. We won't be part of the *community*.'

Angela tore at her hair in mime. 'You really think that scrap of paper you signed, making us subtenants of Tony and Adam . . . you think *that's* what makes us "part of this community?"'

'Besides, it's so far away.'

'It's a hundred and fifteen paces. *My* paces, which makes it about a hundred yards.' A thought struck her. 'I know what it is – the entrance door faces *away from* the Dower House. You feel it's like turning our backs on the community. What if . . . now I don't know if we'd get consent to this, but what if we could swap the two windows on the south side, facing into the Dower House grounds . . . what if we could swap them over with the barn door? Then we could lay a short bit of a gravel drive straight off the existing one. Fifty yards.' He drew breath to speak but she got in first with: 'Or are you just going to say no to everything?'

He let the breath out again and gave it some thought. 'I'd lose the north light.'

'No. You'd still have the two windows. And anyway, you've got no north light at all, here. And as for ownership versus renting . . . don't you think the gravel company will have to give up in the end? They're bound to realize they're *never* going to get consent to demolish the Dower House. Nor will they be able to mine gravel around the park. The law has now made agricultural tenancies as good as title deeds. When they realize that, they'll sell. And the community, as sitting tenants, will be sitting on a bargain. A gold mine. And then we – you and I – will just be the first owners in a community of owners. We'll be the pathfinders!'

Felix eyed her suspiciously. 'Who put such ideas into your head?'

'You should have a little talk with Sally. She has great ideas about—'

'She has great *ambitions*. There's a difference. She wants to enter the halls of architectural fame on the wings of this conversion . . .'

'She also has great ideas about the long-term future of the Dower House. Buying out the lease from the gravel company is only the start of it. Your tea's gone cold.'

She reached for the cup but he pulled it to him. 'It's all right. It's a hot day. I like it like this.'

Angela wondered whether it would be better to leave him to think it over now or to throw a few more thoughts his way . . . which, in the end, is what she decided to do. 'It would be wonderful for Faith and Alex, too, to have the full run of this cottage. And Jasmine – poor little thing! She's been moved from pill box to . . . no! What's the saying? Pillar to post! To belong to The Tribe would transform her.'

'Why don't Faith and Alex buy the Tithe Barn, then? They could easily afford it.'

'Oh, Felix! D'you think they're not already considering it? The part that should be your studio would make a wonderful indoor parking place for an Aston Martin, a Jaguar, and whatever van they buy as a runaround. People will be standing about over there, admiring those cars, when they should be admiring your sculptures. But there! I've said my say and I leave it to you. You won't hear another word from me.'

She hadn't left the room above twenty seconds when she returned: 'Faith comes back from Italy next Wednesday. We have a clear run until then.' She turned away once more . . . but added over her shoulder, 'Possibly.'

Two minutes later she was back again. 'I've said nothing about what it would mean to *me* to have a fully equipped electronic workshop. Things are *really* happening in the field of electronic and synthesized music.'

And finally her voice drifted back into the studio as she climbed the stairs: 'I can just picture you a year from now – pressing your nose against the back window of the studio, squeezing round a sculpture that barely fits here, cursing those cars and all the space they aren't even using.'

In her nursery upstairs Pippin began to grizzle – as she always did on waking.

'And now we've woken her up with all this unnecessary discussion!'

A short while later, as she sang Pippin back to finish her afternoon nap, walking back and forth across the nursery, she

glanced out of the window and saw Felix pacing the distance
from the edge of the Dower House grounds to the nearest
corner of the Tithe Barn . . . then onward to the pair of
windows she had suggested swapping with the barn door . . .
and then he passed out of sight as, no doubt, he went round
the far side to look at the door itself. Just before he vanished
he turned and waved to her. Love, she reminded herself, was
once an unaffordable luxury.

When he returned, she resolved to say nothing, knowing her
silence would irk him. But when they climbed into bed that
night, and he still hadn't spoken, she knew she'd not sleep until
he had.

'Well?' she prompted.

He reached down for the hem of her nightdress and started
to raise it.

'Well?' she insisted, gripping his wrist and holding him there.

'I think . . .' he said, overpowering her grip and raising the
hem a few inches more. 'I think . . .' [and a few inches more]
'. . . we should . . .' [and yet a few more] '. . . start another
baby around now . . .'

'Oh, no!' she cried.

'. . . and make it our deadline to be living over there before
it is born.'

It took a second or two for his meaning to sink in, but then
all she could think of to say was: 'Oh . . . yes!'

Thursday, 30 November 1950

'Champagne!' Faith cried. 'What's the occasion? Are we wetting
Diana's head somewhat belatedly?'

'No. We did that when you were in America.' Hilary handed
her a glass. 'It's hard to catch a time when you're in England
these days.'

'Or even Europe,' Alex added as he took his glass from Terence.

'We're celebrating Terence's appointment to the chair of this
new National Planning Council. So leave a smidgeon in your
glass for a toast when the others arrive.'

'I say!' Alex raised his glass to Terence and looked him up and down. 'The destiny of the nation's now in your hands, eh!' In a stage whisper to Faith he added, 'We must move all our funds abroad at the earliest opportunity.'

'I'm not sure I should be drinking at all,' Faith said, laying a significant hand over her stomach.

'Really? But how wonderful! When's it due?'

'*Now* will you get married?' Terence asked.

'Don't look at *me!*' Alex said.

'Next May,' Faith said. 'But there's many a slip—'

'Oh, don't be so negative,' Hilary said. 'It'll be a Festival of Britain baby.'

Alex said, 'Eric says we can call it Fester. Or Festina.'

'But will it be a Bullen-ffitch or a Findlater?' Terence asked again.

'I have nothing against the name Findlater,' Faith told him. 'But *Faith* Findlater? Find faith later? It's so trite.'

The Breits and Johnsons arrived, stamping slushy snow off their galoshes and rubbing some warmth back into their fingers. And they barely had glasses in their hands when the Palmers and Wilsons turned up, saying, 'Isabella insists on driving down but they're having trouble starting the car.'

'The Lagonda?' Willard asked.

'No, the Morris. They wouldn't take the Lagonda out in this.'

'Who's babysitting?' Terence asked.

'May's got a stinking cold so Arthur's staying up with her,' Nicole said. 'And Pippin's put down with our two. And Lena's there, of course.'

'And Gracie has let Betty sleep over with us tonight,' Adam concluded. 'She knows where to go to find a grown-up.'

Sally added, 'It would be truer to say that Betty has badgered Gracie into agreeing to let her sleep over. The place is becoming more than her *spiritual* home. Are Chris and Anna coming?'

'They were invited but they've gone to the Friday night hop at the Slade. I don't suppose they'll be back tonight at all.'

'They have the key to Robert Street,' Felix said, holding up two sets of crossed fingers.

The Brandons arrived – on foot. 'Bloody Morris!' Eric said. 'Oh, for a decent *Japanese* car – if they make them, that is!'

Everyone laughed at that fantasy – a Japanese car, forsooth!
'It's turning to snow,' Isabella said.
'Did Ruth go down in the end?' Adam asked her.
'I don't know. I just left her crying. It didn't sound too-too
utterly sincere. Gracie was right – one worries far less with the
second one than the first. What's the celebration?'

She was the only who *hadn't* said on arrival, 'Ooh – champagne!,' as if it were special. And several there were thinking
they hadn't noticed her worrying all that much about Calley,
their firstborn, either.

Fourteen was too large a number to seat at the dining-room
table, which was instead laid out, as Hilary put it, 'like the
smörgåsbord we just *lived* off on the ferry to Gothenburg last
summer.' The party divided into parties, who helped themselves
and sat or stood in knots in the kitchen, the parlour, and the
living room.

'Dare I ask how the Tithe Barn's coming along?' Alex asked
Marianne.

She told him, 'We applied for consent even before the purchase
was completed, and got it. I think the Hertford planners liked
the idea of one of their buildings being featured in the AR –
especially as our interior doesn't even touch the medieval fabric.
The builders have already swapped over the door and the two
windows, so we start pouring concrete tomorrow. Seventy-five
yards!'

'Reinforced?'

'As we go. Double the depth where Felix might want to put
any weight of sculpture. It'll load to twenty tons a square foot.'

Faith drifted away. Alex was only tormenting himself that
they had dithered too long; he still had forlorn fantasies of
leaping out of bed in one of Sally and Marianne's cedarwood
boxes, perched on bright aluminium scaffolding, and coming
out to stand on the balcony and gaze lovingly down on two or
three aristocratic sports cars. 'We'll get the second galleys for
the last chapter of the fashion book on Monday,' she told Isabella.
'I'll have a set sent straight round to *Vogue*. So we're going to
be screaming for those last few illustrations before next Friday.
Otherwise you and Eric have done bloody well.'

'Eric?' she asked as if this collaboration were complete news
to her. 'He was just a pain in the neck.'

To the extent that he always managed to cut a thousand words of your text down to the planned four hundred and fifty without losing any of the meat, Faith thought, but she said, 'You must lead a charmed life at *Vogue*. From our perspective at Manutius, yours was the ideal partnership. Fogel's pleased, anyway.'

'How's life treating Stackaprole and Stackaprole?' Eric asked. 'Is yours higher than Willard's or is his higher than yours?'

Adam no longer rose to the bait. 'We prefer to measure it in terms of the green space all around. Theo loves your *Bruno the Piebald Polar Bear*, by the way. He goes off to sleep murmuring, piebald . . . piebald . . . It's sweet.'

'I suggested a sequel in which Bruno marries Brunette – another piebald polar bear – and they have one black, one white, and two piebald cubs. Mendelian genetics for preschool toddlers. You can't start too young, you know.'

'And?'

'They're actually considering it! People are starting to take me seriously – it's *awful.*'

'When we drove with the kids down to Cornwall last summer,' Willard said, 'we stopped at Stonehenge and had a picnic, right in the circle. It was spooky, sitting on those ancient stones, eating sandwiches and thinking of all that history. Then we went over Dartmoor – by moonlight – man, that was really something. Except we had to stop five or six times for Marianne to get out and open gates for me to drive through and then she had to shut them behind us. Two of them were already open. Left that way by drivers who couldn't care less. I'd have driven on, too, but Marianne, being Swedish of course, said, "No. They've got that notice saying please shut the gate behind you," so we did the decent, responsible, upright thing. But I tell you, those couldn't-care-less guys are the real public benefactors. If we all copied them, those farmers would scrap the gates and install cattle grids, PDQ. It's crazy – that's the main highway, the *only* highway, across Dartmoor – barred by five gates!'

Faith said she'd been along main roads worse than that in Wales.

Tony and Nicole could trump them all with one in the Highlands.

All were agreed – in a very British way – that British roads were nothing but a joke.

'My aunt in Paris,' Nicole said, 'thinks they've ended rationing completely in Germany and soon, too, in France.'

'They could do the same here,' Willard said. 'What have the British managed to take off rations this year? *Soap!* If we didn't have this communist government, we could have completely eliminated—'

'Socialist, not communist,' Terence butted in. 'Socialism is what communism aspires to achieve, so it's even worse from your point of view. Communism is when they put up traffic lights in every street but they're all set to red. Socialism is when they take them all away . . .'

'. . . and the streets *run* red,' Eric put in. 'Sorry, Nicole, it was just too good to miss. But you needn't worry, Willard. The Tories will get back soon enough. Then bloated plutocrats like you will inherit the earth. But you'd better make the most of it because I read the other day that we've only got enough oil left to last another twenty years.'

Terence laughed. 'We've *always* only got enough oil for twenty years. The oil companies have no commercial incentive to look farther into the future than that.'

'So what does being chairman of this National Planning Council mean?' Marianne asked him.

'With this socialist government?' he said. 'Mainly it's telling them what they can't afford to do. If the Tories get back in . . .'

'. . . they'll sack all you academics,' Willard said cheerfully, 'and replace you with entrepreneurs who know how to . . .'

'. . . how to rerun the Great Depression,' Eric said. 'Only more thoroughly. This time they'll get it right.'

Willard turned on him. 'Whose side are you on, Eric? You make this great play of sitting on the fence. Time you came down.'

'I'm on Isabella's side – as always.' He smiled at her as if he hadn't known she was passing by.

'You're eating too much,' she said. 'They can't let those trousers out any further.'

★   ★   ★

'Did you listen to *In Town Tonight* last Saturday?' Tony asked. 'Poor John Snagge! I'm sure the editors shove in one item each time to flummox him.'

'What was it?' Sally asked.

'I heard that,' Eric said. 'Some modern poet with an appalling cockney accent that I'm sure wasn't genuine. And his poem ran something like – *When I'm dead don't bury me down. Just saw me up and feed my hound. And tell him this as he'll snarl and roar – There's more where this came from – over there on the floor* . . . Something like that. You can just imagine what poor old Snagge made of it! He said, "Oh, you've got a hound, you say. What sort?" And the poet said, "No, it's figgrative. It's a pome."'

'I heard that, too,' Tony said. And then all he could think of to ask was, 'Do you think you're going to die soon, then? And the poet said, Yeah, probbly.'

'There's a fundamental point about it, though.' Alex joined the group. 'That particular item was slipped in as a last-minute time filler, when they saw they were running short, so it wasn't from a script.'

'Pretty obviously!' Eric said. 'Why have a script, anyway?'

'Because Auntie still has this absurd rule that we can't broadcast the spoken word – the genuinely spoken word, off the cuff. When Stewart MacPherson does *Down Your Way,* for instance, he meets a number of interesting and important people in the district and interviews them – *twice*. The first time, he's asking questions and they're answering just as they would in ordinary conversation. Then the producer turns it into a script – question, answer, question, answer – only this time they're reading it. So they take – for example: *They tell me you've lived here all your life? 'S'right. Born in that 'ouse there, see – with the hydrangeas. Still live there. Never moved.* And they turn it into: *I understand you've lived here all your life, Mister Smith? Oh, yes, indeed, I should say so – man and boy.* And so on. And the poor bugger has to read it out – lines that would tax the powers of a top-class actor. That's why it always sounds so fake.'

'I guess I don't listen that much,' Willard said. 'Why do they do it?'

'Fear,' Alex said. 'Fear that someone will say something libellous. Or worse – slip in a few words of our Anglo-Saxon vernacular. Also it's a leftover from the war, where people might have let some hush-hush cat out of the bag. But we'll have to stop it. There's no real life in anything we do that's supposed to be a slice of real life.'

'You should listen to Jack Jackson on Radio Luxembourg,' Marianne said. 'He's not reading from a script. You're going to need people like him who can just talk.'

'And AFN,' Willard added. 'Their interviews with GIS are recorded just the way they speak – and they blur out any naughty words.'

'Not all of them,' Eric said. 'I tuned in on AFN the other night and an exceedingly hoarse man was yelling at the top of his voice – *If Ah had mah ahms 'n legs cut off – Ah wud craaawl on bleedin' stumps – to the body of the Laaawd – who is mah Sayvyeh! Halleluyah!* And they didn't blur out a single word. Maybe comedy's different, though.'

And so the ashtrays filled, and were emptied, and were filled again; the wine bottles emptied; the liqueurs came out; and the plates that had held some very English smörgåsar were stacked in the Belfast sink, and Tony cut up some envelopes rescued from the salvage basket, making little white squares on each of which he wrote a letter of the alphabet or a number from zero to nine, finally arranging them in alphabetical order, in a two-foot circle on the newly cleared table. When he asked for a smallish tumbler, Terence said, 'Oh, not this! Surely we're all rationalists and humanists here?'

'I've seen some pretty amazing things in India,' Alex said.

'Yes, it's truly wonderful,' Eric agreed, 'how swiftly their ancient spirit guides were able to master the Graeco-Roman alphabet, and I'm told it coincided almost exactly with the circulation of coinage with Queen Victoria's head on it.'

'I'll join in,' Willard challenged, 'if the . . . whatever-it-is can tell us what the initial A in my name stands for.'

Everyone laughed because, of course, they all knew by now that it stood for nothing – like the S in Harry S Truman, which was why there was no 'period,' as Willard called it, after the letter.

'*It* may not know that,' he said, 'and don't anyone here say it out loud.'

And then it turned out that not everyone knew it. Hilary for one. And Angela – who didn't even know he had a middle initial. And Nicole said she had forgotten what name it stood for. So they sat at roughly 120 degrees to each other and placed a finger on the base of the upturned wine glass.

'What now?' Hilary asked.

Tony explained: 'If there's a spirit in the room, it will enter your fingers and move the glass to spell out Willard's middle name, one letter at a time.'

For a good thirty seconds nothing happened; they were just about to give up when the glass moved – jerkily, hesitantly, zigzagging out from the centre of the circle toward the A. Then, still uncertainly, to the S . . .

'Ass?' Eric guessed.

Everyone shushed him.

H. The movements were becoming more decisive. L . . . A . . . N . . .

'My God – no!' Willard said, in little more than a whisper.

'What?' Several voices chorused.

D.

'Ashland!' Willard said. 'I was born in Ashland, New Hampshire. A one-horse town. A *part-time* one-horse town! Which of you guys knew that? Someone must have sneaked a peek at my birth registration. Who was moving that glass?'

All three denied moving it with any intention; each said it felt as if she was following the glass rather than pushing it, even when it moved directly away from her across the table.

'It never occurred to me,' Willard said in amazement. 'I'm going to have to ask Mom and Dad – did they put that A in my name for Ashland. And hey! My sister's name is—'

'Don't say it!' Felix cried. 'See if this so-called spirit knows that one.'

'And I say we stop this right here. Right now,' Terence said, to general noises of disappointment and frustration. 'We did this once at school. Five of us in the house sanitorium with measles, and we had an assistant matron who claimed to be a medium. And it ended up with the table lifting itself off the floor, with us standing up and all our hands on top.'

'So you believe in it,' Felix said.

'Of course not. I don't know what really happened there. A mass hallucination? All this . . . this . . . occult stuff is just playing tricks on the human mind – about which we know very little. And it's dangerous.'

'OK!' Willard yielded. 'We'll do it one evening *chez nous*. My sister has an empty middle initial, just like me. And, it so happens, it's the same as the first letter of the town where *she* was born – which may or may not have been Ashland. But the secret stays with me. So I'll keep my hands off the glass and we'll see if this spirit can work it out.'

'Can we play children's party games instead?' Isabella asked. 'All the ones we played when we were children?'

Everyone turned to her in astonishment.

'It may have escaped your notice,' she said, 'but we will have fifteen birthday parties next year – that's just the children, not counting the adults. We can't play musical chairs, pass the parcel, blind-man's-buff, and pin the tail on the donkey at each and all of them.'

'Fifteen?' Sally asked. 'Are you sure?'

'I'm assuming the Fergusons' three will come to most of ours, and most of ours will go to theirs, so we might as well count them in. And, actually, it'll be sixteen if Lena's Tommy is still with us.'

Seventeen, if Jasmine's included by then, Alex thought but did not press the point.

Eyes vanished into skulls and fingers waved in the air as people anatomized the house and counted imaginary sleeping heads on imaginary pillows . . . and all agreed, with some astonishment, that Isabella was right. What with the children they had made since coming to the Dower House and the ones that some had brought with them, they now had at least fifteen members of The Tribe, ranging in age from William Palmer, Diana Lanyon, and Ruth Brandon, all now less than one year old, up to Betty Ferguson, who had just turned nine.

And so, rather self-consciously, they started playing childhood games other than the ones Isabella had listed. There was Kiss the Queen of Sheba, One-two-three block, Art thou my food partner?, Chinese miming, Whose face is this?, O'Grady says, Murder . . . and many more. They went on so long that Chris and Anna, who had found the Slade hop rather disappointing and so had caught the last train home, were able to join in the final game or two. They all played in a kind of amazed childhood rekindled. They looked at one another – the chairman of the National Planning Council, one of the country's most successful architects, a Very Senior Person at the BBC, and women near the top of their professions, too – they looked at one another with eyes that said, *Can you believe we're actually doing this!*

All except Felix and Angela; he caught her eye from across the room and each knew the other was thinking: *Did we ever believe we might one day actually be doing this?*

Saturday, 13 January 1951

The baby was just beginning to show when Faith capitulated at last and took the name of Findlater, keeping Bullen-ffitch as her professional name. They were married by her brother Michael, who was back on annual leave from Kenya, at a quiet family ceremony (in the circumstances) in Old Sodbury church on Saturday, 13 January, 1951. Jasmine, almost four, was the only bridesmaid. Alex's brother was his best man.

Alex had bought a new Mark IV Bentley, Tudor Grey, with a 4.2-litre straight-six engine and grey hide seats with red piping. The following day the two of them and Jasmine drove to the Dower House, where the real wedding party was held. Two days later, joined now by Delfine Lardan, a distant cousin of Nicole's who was to be nanny to Jasmine and the new baby when it arrived, the four of them set off on a leisurely tour down to the south of France – specifically to Arles, capital of the Camargue, where they could leave Jasmine safely with Delfine while they rode the wilderness of grass and marsh on those magnificent greys they breed down there – the Camaguais. They were lucky with the weather.

At first it was hard to relax – to realize that each day was not snatched from the working timetable, crammed between meetings, presentations, committees, interviews, decisions . . . The urge was strong to pick up the phone each evening and call a colleague to ask what had happened over this or that pending decision . . . who had won an ongoing battle in such-and-such a committee . . . had so-and-so defected to the opposition . . . and so on. It was a full ten days – more than halfway through their time down there, before Faith felt able to say, 'You know what I was telling you about Abnorman Crowley before we came away – how I'm sure he's going to stage his coup while we're down here? And d'you know what now? I don't *give* a damn!'

He caught her stress and chuckled. 'Tara is yours and he can't take that away from you, eh!'

'It's more than that. I actually had to get away from Manutius to understand what's really happening there. I've been drumming up so much new business . . . I mean, I thought I was some kind of super-editorial person who could use *that* skill to sell ideas for books to other publishers. But actually I'm a salesman. Sales*woman*. I've sold new ideas and new series to so many publishers . . . even Japan now. Maybe.' She frowned. 'Did I tell you about that? I met a Japanese publisher at Mondadori in Verona . . .'

He shrugged. 'Perhaps. I can't always keep up.'

'Anyway, it's too much. I can't chase editors, designers, production people the way they have to be chased *and* cope with all this new business. But I couldn't see that – not in the thick of it. All I was thinking was *I've got to keep Abnorman out of my hair*. Wrong! What I've got to do is *let* him steal my job – the super-editor bit – but do it in such a way that he's the super editor of *my* projects and *I'm* still the one who has the final say.'

'He'll squirm,' Alex warned.

'Of course he will. But if I've constructed the boundaries around him right, he'll just squirm himself into fitting them perfectly! And it could even turn out that he won't notice what I've done until after the first editorial conference.'

'And now you want to go back to London tomorrow!'

'He's a highly experienced *American* editor – that's why he won't get it until it's too late.'

'I don't follow.'

'American publishers make books for one market and one language, mostly. And by the standards of Manutius, where we have half the pages in full colour and the rest in two-colour, their books are cheap. And so their editors are the kings of the castle – and queens, too. But at Manutius, to make a living at all, *we* have to sell a British Commonwealth edition, a French edition, Italian edition, German, Dutch, Swedish, Spanish – the Spanish market is huge – and . . . maybe a Japanese edition now. We have to seduce all those publishers into agreeing a common text for each of them to translate. We all share the cost of colour; then each publisher pays for his own text, fitting it around the artwork. It's why Fogel keeps hammering home – "Ve are all prostitoots now." Abnorman understands all that at the intellectual level, but his guts still tell him that the editor-in-chief is cock of the walk. So I won't fight him at all. I will graciously suggest to Fogel that he should offer Abnorman that title, and I'll just be the company's travelling saleswoman. But when I say, "Rohwolt won't accept that, Norman" . . . who's going to have to roll over?' She laughed. 'I love those novels where the villain gets his comeuppance, don't you?'

He wrinkled his nose. 'I prefer them when I'm never quite sure who the villain is. Perhaps it's why I love you so much – *your* villainy is exciting. I asked if you want to go back to London tomorrow?'

'Certainly not! You remember when we drove down to Castle Combe? How I was supposed to be doing some kind of paper-work for Fogel?'

'Yes, though I have more pleasurable reasons for remembering that particular weekend.'

'And just look at the result!' She drew her hands apart to show her belly. 'Not terribly visible yet, is it? It's going to be a small one – at least I hope so. No, I don't want to go back to London until we're due to return anyway – the twenty-ninth. Well . . . maybe just a day or two earlier so that I can have a private word with one or two people. How do you feel?'

They reined in to a halt and stared out over miles of pool-mottled grassland. The horses champed their bits and tossed their heads at the flies. Devils of Mediterranean wind, unseasonably warm for January, hithered and thithered like swarms of invisible mice, rattling the fronds of grass in a panic. 'I shouldn't have spoken,' he said at last. 'We've been so lucky with the weather . . . it's sacrilege to lose ourselves in this utter wilderness, only to talk of publishing and broadcasting. Don't the words sound utterly meaningless when we speak them here?'

When she did not reply he said, 'No?'

She gave a single, sardonic laugh. 'I'm utterly in love with this place . . . swept away by it. But I can still look at . . . all *that,* and think, *Yes, this is far enough away for me to think dispassionately about . . . Manutius . . . Abnorman . . . all that jazz.* And that's what I cannot help doing.' Now her laugh was more genuine. 'You're obviously going to take to retirement, when it comes, much more easily than I ever will!'

'Oh, I've done my share of thinking, too. In fact, it was something you said on that same day at Castle Combe, about the possibilities of commercial TV . . .'

'About jumping ship, actually.'

'Well . . . yes. But not for purely selfish career reasons. In fact, I'm coming round to the view that the only way to change the BBC will be to pit it against a rival system whose aim will be to collar the biggest number of viewers. Commercial TV will be like TV in America: an endless wasteland of bland, trivial, populist pap, much of it actually bought in from America. The government – even a Tory government – will put a quota on it, of course, if only to prevent a haemorrhage of dollars, but commercial TV will buy right up to that quota.'

'I'll tell you another thing that "even a Tory government" will insist on: a certain standard of news broadcasting – not all gossip about film stars and sporting heroes and kittens being rescued after falling down wells.'

He reached a hand across and patted her on the back. 'You're ahead of me, darling. The same will be true of cultural programming . . . they'll also insist on so many hours a week dedicated to culture, drama, science, history . . . and that's where it starts to get interesting.'

'To you.'

'To me. The question is, do I jump ship and join commercial TV and show Auntie how it could be done, or do I stay and scare Auntie into doing it first? Steal their thunder.' He stole a sly glance at her. 'I'd stay with Auntie if *you* were there, too.'

She avoided his gaze. 'And what if I joined commercial TV when it starts up?'

When he did not answer she added, 'They'll come knocking at your door anyway, months before there's anything on air.'

When he still did not answer, she leaned forward and stared into his face. 'By God – they already have!' she said.

He nodded. ''Fraid so, old darling.'

'And you've said you'd think it over? When did this happen?'

'The day before our wedding. So I haven't really considered it too deeply. Yet. In fact, there was something else to think about first: how long it might be before this Labour government falls and the Tories get back in. This is only their first year and they could theoretically last until 'fifty-five . . .'

'But . . .?'

'The flies are bothering these fellows – I thought we'd avoid them in January. And we ought to get back to the hotel, anyway.'

They trotted off inland to the home of the *gardian* – a simple whitewashed cottage roofed in thatch, where they could tether their horses and arrange for tomorrow's ride.

'The Labour government?' she reminded him as they set off at a necessary snail's pace in the Bentley, along a track that even a tank commander might negotiate with care. The suspension control on the steering column was set to its firmest notch.

'Well,' he replied uncertainly, 'I think they'll be lucky to survive until the Festival opens this May. I doubt they'll still be in by Christmas. But even so, it could still be three or four years before any new commercial service is launched.'

'Four years . . . five years . . . six years – what's the difference? Surely the BBC can see it coming? How far ahead do you plan programme changes? Give me an example.'

'OK, did you ever see an American programme called *What's my Line?* any time you were over there? Bennett Cerf, Harold Hoffman, Louis Untermeyer . . . John Daly in the chair? People come on and do a mime—'

'Oh, yes! Good fun.'

'Well, we've taken up the British rights and we've already been planning it in detail for some months – lining up the chairman and "panellists," as they call them – though it won't go out until next year. So, to answer your next question, I'm sure it would take a couple of years to start an entirely new broadcasting company from scratch. Just to give you one little detail: we'd have to start transmitting a test signal about six months before the first programme went out, to reassure people we're serious, to give them time to buy aerials, and to give electricians time to sell, install, and tune the sets. Six months.'

'You said "we!" Is your subconscious running ahead of you?'

He laughed. 'Could be.'

Her fingers played an imaginary piano as she counted the months and years forward to a possible change of government and then onward to the day when transmissions might begin in earnest. 'I think,' she said at last, 'that "we" can safely leave it until the Tories actually win.'

'Hmmm. You don't think that might be too late? They are already recruiting.'

'Nobody of any quality, surely? Just people who suspect their star is already waning . . . people tempted simply by money. But you're a heavyweight, my love. Even if their ship already has a captain, they'll put you on board as the admiral.'

Without taking his eyes off the ruts and potholes, he reached across and gave her arm a squeeze. 'Thank God you're here.'

She kissed his hand and placed it firmly back upon the wheel. 'I met Henry Reed at a Faber literary launch last month, and we were discussing wars and civil wars – as one does, you know – and he said something very striking; one of those ideas that helps a large chunk of the jigsaw to fall into place. He said that a civil war is the supreme kind of war because it puts a general to the severest test. A *successful* general in a civil war is the one who knows, to the nearest hour and minute, when to change sides!'

Thursday, 17 May 1951

'*Please* don't fiddle with those loops!' Angela said sharply.

'Sorry!' Gingerly, Chris placed the one he was holding back on its hook. 'What's *pschuu* stand for, anyway?'

Rather than answer him, Angela hooked it into her tape recorder and pressed *Play*. The volume from the two large studio monitors made him wince. 'My fault,' she said as she modulated the output. Then he heard: *pschuu . . . pschuu . . . pschuu . . . pschuu . . .* as the tape looped endlessly past the read head. She, meanwhile, went on seesawing tape manually through a lash-up connected to her headphones.

'What is it?' he asked.

'You could call it a note. A single note in a future composition. That's what all those other loops are, too.'

He scanned along her handwritten labels, written in black on the shiny white tape that joined the cut ends of each segment to form a similar loop: *skttzz . . . blih . . . ğuh . . .* 'What's g with a little crescent moon over it mean?' he asked.

'Scratchy, like clearing your throat.' She imitated the sound, and then he mimicked her, extending his reading to other labels, too: '*Skttz pschuu kl-k-k-k blih fzzz psss ğuh!* It's poetry! It's the poetry of pure sound rather than meaning! Fan-taaas-tic!'

'I'll play them all to you if you've got the time,' she offered.' And, indeed, she did.

'Well?' she asked when she had exhausted her little store of some twenty loops.

He shook his head, unable for a moment to speak. At last he said, 'I think that's just about the most exciting thing I ever heard. You're going to turn that into music? Strange music?'

'No.' She laughed. 'I'm not a composer. Maybe I shouldn't have said "composition." Compilation is more like it. Or demonstration. I'm making a tape – *compiling* a tape, using all those different sounds and messing them about with electronic distortions. See that old water tank?'

He found it in the shadows at a corner of the old barn. 'That's the one they took out of the tower on the main house.'

'Waste not, want not.'

'I hope it's not still full of dead pigeons and rats.'

'As if! I've fitted a speaker and a mike inside it.' She pushed two banana plugs into her control board, picked up a guitar, and held a mike hard against the sounding board. She gave one of its strings a barely perceptible pluck but the sound that emerged from the speakers was spine-chilling . . . ghostly . . . a dying note escaped from caverns measureless.

'Holy moses!' Chris murmured. 'You can turn *that* into *that?*'

'It's only the beginning,' she said nonchalantly. 'If you think of these discoveries of sounds as like the discoveries of new lands – of America, say – we've not yet reached the Adirondacks. Wait till we reach the Rockies!' She peered into his face. 'Why so glum?'

He shrugged. 'I'm in the wrong sodding trade, that's what. Have you been to the Festival yet?'

'Yes, of course. Felix has a sculpture in—'

'No, I meant the exhibition – *Sixty Paintings for Fifty-One*. Talk about depressing. It's just anarchy. There's no . . . I mean, you can look at any Renaissance painting and say, "Yeah – that's Renaissance, all right." Same with Baroque . . . Classical . . . Romantic . . . I don't mean they're all the same. Delacroix . . . Turner . . . William Blake . . . I mean, they could hardly be more different but they're all part of the Romantic Movement. You can see what they have in common with Wordsworth and Coleridge and . . . I don't know – Chopin. Just like you can see something common in Oscar Wilde and Whistler and Debussy. But now! What's in common between John Minton, Ruskin Spear and Graham Sutherland – just to stick with painters, never mind writers and musicians and poets? And *this*!' He wafted his hand at the tapes.

Angela, who had been fiddling with yet more segments throughout this complaint, said mildly, 'You've been talking with Eric.' She reached out and squeezed his arm. 'It's not a good habit. Try and give it up.' And she went on to repeat Felix's remark about bumblebees that continue to fly even after aerodynamic scientists had proved it impossible for them. 'And anyway,' she concluded, 'I can give you a few names – Joyce's *Finnegans Wake,* Alexander Calder's mobiles, Jackson Pollock's paintings, and the music of Darius Milhaud and Olivier Messiaen. Fragments of words, fragments of shapes, fragments of paint, fragments of music – and in each case they add up to a universe . . .'

Felix entered the sound studio. 'They appear chaotic but the more you look or listen, the more sense they make. Sorry, I couldn't help overhearing. Eric may speak the truth but he's blind to reality.'

'One more thing,' Angela said. 'If you want a hot tip for the future, look out for the name of Pierre Schaeffer. He's been experimenting with tape loops and natural sounds – just like this. He calls it *musique concrète* and he's just joined RTF in Paris, where he's persuaded them to set up a *musique concrète* workshop, which is more than I've been able to do at the BBC, I must say. There will be great things—'

Catching her tone, Chris asked, 'Are you going to quit, then? When is the baby due?'

She glanced at Felix before answering. 'September . . . October. After that, I'm going part-time – three days a week. And the rest of the time, between nappy changes and breastfeeds, I'm going to offer young composers – or even old ones if they feel like it – the chance to make concrete music in England.'

'For free?'

She grinned. 'Corvo says he's sure the Arts Council will come up with a grant to make it possible. Don't tell Eric – you know what he feels about the Arts Council.'

'And I have news for you, too,' Felix said to Chris. 'You know Marianne and Sally have won the competition for the new children's wing at Enfield Hospital – the old infirmary? They were thinking of asking Eric to design the murals, and I just commented casually to Marianne that it was a very *safe* choice, and she took it that I was really saying "unadventurous" – which, in a way, I suppose it would be. Children's author-illustrator . . . children's hospital . . . not terribly imaginative. And then somehow *your* name came up, Chris – something much more likely to intrigue the editors at the *Architectural Review*. Up-and-coming young painter . . . in for the *Prix de Rome*. So it might be as well to have one or two ideas ready, in case she asks – so you can trot them out as if they just spilled off the top of your head.'

Chris punched him lightly on the arm. 'Ta muchly, mate. Enfield? Wasn't Willard's firm in for that competition, too?'

Felix nodded. 'It's a bit of a sore point at the moment. Willard, with more than a hundred draughtsmen's tables, beaten by his own wife with only a dozen – though she'll have to find room for more now! Adam says poor old Willard-A spends half his time boasting about how much Marianne learned while working for him and the other half wondering aloud to anyone who'll listen about whether she and Sally haven't bitten off more than they can chew this time.'

Chris was skipping toward the door, saying, 'I've got to tell Julie!' when Angela called after him: 'Something that might help you, Chris. A very *smart* young man at the BBC was talking to me yesterday about this concrete music idea and he kept referring to "the sonic ambience." So if, instead of talking about "murals" and things, you referred to . . . I don't know – the "painterly ambience?" The "colour ambi . . . ?"'

'The "*graphic* ambience!"' Chris said.

'You've got it!' she agreed.

'Well . . .' He paused at the door. '*Skttz pschuu kl-k-k-k* to one and all!'

When he had gone, she turned to Felix. 'Julie? Who's Julie?'

He shrugged. 'Chris's latest, apparently. It turns out that Anna was a bit of an ice maiden. I've not met her but Adam – who should know these things – says that Julie is "dark and luscious."'

Midsummer, 1951

Taking their cue from the Festival of Britain, the Dower House community decided that their midsummer party should be in fancy dress on the theme *The Great Exhbition of 1851*. The main proponent of this idea was, to be sure, Eric Brandon. 'After all,' he said (once the invitations were out and the decision irrevocable), 'the Victorian festival had so much to display that they had to ask the Duke of Devonshire's head gardener to design a building large enough to hold it all, and that enabled them to build it in a few months. But the whole point of our Festival of Britain is that Britain has absolutely *nothing* to display, so we've had to employ dozens of leading architects to design buildings so eye-catchingly wonderful – from the Dome of Discovery all the way up the scale to those magnificent lavatories – that no one will notice the lack of content. No wonder we've taken a couple of years to build it. I'm sure that all our architects at the Dower House will swell with pride at what their profession has achieved.'

The gusto with which those same architects threw themselves into becoming Victorian ladies and gentlemen was extraordinary, considering the unbridled contumely they would (often quite literally) *spray* in an apoplexy on any building of the Victorian era. When Adam and Tony had been at the Bartlett, before the war, they had only half-jokingly concocted a scheme to dynamite the Euston Arch, built in the year of Queen Victoria's accession. They cooled only when students from the Imperial College trumped them (for subtlety, at least) by blowing the left breast off Britannia on the Albert Memorial in Kensington Gardens, but their contempt for all things Victorian persisted.

And yet, when the day arrived, there they all were, passable imitations of those predecessors who had created such master-pieces as Northumberland House, the General Post Office at St-Martin's-le-Grand and, to be sure, the Euston Arch itself – each of which and many more besides they would gladly have demolished with their own hands. If a different theme had been chosen, the day might have turned out very differently.

It started when Felix drove to Welwyn North to collect Peter Murdoch, who was now editor-in-chief at Manutius, following Abnorman Crowley's angry resignation and return to New York. Felix found two or three other guests – all recognizable by their Victorian fancy dress – looking for a taxi and so gave them a lift, too. One of them, clearly a foreigner, ill at ease with English, had made only a minimal effort with his dress; indeed, with his high-wing collar, morning coat, and pearl-grey spats, he could have passed for one of Neville Chamberlain's 1938 entourage on his return from Munich when he waved that scrap of blank paper on which he pretended to have Hitler's promise of 'peace in our time.' This gentleman had responded with a surprised, 'Yes-yes' (or, rather, *Ja-Ja*) to Felix's 'The Dower House?' and now seemed even more surprised to find himself among a group of apparent Victorian gentlemen and one lady, all making their way to that same destination.

Felix tried speaking with him in German: 'May I ask who has invited you to our party today, sir?'

'Party?'

'I'm sorry, you're not . . . I mean, clearly no one has invited you. Allow me to introduce myself – Felix Breit, artist.'

'So! I know of you, of course, Herr Breit, and I feel honoured to meet you. I am Freiherr Max von Ritter, father of Marianne, Frau Johnson.' His German was impeccable.

Felix pulled over and waved the following traffic to pass him out. 'I regret to tell you, sir, that today is not a good day for your visit. In fact, knowing your daughter as well as I do, I don't think *any* day is a good day. Or ever will be. I'm sorry to say this but we do not have enough time to—'

'I know all that, Herr Breit, but we have written . . . we

have telephoned . . . we have sent messages through third parties
. . . and—'

'But that should have told you . . . warned you . . . that a
visit in person would be the least welcome—'

'It is no business of yours, Herr Breit, but rather than incon-
venience these other people further, I will tell you I also do
not have much time. I mean I do not have long to live and my
wife is . . . not entirely possessed of her right mind . . . and
Marianne is our only child so there are discussions that cannot
be postponed much longer. Indeed, *any* longer.'

With a sigh, Felix slipped the car back into gear and set off
once again for the Dower House.

Von Ritter said, 'I would be grateful, Herr Breit, if you could
accommodate me somewhere while you alert my daughter to
this situation.'

'There at least, sir, we are of one mind,' Felix replied, surprised
at the unaccustomed formality his native language seemed to
impose upon him.

'And,' the man concluded, 'do your best, please, to make her
see the good sense of this meeting.'

Felix passed the remaining mile or so in summarizing the
history and present situation of the Dower House community.

'And Marianne – she is happy?' von Ritter asked as they swept
past the gatelodge, where a rabble of Oliver Twist urchins – Siri
Johnson, Sam Prentice, Andrew Palmer, and Jasmine Findlater
– held their grimy hands out for pennies. Successfully.

Von Ritter laughed and, for the first time, relaxed a little.

'One of those little girls is your granddaughter, Siri, by the
way,' Felix said. And then, since the news seemed to surprise
the man, he added, 'She has a two-year-old brother named
Virgil.'

'*Ach, so!*' There was a sudden hint of a catch in his voice.

Hastily Felix continued: 'And yes, Marianne is very happy
these days.'

In the short distance that remained he explained about the
partnership with Sally Wilson and the successes they were
enjoying.

'Speer!' von Ritter said. 'I was right. She learned so much
with Albert Speer!'

'I have to talk to you,' Felix said.

He let the others off at the point where his own new drive to the Tithe Barn branched off from the main drive to the Dower House and then took Peter Murdoch and von Ritter on to his parking apron, beside the barn. There he hastily explained the situation to Angela, asked her to take care of Peter – and explain the significance of all this to him – while he took von Ritter out to the walled garden by way of the little-used side gate. Also, of course, to ask Marianne to meet them there.

'Why not in our place?' Angela asked.

Felix shrugged. 'Somehow . . . I don't know . . . the open air feels better.'

The old man took one swift look around the garden, as an infantryman might check for snipers. 'This is a disgrace,' he said. 'Why don't you use weedkiller? And those fruit trees need pruning properly. Where are your gardeners?'

Felix ignored these remarks. 'You may tell me again that it's none of my business, Freiherr,' he said, 'but I would advise you not to mention the name of Speer in your daughter's hearing – unless you want to be on the next train back to London.'

'You are very blunt, Herr Breit. You say you know my daughter – how well?'

'How well do you know *me*?' Felix responded.

'I know you are an artist of no small reputation. I think I even know some of your work. I have seen the one at the Festival.'

So he hadn't come hotfoot from the boat train. Getting up courage? Or daughter unimportant . . . deal with her last of all if time permits?

'But do you know how I spent the war?'

It took him aback; he opened his mouth to speak . . . thought better of it . . . and pursed his lips once more.

'But the real question is how well do *you* know Marianne?' Felix went on.

'I . . . her father!' he complained.

'Let me tell you, I spent the last years of the war in a KL and so did my wife, and—'

The man interrupted: 'I'm sorry, Herr Breit. I'm sure that in your case and hers it was completely undeserved, but in the heat of battle, mistakes occur—'

'Never mind that.' Felix spoke sharply, surprising him to

silence. 'The fact is that she – my wife, that is – and I, and others here in this community who all suffered because of what the Nazis did, we would all now defend Marianne with our lives. She was braver than any of us. I'll say no more than that – she can tell you if she wishes, but that one fact alone should make you think. It should make you wonder if you know your daughter *at all*!' A movement at the regular gateway caught his eye. 'Here she comes. I advise you to do more listening than talking, sir. Marianne!' he shouted, for she had stopped halfway.

'What does he want?' she asked in English.

'I'm not going to act as go between,' Felix replied, starting to walk toward her.

She turned on her heel and began to retrace her path to the gate.

'It's no good,' he called. 'Your father says he may not be here much longer.'

She did not falter.

'He means here on earth.'

She faltered then, and turned about to face them. 'Blackmail,' she said.

'Life!' he countered. 'Just at this moment they are synonyms.'

Von Ritter paused when a dozen yards still separated them. 'Marianne!' he said, holding out his arms, and then tilted his head toward the overgrown garden. 'I hope none of this mess is yours.'

Felix continued walking, intending to leave them alone.

She stood her ground and bobbed an ironic little curtsy. 'Pappa.' She caught Felix by the elbow as he passed. 'Stay! Please?'

He glanced back at her father, who simply shrugged.

Felix sighed and then added, in German, 'I am not an audience. The moment either of you appeals to me instead of talking to the other, I will go.'

'*Vi talar svenska*,' her father suggested to her.

'That will make it a lot easier – for me,' Felix said.

'*Om Pappa vill*,' she agreed with a shrug.

Throughout their conversation Felix noted that she continued to use the third person *Pappa* – 'Pappa must understand . . . Pappa has no right . . .' – never the formal *ni* – equivalent of the German *Sie* or the French *vous* – and certainly not the familiar *du*. He wondered if it had always been so between a daughter and her father – or between this daughter and such a father.

In fact, Swedish is close enough to German for him not to lose the thread entirely. They stood an incongruous dozen paces apart and spoke as near-strangers would speak over a swollen river that neither dared to cross – which, he thought, was not a bad metaphor for what was actually taking place here. The gist of it was (as best he could gather) that von Ritter was reconciled to *never* being reconciled with Marianne. His doctors had told him his heart could give out at any time. His principal worry was that his wife was already beginning to lose her mind . . . forget everyday things . . . not recognize people . . . tell the same story twice within twenty minutes. He had brought papers [here he fished them from his pocket] . . . he spoke of *befogenhet,* which would only begin to operate after his death . . . he assumed she would come home for *that*!

At this Felix glanced toward Marianne and saw she was close to tears. He reached out and touched her elbow but she shook him off impatiently and murmured again, 'Blackmail.'

So could they now go somewhere to sign the papers . . . and would Herr Breit kindly witness their signatures . . . and perhaps they could then sit alone together and have a mature discussion about the arrangements to be made for her mother, the selling of the castle and the business, the finances involved . . . the trusts . . .

'Honey! Freiherr von Ritter . . . Father-in-law? What gives? How wonderful to meet you at last!'

When first glimpsed, Willard stood, framed in the arched gateway, arms outstretched as in an Old Testament tableau, but by the time this gesture registered he was already striding down the path to greet his father-in-law.

Marianne stepped into his way. 'No, honey – really – no.'

He stopped. 'Why not? What? Your father comes all this way—'

'No. It's just some necessary . . . it's not a reconciliation. There will never be a reconciliation. It's just about Mamma. She's not well and nor is Pappa and he wants to give me . . . *befogenhet*—'

'Power of attorney?' Felix suggested.

Willard hesitated, staring at Felix as if wondering why he was there at all.

'He was at the station when I went to collect Murdoch,' Felix explained.

Willard nodded, still not happy. 'Introduce me.' He smiled at von Ritter. 'I've forgotten the German for son-in-law.'

'It's not necessary,' Marianne insisted. 'We'll just sign the papers and Felix can be witness, and then I can discuss all the . . . what they involve, and then he'll go. I don't want him here – especially not today.'

The two men looked at her father, who merely shrugged and opened his hands in a hopeless gesture; there was no doubting that he understood.

Willard shrugged. 'OK – I'll butt out.' Then, in German: 'Father-in-law – my felicitations! I'm sorry we won't get to know each other better.'

'You can go that way' – Felix pointed Marianne toward the old side gate – 'and settle all this business in our place. Call me when your father wants me to witness things and then I'll take him back to the station.'

When they were beyond earshot, Willard gripped Felix by the elbow. 'Listen, you've gotta help me, buddy boy. We really can't let the guy go . . . just like that.'

'Isn't it really a matter for Marianne and her old man? Between them?'

'That "old man" is worth millions – that's what I mean. Look, I know how Marianne feels about him. Boy do I know! But—'

'I think you'll find all that is settled . . . taken care of—'

'How can you possibly know that?' His eyes narrowed. 'How long have they been here?'

'Ten minutes – but he's got it all sewn up. I heard enough to know that. Marianne may inherit but it will all be tied up in trusts. I'm sure she'll be in charge of the trust that takes care of her mother but there are bound to be strict conditions. And—'

'Trusts? Did you say trusts? But if her inheritance is administered by *trusts,* I want a seat among the trustees. She's *my* wife for God's sake! What sort of wimp would want a bunch of gray-faced Swedes having power over his wife's inheritance? No – you've got to help me – if only to interpret. I've forgotten most of what legalistic German I once knew. I'll go back to

Welwyn North with you when he goes. OK? I'll fix something
with him.'

As things turned out, it was not necessary.

Half an hour later, Siri and Jasmine came running up the
drive in great excitement; seeing Willard standing outside
the Tithe Barn with Felix, they veered off toward him and
opened their clenched hands to show fists full of copper and
silver. 'Look what we earned! Where's Marianne? We must show
Marianne, too.'

Willard made the mistake of telling them, and they were
through the door before he finished saying, 'But don't disturb
. . . her . . . now . . . what's the point!' He turned to Felix.
'This place is anarchy in spades.'

'The world's best political system. In hearts.'

'Yeah-yeah, OK.' He gazed over the Breits' new grass toward
the big lawn, now fairly populated with Disraelis, Livingstones,
Sarah Bernhardts, and Vesta Tillies. 'I guess we'd better do our
duty as hosts while we can.'

A few moments later the two girls came running out again,
each now sporting a new fiver tucked into her bonnet ribbon.
The two men pounced.

'We'd better take care of these, honey,' Willard told Siri. 'This
one piece of paper is worth a hundred times more than all the
rest of that money you've got. You could buy enough candy
for a year . . . or ten dolls – think of that! So I'd better keep
it safe, huh? What if the wind just blew it away!'

The girls stared at the bits of paper with awe.

Felix took Jasmine's fiver, saying, 'I'll give this to Faith, OK?
Did the old man in there give them to you?'

Siri nodded. 'Marianne said he's my *morfar*. He looks very
sad.'

Then, with all the empathy of four year olds, they went skipping back down the drive toward the party, chanting: 'Sad . . .
sad . . . sad . . .' in time with each footfall.

Marianne came out and joined them, looking somewhat
crushed.

'The old man?' Willard asked.

'Using the facilities. What's all *that* about?' She nodded toward
the girls.

'They think your father looks sad.'

Marianne shut her eyes – tight. 'He does.' A moment later she added, 'Oh, God! I *can't* send him away, can I? I just can't. Sad? If he goes now, that'll be Siri's last memory of her *morfar*.' She turned to Willard. 'Would you mind terribly?'

'If he stayed? I'd like nothing better.'

She turned to Felix, who had spotted Angela near the house and was signalling to her to come over, which she seemed to have every intention of doing, anyway. 'You're about the same build as my father, Felix. Could you rustle up some clothes for him? It doesn't need to be fancy dress, but what he's wearing is so out of place.'

'Sure. But does he know I'm Jewish? Probably. I told him I was in a KL in the war.'

Angela was close enough to call: 'How has it turned out? What's been happening? My God, Marianne, you look washed out. Come inside and have a brandy. I imagine we could all do with one.'

Nobody objected.

They gathered around a large, complex abstract still only half liberated from its marble prison. Chips of it crunched underfoot. Von Ritter joined them just as Felix was pouring the last glass, which Marianne handed to him. She stayed his arm before he could raise it for a toast. '*Pappa får vila sig här hos oss inatt,*' she said, even managing to smile at last. '*Vi måsste ju diskutera lite vidare. Skål!*'

He bowed a few degrees and said, '*Jag har ingen möglighet att avböja en sån älskvärd inbjudan!*' [I see no possibility of turning down such an amiable invitation.]

Skål . . . Prosit . . . Cheers! The glasses clinked, the brandy burned the throat and mellowed the hour . . . and Marianne just wished that young Siri could see her *morfar* now.

Taking the bottle with them they drifted between the aluminium scaffolding poles into the sitting-dining area beneath the cedar-box bedrooms. Von Ritter complimented Felix and Angela on their conversion of the Tithe Barn but they, of course, waved the praise onward to Marianne.

'So!' he murmured, looking at it – and her – in a new light. 'It's clear that from Speer you have learned nothing. I was wrong.' He glanced at Felix for approval.

Felix held his breath and waited for Marianne to explode.

But all she said was, 'Pappa can speak English!'

Felix laughed, amazed he had not noticed.

'I can English,' von Ritter admitted. 'A little. All the Europe must now English.' He glanced at Willard and added, 'Americanish.' Then, having broken the linguistic ice, he poked his glass toward the unfinished sculpture and said, 'Men buy that *Kvatsch* with money – good money?'

The laughter was a little nervous. 'Very good money,' Angela assured him.

'Did you hear Alfred Munnings – *Sir* Alfred Munnings – slagging off Matisse's *La forêt* at the Royal Academy banquet?' Felix asked the group in general (while Marianne translated for her father). 'He called it *Le forêt* throughout. The man's a barbarian.'

'Like I,' von Ritter said emphatically. Marianne translated the rest from his Swedish. 'To get anywhere in life you must study hard when you're young, form your opinions early, and then be loyal to them – which is really no more than being loyal to yourself – for the rest of your life. You must be a rock in a wish-washy sea of changing opinions, flickering loyalties . . . that way, everyone will know where you stand. They will know they can count on you through good times and bad.'

Willard smiled and nodded throughout this manifesto for the Good Life. Watching him, Felix could not help wondering whether Marianne had not jumped from frying pan to fire – by not realizing that Willard's easy manner, his smile, his bonhomie was all shaped around an inner man who could nod and smile with approval at her father's self-advertisement. Did she understand it even now?

Angela, knowing whither several glasses of brandy might lead, crossed into the kitchen to find some biscuits, or cake if any was left after yesterday's invasion by The Tribe. Marianne came with her. 'I'm not going to translate any more of that *Kvatsch*,' she said.

Back at the table, von Ritter produced the documents for Felix to witness. Willard glanced at a couple but, of course, they were all in Swedish – and legal Swedish at that.

In the kitchen Angela said, 'I think I'll brew some coffee, too. Actually, I was wondering if you might give him my transcription of the Wannsee meeting to read – the original German, of course?'

Marianne's eyes gleamed but almost immediately dulled again. 'No . . . it won't do.'

'Why not? Especially after what he's just said!'

'Because it would involve explaining you . . . me . . . the communist connection . . . with Willard there.'

Angela had tried to persuade her to enlighten her husband too often to try again now. 'We can just say *I* did it, on Heydrich's orders, and after he was killed they blamed me for not telling them at once, and so they sent me to Ravensbrück . . . no need to bring you into it at all.'

Marianne saw the logic of it. 'And yet . . .' she said. 'And yet.'

'You want him to know . . . that you were also . . .'

Marianne nodded.

'Well, there were *other* anti-Nazi groups. The White Rose . . . We could stick to the facts – just not all the facts . . . the documentary in Speer's office . . . making friends with you . . . knowing you were Swedish . . . asking you to get the transcript to the Swedish embassy . . . in fact, it doesn't need to involve *any* anti-Nazi group. Just me and you and the embassy.'

Still Marianne hesitated.

'After what he's just said?' Angela pressed her. 'He was practically asking for it.'

'OK,' she said at last. 'Let's do it.'

They returned with both cake and biscuits. 'Coffee's coming along in a minute,' Angela promised.

The cake induced a gentler mood. 'You say I know not my own daughter, Herr Breit,' von Ritter challenged. 'Tell me now any more.'

Felix turned to Marianne. 'There may never be a better time.'

'Oddly enough,' she said deliberately, 'Angela and I were discussing that same idea out there.' She glanced at Angela.

The atmosphere was suddenly tense; von Ritter felt it at once and sat up ramrod-straight. '*Also?*'

Angela said quietly, 'I don't know how much my husband has explained of our history . . . my past . . .'

'He says it was in a KL you were in the war.' He broke back into German to repeat what he had said to Felix – that in the heat of battle . . .

She, too, cut him short. 'No mistake was made in my case,

Freiherr. On the orders of Reinhard Heydrich, I, a recording specialist in the *Schutzstaffel*, made a secret recording of a conference over which he presided in January, nineteen forty-two. Six other senior members of the ss were present but not even they knew they were being recorded. That was Heydrich's wish – his command. Within a few months – as you know – he was assassinated. And shortly after that Eichmann – Adolf Eichmann, who may still be alive somewhere, discovered what I had done. I was lucky to escape with my life because, in fact, I went beyond Heydrich's orders and actually made a transcript of my recordings. Two transcripts, in fact. If they had known that, they would have hanged me. Instead, they sent me to die more slowly in the Ravensbrück KL.'

He gave a baffled shrug and, speaking now in voluble German, said, 'Madame, I cannot continue this conversation under your roof.' He made a gesture out of putting down his half-drained brandy balloon and pushing his cake plate away. 'You have confessed to actions that would lead me to brand you by a name I cannot utter in these surroundings. And so—'

Marianne butted in: 'Pappa should read that transcript before he says another word.'

'What has this to do with you?' he asked.

'Everything. The copy Pappa will read was the copy Frau Breit – then Fräulein Wirth – handed to me – yes, to *me*! – to pass on to the Swedish ambassador in Berlin. In nineteen forty-two.'

'You?' He looked from one to the other. 'And you? You both did such a—'

'Yes!' Marianne insisted. 'And I can tell Pappa this: if he does not read what was said at that meeting and if he lives another *hundred* years, he will still go to his grave in complete ignorance of this entire century . . . the war . . . his own life . . . his very self! He will understand *nothing*.'

Unable to speak, he turned to the two men. Felix nodded; Willard said, 'Honey? Maybe another time, huh? We're forgetting what day it is and where our duty—'

'No!' Von Ritter was suddenly galvanized. 'I will read.' He reached again for his brandy and patted his daughter's hand. '*Pappa skall läsa det.*'

He smiled.

She smiled and said, 'Good.'

Angela said, 'But Willard is right. Today is our midsummer party. I'll bring my transcript over this evening.'

In the kitchen the coffee grounds fell slowly, of their own volition, to the bottom of the cafetière.

Sunday, 24 June 1951

Whenever Eric let a deadline slip – which happened with almost every one of them, whether imposed by a publisher or by himself – he was experienced enough to avoid the trap of an early rise, a cup of double-strength coffee, and a blank sheet in the type-writer while he was still unshaven and in his pyjamas. Instead, he would rise at his normal hour of seven, shave, eat a substantial and unhurried breakfast while exchanging pleasantries with Isabella (if she happened to be conscious by then), followed by a bracing walk in the woods. The morning after the midsummer party was no different. He set out as the communion bell began ringing from Dormer Green Church.

He was rather surprised to see Nicole who, to his certain knowledge, had not gone to bed before three that morning, standing with a laundry basket on her hip, staring into the pheasant run. 'Didn't expect to see *you* up and about,' he said.

'Bloody kids!' She replied. 'I'll bet it's Tommy and Andrew.' She raised her voice to a shout. 'Tommeee! Andreeewww!' To Eric she added, 'I'll kill them.'

'What is the capital crime this time?' Eric asked.

'They must have liberated my washing line. They know enough to leave everyone else's alone. Can I hang these up on yours? Is Isabella doing any washing today? I wouldn't think so.'

'If she manages to push the flannel as far as her own eyebrows, that will be heroic enough. In Isabella-land champagne is more common that water. Be our guest!' And with a *heigh-ho* he was off into the woods.

There was a flash of movement away to his right – a flash that was distinctly reddish. His eyes focused and he was surprised to see . . . a red squirrel. It was his first sighting of the year;

of course, the creature would have hibernated in the winter but it would still have been out and about since April, if not earlier. He had been thinking of writing to *The Times,* adding Gideon's Coppice to the list of woodlands where the American gray squirrel had ousted the native English red. Now he would have to find out if this solitary red had found a mate. But not this morning. This morning he would do the strict circuit, have a quick look at Bob Ambrose's snares and gin traps (and dispatch any animals they had caught) and then . . . the magic with the typewriter: a piece for the *The Studio* about Chris Riley-Potter's designs for the new children's wing at Enfield hospital – the intention being to follow them over the months from conception to completion.

He already knew, almost to the last comma, what he was going to write – which was why he had left it to the very last moment, of course. Chris had had the brilliant idea to get himself parked on an operating theatre trolley in the existing hospital and wheeled from a ward along the corridor to the operating theatre; and, as a result, he had put all his decorations for the new children's wing – or almost all – up on the ceiling. Carrying out the actual commission would probably leave him with pains in the back and neck that Michelangelo himself would have understood, but . . .

But . . .

There was someone up ahead, sitting on the woodland floor, leaning against a tree . . .

A man in . . . pyjamas . . .

'I say!' Eric called out.

The fellow did not stir.

But a bush slightly up the hill and behind him did, and from it emerged a very hesitant Tommy Marshall and Andrew Palmer.

'We found him,' Tommy said, running to Eric.

'We think he must be dead,' Andrew added, hard on his heels. 'It's that old German man staying with the Johnsons.'

There was no doubting it. The man – or body, rather – was Marianne's father and he must have been dead for several hours, for, when Eric bent to touch him, his flesh was quite cold. Two flies, experimenting with his bald scalp, flew away; one returned and flew away again instantly.

'Did you touch anything?' Eric asked the boys – casually . . .

not wanting to make a drama of it when they realized what had actually happened here. Death meant little more to them than the death of a hamster as yet, but the formalities that would soon visit them all at the Dower House in connection with this event would change that.

'No!'

'We called *Mister* several times and then we took back the rope, which—'

'What rope?'

Tommy ran to the bush where they had hidden and returned with Nicole's washing line. Meanwhile, Andrew pointed to a branch directly above the corpse, and said, 'It was hanging over that, there.'

Eric took the line and examined it. 'Was there a . . . I mean . . . did you untie it? Did you have to untie *anything*?'

'No,' both boys said. Andrew added, 'It was what I said. It went up there and over that branch and straight down again. No knots.'

'OK.' Eric sighed with relief. 'He was probably a birdwatcher and he probably wanted to use the rope to help him climb up into the tree to get a better view. And then . . . I don't know . . . the effort was too much for him? He had a heart attack? Anyway, he dropped down dead. Look, he must have leaned back against the tree first and then slid down as he got weaker and weaker. D'you see how his pyjama top is all rucked up at the back? That's what happened. But listen, chaps. When people die like this – not in a hospital nor at home with the doctor coming to visit – the police may have to make enquiries. I'm going to get Doctor Wallace to come out here and look at the body and sign a certificate to say he died naturally, which he did. But if you breathe the smallest, teeniest word about the rope, the police will come swarming all over the place. Which will be awful, because Marianne is going to be upset quite enough as it is. So we don't want any complications, OK? D'you know what I mean? No one must say a *word* about the washing line. That could set the police off on a complete wild-goose chase. They might even think he meant to hang himself – which is ridiculous because there wasn't even a noose, was there. But the police would think it their duty to take you, one after another, into a room, all alone – just you and three or four coppers – and ask you lots of questions. You understand, don't you? So, to cut all that out, we're going to say *nothing* about the washing line. You two are going to bring it back to Nicole and say *you* took it and you're very sorry but you didn't think she was going to need it so early in the morning. And this is *our* secret, right? You mustn't even tell the rest of The Tribe. You can boast all you like that you were the ones who found him but you'll say nothing about the washing line. The three of us will be the only ones who will *ever* know about that. Now put your hands on mine and we'll swear an oath about it.'

When they had done, Tommy looked wistfully at the corpse and said, 'Couldn't we just loop the rope under his arms and sort-of drag him back to the house?'

Eric laughed. 'A Roman triumph, eh? We won the war! Wouldn't that be wonderful! But no. For one thing, just think what Marianne would feel to see you dragging him home like that. And for another, Doctor Wallace must see him exactly as he is because it proves he died of natural causes. So you two cut along now. I'll stay here to see that foxes and badgers don't try to eat him.'

'Eeeurgh!' they chorused.

'Oh, but they would, you know. Go straight to Felix and Angela and tell them what's happened – but nothing about the washing line. Just tell them that I think Marianne's father has died of a heart attack here in Gideon's Coppice and could he ring for Doctor Wallace to come out and sign a death certificate. Can you remember those two words: death . . . certificate.

And off they ran, muttering 'death cer-tifi-cate . . . death cer-tifi-cate . . .' every fourth step.

Left alone, Eric turned to the Freiherr. 'Well, old boy,' he said. 'Man proposes, God disposes, eh!' He folded his jacket and sat down beside him. 'And you never did manage to hang yourself, by the look of your neck. Which is good. You probably don't know it, but you've had a narrow escape. Suicide is actually a *crime* in this enlightened country. If you had been English, all your property would have gone to the Crown. And even if you had bungled it, they'd have arrested you and put you on trial. Things are probably much more enlightened in Sweden but that's the way things are here. I'm only telling you this because, although I don't believe anything but a few shillings-worth of chemicals survive after death, I have to allow the slimmest chance that something may linger around for a bit. So . . . we are rearranging history a bit here.

'What else can I tell you on this bright midsummer morn? To keep our spirits up, eh? I think the most important thing is to let you know how pleased we are – and I mean everyone here at the Dower House – we're pleased that you and Marianne were able to make some sort of a peace before . . . well, *this*. She always made out that the breach between you was absolute and that that was fine by her. But it wasn't true. No one is that implacable. No one can sustain an emotion of that intensity unless some fire is keeping it hot. I saw you walking arm in arm with her last night, around our midsummer fire – which seems to be a big deal in Sweden – I mean, usually she's in there dancing like a Dervish. But not last night. What were you talking about, I wonder? She had that look grown-ups get when they remember donkey rides . . . wild strawberries . . . turning over pebbles in rock pools. Was that it? I'll bet it was.'

'It was,' Marianne said quietly.

He turned, saw her, sprang to his feet, and waved an awkward hand toward the body of her father. 'Marianne – I'm so sorry.'

She shrugged. 'You knew I was here.'

'I knew *someone* was here – whoever untied the noose before the boys came down.' He offered her his handkerchief. 'It's clean. I hoped it was you.'

She coughed up a wheezy sort of laugh. 'The one thing I forgot. I've cried my tear . . . cisterns . . .?'

'Glands.'

'I've cried them dry. But I didn't know what to do, even when Tommy and Andrew came. I just hid. I had the noose untied but when I heard them I just ran and hid. I wanted to stop them but I was . . . like paralyzed. I wanted someone else to take over – not the boys – and then you came, thank God. What you did was so good.' She squeezed his arm. 'Thank you.'

They moved a little way away from the body.

'But why did you . . . I mean, were you somehow *expecting* this?'

She nodded. 'He left a note. It's too complicated to explain, but when I read it I just knew he was going to do this. In his place, I think I'd have done the same.'

'But it wasn't suicide.'

'Of course it was. His intention, anyway. The noose was round his neck.'

'But it hadn't tightened. No marks. His heart gave out. He slumped against the tree. Slid down. That's not suicide. Just a heart attack. Lose the rope. He was . . . I don't know – sleep-walking . . . wandering in his mind . . .'

'And what about the note?'

'What did it say? Marianne – this is vital!'

'Exactly?' She was beginning to lose her composure.

'Yes.'

'I have it here.' She fished it out of her pocket. 'I couldn't leave it for Willard to find.'

It read: *Hur får jag se migsjälv i ögonen efter det här?* She trans-lated: 'How can I look myself in the eyes after this?'

'That's all? What does he mean – *did* he mean? After *what?*'

'Last night he read Angela's original transcript of the Wannsee meeting.'

'No! For God's sake! What was she thinking of?'

'No – it was me. Me. I gave it to him. So the question is how can *I* face *myself* after' – she waved a hand over her shoulder – 'this!' She turned and took a step back toward her dead father, shouting at him: '*Du . . . du . . . !*'

By the time Dr Wallace arrived, almost everyone in the community had been down to Gideon's Coppice. Marianne, who was by then too numb to show any of the expected emotions, was easily persuaded by Willard to return to the house, from where she could call friends of her mother's and ask them to break the news as and when they saw fit. She could leave the transport and funeral arrangements to him if she wished.

'I'll miss the site meeting at Enfield,' she said, and then burst into tears but simultaneously laughed, saying, 'Dear God! As if that's the only important thing now, and the only thing left that can still make me cry!'

The doctor had no hesitation in certifying a death by natural causes, assessing the time of death as between three and four last night. 'I'll give you something to help Mrs Johnson sleep,' he told Willard, who had arrived back with a makeshift stretcher. Willard took the bottle though he knew Marianne wouldn't touch the stuff, just as she would never get drunk or go on violent fairground machines or do anything that might threaten her moment-by-moment control of her everyday self.

Angela went only halfway down the woodland path, just far enough to glimpse von Ritter, still propped against the tree with his pyjama top rucked halfway up his back. Then she turned and fled to Marianne, by now back in their flat at the top of the house. 'It's all my fault,' she called out before she was even through the sitting-room door. But the moment she stepped inside she could only stop and stare. Of all the activities you might expect a bereaved daughter to be doing in such circumstances, the last thing of all would be ironing; but, indeed, Marianne was standing at the ironing board, pressing the grey pinstripe trousers her father had been wearing on his arrival yesterday morning.

'It's not your fault at all,' Marianne replied wearily. 'I'm the one who suggested it.'

'No. I suggested it. You just agreed. It's me and those hanging movies all over again. I couldn't bear his ignorance . . . and his arrogance—'

'You think I could?' Marianne asked, but Angela went on talking over her: 'I wanted him to understand . . . you know. He was so damned . . .' She sighed. 'I'm sorry. He was your father, after all. Well, it's done now and talking won't undo anything. I must just learn to live with the vengeful, spiteful creature that I am.'

Marianne gave a hollow laugh and fished out her father's note. 'First him,' she said, passing it over. 'Then me. Now you. Felix will probably think it was all *his* fault for accidentally collecting him at Welwyn North. Where does responsibility end?'

The phone rang. 'Shall I finish that?' Angela offered.

Marianne went to answer it. 'You can do the shirt if you wouldn't mind.'

The shirt was finished by the time she returned. 'They say my mother seemed to understand it for about five minutes. Then all she could remember was that there was some sort of message about my father. Was it about him coming home . . . dates and times and so on? It doesn't look good. His manager . . . or deputy? . . . anyway, his right-hand man says my father several times expressed a wish to be cremated. I wonder if we should do it over here? It's Golders Green, isn't it? But who to inform? The Swedish embassy . . . the German embassy, I suppose . . . Oh, God, I'm going to make such a mess of it and Pappa will think I've done it deliberately!'

Angela let the implications of that curious remark pass by. 'Surely Willard will know exactly what's to be done?'

'Yes!' She brightened, as if she had completely forgotten him. 'Look, he's already doing it. He made that stretcher in minutes, you know – the door off Rosy Primrose and two clothes-line props. And half-a-dozen nails. Willard will fix *everything*. Pappa will have a perfect cremation!'

And Angela silently heaped yet more cause for shame upon herself by trying – but failing – to suppress the thought that she might steal a few grams of the ashes to sprinkle over the site of one or other former KL – not Ravensbrück nor Mauthausen, to be sure – but that still left over a thousand from which to choose.

Eric finished his review by lunchtime and walked into the village to post it – along with, and more importantly, his invoice. He seemed to be getting lots of work lately but all of it for very tardy payers. In Gideon's Coppice there were few signs of that morning's drama – trampled bushes, stirred-up leaf mould, the faintest scrape where von Ritter's spine had rubbed some lichen off the tree trunk; Mother Nature was closing in as always, an Old Maid, fastidious about death. On his way back, at the edge of the wood, he found Tommy and Andrew, pretending they were only half there.

'Skulking is the word that comes to mind,' he told them. 'Were you going back to visit the scene of your discoveries this morning?'

Andrew said, 'Yes.'

Thomas said, 'No.'

Then both said, 'Could be.'

'Well, all you'd see now is how quickly nature gets everything back to normal. By next week you'd never know anything had happened there. Tell me – suppose all the grown-ups in the community went away for two weeks, leaving you enough food and money and all that, what d'you think would happen? What would The Tribe do?'

They looked at each other and giggled. Thoughts of death coming closer to home had not yet struck them, then.

'I'm serious,' Eric said.

After a moment's thought, Tommy said, 'We wouldn't have to wash every day.'

'And we wouldn't wear socks at all,' Andrew added.

'And eat when we liked . . .'

They warmed to the fantasy.

'And leave the washing-up until it fell over by itself . . .'

'. . . like Chris and Julie did.'

'And go in the secret passage anytime we liked.'

Tommy nudged Andrew and looked daggers at him.

'What's this secret passage, then?' Eric asked.

'Nothing.'

'It's just a . . . just a story.'

'Where is it, though?'

'Nowhere,' Tommy insisted.

Eric fixed a friendly eye on Andrew and waited.

Andrew said, 'We don't let the little ones go in there.'

Tommy flailed the air and tore out notional clumps of hair, shouting, 'Now you've done it! Now you've done it!'

'He won't split.' Andrew looked pleadingly at Eric. 'You won't split, will you!'

'I'd better see it for myself before I answer that, don't you think?' he replied.

Saturday, 30 June 1951

The Dower House Residents Association
Notice of an Extraordinary General Meeting
Agenda – Saturday, June 30
Discussion of The Tribe's 'secret passage'
to be held in the Brandons' sitting room at 6.00 p.m.
NO OTHER BUSINESS PLEASE

'Why is Eric in the chair?' Isabella asked as soon as her husband declared the meeting open.

'Because you chose to sit on the sofa, my dearest,' he told her. 'Do you want to swap? I'd much rather sit quietly at the back, *not interrupting the chairman before he's managed to speak a word*, and take down the minutes – I adore anything to do with creative writing, as you know.'

'No, no – just don't bore everybody.'

'For example! No, please don't answer. It was demonstrative, not interrogatory. Well, I'll call upon Tony to give us his—'

'One other thing,' Isabella continued. 'Why is it "Residents Association" without an apostrophe? "Residents" has always had an apostrophe before.'

'Because, my dearest one, it's an association *of* residents, not an association *owned by* residents.'

'Don't we own it, then?'

'Not as an independent entity – an *ipsos res*. If we all went to live elsewhere, it would cease to exist, though it might very well be replaced by a *different* association *of* different residents, *mutatis mutandis*, as it were. Now may I call on—'

'You always add in bits of Latin when you know your argument is weak.'

'Ah, but you only ever point that out *after* you've already lost. Can Tony now give us his report? Brave fellow – he has actually ventured into these catacombs that surround us all.'

'They're nothing extraordinary,' Tony assured them. 'They're the original kind of *tanking* – literally "tanks" of air surrounding the foundations and cellar walls of a house so as to ventilate them and keep them dry. Today we use heavy-duty plastic sheeting, of course, but back in the eighteenth century they'd build a wall about so far away from the actual cellar wall – I mean, I could just about walk straight on but it was easier to go sideways-on. Anyway, this wall comes up to about a foot below ground level and they've bridged across the top with a couple of layers of thick slate and then lead, which they bent upward and took it up to ground level. And then they covered all that over with a flower border, which is all that we can see above ground, of course. And the actual cellar walls all have a thick, damp course down there at the base – several layers of slate – *this* thick. So moisture has a pretty hard job getting through anywhere. That's why our cellars are so remarkably dry.'

'I guess the only question we really want answered,' Hilary said, 'is "is it safe?"'

'You'd be happy for Andrew and Guy to go down there?' Faith asked.

'To *carry on* going down there,' Tony said. 'Yes, frankly, though I'd like to build something more permanent to replace the stool that Arthur and May have so generously donated.'

'We don't want that thing back,' May said hastily. 'Not after what they've done to it, thank you very much.'

'Willard went down there, too,' Eric said. 'Before he and Marianne went to Sweden. He asked me to tell the meeting he thought it safe enough. In fact, considering all the other opportunities for sudden death and injury that surround us here, they're probably more out of harm's way down there than in most other places.'

'Me, too,' Sally put in. 'I agree with Tony and Willard. It's scary because it's pitch black but structurally it's safe. Safer than Rosy Primrose. We really ought to fix that slate lean-to roof at the back.'

'Not on the agenda,' Eric insisted. 'We dealt with that at the last regular meeting.'

'But that's all we *ever* do – deal with it at meetings – never out there on the site.'

'And there's hardly any putty left on the glazing on the glasshouse-side,' Nicole added. 'The bits that the Johnsons never quite finished. Those panes of glass could do serious . . .'

'Not on the agenda!' Eric trumpeted before either of the Johnsons could leap in.

'Not on *your* agenda, maybe, but they ought to be on everyone's . . .'

'Maynard told us a pane fell out last week and almost hit Theo,' Hilary said.

'Theo never breathed a word about that,' Sally told her.

'The agenda . . .' Eric began.

'Can't we move on and discuss this as Any Other Business?' Adam suggested.

'There isn't Any Other Business. This is an Extraordinary General Meeting to discuss just . . .'

'Did it break?' Sally asked. 'The pane of glass?'

'Maynard didn't say.'

Faith winked at Alex; whenever he had complained of point-less admin meetings at the BBC, she had told him, 'Just you wait!'

Isabella wanted to bring up the subject of the cleaning rota for the back hall. 'This week it's . . .'

'This week it's not on the agenda,' Eric insisted again.

'. . . it's supposed to be Chris and Judith who . . .'

'Her name is Julie,' Chris said.

'Yes. It's supposed to be your turn. I had to put on wellington boots just to walk across to collect our milk and the post. It's disgusting.'

'But it's not the weekend until tomorrow,' Chris objected. 'Our week still has a day to run – before we *have to* clean it. We always leave it to the last possible day.'

'All right!' Eric shouted. 'We can declare ourselves content that The Tribe should continue to enjoy their secret passage unhindered until they're too fat, too lazy, too old, or too bored to want to any more. And then we can discuss what to do about Rosy Primrose *ad terrorem omnium*. All in favour?'

'Oh, but I didn't think we'd finished discussing that subject yet,' Nicole objected.

'We had – *de facto* but not *de jure*,' Eric assured her, wondering why Isabella was no longer rising to his cod-Latin. 'All in favour of continuing with consideration of the agenda?'

'You haven't made any notes yet,' Isabella pointed out.

'*De minimis non curant lex*,' he assured her.

She rose and walked toward the kitchen, saying, 'I'm going to make us some caviar canapés.'

'Fishpaste nibbles,' Eric assured them in a stage whisper. 'Now who has a further point to make on the subject of The Tribe's secret passage?'

They actually managed another ten minutes of 'further points.' Sally wondered if it wouldn't benefit from lighting; others thought that would rob the place of its mystery, scariness, and attraction; some thought that not a bad idea; some said that childhood should have its moments of danger and threat – as long as they were more apparent than real; there was agreement that candles and matches should be so strictly forbidden that the entry hole would be bricked up at the first violation (but all realized that that was just a decision on paper); the architects insisted that ventilation bricks, not solid ones, would be used in that case. And should there be a cut-off age – say, no child under four? Many thought that a good idea until Arthur pointed out that children mature at different ages, so the best cut-off would be decided by the child him- or herself; some would go down without a qualm at the age of three while another five-year-old might get scared in less than a minute down there and scream to go out. Eric noted (but did not minute) that the permissive parents leaned toward the political right while the proscriptive ones were of a more leftward slant – just as he had expected. In fact, he was able to close the entire discussion happy in the knowledge that its conclusions were near enough to the minutes he had already written earlier that day for them not to need retyping.

Isabella reappeared with the caviar canapés and two bottles of Krug, which opened with a satisfactory, *pop!*

'Someone's not short of a bob or two,' Tony commented.

'Don't you believe it,' Isabella assured him. 'The caviar is left over from the Crespigny show, yesterday, and the champers is courtesy of Faith and Alex.'

'Faith, actually,' Alex said.

'Doubleday, actually,' Faith added. 'We launched a new series last week and I was rather ambitious with the drinks requisition. Wartime habits die hard.'

Cigarettes were stubbed and the meeting broke up into gossiping groups.

'Don't quote me on this,' Terence said, 'but Rex, a friend of mine on *The Telegraph,* tells me that these two missing diplomats have gone over to Moscow. One of them, Maclean – this'll interest some of you – Maclean ate his last meal in London at Schmidt's in Charlotte Street! Anyway, it's all going to come out in the next week or so. We'll now have paranoid govern-ments for years to come – of either party.'

'What about those telegrams?' Tony asked between puffs as he rekindled his pipe.

'It seems they weren't actually from them. Some woman friend of theirs in Cairo sent them – making it look as if they'd run away there. But they're already in Moscow – and the real stink is that they aren't diplomats at all. They were actually at the top of the Secret Service. It'll be . . . I mean, it could bring down the government.'

'Too late!' Nicole put in. 'This government has already fell. Fallen. Back in the spring, when Bevan, the only true socialist, resigned over the health service. That was the kiss of death.'

'*Á la* Judas Iscariot?' Eric asked.

'Ignore him,' Isabella advised.

Nicole ignored him. 'We'll have another general election soon and all the Bevanites will get back and then we'll have a truly socialist government at last.'

'Unless, of course, the Tories win,' Eric said.

Nicole just laughed.

'We kicked Churchill out once and we can do it again,' Tony said.

Eric began to sing – to the tune of *The Red Flag*: 'The working class / Can kiss my arse—' at which Nicole rammed a fish-paste nibble into his conveniently wide open mouth.

Angela, rummaging in Felix's shoulder bag in vain hope of finding a box of tissues, pulled out a notebook. She was about to stuff it back when Felix took it from her and opened it at a certain page. He passed it, still open, back to her and said, 'Who's that?'

She saw the likeness in a flash and laughed, saying, 'You've caught him to a T!' She held up the book for all to see. 'Look, everyone! Who's this?'

Immediately several voices cried, 'Tony!'

The man himself stared at it and said, 'You sod! You're not going to make a sculpture of me like that, I hope?'

'You'd never hold the pose,' Felix said.

On their way back to the Tithe Barn after the meeting, Angela repeated Tony's question about turning the sketch of him into a sculpture.

Felix laughed. 'I would do it if I got one particular commission for one particular place – the main gate at Mauthausen.'

It shocked her. Felix went on to explain that almost his last conscious memory, as they carried him on a stretcher to a waiting ambulance on the day of liberation, was the sight of Tony standing on one leg and raising the other boot in order to tap his pipe on its heel so as to dislodge the tobacco ash.

'And so it was the first drawing you did when you began to convalesce?'

'No. I did it here, in town, after my first visit – my very first visit – to the Dower House. I was standing on the front steps and Tony and Nicole came up from inspecting the septic tanks and Tony stopped at the edge of the drive and tapped out the tobacco ash . . . exactly the same. At the time I thought it was hugely symbolic – the same gesture at my liberation and again at my . . . well, what was to be my homecoming.'

'And don't you still think so?' she asked.

They were home by now. As soon as they were through the door she flung her arms around him and kissed him passionately; something about his use of that phrase 'at the time . . .' worried her.

'There's a deeper level to it,' he said. 'Something I only realized a few days ago when I was skimming through that sketchbook. There's no face. I didn't give Tony a face.'

She was even more worried now; there was a hint of controlled agitation in his manner – a tension between wanting to tell and wanting not to tell. 'But it's only about four inches high, darling, hardly—'

'No. It's nothing to do with the size of the sketch. Even if I'd drawn it . . .' He paused and then abandoned that line of explanation. 'I don't know if it was the same for you, but I found . . . after a while in the KL . . . I no longer looked at faces.'

'Other prisoners' faces,' she said.

'Yes, of course. You never looked the ss in the face.'

'Well . . . there was one – ss-*Aufseherin* Heugel – Irma Heugel – who sometimes insisted I look her in the face, and hit me when I forgot, and then after a few weeks of that she'd hit me for doing it. That was her game. One of them. They didn't hang her – just prison.'

'But I'm talking about fellow prisoners. Even if I *did* look at them, I didn't expect to get any information. Because they were expressionless. They told you nothing. They weren't blank, but they were sort of frozen in some set attitude. I only realized this recently. There was a man who swept our ward, the medical experiments ward, twice a day and he had a permanent . . . *mask* – you couldn't call it anything else – a mask of idiot cheerfulness. Olive-coloured skin and pale turquoise eyes. Blank. Filled with meaningless cheer. But he

wasn't the only one. There were hundreds like him – with
different frozen expressions – but never changing. Me, too,
probably.'

'Has it upset you?' she asked. 'You haven't shown any—'

'No. Upset me? No.' He paused; the stillness was only faintly
stirred by his breathing. 'Upset me? No, but it disappointed me.
Shall we go for a walk? We could go to the Plume of Feathers?
See if they'll do us a sandwich?'

Angela was now on the borders of her third trimester, so it
wasn't the way she would have chosen to pass this summer
evening – but . . .

They fed Pippin, bathed her, read her a story, popped her
into her portable cot, and left her happily enjoying a second
bedtime story with Rachel at the Wilsons.

'You said "disappointed,"' Angela reminded him as they set
off through Gideon's Coppice. 'The fact that you only
remembered—'

'Yes, I know. Disappointed. What I meant was . . . every
time I think I've put Mauthausen behind me . . . No! It's not
a deliberate, conscious thing. It's not something I'm *striving* to
do. Every time I think it has just withered and faded into the
background—'

'Like the way mountains lose all detail and turn blue or gray
or . . . just one single colour, anyway . . . as they fade into the
distance?'

He turned the image over in his mind and said, slightly
surprised, 'Yes! That's exactly right. It's still big – because, of
course, it's a mountain – but there's no detail and only a bleached-
out tone to it. Every time I think the memories have done just
that – *pfff!* back comes something vivid. *Still* vivid. Like remembering how facial expressions became meaningless. And it disap-
points me because now I've got to wait for *that* to fade into a
blue-gray emptiness. And then I wonder what else is locked
away in here' – he tapped his forehead – 'waiting its turn? It's
a thousand-headed Hydra.'

'And all this came about because you looked at that sketch
of Tony?'

He did not answer at once. They were approaching the tree
beneath which Eric had discovered the body of Marianne's father
– another reason why Angela had not relished this particular

outing. 'I still feel guilty, you know,' she told him, 'despite everything Marianne says.'

Felix stopped and stared at her in surprise. 'But the man knew exactly what to expect. You told him. Marianne told him. He accepted it because he was so cocksure he could pick holes in it. He thought it was another milk-and-water document like the so-called 'official' Wannsee protocol. You saw that patronizing twinkle in his eye. Believe me – he forfeited every claim on your conscience, or Marianne's, when he agreed to read it in that spirit. I know he was Marianne's father and in some perverse way she loved him so much she could only hate what he had become, but the world is better off without him.'

She responded with a tight little smile and, taking his arm, she pushed him onward, down the path, saying, 'Oh, darling, you are so strong in things like that.'

'Well . . .' He gave a sardonic grunt. 'That's more or less what we were talking about, isn't it – when will our freedom be one hundred per cent?'

The silence between them was thoughtful rather than tense.

'I ran across another Mauthausen survivor last week,' he said at length. 'A designer. A brilliant designer – three-dimensional stuff as well as illustrations and book design. He has no discipline in himself but he understands the discipline of the medium, the materials, the intention. He throws his own wildness at it and the result is . . . electrifying. Fogel is very excited because he's just what Manutius needs as it expands into serious adult books on philosophy . . . maths . . . psychology . . . all that.'

'Does he have a name?' she prompted.

'Oh, sorry.' He laughed. 'Germano Facetti. Italian, obviously. A young resistance fighter. Our paths never crossed in Mauthausen. He was sweeper-upper and keep-*alles-in-Ordnung* in the headquarters block.' Felix laughed again. 'And you'll never guess. The other day he had a row with Fogel – because he's quite temperamental – and he came back to the design studio, to the corner where he works, he must have been worried that he'd gone too far, because he did the same thing as you: he took everything off his pinboard and sorted it all out and smoothed out the scrunched-up bits and then pinned them all back up again, lined across and down like soldiers on parade . . .'

Angela felt the hair prickle on the nape of her neck. She did

not join his laughter. 'You're right — we won't ever be *really*
free, will we? I thought I'd be free after the hanging movies.'

'But . . .?'

By now they were out of the woodland, walking uphill across
the open fields. She stopped.

'But?' he prompted again.

'Listen!' High above them a pair of skylarks were singing their
endless songs, one almost overhead, the other down the valley
a bit, toward the church. 'Eric says they're like manic auctioneers,
inviting lunatics like us to bid on their territory.' She sighed.
'To anyone else at the Dower House it would seem ridiculous
to be holding this conversation in such a tranquil landscape on
such a beautiful evening.'

'There was a skylark over Mauthausen one day, I remember.
Birds were pretty rare. It brought on a fantasy of flying away
— a helicopter landing and taking me away — taking me here to
England.'

'Fantasy, all right,' she said.

'Suppose it had happened, though — to you. If a plane had
spirited you away to England, would you have joined up and
fought against Germany?'

The 'manic auction' of the skylarks came flooding back.

At length she said, 'I'd have offered my technical skills in
electronics to the English, yes. But would I have pointed a rifle
at an ordinary soldier in the Wehrmacht and pulled the trigger?
No, I don't think I could have done that.'

As they resumed their walk he said, 'The English can't possibly
realize how lucky they are. No foreign armies have fought across
these fields or up and down these lanes for almost a thousand
years. No foreigner has kicked them out, confiscated their goods,
demanded a tax or a ransom. All this has been theirs and only
theirs all that time. To them it must seem the most natural thing
in the world. But Nicole was telling me at the midsummer party
— we were talking about this very thing — she told me she had
an uncle who is still alive at eighty and he has property near
the border which was French — his family's — until eighteen
seventy, then Prussian, then French again, then German in
nineteen fourteen, then French again in nineteen eighteen, then
German in nineteen forty, and now French again. And that's
just in *one* lifetime!'

'And we live among them – Nicole and Marianne are even married to them. I mean, the Americans are the same, and still they can't really comprehend it. They think we and our parents and grandparents all just had a bit of bad luck, a deviation from normality. They'll never grasp that it *is* normality for us, that borders are *always* changing, and that power, currency, law . . . everything – changes along with them . . .'

'So? Are we finally giving up our attempts to persuade the English it's their duty to balance France and Germany *within* Europe?'

She threw up her hands and let them drop, flopping at her side. 'Ever since I got to know Alex – a man of the world, a man who knows more than he'll ever allow you to guess . . . he knows so much about the world that he can't see the slightest reason why England should get bogged down in parochial little squabbles in Europe. That's Alex almost word for word.' A new thought struck her. 'Speaking of Nicole . . . she said something else, just the other day . . . we were discussing the English and she pointed out they have no word for *patrie* . . . *Heimat* . . . and Marianne had a word . . . *hem* . . . something—'

'*Hembygd* – I've heard her use it.'

'Something like that. Anyway, Nicole pointed out that probably every European country has a word for that bit of country where you're born. Where you come from. Where you really belong. But the English don't, because for them there's never been any difference between *patrie* and *pays* . . . between *Heimat* and *Vaterland*. That's why they don't understand us. And never will.' She let out a brief, explosive sigh, partly of exhaustion, partly of satisfaction at having nailed the idea down at last. 'However,' she went on, 'for me, concrete music is so much more rewarding than . . . all that. I must get that skylark, or I could see if Ludwig Koch has a good one.'

And so their conversation drifted along this well-trodden path, though each knew that the subject they had started by discussing . . . the questions Felix had raised . . . the answers she had not given – they knew that all of these had been merely shelved . . . yet again.

Wednesday, 18 July 1951

Apart from their castle out in the sticks, the von Ritters had a villa on a peninsula jutting out into a small lake in Mölndal, on the eastern outskirts of Gothenburg. The steelworks were in Eskilstuna, two hundred miles away on the far side of the country.

'This is one incredible place,' Willard murmured, linking his hands behind his head to brace himself off the pillow and drink in the view from their bedroom, which was at the top of a romantic turret in the style of a French château. It was not yet eight but the day was already a little too hot for comfort. 'Honey?'

He glanced slantwise across the bed and found it empty.

He rose, slipped on his pyjamas and dressing gown and padded to the door. There he heard her labouring up the winding stair. He went down to meet her but it was too narrow for him to offer her any practical help. 'You look all in,' he said.

'Thanks!'

'No, I mean it. We'll take a vacation when everything's wrapped up here.'

'Wrapped up!' Her eyes almost vanished upward in their sockets but she waved away any further conversation until they achieved the stairhead. Even then she waited until they were in their room and the door was shut.

'Oh,' Willard said. 'I was welcoming the draft.'

She shook her head. 'Her hearing is amazing and she understands English perfectly – she has some remarkably lucid moments.' She sat on the edge of the bed and slumped. 'I don't know what we're going to do with her. She couldn't possibly come to the Dower House and—'

'We can afford – or *you* can afford the absolute tops in care for—'

'Unh-unhhh. This has been her home for donkey's ears.'

'Years.'

'She'd just curl up and die if we moved her anywhere. No, Pappa has left everything to me precisely because he knows I won't touch a penny of it. So there's absolutely no question that—'

'Well, honey, that's something I want to talk about.'

But as he drew breath to do just that she cut in: 'No, Willard – darling, darling Willard. No! I realize how much it would mean to you. And I, too, long for all the things we could do with it, but to me it's stolen money. *Worse* than stolen. Every *krona* is a Jew's life, a Gipsy's life, a resister's life, a Red Army soldier's life. I won't touch a penny of it for us, for our own personal use.'

'But that's absurd!' he said angrily.

'I'll tell you when I'd make an exception.'

He bit off what he had been going to say and listened.

'If Siri or Virgil . . . if any of us had an accident or got desperately ill and only some hideously expensive treatment would save us, then that would cleanse the money. It would be "absurd" – as you say – not to use some of it then. And I will also use it to pay for every visit I have to make to Sweden . . . everything connected with Mamma's affairs. Clearly she'll have to stay here. And I'll have to visit quite often, too. That also is reasonable and it's what Pappa wants.'

'Why d'you always talk about him in the present tense?'

'Because he hasn't gone!' she shouted, not at Willard but at one of the open windows. 'His body may have gone but he lives on in every line of that *fucking* will! It's his revenge for my rebellion.' Her voice broke.

There was a silence between them after that.

Willard broke it first: 'You're right, honey.' He sighed. 'As always. In fact, you're more than simply right – you're *absolutely* right.'

She smiled at him and, reaching out, gave his arm a grateful squeeze – even though, in her heart of hearts, she knew this was just the *other* Willard speaking; he was his own good cop, bad cop.

'But,' he said brightly, 'may we now take it – now that the war is over and the Nazis are either hanged or shot or rehabilitated or hiding out somewhere – may we now take it that von Ritter steel is clean?'

'No! Certainly not! The entire business was built up with the same blood money!'

'So what are we . . . what are you going to do with it?'

'Take legal advice. Make it a cooperative? Make it a charity, like Carlsberg? Turn it into a public company to go on making profits—'

'Now you're talkin' turkey!'

'. . . but keep a controlling share and turn those profits over to some good cause? Helping the victims of Naziism? I don't know. I'll have to take legal advice. Come on! Breakfast's waiting, and we have quite a day ahead.'

She kept the Big Possibility in reserve.

Breakfast, served out on the terrace overlooking the lake, was of moist, thin slices of ham, a very mild, soft cheese, rounds of bread that looked artificial, with all the aerated bubbles evenly sized and equally spaced – though it tasted good. There was also a bowl of a thready kind of yoghurt, called 'long milk,' into which they broke chips of a hard, flat, unleavened bread, served in rounds the size of a twelve-inch record.

'Do they ever do French toast here?' Willard asked.

She laughed. 'We have a much more romantic name for it – *fattiga riddare* . . . poverty-stricken knights – that's knights with a 'k.' Don't ask me why!'

'Jesus! *Arme Ritter!* I'd forgotten that – when I wanted french toast in Germany . . . *Arme Ritter!* It means the same.'

She thought he was about to connect the name with her own and make some comment about money and poverty, but he gazed far out across the little lake and said, with a sigh: 'It's all so . . . faded and far away.'

'The view?'

'No. The war. The way of life we led back then.'

'Do you ever hanker after them – those days?'

He was genuinely shocked. 'Hell, no! All the things we're doing now . . . our careers . . . our work . . . our friends – that's what we were fighting to attain. Surely you don't miss *anything* about the war years? Do you?'

She wondered if it was time to come clean at last about her links with the communist resistance in Berlin . . . the excitement . . . the danger . . . the feeling of doing something useful on behalf of . . . well, the whole of Europe . . . the future . . . now – the 'things' he was talking about.

He respected her hesitation and regretted putting the question to her so bluntly. 'Anyway,' he said, 'we can't come to Sweden without calling on Sven Markelius. I'd like to see his plans for this new garden-city outside Stockholm . . .'

'Vällingby.'

'That's the one. Also to see if he's likely to be Sweden's nominee on the committee to design the new UN headquarters in Manhattan. He'd have quite a lot of sway there.'

'I certainly won't have time for that,' she said.

'I understand.' He cultivated a brief silence. 'On the other hand . . . I'm not going to be much practical use to you here . . .'

Marianne laughed. 'Clicketty-click, honey!'

'Clicketty-click,' he agreed.

Monday, 17 September 1951

When Faith told Alex that, in a few weeks' time, she was going to Tehran to discuss a possible book to mark the 450th anniversary of the foundation of modern Iran under Shah Ismail in 1509, he said, 'But that's eight years from now.'

'The inspiration for the book is theirs, not ours,' she replied. 'They want to commission it from us. And believe me, what with the lavish sort of book they're planning, in a dozen different language editions, to say nothing of the multiple international exhibitions of Persian art and crafts to coincide with its launch, it could easily take us every minute between now and then to put it all together. Besides, it's all got to be very hush-hush for a few years – so "not a word to Bessie about this," eh!'

He laughed. 'When you say it's *their* idea . . .?'

'Yes. That's typical of Fogel – the unplanned way it came about. The Iranian embassy held a party last year to launch a new edition of one of their ancient poets, Ferdowsi, who'd been translated into English – published by Blond but with a hefty subsidy from the Shah. Bound in silk . . . cased in leather . . . hand-laid paper from Barcham and Green . . . no expense spared.'

Alex laughed. 'I'll bet old Fogel's eyes gleamed at the mere sight of it!'

'More than that. He immediately started asking the ambassador about the history of Persia . . . and about three seconds after the man said the country was united inside its modern boundaries in fifteen oh-nine, Fogel said, "But that means the four hundred and fiftieth anniversary is only nine years away!" which it was, then . . . and the rest is history – Persian history! So now we've got a *disgracefully* huge budget to produce what will probably be the most lavish book of . . . well, certainly since the war. We're already talking about seven-colour gravure, including gold . . . it'll outshine anything from Lund-Humphries.'

'And all to the greater glory of Mohammad Reza Pahlavi, no doubt!'

'Ve are all prostitoots now.' She gave an expansive, Fogel-type shrug and added, casually, 'He's asked me – Fogel, that is – to come back from Persia with a detour via Tel Aviv.'

'Oh?'

Faith would have sworn that his ears physically twitched. 'Yes. The Persian book has woken him to the fact that nation states have even more loose cash than do American publishers. I bet I'll be off to Ghana before long. He's well in with Nkrumah. Took him to a picnic at Whipsnade last Sunday. Gave him a birthday present of an air gun.' She chuckled.

'What's funny about that?'

'Oh . . . years ago, Fogel asked him what he'd like for his birthday and Nkrumah said, "An air gun – and when you can give it to me legally, you'll know that Ghana is at last free from imperialism!"'

'About Israel?' Alex prompted.

'That's very current. Our previous overtures toward the Zionists were a little premature. But now Fogel thinks that – what with the criticism Israel's having to endure at the UN these days – Ben Gurion might see the wisdom of doing a book on the Zionist claim to the Holy Land. The *Promised* Land, after all.'

'And, to be sure, Ben Gurion will be even more inclined to see the wisdom of commissioning such a book once he claps eyes on the dummy pages you'll be taking to His Supreme Majesty in Tehran?'

She smiled archly and said, 'That might just have formed part of Fogel's thinking.'

'After *you* had planted the seed of it in his mind, no doubt?' he asked with pantomime casualness.

'Me?' Her mouth was an O of surprise. 'Moi? Perish the thought! I'm just the company messenger.'

'It's beginning to look as if BG has worked out a deal to end the stalemate.'

'That's the other thing – he'll be too busy to start nit-picking over every small detail in the text. If we say "so-and-so was armed," they'd want it corrected to "so-and-so was *furnished with arms.*" Stuff like that is an editor's nightmare.'

A few weeks later and some ten days before she was due to leave for Tehran, Alex rang her from the BBC to suggest they should stay up in town for dinner at the Lansdowne. 'I've spoken to Delfine,' he added. 'She'll bath the brats and put them to bed. I said we'd be back before midnight. Oh, and I've asked a friend to join us.'

'Do I know him?'

'Philip Anderson. He and I occasionally lunch at the Lansdowne. You may have met him there.'

Her heart sank. 'Oh, yes.' She had met him once before, lunching with Alex at the carvery bar in the Lansdowne. He had clearly been annoyed with her for turning up unannounced and she guessed he had some business with Alex that could not be talked of in front of her. In fact, Alex – instead of walking back with her as far as Broadcasting House – had gone off with him at the end of their lunch. Out of curiosity she had followed, and was just in time to see them disappear into that huge, ugly, concrete Ministry of Education building just round the corner from the Lansdowne, in Curzon Street. But when she had gone to the main desk there, the receptionist denied that two people had just entered the building and that anyone named Philip Anderson worked there or had *ever* worked there. Tony and Adam later told her what 'everyone in London knows' – that the 'Ministry of Education' in Curzon Street was actually the HQ of MI6 and people who worked there liked to meet at the carvery in the Lansdowne because it overlooked the swimming pool, where the splashing and the echoes rendered it almost impossible to make clandestine recordings of conversations there.

'You don't sound too enthusiastic,' Alex said. 'Shall I put him off?'

'No! I only met him the once but I got the impression he wasn't too happy to see me.'

'Ah, well, believe me – he'll be more than happy to see you tonight!' Alex promised.

The Lansdowne dining room had been très chic back in the thirties – all peach-pink lighting and warm-tinted mirrors and a deep pile carpet that a regiment could have marched over in utter silence; unobtrusive screens of frosted glass in art-deco patterns baffled conversations between each table and its neighbour so that only people up from the shires, accustomed to conversing over hunting horns, shotguns, and howling draughts, ever spoke loud enough to be overheard. Now, in the austerity fifties, it seemed almost sinful to be sitting there, basking in glories that only last year seemed gone forever.

But Philip Anderson was, indeed, pleased to see her; he sprang to his feet and clapped and dry-soaped his hands and helped her into her seat with a beaming smile. 'I've been *so* looking forward to meeting you again,' he said. 'Alex has been telling me what a globetrotter you are. I long to hear all about it.'

'I've ordered you a dry Martini,' Alex said.

And a moment later it was there.

'Oh! This menu has improved out of all recognition since they abolished the four-shilling limit on meals,' she said.

'And it can only get better now we've kicked out the socialists,' Anderson said.

She raised an eyebrow at Alex. 'You agree?'

He shook his head. 'I wish it were so, but . . . no.'

Anderson looked at him in surprise. 'Really?'

'Really. Churchill's not actually in charge, these days. The first thing they moved back into Downing Street was his bed from Hyde Park Gate – symbolic, what? We ought to order, chaps.'

They decided on a selection of hors d'oeuvres from the trolley, followed by Dover sole for Faith, devilled kidneys and bacon for Anderson, and beef carved from the joint for Alex – and agreed, once again, that the abolition of the old cash limit was an utter boon. To wash it down they chose the house white and the house red. 'So abstemious!' Anderson remarked.

Conversation over the hors d'oeuvres was light enough, mainly about the gossip then circulating around town. Anderson had seen Tallulah Bankhead arriving at the Ritz – her first return to London since before the war; the newspapers said she was afraid all her old friends would be in wheelchairs or on crutches. Faith's mother had been at a house party where Lady Diana Cooper was one of the guests; everyone had been dying to hear about that fabulous party Charles de Beistegui had held in Venice at the Palazzo Labia, which the Aga Khan said was the best party he'd been to since the days of Queen Victoria. Nobody mentioned the incident in which someone threw a glass of water over Lady Diana, and she hadn't spoken of it herself.

'I wonder – did she mention Johnny Russell?' Anderson asked with a grin.

'Of the embassy in Rome?' Alex said. 'First secretary, isn't he?'

'The same.'

'Oh, yes!' The penny dropped with Faith. 'He was the one whose feathered headdress caught fire. Yes, she told them about that.'

'I've got one for you, Findlater,' Anderson said. 'Remember an old Gaiety Girl called Rosie Boote? Married the Marquis of Headfort.'

'Vaguely, but nothing to do with me. We've never met.'

'Wait till I tell you! She lives in St John's Wood and sends out invitations to what she calls "TeeVee dinners." The guests all sit around with dinner trays on their laps and watch television! Sign of the times eh, what? What?'

'Well! Funny you should say that. I wish I'd heard of it yesterday. We had a meeting this morning and it would have gone down well. We were talking about the division of resources between radio and television and up until now I've had the feeling that people considered—'

'People?' Faith asked.

'"The men upstairs," as Arthur Askey calls us. The feeling among us has been that television was at the undignified end of broadcasting, while radio was the plum, with the Third Programme at the summit.'

'Radio certainly has all the plummy voices,' Faith commented.

'Sorry. D'you two realize, these olives are stuffed with real anchovies? It used to be sardines. Another sign of the times.'

'But now?' Anderson prompted, looking at Alex.

'Well . . . writers who previously wouldn't have dreamed of writing for TV . . . and actors and actresses who wouldn't have stooped to appearing on it . . . they're all beginning to change their minds. Not en masse but . . . straws in the wind, don't-you-know. I give it a couple of years before radio will be fighting for its share – not struggling but certainly fighting.'

'We should let Eric know,' Faith commented.

'Eric Brandon?' Anderson asked.

'You know him?' Faith was intrigued.

'*Of* him.'

In the corner of her eye she saw Alex shaking his head at Anderson. 'What's going on here?' she asked.

Neither man answered. She turned to her husband. 'Why are we entertaining Mister Anderson?' She turned to him. 'Not that I'm anything other than enchanted by your company, dear sir, but it was all arranged quite suddenly and Alex hinted very strongly that you'd be delighted to see me, especially as I'm about to go to Tehran. And actually I'm—'

'And now Israel,' Anderson said, turning to Alex. 'The ball's in your court, chum.'

Reluctantly Alex explained: 'Philip works for a branch of the Civil Service that—'

'The . . . er . . . "Ministry of Education" just round the corner. Yes, I know all about that. What I want to—'

'You do?' Both men were surprised.

'Of course! Everyone in London knows. I'm just interested to know how he' – again she turned to Anderson – 'how *you* come to know Eric Brandon.'

'Know *of* him,' he replied. 'I used to work at the BBC, in the legal department, vetting scripts for possible . . . difficulties.' He smiled. 'I don't think I need tell *you* which particular script fastened *his* name in my memory!'

The waiters brought their main-course dishes. By the time they withdrew, the tension around the table had subsided.

'Iran,' Faith prompted. 'And now Israel.'

'Oh, it's very simple,' Anderson assured her. 'So trivial it's hardly worth mentioning. But I have a document – this is in connection with a family trust – that needs to be signed by a colleague in our embassy in Tehran. So . . . I was wondering—'

'Hold on! I was about to tell you a moment ago that I'm not actually going to Tehran now.'

Anderson's face fell, but so, too, did Alex's, she noticed as she went on to explain: 'We got a cable today saying that our contact on this book project would prefer – for various unspecified reasons – that we should meet in Istanbul instead. Fogel suspects there are half-a-dozen factions in the Shah's court, all jockeying to honour the top man with some grand scheme, and our particular man there doesn't want the others to know about the book project just yet. But if I were seen meeting him in Tehran, the cat would be out of the bag. Byzantine courts aren't exclusive to Constantinople – which is where, appropriately enough, I shall now be meeting Mister Rowhani.'

Anderson did a double-take. 'Baqer Rowhani?' he said.

Alex began to laugh.

She looked from one to the other in bewilderment. 'You know him?'

'Quite well,' Alex said. 'He's a pearl merchant – Iranian, but he lives in Istanbul – or, rather, he maintains a magnificent . . . almost a palace there.'

'More than that,' Anderson added, 'his well-greased palm was the ultimate destination of the family papers I mentioned.' He paused before adding, 'And actually, now that things are more or less out in the open . . . it occurs to me . . . you're going to Tel Aviv, you say?'

'More family papers?'

'No.' He laughed. 'Scholarly interest, really. The history of the Middle East is a bit of a hobby with me. The heart of your book will, of course, be Zionism, which is about ten times older than the new Zionist state of Israel. I just wonder what sort of questions you'll be raising with Ben Gurion. Or his associates.'

Faith was not fooled for an instant, but she was interested to see how persistent Anderson would be. 'I'm a sales person, not an editor,' she assured him.

But two could play that game. 'Ah!' Anderson dropped the subject with a very Middle Eastern shrug.

'I've no doubt that the content of the book would form an

important part of my discussions,' Faith went on. 'But I wouldn't make any detailed editorial comments or suggestions. I'd be more interested to know how many copies *they* will guarantee, because *our* profit will come from the run-on.'

'But you're almost bound to conclude with a chapter that looks toward the future. I'd be interested to hear how they think Zionism's going to develop now it has roots. Ben Gurion would like it to be secular, of course, but he's just spent the best part of a year learning to live with its religious incarnation—'

'Learning?' Alex interposed. 'Scheming, surely.'

'In politics . . . is there a difference? I'd contend there's no such thing as *pure* Zionism. Some Zionists would say it exists to return *all* of the Promised Land to the Jewish people and kick out whoever's living there now. Others will say it's to promote and enforce the religious laws. Idealists would say it's to repair the world and reconcile the West and the East. In general those on the left want a Jewish state that is nonetheless democratic and secular. But those on the right would happily sacrifice the secular bit and really don't want democracy if it dilutes the Jewishness.'

'Quite a tall order!' Faith commented.

Anderson's smile narrowed his eyes to slits. 'Perhaps you'd prefer – at this stage – to let them think they have carte blanche over what to put in the book and what to leave out?'

'That might very well be true,' Faith allowed. 'But I'd still like to know all the *potential* points I might make, even if I keep my powder dry when it comes to the crunch.'

He grinned at Alex. 'No flies on her, eh!' Then, turning again to Faith, 'If they answer your questions about what flavours of Zionism they want to cover, you might follow it up with a discussion of the wider . . . or external aspects. What will the diaspora make of the developing Zionist state? At the moment I think they see it as a safe haven for *all* the world's Jews. But if Israel gets attacked again and becomes aggressive . . . tension feeding tension . . . the diaspora will start to think it's better off where it is. How will Israel then expand, as it must in order to survive? But the question I'd most like to hear them answer is: do they think Arab-Israelis will always feel *Arab*-Israeli or will they one day feel as Israeli as our Jews feel British, or American Jews feel they're American? That's at the very heart of their future there and, I hope, it's at the heart of their book and yours.'

'Is that all?' Faith asked with a laugh.

'Not quite,' he replied evenly. 'If you wouldn't mind awfully, I'd love to hear their responses to whichever of these questions you choose to raise. It's a hobby of mine, as I say. Our friends at the FO do raise them at the diplomatic level, of course, but the replies are also rather . . .'

'Diplomatic?' she suggested.

'Quite so.'

In the taxi on their way back to King's Cross, Faith said, 'You wouldn't be putting me in any sort of danger, darling? I don't for one moment suppose you are, but I feel I have to ask.'

'We're in danger now,' he said. 'We're in danger crossing the road . . . taking a train . . . cutting our fingernails. But what Anderson was asking of you puts you in no greater danger than that.'

'But it's not just Anderson who's asking this of me, is it?'

After a pause he said, 'Sometimes it's *knowledge* that offers the greatest danger. The less one knows, the safer one is. To be genuinely innocent is easier than having to act innocence.' When she remained silent, he added, 'Don't you agree?'

'I wasn't thinking of innocence so much as of ignorance.'

'For example?'

She drew a deep breath. 'All right. I suppose the question has to be asked sooner or later: our meeting in Paris? Was that entirely a matter of chance? And your telling Marianne about falling in love with me years back at a meet of the—'

'Of course! Of *course* it was a matter of chance. Dear God, how Machiavellian do you think I am?'

She started to laugh. 'Dear, sweet Alex! I think *every*one and *every*thing is Machiavellian, until proved otherwise. My suspicion isn't something I just cooked up this evening. It crossed my mind the moment you spoke to me in Paris that night, back in April last year. I thought you were just too, too wonderful to have come into my life by chance.'

'Oh, yeah?' He, too, laughed.

'Now drop the other boot.'

He made no reply.

She continued: 'Well . . . when you said you were at the BBC, and it was only one month after Eric had sent in that Wannsee conference play . . . and there had been all that trouble Angela had with British Intelligence – losing or claiming to have lost her transcript . . . I was bound to wonder, wasn't I?' When he continued to hold his silence she repeated, 'Wasn't I?'

'All right,' he said. 'Here's what really happened in Paris. I saw your name in the register, and everything I've ever told you about falling in love at that hunt meeting all those years ago is all true. So of course I was overjoyed. And the address you gave was for Manutius Books, which made it rather easy for me to check on you . . . that led to the Dower House . . . and that led someone at the BBC to recall Eric's submission—'

'Anderson?'

'Oh, no – that play, or whatever it was, ruffled quite a few feathers. There are plenty of people, at Auntie's and elsewhere, who, if you just mentioned Eric's name, would say, "Ah yes – the Wannsee script wallah!" And don't you go telling him this – you're on our side of the fence now. Talking of which, it might be an idea for you to drop into my office and swear to the Official Secrets Act.'

'At Broadcasting House?'

'No. My other office. I'll give you a pass.'

Tuesday, 30 October 1951

Baqer Rowhani was a short, slim, dynamic man in his early forties who dressed in Paris, manicured in Rome, lived in Tehran . . . and blossomed in Istanbul – or rather, as he explained to Faith, in Constantinople. 'Istanbul,' he pointed out, 'is three cities, bound together by a paradox. Pera and Scutari are its Oriental components while Constantinople is supposed to be its European counterweight, and yet it is the most Oriental of the three. All that "Mysterious East" stuff that Europeans come here to discover – it's all in Constantinople, give or take the odd Dervish and the Old Seraglio. Talking of which . . . I thought we might spend the afternoon there, now that this morning's discussions have been so very satisfactory.'

His English was impeccable – as one might expect from someone who had completed his education at Eton in the thirties. She accepted with pleasure, glad that the most intense morning of questioning and planning she had ever experienced was now behind them. The Shah – or the court faction that was going to make him a present of this book – was surely going to get his (or their) money's worth.

They drove in his Silver Wraith down to the Top Haneh landing stage. When she admired the car he told her it had come off the assembly line at Derby immediately ahead of the one bought by George Bernard Shaw, which had recently been sold after the great man's death to 'my London stockbroker, Charles Goff.'

'I'll bet *he* doesn't travel in front, beside his chauffeur,' Faith commented primly.

Rowhani shot her a penetrating glance. 'I hope you don't object to my hauling you out of the Pera,' he said. 'Socialists who are compelled to stay there usually find it distressingly enjoyable.'

She smiled sweetly. 'Don't leap to conclusions, Mister Rowhani. As for the Pera, they told me I had the room where Agatha Christie wrote *Murder on the Orient Express* but even if it was true, I don't think much survived from her time, not even the wallpaper. And besides, your palace is . . . well . . . beyond any socialist's dreams.'

'Or reach, I hope. The Orient Express, eh – such a pity the Bulgarians have closed the border with Turkey.'

'I enjoyed it as far as Athens, anyway. It still is one of the great railway journeys of Europe.'

'Of the *world*.'

When was he going to mention Anderson? Her instructions were to keep the 'family papers' by her until he asked if she knew Philip Anderson. Then there was a little rigmarole before she handed over the papers – all very exciting in a childish fashion.

At Top Haneh they boarded a ferry headed along the Bosporus toward the Seraglio Point.

'That's Scutari, over there across the water.' He pointed it out.

'Üsküdar, nowadays. It's where Florence Nightingale had her hospital.'

'Goodness! That must be quite a way from the Crimea?'

'About five-fifty kilometres. I suppose it made sure they weren't troubled by the really hopeless cases.'

They stopped at the Kaik Haneh landing stage, where other visitors to the Old Seraglio trooped off toward the official entrance; but Rowhani led her away from them, around the foot of the ancient fortifications to an enceinte on its western flank, something like a medieval fortress. There, he tapped his silver-knobbed cane lightly on a small, iron-studded door, which was opened immediately to let them in.

He smiled at Faith. 'The administrator is a kinsman.'

But Faith was simply bowled over by the vista that now spread out before them, for this was once the ancient palace of the caliphs of Turkey. It was a world within a world, and a hidden one at that, for high walls excluded not just the sight of the three teeming cities that make up Istanbul but even their noise and their bustle – tugboat hooters, the sirens of larger vessels negotiating the narrow passage to and from the Black Sea, the hooting of taxis . . . instead, a sudden and profound silence reigned. Cypresses as tall as minarets, and of a green so dark it was almost black, towered over ancient plane trees, grotesquely withered and contorted with age. Around their feet tall, dry grasses shivered between the untrodden flagstones. And beyond – steeped in shadow – were the galleries of the Seraglio itself, long colonnades in the ancient Turkish style whose verandahs were still covered in their medieval frescoes.

Rowhani stretched a hand toward it. 'Imagine ambassadors from every European country – but especially our nearest neighbours – imagine them lined up there, trembling as they waited on the sultan's pleasure. "The sick man of Europe" lay centuries in the future, then.'

'Are you Persian or Turkish yourself?' she asked.

He laughed. 'Dear Miss Bullen-ffitch!' he said. 'Do you know which people we Orientals fear dealing with the most, whether we are Persian or Turkish?'

'The Arabs?' she guessed.

'No! The English! You are so direct. If you want to know something, you simply ask. It unnerves us because then we feel obliged to answer with equal directness.' He shivered theatrically.

Then it was her turn to laugh. 'I seem to remember someone asking an almost endless string of questions this morning . . .'

'Direct questions? Blunt questions?'

She cast her mind back and realized he was right, and at last she put her finger on what had made it so intense and so tiring. All his questions had been oblique. Instead of asking, for instance, 'Shall we be using seven-colour gravure?' he'd say something like: 'Help me escape from my own ignorance . . . I've heard of a printing process called seven-colour gravure. Can you perhaps explain?' Again and again it had given her the feeling that he was somehow nudging her into a trap – having to commit Manutius to such an expensive process without his having to ask for it directly.

She turned to him with a smile. 'Let me rephrase that. I suppose . . . what with knowing so many useful people in Istanbul, and having such a superb house here in quite the best quarter of the city – not to mention useful kinsmen – you must hope that political developments outside your control will never require you to make a very uncomfortable choice?'

He conceded with a nod. 'On the other hand, to have any sort of choice at all is one step up from having none.'

He led her back almost to the point where they had landed, except that they were now inside the wall. Their way passed through several courtyards, each filled with a seemingly impenetrable garden, over whose hedges and walls she could glimpse, amid groves of cypresses, a series of ancient kiosks, all with shuttered windows.

'Does anyone live in those places?' she asked.

'They were reserved for imperial widows . . . elderly princesses, and so on – to live out their days. A foretaste of paradise, it was claimed. How our aspirations have changed, eh!'

Toward Seraglio Point they climbed a series of marble staircases to a lofty, white promenade where, for the first time, they mingled with tourists. 'Asia!' Rowhani waved a hand across the blue expanse of the sea toward the rest of the city. 'Here we stand at the very limit of Europe.'

She tried to muster a complex thought, wondering whether European institutions and values would push that boundary farther east or would Eastern mores gently subvert those of the West and so push it in the opposite direction? It was the question that now overhung all future dealings between Manutius and Rowhani's . . . clique? . . . faction? . . . cabal? The very fact that no reach-me-down English word exactly fitted the situation that had been revealed in that morning's negotiations was itself indicative. And the complexity baffled her or, more precisely, frightened her with the thought that a single ill-chosen word here would carry nuances undreamed of back in Rathbone Mews.

She took refuge in obscurity. 'I work for a man whose attitude to limits is actually his driving force.'

'Interesting . . .?' There was just a hint of a question mark in the word.

'I'm sure you know the cliché: "Stone walls do not a prison make, Nor iron bars a cage . . ." When he hears that, he thinks, "Ah yes, but limits do!" Limits are a prison to him and he immediately starts digging tunnels.'

'*Very* interesting,' Rowhani murmured.

Well, when it came to signing contracts he couldn't claim he hadn't been warned.

He took her on a tour of the remaining kiosks. The first was closed 'even to the Faithful, for it houses the mantle of the Prophet,' he explained in a tone of public reverence that (she felt sure) masked a private amusement. Then, with undoubted pride on his part, came the Kiosk of Baghdad, crammed with priceless Persian porcelains.

'Those red flowers . . .' he pointed to a detail in the decoration. 'The pigment is derived from real coral but the art has been lost.'

The crowning of their tour was the imperial treasury – a scene out of the Arabian Nights. But no cave of Aladdin or Ali Baba could match these riches, the hoarding of eight centuries of rulers who, for most of that time, had been the lords of the ancient world. There were caskets for spices, jewel boxes, gem-studded robes, ceremonial swords . . . weapons from the time of Yenghis Khan, and even from the days of Mohammed: daggers and scimitars of silver and gold, encrusted with precious stones . . . and golden chests of every size, one decked with rubies, another with sapphires. On one table, quite casually displayed, stood a casket carved from a single giant emerald, which must have been as large as an ostrich egg. Another room was filled with coffee services and flagons and pitchers, all quite exquisite; yet another was given over to precious cloths – from tissues of fairylike daintiness to great caparisons of gold thread for camels and horses; also saddle cloths of silver and gold, bordered with flowers of precious stones.

'Did it do them any good, I wonder?' Faith murmured.

Rowhani turned to her, bewildered.

'If one of the sultans woke up with a hangover – no! They were Muslim, of course. OK – a headache. If one of them woke up with a headache, did the pain go away when they remembered they owned all this? Did they gloat over it? You couldn't do it all in one day. Did they spin it out? A flagon today, a gold chest tomorrow, a cloth of woven air the next day? There's a maharajah in India who has a hundred or more Rolls-Royces. Why?'

He clearly did not welcome this sort of speculation; she had a fleeting intuition that the accumulation of wealth was, for him, an end in itself. The very idea that it might be for something *other* – beyond the simple act of acquisition – was perhaps impossible for him to grasp. 'On certain festive days the sultan would throw handfuls of gold coins into the hareem of the concubines for them to fight over,' he offered.

'Ah! Well, if one is going to behave like that, I suppose one would want a fair bit of accumulated wealth to fall back on.'

For the first time in any of her international travels she wished Eric Brandon could be with her; he would know the *mot juste* for all this.

Still slightly nonplussed, Rowhani led her toward the end of the chamber, where stood a collection of ancient thrones of state, made for sitting cross-legged in the former royal manner. One was a blaze of rubies and pearls; another was studded with emeralds and sapphires, making it seem to ripple like the sea; even Faith, in her present mood, was slightly awestruck.

'And this is the climax,' he announced dramatically as he led her into the final chamber. And there, standing motionless and terrifying behind sheets of glass, were the twenty-eight life-sized puppets of the sultans who had ruled between the fall of Constantinople and the end of the eighteenth century; as each of them died he was brought here in effigy, wearing his court costume and ceremonial arms. And there they now stood, shoulder to shoulder, grotesquely lifelike, dressed in wonderful brocades embroidered with mysterious designs that no doubt held some occult significance, turbaned in silk with magnificent aigrettes and epaulettes of jewels . . . and more than slightly dusty.

Now Faith was in a quandary. Rowhani clearly expected her to be impressed . . . bowled over, even, by this gross display of riches. True, it was a museum these days but it displayed what had once been the accumulated *personal* riches of one man – the supreme sultan of his day. Should she play the acquiescent guest and let herself be bowled over?

No. It was impossible. If she was expected to understand his attitude, then he must equally understand hers. Ve are not *always* prostitoots now!

She drew a deep breath and said, 'They had no idea what wealth was *for*, did they!'

He took a step back and stared at her. 'In what way?'

'Think! If they had cashed in this lot and put the proceeds into universities . . . inventions . . . sewerage systems . . . shipping . . . engineering . . . they could have done it all, way ahead of the rest of the world. They would never have become the "Sick Man of Europe." They had the cure right here, under their noses. And the new wealth it would have generated would have turned this display into a mere sideshow.'

Even as she spoke, she knew how close to the wind she was sailing. The court of the Shah was patterned more on these old Turkish courts than on . . . well, Buckingham Palace. The very book they had planned in outline that same morning would be modern publishing's equivalent to these ancient treasures, which was no doubt why, or partly why, he had brought her here. She waited for his response.

When it came, he took her by surprise.

He ushered her outside and led her, in silence, a good hundred paces out into the surrounding parkland, under the trees. There he looked all about and, grinning broadly, said, 'I am going to shock you now, and I wouldn't like what I'm going to say to be overheard. In short, Miss Bullen-ffitch, I am going to ask you a direct question: what you said back there – about the proper use of public wealth – were you hoping to test me?'

Faith stared uncomfortably over his shoulder; now that she knew the man's technique: always oblique, never advancing to a position from which he could not retreat. This sudden burst of directness was especially unnerving.

'*En passant,* perhaps,' she said. 'You seemed to expect me to be dumbstruck by . . . all that.' She waved a hand toward the kiosks and treasure chambers. 'I thought it only fair to let you know my true feelings.'

'All I was hoping . . .' He began to laugh. 'I hoped you would see some parallel between the magnificent book on which we are about to embark and some of these treasures around us here.'

'Oh, but I saw it only too clearly. However, I want it to be quite understood that – for Manutius – this is a straightforward commercial venture. We happen to be *the* master-craftsmen in our field, with the best designers, the best editors, the most assiduous researchers—'

'Yes, yes, yes. I knew all that before I even approached your Mister Fogel—'

Here's an interesting reversal of history, she thought. Had it not been Fogel who had approached the Iranian ambassador?

'So!' she said. 'Understanding all around!'

'Hmmm,' was all he said to that. Then, suddenly belligerent (and, she suspected, more so than he intended) he said, 'You're off to Israel next?'

She nodded.

'They'll probably tell you that when Theodor Herzl met the Sultan Abdul Hamid the Second – you know about Herzl?'

'Founder of Zionism . . . *political* Zionism, anyway.'

'Yes. When he asked the Sultan to donate Palestine to the Zionists, the reply was, in effect, "not while I live and not while the empire exists." Well . . . he's dead and so is the empire but that reply is hardly a legal document.'

'I'll certainly bear that in mind,' she assured him – straight-faced.

Dinner – a feast of Turkish cuisine – was over and still he had not started the rigmarole that would lead her to hand over the envelope Alex had given her. How many Rowhanis were there – perhaps he was not the one they had in mind? Or perhaps he would wait until his wife had retired – not that Faith was eager for that moment, for, apart from anything else, Yasmin Rowhani, was a philosophy graduate from the Sorbonne whose doctorate, from Uppsala, had concerned Kierkegaard and his role in the development of existentialism. She and Faith had quite some conversation on the subject during the many courses of their dinner, and – again – Faith found herself wishing that Eric were here, if only to allow her to watch while his attachment to Wittgenstein and the Positivists took a nasty knock. She was sure Eric had too much influence over Felix, steering him away from those irrational, self-contradictory impulses that were the true source of his art. And if anyone could shake Eric out of his complacency it was this intellectual giant of a woman.

'If you ever come to London, you simply must visit us,' she told them, and went on to describe the Dower House community. 'There's one man in particular – Eric Brandon, a writer and illustrator, who knows everything about the "thatness" of things, in the positivist sense, and nothing about the "whatness" of things in Kierkegaard's sense. I mean, he knows *that* a thing exists without necessarily knowing, or even wanting to know, *what* it is. He needs some re-education, I think.'

Yasmin raised a sardonic eyebrow. 'You seem well qualified to take him in hand yourself.'

'Unfortunately, all I know is what I've gleaned from reading the galleys of a book Bertrand Russell is writing for us—'

'Really?' She sat upright and leaned forward. 'He's a great thinker *and* a great doer.'

'And a model author. But I have to confess that until about five weeks ago, Kierkegaard was just a name to me.'

'This book—'

'It's a kind of history of Western thinking. A layman's guide to every important strand in the development of Western philosophy – including, of course, influences from Islam. Unfortunately, it's proving difficult to illustrate . . . portraits, facsimile signatures, pictures of birthplaces, statues, title pages in Latin . . . it becomes very repetitive. And parallels in art are non-existent. Who is the greatest philosopher in the age of the baroque? Descartes!'

'So, that's one more reason to come to London!' She looked provocatively at her husband, who did not rise to it. Instead he asked, 'Why does it worry you – this Eric Brandon's positivism?'

'Because I think he's a bad influence on Felix Breit, the sculptor, who is a very dear friend of mine. An artist – especially an artist like Felix – needs to experience things from the inside outwards. It's nothing like a scientist's experience, which is from the outside inwards.'

'Get him to look at Leonardo's anatomical drawings,' Yasmin said. 'In fact, *any* of Leonardo's engineering drawings and inventions. And then make him compare them to the drawings in an anatomy textbook or any engineering drawing. Long before he puts pen to paper, Leonardo understands the flayed human corpse – he probably flayed it himself! So the drawing starts from that understanding and works its way outward to the external appearance, refined to one particular viewpoint. But the *whole anatomy* is not sacrificed *to* that viewpoint.'

'Oh!' Faith was ecstatic. 'You simply must visit us when you're next in London. You *do* visit London, I hope?'

'As a matter of fact,' Rowhani said casually, 'we were thinking of making a visit quite soon. We must set up a research unit – jointly with Manutius – and go through all the British Library catalogues of Persian material . . . and the British Museum—'

'And the Chester Beatty collection—'

'Naturally. And also to look up old friends—'

'Especially old Philip!' Yasmin said.

'Yes, indeed.' He turned to Faith. 'Philip Anderson – d'you know him by any chance?'

'He's a keen swimmer,' she said, thinking: Lord, how fake this sounds . . . and why are we bothering, anyway? And, more worryingly, why did no one tell me that Yasmin would be part of the script?

'I didn't know that,' Rowhani replied; he was far more convincing than she felt herself to be.

'I'm a member of the Lansdowne Club – just off Berkeley Square, you know. My husband and Philip often indulge in races in the club swimming pool before joining me for lunch at the poolside buttery. And, as a matter of fact, I'm glad you reminded me – he gave me a letter for you.' She fished in her bag. 'Yes, here it is.'

He took it and made at once for the door, saying, 'I'd better see if he wants an immediate reply.'

Left alone, Faith and Yasmin smiled self-consciously at each other. 'What an unconvincing rigmarole,' Faith said.

'Well, it was intended for a restaurant or some other public space.'

'I wasn't told you'd be part of it.'

'I wasn't intended to be part of it, but the moment I set eyes on your photograph—' Seeing Faith's surprise, she said, 'Oh, yes, Alexander sent your photograph ahead of you, and the moment I saw it, I said to Baqer: "I'm coming, too!"' She smiled a very feline smile. 'You see, I know the *thatness* of my husband and I know the *whatness* of him, too!'

Monday, 5 November 1951

Fritz flapped a none-too-clean napkin at the tablecloth until Fogel at last told him to stop it and go away.

'They must be the rudest waiters in London,' Alex commented.

'New York is worse,' Faith assured him. 'Last time I was there I had an incomprehensible menu shouted at me by an ex-tobacco-auctioneer posing as a waiter, who finished – without pausing for breath – "makeyaminduplady."'

'Something still bothering you, Wolf?' Alex asked.

Fogel nodded. 'Ben Gurion. In one way we want his intimate cooperation for *Land of Promise*. It opens so many doors. But, in another way, we want mainly a go-between. We must sell this book in America—'

'Will that be difficult? Surely not?'

'Because of the big Jewish population . . . not longer poor?' Fogel turned to Faith. 'Explain to him our problem.'

'They are rich. They are liberal. But they are *American* liberal, which is not socialist. Ben Gurion is a socialist. I met him just a few days after he managed to put together this new coalition, after eight months of squabbling over religious education. That squabbling – it doesn't go down well. The Jews in America want only positive thoughts . . . successes . . . struggles and battles, yes, but always with positive outcomes. We think it would be better in the long run if we had a go-between, someone we can talk to frankly about the market for this book, who can then rephrase it in the most tactful way for Ben Gurion.'

'A buffer zone,' Alex commented. 'How appropriate.'

'We need impartial advice on this,' Fogel said. 'And when I hear the word "impartial" I think of the BBC. You have a correspondent there, yes?'

Alex nodded. 'P.J. Kennedy. But I'm not sure what his contract would allow in the way of—'

'Just advice,' Faith explained. 'He must know all the ins and outs of their politics. He could give us a few names? I must admit, I have forebodings about this book. Weizman once complained that every Jew wanted to be president of Israel . . . My complaint is that every Jew I met is certain that he has the one true, unchallengeable account of Erez Israel. And I'll give you an extreme example. One ultra-orthodox religious Jew I spoke with – no names, no pack drill – told me to read Jeremiah sixteen because it proves that Hitler was an instrument of God's will and the *Vernichtung* was precisely foretold in chapter sixteen. "It is we Jews who should be ashamed of the *Vernichtung*," he said, "not the Germans. They were the righteous instruments of God's wrath and should hold their heads high." Our editors will have to cope with everything between that extreme and its opposite. However . . .' she added in the glum silence that followed, 'here's an idea that has just occurred to me . . .' She turned to Fogel. 'You remember how when you were doing *Forward!* and *Illustrated Britain* you went inside various branches of British industry – steel . . . transport . . . shipbuilding – and explained how they worked—'

He chuckled. 'And how they *didn't* work. Ernest Bevin told me we made nationalization much easier for Labour. I told it to Shinwell at Bevin's funeral and he agreed. Why?'

'Well, Manutius has pioneered a new type of publishing, partly out of commercial necessity but also to make books genuinely international. I look at books published before the war – illustrated books on science, engineering, history . . . anything – and I *cringe*. I curl up inside with embarrassment at how parochial they are. But now, just because we have to have simultaneous printing in eight, nine, ten different languages to pay for the colour and the design and research, we are forced to think internationally. And we've been doing it so long now that it's second nature. We do it automatically. And that's a revolution. *You* have done this, Wolf. You started a revolution in your own backyard. We have radio documentaries and TV documentaries on Fleming and penicillin, Whittle and the jet engine, Baird and television – even though his system was hopeless and never worked properly. So wouldn't it make a fascinating documentary to follow the progress – the *international* progress – of one of Manutius's books?'

Faith knew something was wrong when Fogel decided to walk the half-mile back to the office rather than take a taxi. 'This idea is a disaster,' he said, breaking a long and ominous silence. 'The more I think about it, the more terrible it is.'

'You were happy enough back there when I first—'

'Because you flatter me. "*You* have done this, Wolf. It's *your* revolution in *your* own courtyard!" But now I say no. Manutius survives . . . *I* survive . . . because it's a mystique all round how we work. *Anyone* can hire artists, designers, editors. Why don't they? Because they think Wolf Fogel has a crystal ball or a guardian angel or something they can never have, and so—'

'But you do! Slow down, for God's sake! Who else can pick up the phone and get Bertrand Russell, Julian Huxley . . . Gerald Barry . . . Boyd-Orr . . . to listen and say yes?'

'This is not a crystal ball – this is my point.'

'It's half a crystal ball. Or a magic bullet – that's a better name for it. You're probably not even aware of the other half.'

For fifty paces he maintained a stubborn silence but was at last compelled to ask, 'What other half?'

'Think back to the Iranian embassy party – how many other publishers do you know who would immediately think *book contract* when they hear that a four hundred and fiftieth anniversary of a distant country is almost *ten years* in the future? And that *still* isn't the full "other half."'

Again she waited until he felt compelled to ask – only fifteen paces this time.

'Russell, Huxley, and Barry and so on are yesterday's trophies, but you're still bagging the next generation. Alan Bullock, A.L. Rowse, F.R. Leavis, Ritchie Calder . . . you've got them all sniffing the Manutius bait. You're worried that if we were in a documentary on how international co-production works, every other publisher in the world could use it as a textbook on how to do it? They'd fall flat on their faces, because they'd only see the physical process and the costs. They'd see nothing of all those background costs – the network of contacts, the bait, the Hampstead parties, the *snish-snish* of keeping a hundred streams of information flowing just for the sake of the one we can exploit. They wouldn't even know where to start.'

'Some of them would.'

'Never! They are *English* publishers. Europe exists in a different dimension of space-time for them. They'd have night terrors at the thought of having to collaborate with just *one* other European publisher. Imagine telling them that their editor would have to work with editors from Hachette, Sansoni, Ullstein, Bonniers . . . and half a dozen more. They'd say "Thank God we still have the Empire," and so they'd leave the field to us. Besides, we've got a ten-year head start on them.'

They were nearing the office by now and, for the moment, he seemed to have run out of objections. But long experience had taught her that logic alone never went very far with Fogel. She judged it time for a distraction. 'Alex and I went cubbing in Gloucestershire last weekend,' she said. 'And Felix asked us to say hello to a sculptor friend of his who lives in Cheltenham, John Bowes. And through him we met a man I think we – meaning Manutius – ought to cultivate.'

'Go on.' Fogel's tone said she still had not won him over.

She continued as they walked up Rathbone Mews. 'If I say he's a mathematician who worked in Operations Research in the war, that he's a friend of Laura Riding and Robert Graves, that he wrote a marvellous study of William Blake published by Secker, which is already in its third printing, and that he's now in charge of research at the National Coal Board, I wouldn't even be scratching the surface. He's a remarkable man – a truly renaissance man.'

Fogel paused at the main entrance door. 'His name?'

They entered the building and rang for the lift.

'His family came to England when he was twelve, just after the Great War. He learned English mainly through Shakespeare but he told me he still didn't think it good enough when he was about eighteen and in a public lavatory near Fleet Street and he recognized the great G.K. Chesterton struggling to do up his flies, which were out of reach under that enormous belly.'

The lift arrived and they started the ascent. 'His name?' Fogel asked again.

'He says that to this day he regrets not offering to help the poor old fellow.'

Fogel drew an exasperated breath to ask one last time but she cut him short with: 'His name is Jacob Bronowski.'

Rather than waste the breath, he said, 'We give him lunch next time he comes to Coal Board head office. I still don't want your documentary spies.'

'How did it go after lunch with Fogel?' Alex asked as they drove back in the Bentley to the Dower House that evening. 'I saw you *walking* back with him – is that a good sign?'

'He wasn't happy with my suggestion for a documentary.'

'Oh? He seemed to like it at lunch.'

'That's a thing with Fogel. He'll work like a slave to secure a contract with some big overseas publisher but then – as soon as it's signed and sealed . . . bang! Down comes a cloud of gloom and he's thinking of ways to tweak it even more to our advantage. Or even break it. He hates being fettered.'

Alex considered this awhile and then said, 'But what's "being fettered" about being the star of a documentary on the BBC?'

'Exactly! I couldn't see it, either. I've been turning it over all afternoon and I think it's part of the same thing but in a more complex way. Remember when I was trying to describe him to Bronowski? I had a fleeting intuition of this . . . problem or whatever you'd call it. Fogel's innermost fear is that he'll lose control. A contract is something that takes control away from him and hands it over to the law. A TV documentary on the BBC might create such interest and bring in so much new business that Manutius would have to expand. Inevitably then there'd be so many layers of management and such a formal structure that he'd lose control. Or he'd lose the sort of control he enjoys now, where he just picks up the phone and says, "Come!" And where he can praise you for something on Friday and bawl your head off for the same thing on Tuesday.'

'So! He doesn't want Manutius to expand, eh!'

She sighed. 'Yes. He doesn't want expansion. That was what

was gnawing away at the back of my mind when we were with Bruno last weekend. I suppose I've only dared admit it to myself today.' He drew breath to speak but she cut him short: 'And I know what you're going to say next, my darling. And you may very well be right. But the question is – do I stay and fight it? *Force* the business to expand? Because I really do want to be a big fish in a big pond. Or—'

'There's a big pond already waiting!'

'Yes, but it already has a big fish swimming around in it by the name of Grace Wyndham Goldie.'

Alex held his fire.

'I'll just have to think about it. There's a kind of paradox in it. I could never have started with nothing and created Manutius as it is today. Fogel is an absolute genius to have done that. But those same qualities make it impossible for him to grow the firm beyond where it is now – to give it the power of its full potential. But I think I can. I *know* I can – and I think I could do it by stealth, behind his back, against his wishes. *Fait accompli!* But do I have the moral right? Is there even such a thing as "moral right" in business? Or is it all a matter of cold logic and commercial imperatives? If so, perhaps it's my *duty* to take the initiative from him and destroy his nice little outfit in order to give him something bigger, better, ten times more valuable—'

'. . . which he doesn't want!'

'. . . which he'd hate.'

'Oh, by the way, Anderson was very pleased with whatever it was you told him about the Ben Gurion meeting.'

She grinned. 'Which you have studiously avoided asking about!'

'Well . . . I can't claim to be *completely* uninterested,' he admitted.

'I'll tell you, anyway, but I'm surprised Anderson is pleased. It was quite clear to me that all those big, universal, global sort of issues he put to me at the Lansdowne are of almost no interest to the present Israeli government. The whole state is so riddled with factions and infighting and jockeying for advantage that no one can raise his sights to look beyond the next vote in the Knesset . . . the next election . . . all the most immediate things. Felix told me they had a joke in Mauthausen that if you locked

two Jews in a cell they'd immediately form three escape committees who wouldn't talk to each other. It's like that.'

'But of course Anderson is delighted. Our embassy would
never be quite so positive in their assessment. They'd hedge it
with "on the one hand" . . . "on the other" . . . What about
the book?'

'The book's fine. It'll be a straightforward justification of the
establishment and expansion of the homeland . . . a hymn of
praise to past heroes . . . a warning about departing from BG's
secularist ideal, and de-dah-de-dah-de-dah. We never really
expected anything else. But we'll sell several hundred thousand
copies and our upfront costs are already covered . . . so everyone's ecstatic.'

Friday, 29 February 1952

Marianne found Chris, still in his pyjamas, collecting their milk
from the shelf in the back hall. 'Not dressed yet?' she asked.
'You're supposed to start painting at Enfield today.' She checked
her watch. 'I can wait ten minutes if you want a lift.'

'It's Julie's birthday,' he said. 'It's only her fifth so I thought
we ought to make something of it.'

'She's a . . . whatsit? Leap-year girl! I didn't know that – you
should have said. Are you having a party?'

'Probably. I don't know. Anyway, I can't paint in this mood.'

'What mood?' Marianne asked wearily.

'This announcement of Churchill's.'

She frowned.

'About the atomic bomb. Britain's only gone and made one.'

Her frown deepened. 'But . . . Japan . . . Hiroshima—'

'They were American. This one that Churchill's on about is
independent. Exclusive or whatever you want to call it. The
RAF doesn't need to ask anyone . . . NATO, or . . . anyone else.
Just . . . you know . . . *bang!*'

'And so?' She checked her watch again; she was going to
hit the rush hour. And the baby always kicked when she got
het up.

'Well, it'll just take one lunatic and we're done for. It's awful, just thinking about it.'

'Thinking? Thinking's not going to change anything. And you can't *do* anything about it either, so—'

'We can vote for a return of the Labour government.'

'Hah!' She raised her hands in despair. 'Churchill's only been back in since last October. D'you imagine they've made this bomb from scratch since then? Look, I've got to go.' Over her shoulder as she left she called: 'This is not a good start, Chris!'

Morosely he padded back upstairs, where the first thing Julie said was, 'She's right. You've got a contract. You can't let the Tory government put you off your stride.'

'I can't help it, bonny lass.' He found enough space on the kitchen counter to put down the milk bottle and then he folded her in his arms. 'I keep thinking that somewhere out there along the A4 there's a . . . a *thing* of metal, a bomb, smaller than our car, and it could completely obliterate half of London. You remember the pictures – what it did in Japan – and now we've gone and made one for ourselves.'

'But, as Marianne just said, there's precious little you or I can—'

'No-no-no – there must be something. I want kids, don't you?' He checked his flow and added, 'One day. How could we bring kids into a world where every bleeding country's got its own stock of atomic bombs? Because now we've got one, everyone will want their own.'

'I don't want kids,' she said.

'No. Of course. Not yet.'

'Not ever.'

'I'll take them if you like,' Eric said as Isabella started a hunt for her boots. 'D'you want any fags?'

'Capstan Full Strength?' she replied. 'No, thanks. If they've any Gaulloises . . .'

'I'll see. You can come with us if you like, Calley – just for the walk.'

It was quite a little platoon that was now daily ferried to and from the school across the fields – Sam and Hannah Prentice, Jasmine Findlater, Tommy Marshall, and Siri Johnson. Strictly speaking Siri, who would not be four until July, ought not to have been included, but she had been allowed into school when it became clear that she could not only read quite fluently and write, after a fashion, and was bored to the point of mischief at home; the actual turning point had come when, determined to progress from pencil to ink, she had spilled a whole bottle of Waterman's permanent blue over the magnificent pine table Willard and Marianne had made so lovingly during that first spring at the Dower House, five years ago.

In all, there were now twenty children under the age of nine in the community, ranging in age from Sam, who was nine, down to Karl Lanyon, just fifty-seven days old; and Nicole was expecting again in July, followed by Marianne sometime in September – if, as she often said, 'she doesn't kick her own way out before that.' In half-a-dozen years, if they kept it up at this rate, they could start a school of their own.

A fine drizzle was falling – or, rather, wafting uncertainly all around them – as they set off from the assembly point in the back hall.

'Can't we go by car?' Siri asked.

'No!' Sam and Tommy shouted together as they jumped into a puddle to prove their point.

'If you get any mud over yourselves or anyone else,' Eric warned them, 'I'll pull your arms off and beat you both round the head with the soggy ends.'

'Then we'd have blood on us, too,' Tommy said.

'It wouldn't show much on you,' Sam pointed out.

'I don't think the odd smear of blood would be your biggest worry, though,' Eric said. 'Deep breaths now, everybody! In through the nose, out through the mouth. Every deep breath is worth a guinea in the Bank of Health!'

And off they set.

'The first child to spot a double-breasted backchat can have my entire sweet ration for the month,' Eric announced.

'How can we tell a double . . . whatsit?' Sam asked.

'A double-breasted backchat. Well, it has a reddish-brown double-breasted jacket – and you can easily tell the cock from the hen because it buttons up on different sides. And whatever you say to it, it says something cheeky back at you.'

'Do-o-o-uh!' they moaned as the prospect of a month's sweet ration receded.

'Tell us a story,' Jasmine begged.

'I just did.'

'No! A *proper* story!'

'Oh . . . very well.' Eric began: 'It was a dark and stormy night—'

'Noooo!' they all shouted.

'OK,' he said. 'This is how to catch a pink elephant—'

'Noooooooo!' they cried.

'OK. Did I ever warn you against the Old Woman of Gideon's Coppice?'

'No,' they lied. 'Tell us that one.'

The hazy drifts of drizzle let up as they passed Rosy Primrose on their way to the coppice, but every branch dripped a line of rain and the grass and clay squelched underfoot and popped and crackled behind them.

'It's a very serious story, not just for amusement, you know. It's a dark and dismal warning not to go down these paths alone, or the Old Woman of Gideon's Coppice will get you. I know, because I have met her and, more importantly, I have lived to tell the tale. You may not be so lucky but the way of it was this. I came down here one evening, just before sunset it was, after one of those strange summer days when the sky is blue and the sun beats down but a thin, cold mist slithers across the fields and distant objects seem to quiver and shrink even as you stare at them. But I didn't have a lot of time to notice things like that because I came down here, on this very path – Siri, don't wander that way; even dead stinging nettles can still sting, you know. Anyway, I came down here to check on Bob Ambrose's traps, to see if he'd caught any rabbits, and—'

'What d'you do if you find them?' Calley asked.

'I deal with them. But sometimes the snares catch badgers or foxes and then I throw my jacket over them and undo the trap and let them go.'

'Why d'you throw your jacket over them?'

'It's a good thing you asked that, Tommy, because – listen all of you – if you see any wild animal caught in a trap, or even a dog, even your own dog who loves you, they may be in such pain that they'll just bite anything that comes near them. But if you throw a jacket over them and hold it there you can then open the trap and let them go. But it's best even so to go and get a grown-up. Look, that ditch is rather full so I think we'll go up to the log by the pond. OK, Tommy – you're a great example, I must say. So now you can just stand there and wait for us to come round. What were we doing?'

'You were telling us a story.'

'Was I? I don't remember.'

'You doooo! The old woman one.'

'Oh! Surely you don't want to hear that old tale again?'

'Yeeeees!'

'Oh, very well. It happened just back there, where the path bends . . . see?'

Tommy jumped back over the ditch and trotted to join them. 'It happened at the bend before that last time you told us,' he said.

'Oh, Mister Smarty pants – who said it only happened to me once, eh? Anyway, that's where it happened this time – the time I'm telling you about *now* – OK? The slithery mist thickened until I quite lost my way and I was actually stumbling toward Dormer Green when I thought I was heading straight for home. Because, in a mist you know, one hill is very much like another hill. But there was this old woman standing there. I mean, she suddenly loomed up out of the mist. At first she was just a dark shape and I thought she was a broken-off tree trunk. A bit of a dead tree. But when I got really close – I mean, as close as this – I saw it was an old woman. Quite a good-looking old woman, not at all witchlike, but dressed in old-fashioned clothes. "You're going the wrong way, young man," she said. Well, compared with her, I *was* a young man. "That's your way home." And she pointed back up the hill. Siri, pet – the farmer's planted corn there. Just keep to the path, eh? So we chatted a while, the old woman and me, and she told me she had once lived at the Dower House and she remembered when the coppice was first planted. And so, of course, I knew she was just having fun with me, because to make a coppice like this you have to let the trees grow forty or fifty years and then cut them down and then let new little trees sprout up again all round the old stump. So Gideon's Coppice is well over a hundred years old and this old woman didn't look a day past seventy. So anyway, we parted company and I set off home and the mist had lifted by then so I could see the way. And I'd only gone about twenty paces when I realized I'd forgotten to thank her. Siri – yes, darling, it's a bird's nest left over from last year but the birds might just want to come back to it again next month, so let's just leave it there, shall we? Maybe Mrs Walker will let you do a drawing of it when we get to school. So – I'd forgotten to thank the old woman, so I turned round and said, "Ta muchly," or something extremely polite like that. But instead of saying, "You're welcome," or "Not at all," or something extremely polite like that back to me, she raised her hand up like this and she put it on her forehead. And then she slowly . . . lowered it . . . down . . . down . . . down . . . over her entire face. And when her hand was here, she had two bright, coal-black eyes; but when it reached here – *the eyes were gone!* And when her hand was here, she had a slender, aquiline nose; but when it reached here, *the nose was gone!* And when her hand was here, she had a full red mouth; but when it reached here – *her mouth had vanished!* Her whole face was as smooth . . . and as plain . . . and as white . . . as the side of an egg!'

The children halted and stared at him, open-mouthed; but they knew the tale well and wanted to hurry on to the climax. 'What did you do? What did you do?'

'This!' He ran the few remaining paces and vaulted the stile into the lane that led up to the school. 'Except that I didn't just jump over some little fallen-down log. I jumped clear over one of the *trees!*'

Laughing, they all ran to join him and he helped them over. 'What then? What then?'

'Well, you can imagine – I ran for my life. I crashed through brambles, tearing my clothes. Isabella was furious but I forgave her. I got stung on those nettles, Siri, which is how I know they can sting—'

'You said summer. They're green in summer.'

He sighed. 'Then you have my permission to wander among them on your way back from school. Then we'll see whether I'm right or not.'

'The girl!' The other children shouted. 'The Young Girl by Rosy Primrose!'

'Yes! How did you know that! You're right, though. When I was almost home again I met a young girl standing between the pheasant run and Rosy Primrose.'

'Was she pretty?'

'Yes, Jasmine, she was devastatingly pretty. "My oh my!" she cried out to me. "You are in a sweat! And you look as if you've seen a ghost." So I stopped and just stood there, panting for breath, and glad – oh, so glad – to meet another human being after that terrible sight down in Gideon's Coppice. "I don't know what I've just seen down there," I told her. "But I hope I'll never see the like of it again – that I can tell you." "Yes," she said. "Please – *do* tell me." So I described what had just happened as best I could, and when I'd finished, the young girl said, "D'you mean she did *this*?" And she, too, raised her hand to her brow and then she slowly lowered it, down, down, down, over her entire face. And when her hand was here, she had two bright, sparkling eyes; but when it reached here, *the eyes were gone*! And when her hand was here, she had a slender, very pleasing little retroussé nose; but when it reached here, *the nose was gone*! And when her hand was here, she had a pretty little rosebud mouth that any man would want to kiss; but when it reached here, *her mouth had vanished*! Her whole face was as smooth . . . and as plain . . . and as white . . . as the side of an egg!'

They all ran off screaming and laughing into the playground – except Calley, who took her father's hand and tried to drag him to the village shop. And Siri, who came back out of the playground and said, 'That wasn't true, was it? It didn't happen.'

He looked her in the eyes a moment and then said, 'Some things happen out here, Siri – in the world of trees and grass and stones and birds' nests and things. And some things happen inside here among the double-breasted back chats.' He tapped his forehead. 'And if you can work out the difference and tell it to me when you come back from school this evening . . . well, what would you like by way of reward?'

The little girl drew breath to answer, as if it were the easiest question in the world, but then a cunning look crept into her eyes and she said, 'I can tell you that, too, when I come home from school.'

'That little madam!' Eric said to Calley as they set off for the village shop. 'She is going to be a handful.'

'I know the difference,' Calley said.

'Tell me then.'

'Things in your head are more fun.'

'That's not bad. We'll see if she gets it, too. Can you remember why Peter Rabbit doesn't like lettuce?'

'Because it's sop-or-ific.'

'Very good! What does soporific mean?'

'Yawny and sleepy.'

'Wonderful. And Isabella works on *Vogue* – what does vogue mean?'

'Fashion.'

'And what is fashion?'

'It's what people do when they haven't got any ideas of their own.'

'Better and better! It pays to increase your word power, you know. You keep on like this and when you grow up you'll be the editor of *Reader's Digest!*'

At the village shop he asked for twenty Capstan Full Strength but Calley shouted, 'Gaulloises! Gaulloises!' and pointed to where the packets stood on the shelf.

'You've been talking to Isabella,' Eric accused.

'Two packets,' Calley said.

'You *have* been talking to Isabella!'

Going back across the fields she counted the number of birds she saw flying – forty-seven; and that way she forgot that her legs were getting a bit tired. In the coppice Eric suggested they should stop and look hard at the first bird they saw sitting still, either in a tree or on the ground. 'And then, when we get home, you can look for it in *The Observer's Book of British Birds* and then you can do your own drawing of it.'

The one she picked was a goldfinch but he didn't name it for her, so that she'd have to search for it by its appearance.

When they arrived back indoors she ran up the short flight of stairs shouting, 'Isabella! Isabella! When I grow up I'm going to be editor of *Reader's Digest!*'

Isabella looked at her husband with a sort of amused weariness.

He shrugged. '*Calme-toi, chérie* – it's just a phase she's going through. Don't you remember when that was all *you* wanted in life and *Vogue* just seemed impossibly distant? She'll grow out of it.'

Wednesday, 4 June 1952

For half an hour Felix accompanied Reg Butler, the external adjudicator, on a tour of the sculpture diploma exhibits at the Slade. 'So that's about it, Reg,' he said when the tour was complete. 'I'll leave you to make your mind up. I'll be looking at the painting exhibits if you want me again. Up on the first floor.'

In the still-life room and spilling out into the corridor, an eclectic mix of classical plaster casts, from a scaled-down *Laocöon* to a half-sized *David* by Michelangelo, was scattered among spiky palmettos and improbable rubber plants. The sight, though by now familiar, still amazed him. These things belonged to a vanished world in which students had to prove they could draw and paint *properly* before embarking on more experimental work. There was even an Augustus John life study hanging on one of the walls to underline the point; there was nothing of the later John about the figure; it might have been painted by a French classicist – an Ingres or a David. Today, in passing, he noticed that the Venus de Milo was back on her plinth, after a meticulous repair that left no trace of the anatomically accurate hole one of the students had drilled in her plaster.

He found Bill Coldstream and Claude Rogers wandering around the diploma-painting exhibition.

'What d'you think?' Coldstream asked as he joined them.

Felix answered with a mirthless chuckle. 'I wish I were Wildenstein.'

'Why?' they both asked.

'I was following him round Helen Lessore's gallery in Bruton Street the other day – the Lefevre. She's got a Bratby exhibition on there at the moment. He looked at each picture in complete silence, with Helen, all anxiety, at his side, and then he reached the doorway to her little office and opened it and said, "No." And then he ushered her inside and followed her and shut the door behind them. But just as he shut it I heard him say, "And I'll tell you why." For myself, I thought Bratby's work was pretty powerful but I'll never know what Wildenstein disliked about it.'

'Probably the prices,' Rogers said, with some feeling, for he exhibited at the Lefevre, too.

'So you just want to say no?' Coldstream asked, waving a hand at the paintings generally. 'But you don't want to say why?'

Felix shrugged awkwardly. 'I find it all just a bit unadventurous, Bill. Remember Chris Riley-Potter – got his diploma in 'forty-nine?'

'Adventurous, all right,' Coldstream said, with feeling.

'There's nothing dangerous like that here, this year. It's the same with the sculpture. There's more adventurous stuff being done in the first year than we can see in any of the diploma work.'

Coldstream nodded. 'Rogers and I were just discussing that. It's because most of these students are on ex-service grants. They're older, they went through the war, they're married, a lot of them, and some have children, too. They weren't demobbed until 'forty-eight, so they're in a hurry to catch up. When they leave here this summer, they're not going to live on half-nothing in some garret in Whitechapel or Montmartre. They want to go straight into teaching . . . or curating—'

'Or one of the auction houses,' Rogers added. 'It's sad, but they were fighting a war when they should have been letting off the visual fireworks.'

'I can see all that,' Felix said. He wanted to add that, even so, they weren't exactly compelled to paint in that drab, post-Sickert-and-a-long-way-post-Post-Impressionist style known as 'Euston Road.' But, as Coldstream was one of the founders of that school and Rogers, to a lesser extent, had been a practitioner, all he said was, 'One can't withhold the diploma, really, because they're all pretty competent and professional-looking, and workmanlike, but one can say that if they were reaching for Bonnard, they didn't even make it as far as Vuillard.'

'If you want "adventure,"' Rogers replied, 'Ruskin Spear tells me there's a student at the Royal College who's dripping paint on his bicycle tyres and cycling up and down a strip of primed canvas. He then cuts it into squares and stretches them on frames, which he hangs in random order with titles like *bicycle ride one, bicycle ride two, bicycle ride three* . . . That's the sort of thing we'll be judging for diplomas *here* next year.'

As Felix left the Slade, treading a careful path over the lawns, between and over the collapsed, sun-drenched bodies of a dozen or more students, he was almost tripped by one who suddenly rose to a sitting position as he was about to step over her. Debbie something.

'Oh, Mister Breit,' she said, shielding her eyes against the glare of the sky.

A pretty little girl – a natural for casting as an upper-class English rose, except for the brilliant red hair. She would look even more natural in a twinset and pearls, with a Doris Day haircut, rather than the denim slacks, the fisherman's smock, and the tangled ponytail that actually adorned her.

'Debbie . . . ah . . .'

'Kennedy,' she said. 'You know Chris Riley-Potter, don't you?'

'Quite well. Why?'

She glanced about her, at all her somnolent companions. 'Can I talk with you a bit? I don't want to hold you up but I could walk with you . . . if you're going to walk, that is.'

He reached out to haul her to her feet. 'By all means. I'm going sketching in Regent's Park. Bring your own sketchbook along if you wish.'

'No.' She dusted herself off. 'I just want to . . . it won't take long.'

It was a pleasure to watch someone move with such lithe and easy grace, without those little twinges of discomfort that attended almost every move he made these days. *Anno domini* according to Dr Wallace. At forty? The outlook was bleak, then. He hoped she admired the controlled strength with which he had raised her.

'What about Chris?' he asked as they tipped a farewell finger to the porter at the gate.

'How well d'you know him?' she countered as they headed off north, up Gower Street.

'We both live in the same community out near Hertford – a big house divided into flats. I've been there five years. He's been there two. Why?'

'He's living with a girl, I suppose? Jenny?'

He sighed. 'D'you think it's fair to ask me that?'

When she didn't reply he turned toward her and saw a tear, just starting down her cheek. 'Oh, dear,' he said. 'I should warn you I'm not very good at this sort of thing.'

She sniffed glutinously and wiped her nose on the sleeve of her smock. He offered her his handkerchief, which she then half-filled.

'Listen,' he said. 'This street is hardly the place. I've an idea. I have a flat just across the Euston Road in Robert Street. A *pied-à-terre*. We could go there and make a cup of tea and you could tell me all about it.'

The change in her was astonishing. She grinned at him broadly, punched the tear off her cheek with a bare-knuckle jab, linked arms with him, and dragged him up the street past Lewis's bookshop toward the Euston Road. 'That would be the best thing possible,' she said. 'But would you have beer rather than tea? I mean I don't mind tea but . . . you know . . .'

'We have beer,' he assured her.

'We?'

'My wife and I.' For some reason he added, 'She won't be there,' and for some reason her *joie de vivre* did not return until he said it.

But Angela was there. The sound of his key in the lock and the sudden inrush of street noises brought her into the hallway.

'Felix!' she cried. 'Oh! And Miss . . .?'

'Debbie Kennedy. She's a fourth year. My wife, Angela.'

They shook hands, eyeing each other guardedly as Felix added, 'Actually, she wants to discuss something to do with Chris. You might be better at it than me. I've already told her I'm not very good at this sort of thing.' He turned to the girl. 'Would you mind?'

'This sort of thing . . .' Angela quoted, her eyes flickering rapidly from one to the other; she still held Debbie's hand in a light grip.

'I think I'm going to have Chris's baby,' Debbie blurted out, looking wildly at each of them in rapid turns before flinging her arms around them both and hugging them into a knot of three, in which she buried her face and howled.

Over her heaving back Angela shot a look at Felix that might have said, *And you thought you could handle this?* Or it might have said, *I'm still only half persuaded that everything's kosher here.* Or it might have said . . . But why pursue it? The air was heavy with the reek of emotionally costly sequels.

'I'll make a pot of tea,' Felix muttered, wriggling into a disengagement.

'Thanks *so* much,' Angela replied, with an ambiguity to match her earlier *look*.

Debbie wiped her eyes and nose into her sleeve and then, remembering Felix's handkerchief, produced it and blew massively before crushing it in her hand and offering it to Angela, saying, 'It's his – Mister Breit's.'

'Keep it,' Angela said with a shudder. 'Let's sit down here and you can tell me all about it. First, how late are you?'

For a moment Debbie seemed not to understand; then she said, 'Oh! Three weeks. It's been three weeks since . . . you know.'

'I'm not sure I do know, Debbie – may I call you Debbie? And we'll be Angela and Felix, OK? D'you mean three weeks since you and Chris "you know?" Or three weeks since "you know what" should have happened. And didn't?'

'The second – the flowers.'

Angela laughed. 'Oh Debbie – forgive me! I only ever saw that word for it written down, and I thought it was "flowers" like in a bouquet. I never thought of "flow" as in like a river flowing. Of course! I didn't mean to laugh.'

By now Debbie was laughing, too – at which moment Felix stuck his head round the door and said, 'Splendid! Would you still prefer beer, Miss Kennedy?'

'No. Tea,' she replied.

'And we're Debbie, Angela, and Felix, OK?' Angela added. When he returned to the kitchen she asked, 'And how regular are you usually?'

'Not completely, I suppose.'

'Have you missed three weeks before?'

She shrugged. 'Two, anyway.'

'In the war I missed "the flowers" for three years – but that's because I was more than half starved. But it doesn't look as if you starve yourself much. I don't mean you're fat, but—'

'I don't eat all that much. Sometimes I drink rather than eat.' She gave a bitter laugh. 'I've certainly been drinking these past ten days – gin and a scalding-hot bath, and jumping down the stairs backwards after it. Not that it's done any good.'

'I shouldn't think it would do any good. In fact, if you are carrying, you could be doing the little mite a lot of harm. If he's about four weeks old, he's only about *this* big. A gulp of gin could do him a lot of harm. Oh, don't cry again, please! We've got to be practical. D'you want Felix here or can we sort it out – the two of us?'

She gazed at the kitchen door and said, 'He told me he was going sketching in Regent's Park.'

Felix brought in a tray with three assorted mugs of tea, a half-pint milk bottle three-quarters full, a ripped-open packet of ginger snaps, and a Tate & Lyle sugar carton on which Mr Cube was still lecturing the nation on the evils of nationalization, almost a year after all danger of it had receded.

Angela gave an exasperated sigh. 'We do have matching cups, saucers, milk jug, and sugar bowl,' she assured Debbie.

'I thought a certain informality would go down better,' he said. 'Help yourself to the ginger snaps, Debbie.' He took one himself and sat down facing her, beside Angela.

'You didn't really say whether you wanted Felix here or not,' Angela said, not shifting up to yield him half the sofa.

The girl shrugged awkwardly. 'I suppose . . . if he knows Chris well . . . knows how he might behave . . .'

'But that's not really the point. The question is, what do *you* really want to do about it, assuming you really are carrying and not just late, which I'm not convinced about yet. But assume you are. The two extremes are . . . one, Chris is delighted, wants to marry you, and you have the baby in wedlock . . . or, two, Chris denies everything, says you're making it all up, and so you're left to have the baby alone and bring it up alone.'

'Or get rid of it,' Debbie put in.

'We haven't got there yet, and don't think it's easy. You should pop across the road from the Slade – to the women's wards in UCH. You'll find women who've done just that and it's not pretty. Well?'

Debbie glanced toward Felix, as if for support, 'I suppose . . . if he'd marry me . . . if he's delighted . . .' She shrugged.

'All right. Let's say he'd agree to marry but he's very far from delighted? What then?'

'At least the baby would have a father. He wouldn't have "illegitimate" stamped all over his birth certificate.'

'I don't think they do that any more. But stick to the point – what sort of marriage d'you think that would be?'

Debbie took too large a gulp of tea and had a fit of coughing. 'That's what I wanted to ask . . . Felix.' She smiled at him shyly. 'Is Chris living with someone? How serious is it? And could he ask if Chris would face his responsibilities and marry me?'

'Ooooh!' Angela let out a quiet, despairing sigh and, at last, yielded half the sofa to Felix.

'Sorry if I was asking too much,' Debbie said.

Felix started to assure her he'd do what she was asking but Angela spoke over him: 'No, no, no! It's not the point. You're fixated on marriage, as if it's going to make everything come out right. But of all the *bad* reasons for getting married, this one is the most disastrous. Look, why don't you wait until you're absolutely sure? I don't want to pry but how well do you know Chris?'

'About a year.'

'That's how long, not how well.'

She sighed. 'OK. He's been popping in and out of the Slade every so often . . . two or three times a month . . . and he sort of took an interest in me, in my work. He suggested things where I was lost.'

'He's not a tutor there,' Felix said.

'No, it was personal. He just wanted to help. And then he'd treat me to a meal sometimes – a mixed grill or something up in Camden Town. There's a porters' café there beside the Bedford. And we'd talk about art. And he took a real interest in my work.' She saw the scepticism in Angela's face and said, 'It was genuine. He never took liberties. He never even tried to kiss me, though I wouldn't have minded. He'd walk arm-in-arm with me up to Camden Town but that was all. He was interested in *me.*'

'*Very* interested on at least one occasion! Tell us about that.'

'I was down in the workshop and he showed me a cheap way of framing my work for the diploma show and . . .' She made a vague gesture with her hands.

'And one thing led to another.'

She fixed her eyes on the floor. 'Yes.'

'Just the once?'

She nodded.

'He never brought you out to the Dower House?'

She shook her head.

'And never mentioned Nina? Nor Anna? Nor Julie . . .?'

Her mouth was an O of shock, filled with chewed ginger snap.

'Darling!' Felix chided. Ginger-snap cud complimented her hair rather well, actually.

'Look, if ever there was a time for the truth – time for a dose of realism, it's now.' Angela turned to the girl. 'Listen, my dear – I think I know Chris Riley-Potter better than my husband. And I can assure you that he's just not ready for marriage – if he ever will be. And the sort of marriage you're thinking of would be . . . I'll say it again – a disaster.'

Debbie nodded morosely but said nothing.

'Besides, it may just be a false alarm – if you only did it once. Why not wait a couple of weeks until we're certain, eh?'

'The thing is,' Debbie began, and then lapsed into silence, staring at the floor.

'What?' Felix prompted.

Once again tears rolled down her cheeks, this time in silence. Then, in a small, strangulated voice, she said, 'My parents have kicked me out.'

Thursday, 5 June 1952

Felix and Angela were just turning off the main drive when she said, 'Talk of the devil!' Felix glanced away to their left and saw Chris Riley-Potter running toward them from the main house; he knocked the car into neutral and let it freewheel to a halt. 'Flat tyre,' Chris said between gasps. 'Punctured spare. Pump leaks. Can you . . . could we . . . I mean . . . mate of mine in trouble . . . mate from Camberwell . . . needs to lie low . . . could I borrow your car and collect him at Welwyn North?'

Felix was about to get out and hand the car over when Angela said, 'No! You hop in the back. We'll all go – and there's something else we can talk about on the way.'

He hesitated, 'What?'

'D'you want to collect him or not? Because that's the only offer you'll get from us.'

'Blimey!' He climbed in and slammed the door. 'Sounds ominous, what.'

Felix backed the short distance to the main drive and set off again for the station.

'This is about a girl named Debbie Kennedy,' Angela told him.

'Shit!' he said.

'Yes,' Angela said. 'A whole creek full of it.'

'What did she . . . I mean, where is she now?'

'At Robert Street. Her parents have slung her out – she *says*.'

Felix looked at her sharply. 'Don't you believe her?'

'I'll believe it when *they* tell me. This is none of our business, Felix. It's between them and her and' – she turned to the back – 'you, Chris. Between you three. You've got to sort this mess out between you.'

Felix turned on to the Dormer Green Road. Angela broke off and asked, in surprise, 'You're going this way?'

'We need petrol. I should have come back this way and filled up.'

'See!' She turned again to Chris. 'It's throwing us out in every way.'

He licked his lips nervously. 'What has she been telling you?'

'You tell us, Chris. What do you *think* she's been telling us? What would induce her parents to chuck her out?'

'You're not going to see her parents?' Felix asked anxiously.

'I certainly am, if it's not cleared up PDQ.'

'You won't get anywhere with them,' Chris warned. 'He's an old Victorian father and she's worse. When they speak, dust comes out of their mouths, I'll swear. Being kicked out is the best thing that could happen to Jenny.'

'Debbie.'

'Yeah, Debbie, sorry. I'm worried about Terry, that's what.'

'Terry who?'

'Garlick. That's his name. Terry Garlick. He got in a fight with a barman in Deptford and something happened and now he's got to make himself scarce for a bit.'

'Not here he won't,' Angela said.

'He's got nowhere else. Come on! He's a mate.'

'"Nowhere else" includes the Dower House, Chris,' Felix said. 'We've got twenty children living there. You can't go introducing people who damage someone so badly they have to—'

'What exactly did he do to this barman?' Angela asked. 'It sounds pretty bad.'

Chris just sniffed and looked away across the fields.

'Either you come clean – completely clean, Chris, or we're turning round as soon as we've tanked.'

'Filled up,' Felix said.

Chris sighed. 'It seems he may have blinded the barman.'

'Right!' Angela said. 'He's not coming within a mile of the Dower House. We'll drop you off at the station and you can talk it over with him and . . . take a taxi to wherever you decide is best for him. Have you got enough money? Here.' She fished out a crisp, white fiver and thrust it into his hand.

'You're a bit hard, Ange,' he complained while Felix was out paying for the petrol.

'And you're a bit . . . off your head,' she replied. 'The very *idea* of bringing a creature like that into the community.'

'He's not "a creature like that." I admit, when he's had a skinful, he can be a bit . . . you know. But he writes poetry. He was on *In Town Tonight* a couple of years ago. He's had it published and all.'

When Felix got back in she brought him up to date. 'He's a poet who happens to have blinded a barman in a fight. He's been on the wireless with his poetry. Chris still thinks he's harmless.'

'He could sleep in a tent in the walled garden,' Felix suggested. 'I don't suppose he's likely to blind any of the children. Or any of us, come to that.'

'But we'd be harbouring a criminal on the run.'

'You don't know that,' Chris said eagerly. 'I never breathed a word to you – and I wish I never had, come to that. As far as anyone else knew, he was just a mate visiting us for the weekend. When you meet him, you'll see how gentle he is.'

'I'll say no more until I see him,' Angela responded. 'And I'll have my fiver back, please? Thank you. Meanwhile we can get this Debbie Kennedy business sorted out. She's three weeks overdue and she's sure she's pregnant. Is she just being hysterical or is that possible? More to the point, is it probable?'

'Hysterical,' he said at once. 'Most likely.'

'That would be good for you, wouldn't it!'

'Well . . . it's *possible*. Just about. But probable? No. I mean, I pulled out in time. In good time. Fuck it, I came into her knickers, which she was holding in her hand. She was squeezing and—'

'Enough already!' Angela cried. 'You can spare us *those* details.'

Chris caught Felix in the mirror, corpsing. He tried desperately not to laugh, but to no avail. Soon all three of them were hysterical. Felix had to pull over into the mouth of someone's driveway, where they laughed while the tears ran down their cheeks. They stopped only when someone knocked on the window and said, 'Either share the joke, old man, or let me out, eh?'

'Couldn't . . . possibly share . . . the joke,' Felix assured him breathlessly. 'Sorry. I'll pull forward.'

'Well,' Angela said as they set off for the station again. 'I think we've heard sufficient detail to be fairly sure that Miss Kennedy is more hysterical than actually pregnant. Which' – she rounded on Chris – 'does not let *you* off the hook. Pregnant or hysterical, she's in that state entirely because of you.'

'One way or the other it's your baby!' Felix grinned.

'I'm serious, darling,' she said sharply. 'I want her out of Robert Street . . . I was going to say in three days, Chris, but, seeing what problems you may yet have with the gentle Mister Garlick, I'll say a week. By this time next week you will have sorted out her situation – agreed?'

'You're true blue – both of you,' Chris said.

'Agreed?'

'I suppose so. No choice, have I?'

'Not really, no.'

Terry Garlick did not resemble the mind's-eye image of a man who would blind a barman – or anyone else. His suit was the suit of a thin man but even so he seemed to sway around loosely inside it. The hollow eyes and day-old stubble were easily explained but the cavities under his cheekbones, the half ping-pong balls of bone behind his ears, and the ropes of sinews that controlled all the movements of his head revealed a man who could not get muscle-bound in a dozen courses with Charles

Atlas. Yet nor was he an obvious candidate for having sand kicked in his face on that eternal cartoon beach. His lips formed a grimly determined line and when he smiled, the lower one jutted pugnaciously forward. Not a man to meet in a dark alley, Angela decided.

'Cor, thanks mate,' he said when he saw Chris leap from the car. 'I'm in a bad way, I tell ya. Every city gent's a rozzer and every Austin Seven's a Black Maria. Look at me shake.' He held out a trembling hand.

'These two friends' – Chris nodded toward the car – 'live same place as me, right? I've explained what—'

'No, you can't have.' Garlick thrust him aside and strode to the car. 'It's only for the night, honest,' he said as Felix wound down the window. 'Just till my brief has talked it over with the rozzers so I can give myself up without falling victim to an epidemic of black eyes and broken teeth. You understand? It's just for tonight. If I delay more, it'll count against me, anyway.'

'Hop in, Mister Garlick,' Felix said. 'Officially we know nothing of your story. You're just a friend of Chris's who's staying the night. Do *you* understand?'

'Perfickly, squire.'

'That was what I was going to tell you,' Chris said as he climbed in on the far side. 'They don't know anything about what happened in Deptford.' After a pause he added, 'How *did* it happen? Blinded – Jesus!'

'Penny on the drum?' Garlick replied. 'I don't think I did blind the poor bugger. I think he fell on a bottle standing up – crown cap and all on. My hammer couldn't have done all that damage.'

'*Your* hammer?' Angela echoed.

'Yeah, it was only a little tack-hammer, like what we use in delicate upholstery. It *couldn't* have done that much damage.'

Later that evening, Felix closed his book and laid it on his bedside table.

'Don't put the light out yet,' Angela pleaded. 'I've only got a page to go.'

'What did you think when you saw me coming into the flat with that Debbie girl?' he asked casually.

She chuckled. 'D'you really want to know?'

'No. I think I already do.'

She responded in a sing-song, 'I don't thi-ink so!' and went on reading.

Slightly miffed, he said, eventually, 'You're ashamed of it now.'

She laid the book flat and turned to him with a sort of motherly exasperation. 'If you really want to know, I was thinking, *Don't laugh! Whatever you do, don't laugh!*'

'Laugh?'

She snapped the book shut, put it on her bedside table, lay down full length, and pulled the duvet up to her neck. 'Think about it, darling – I'm off to sleep!'

Saturday, 14 June 1952

The theme for the midsummer party of 1952 was *My Inner Self,* which was proposed – once again – by Eric and accepted by the others without much opposition, much to their later bewilderment as they went about their business, the house, the gardens . . . Hertford . . . London . . . staring at one another and wondering, silently, what had possessed them, and what *was* their 'inner self,' anyway? The worst part of all was that no one felt able to discuss it with anyone else for fear of revealing more about their 'inner selves' than they imagined they were revealing – that plus the fear of having a good idea nicked.

The backlash against Eric was all the stronger as these gripes took hold. 'We missed one vital little clue,' Sally said to Marianne as they both sat at their drawing boards one Sunday afternoon, a week before the party. They had been awarded a contract for an extension to the cottage hospital in Old Welwyn. 'When Eric put forward this ridiculous suggestion, there wasn't a breath of opposition or criticism out of Isabella. How could we have missed that? It has *never* happened before. Usually she can't let even the smallest comment of his pass her by. The other day I heard him say what a perfect blue sky we had and she turned on him like a she-cat and snapped, "Azure!"'

'To which I'll bet he responded, "Cerulean!"?'

'No, he just said, "Azure wish, Chuckles, my pet." He calls

her Chuckles now. They are definitely mellowing – those two. Or *he* is. She's still, well, *Isabella*. The other day I heard her telling Faith that Eric carries bags of sugar round with him. I have no idea what she meant. I'm sure Faith didn't either.'

Marianne laughed. 'It's just her way of saying she thinks Eric is too fat. But did you hear about Chris and the Breits last week? Julie told me – in strict confidence, so keep it to yourself. There's a girl at the Slade called Debbie something and she thinks Chris has got her pregnant, and—'

'Julie doesn't mind?'

'She knows him pretty well. She knew what he's like before she even moved in. She even spoke to me about it. I told her the best way to break a wild horse is slowly and gently, not like you see in the movies. Anyway, this Debbie apparently collared Felix in the street, told him all about it, and then turned on the waterworks. And poor old Felix – you can just imagine it – him standing there in the middle of London with a weeping adolescent hanging on his arm! Poor old Felix panics and thinks of getting her under cover somewhere . . . and seeing as it was just a hundred yards or so from their place in Robert Street, and—'

'He didn't!' Sally laughed in disbelief.

'He did. But wait, what he didn't know was that Angela was there. She'd just bought some new shoes and she wanted to try them on with a dress she keeps there. So Felix ushers Debbie in at the door and . . . tableau!'

'Oh, I wish I'd been there – a fly on the wall! Are you using the nought-point-one?'

Marianne handed the pen across to her.

Sally went on: 'But I wouldn't have thought Felix is that type, you know.' There was a short pause before she added, 'Would you?'

'I think Faith was perfect for him,' she said. 'His time "living in sin" with her gave him the courage to think that marriage with Angela might not be an utter disaster. We're using standard four-foot windows across the entire first floor, right?'

'On a fifteen-foot module. It leaves us three inches short but we'll cheat that back in again with the lead lining round the X-ray suite. Also it suited them both for their careers. He got lots of patronage through Fogel and his Hampstead parties and she got feathers in her cap as his agent.' After a pause she added, 'And he didn't have to go to prostitutes after that.'

'My God! You know about that?'

'Adam told me. I also promised never to tell anyone else! How do *you* know?'

'He told me, himself. He said he hated it, but . . . he thought it was all he'd ever be able to manage after Mauthausen.'

They worked in silence for a while before Marianne returned to the subject. 'When we had our first offices in Curzon Street we had to run a gauntlet of them – in short skirts and fishnet stockings, tapping their stiletto heels on the pavements, all the way from Shepherd Market to Park Lane – and halfway up South Audley Street, too.'

'Yes, I've seen them. One can hardly miss them there. Weren't you afraid sometimes to leave Willard working there at night on his own?'

'My attitude is that I don't mind where he works up his appetite as long as he dines at home.' She chuckled. 'In fact, that's exactly what I told him when we were in Sweden last year and I found he'd bought one of those magazines where young ladies lie around in positions that only their gynaecologists would expect to see. They sell them quite openly there. And he started some excuse about "gaining sociological insight into an important new market for us." I feel sorry for them, actually – men. It's a kind of slavery. And look at the mess it's got Chris in now!'

'Have you got the razor blade?' Sally asked. 'This line's out by six inches. That's what comes of talking!' She started scraping the dry ink off the Kodatrace. 'Personally, I can't imagine what all these women see in Chris. First Nina, then Anna, and now Julie – and Debbie, obviously! What is it about him? Have you got the spec? What does it say about the interior walls on the first-floor wards – stud or solid – d'you remember?'

'Solid, to reduce acoustic penetration. Hush a mo. I think I can hear . . .'

They held their breaths and . . . silence. They breathed a sigh of relief.

'Let's break for a cuppa now,' Sally suggested, 'and then get them up.'

'No, I think we should get them up now or they'll never go

down tonight – or Virgil won't, anyway.' She stood up and winced. 'This one's kicking again. I'm sure it's a boy. He'll play football for England.'

'We're stopping at two,' Sally said firmly. 'I'm too old to go through all that again.'

The two children, Virgil and Rachel, were fast asleep, side by side, in his bed. 'Sprinkle them with leaves and they'd be Hansel and Gretel,' Sally murmured. She reached down and began gently stroking her daughter's temple. 'Wake up! Wake up, you sleepyhead. Get up! Get up! Get out of bed . . .' she sang softly.

But it was Virgil who woke, blinked, focused, smiled . . . and then, becoming aware of Rachel at his side, gave a little cry of dismay and crabbed himself a foot away from her. 'There'll come a time when you may not be so hasty!' Sally told him with a grin.

Ten minutes later, when the two children were happily absorbed in scribbling, each with their own pad of detail paper, their mothers took tea and digestive biscuits onto the balcony, where they sat on canvas chairs and gazed out over the parkland to the south of the big lawn. Trees, lifeless in the breezeless air, shimmered under the westering sun; the farther side of the valley was bleached in the heat-haze.

'Peace is becoming the norm at last,' Sally murmured. 'It's taken long enough. Ciggy?'

Marianne took one and parked it behind her ear for the moment. 'The big difference is in the news – have you noticed? In the war, every bulletin was like a continuation of the last one. People had maps on their dining-room walls and they moved pins across them as armies advanced or retreated – at least, we did in Germany, until it got too depressing. Then it was somehow unpatriotic.'

'We did that, too – except that it got better and better.'

'But now . . .' Marianne continued, 'it's riots in Egypt and France and Germany squabbling over the Saar and the King is dead and England's got The Bomb and anti-French riots in Tangier and on and on and on. Nothing's connected any more. Life is just random events, one after another.'

'At least I'm designing hospitals for the sick and not barracks for soldiers.'

'That's true.' After an easy silence Marianne added, 'We got a food parcel from Germany last week!' Then, seeing the surprise in Sally's face, she added, 'It's a joke. From friends of Felix and Angela – Birgit and Hermann Treite of Hamburg. Hermann was my contact to the resistance in the war. He joked with them when they went back to Germany that time, remember? He joked that Germany would soon be sending food parcels to England. Every year after that he sent them stuff, just once a year. And this year he sent one to us, too.'

'What was it?'

'Sausage. Cheese . . . Sally   that joke you made back there, when Virgil woke up and leaped away from Rachel . . .'

'Yes?'

'I don't think they will. I don't think there'll be any affairs, not even puppy-love, between any of The Tribe as they grow up. They'll feel too much like brothers and sisters – you'll see. And I think it's the same between all the husbands and wives—'

'But I don't feel anyone's like a brother or sister to me here. Damn! I've dropped half my biscuit into the tea.'

'I don't mean that. I mean that the emotional cost of it, the bad blood it would cause, the upheaval to his or her life – to everyone's lives . . . it would all be just too awful.'

A delegation descended on the Brandons around eight o'clock that same Saturday. 'We want to know what *you* mean by *inner self*,' Willard said to Eric. 'And no pussyfooting about, now.'

'*Exactly* what you mean,' Nicole explained.

'Ah!' He folded the book he had been reading (*Prisoner of Grace* by Joyce Cary), clasped his hands together, made a steeple of his two index fingers, and dug it into his chin, just beneath his lower lip. 'There's more than a touch of Heisenberg's Uncertainty Principle involved here—'

'Just tell us,' Tony urged.

'Never mind all the fancy footwork,' Faith said.

'D'you want to know what I *mean* or the *meaning* of what I mean? It's not quite up to Heisenberg, I know, but give me time and we'll get there.'

'What's the difference?' Angela asked.

'For God's sake, don't take the bait!' Willard told her. Then, turning to Eric: 'The first one will do – what you mean.'

'Well, obviously, your inner self won't be identical to your outward self – because it would be like advertising that you're a monochrome, one-dimensional character. So it *could* be the exact opposite of your outward self. For instance, *your* inner self, Willard, could actually be quite a decent fellow! And Chuckles's inner self could be the sort of woman who's always looking for faults and criticizing everyone—'

'Stop being such a pompous ass and just answer the question!' Isabella shouted at him.

'See!' He was delighted. 'She's got the idea, already. She's so quick! But your inner self needn't be the opposite. It could be an *alternative* you – the you that got nipped in the bud when you came down in favour of . . . being an architect . . . marrying an architect . . . taking up sculpture . . . tape recording. Just decide which alternative-you never got a look-in after that. Or it could be a *frightening* you – the *you* you never *dared* to become but whose potential existence still haunts you . . . even thrills you – the public hangman . . . a criminal mastermind . . . a mistress of *Le Roi Soleil* . . . or – hold on to your hats! – *a Tory archbishop!*' He smiled around at them benignly. 'Or d'you think I'm being too restrictive?'

Angela repeated her question. 'What's the difference between all that and the *meaning* of all that?'

'I'm out of here,' Willard announced – then, to Angela: 'You'll regret asking that!'

Eric went on calmly: 'The meaning of what I mean involves a speaker – me – and a hearer – you. This dualism neatly links Descartes to present-day Positivists via Kierkegaard.'

'Thanks!' Angela followed Willard to the door. 'That's really all I wanted to know. See you at the Barn.'

'You see!' Isabella said triumphantly.

'Angela was taking revenge on Willard for shutting her up, my dear. I was but her humble instrument.'

'She shut you up, too, though!'

'Of course! It's like a game of Tag – *if* you can take the hint? What was that about "see you at the Barn"? Is her scandalous inner self taking over already?' he asked hopefully.

Tony said, 'We're all invited over to the old Tithe Barn for drinks. She must have assumed you'd already heard. Willard's flying to Stockholm tomorrow so he won't be coming. Marianne will, for a bit.'

'Before you lot go – do take a pew – what's all this about Chris and Felix and a Slade student up the spout? I don't want to put my foot in it.'

Tony, Nicole, and Faith exchanged awkward glances. 'Didn't you tell him?' Faith asked Isabella.

'No,' she replied calmly. 'He'd only go and put his foot in it.'

All eyes turned to Eric, who said, 'I fear that *in my ignorance* I might put my foot in it. By contrast, my darling Chuckles fears that *with my ignorance dispelled* I might put my foot in it. You know – something very strange happens to the science of Logic, just in this corner of the house. Isn't anyone going to enlighten me?'

'How much d'you know?' Faith asked.

'Only what I hear Chris and Julie screaming at each other through my studio ceiling.'

'Really?' The three of them leaned forward eagerly.

'The bugger knows more than we do,' Tony said.

'I gather that Chris enjoyed a bit on the side with some girl called Debbie, who's just done her Slade diploma show and she tried to get to Chris through Felix and then Angela got involved and worked out that if Debbie thinks she's got a bun in the oven it's more likely due to an hysterical insecurity rather than to an historical insemination – how'm I doing?'

'Spot on, mate,' Tony replied. 'What are they screaming about up there?'

'I'm more interested in what they're not screaming about – or not openly. It's layer upon layer and only the top one is verbal.'

'Here we go!' Isabella sighed. 'I'm off to do my nails if we're going out.'

Eric blew a kiss at her departing back. 'The bottom layer,' he said, 'is that Julie is establishing her supremacy over Chris once and for all. This is all non-verbal. She's now the alpha female, as zoologists call it, and he's the ex-alpha male up there and she's looking round for some way to consolidate her victory. She needs an audience.' He chuckled. 'We're not so very different from wolves, you know – which explains how we were able to hive off a wolf cline thirty/forty thousand years ago and turn them into dogs.' He looked at Faith. 'I was talking to Huxley about it after the last editorial meeting. Fascinating stuff. It seems that an alpha wolf will often let a lower-order male share the

den with his mate, the alpha female, as a sort of "uncle" to the
cubs. This uncle never mates with the alpha female. Never. And
it sometimes happens the other way round – the alpha female
permits an "Auntie" female into the den. Again with no hanky-
panky and how's-your-father. It's a way for the alphas to say,
"You lesser beings are no threat to me but you could have your
uses!" And that's what I'm hearing from upstairs.'

'What?' Tony, Nicole, and Faith looked at one another in
bewilderment.

Isabella came bounding back into the room. 'What's all that
nonsense?' she asked.

'In plain English . . .?' Faith urged.

'In plain English, the alpha female is telling her beta-mate
that she wants this Debbie girl, who will be very much a delta
female, to take up the spare room in their flat, since her parents
have cast her out in the snow.'

'It's June,' Isabella said.

'Which makes the snow quite metaphorical, darling. Personally,
I think the poor girl will be an epsilon semi-moron if she
accepts, but that's the lie of the land right now.'

'Is she crazy?' Tony asked.

The three women were less certain; something in Julie's
behaviour struck a chord with them.

'How d'you train a dog to stop chasing chickens?' Eric asked.
'You hang his latest carcass round his neck and keep it there as
a reminder of his crime, day and night, until it rots and falls
away. Debbie is to be that carcass around Chris's neck. Debbie,
demurely sleeping a foot away from him but in the next room
(touch her if you dare) . . . Debbie in man's pyjamas, slopping
along the corridor, her eyes full of sleep and her hair in rats-tails
(touch her if you dare) . . . Debbie's angelic little jaw and Cupid's
lips chomping Rice Krispies across the breakfast table (kiss them
if you dare) . . . she's going to be the purification and domes-
tication – not to say castration – of the dear old Chris we all
love and admire.' He looked down and, using a right-hand
fingernail, scraped nothing in particular from under his left
thumbnail, adding, as if to himself, 'Unless his friends rally round
and save him, of course.'

Saturday, 21 June 1952

The Sun King was an early arrival. 'Good God,' he said, 'what *are* you?' He knew *who* she was, of course.

'I'm the concubine – *the* concubine, please note – of an Ottoman sultan. What else? My one fear was that *you* would come as the Sultan himself, which would certainly have set the tongues wagging. So I'm relieved to see your wife as Marie Antoinette. Although,' she dug a finger into his expanding waistline, 'she shouldn't let you eat so much cake!'

'But,' he objected, 'you . . . a concubine? It's really the inner you?'

'Ve are all prostitoots now, Fogel. Actually, Madame Rowhani gave it me, last October in Istanbul.'

'Also,' said Alex, as Lawrence of Arabia, naturally, 'she has the legs for it. So why not? The same is true, by the way, of our Lady Lion Tamer in the fishnet stockings. I wonder if that whip is real?'

'There's one person who wouldn't dare doubt it.' Faith gestured toward the greenery-yallery Grosvenor-Street-Gallery foot-in-the-grave young man who was, figuratively, clinging to the tails of her frock coat. 'She has the whip hand there, by now.' And she went on to explain to the Fogels how Chris had been tamed by Julie, including the *coup de grâce*: taking in Debbie Kennedy as a lodger.

'Debbie's inner self,' Alex remarked, 'seems to be a National Hunt jockey.'

'One-all wouldn't you say?' Pierrot-Eric asked, picking up the conversational fag-end as he joined them. 'How will the Lion Tamer respond?'

Isabella's inner self, apparently, was Pierrette, in a very fetching creation, reminiscent of Balmain or Jacques Fath, which was why she had so uncharacteristically agreed without a murmur to Eric's suggestion of today's theme. Everyone saw the joke, of course, though no one could be certain that *she* did.

'How would *you* know whether or not she's a jockey?' Alex asked. 'Is this personal experience speaking?'

'Inside information.' Eric winked. 'Her cousin's a National Hunt jockey in Ireland. He's always worth a bob or two to win at Cheltenham, by the way. The course suits him.'

'Keep an eye on Felix today,' Angela begged Marianne. 'If you can actually see through those pince-nez, that is. What are you supposed to be?'

They were arranging smörgåsar on trays, ready to take down to the stands that Willard and Tony were even then putting up on the side lawn, in what was now a firm tradition of these Dower House midsummer events.

'Isn't it obvious? How did German schoolmarms dress before the war?'

'Before the *First* World War – like *that*. But is it the inner *you*? Really?'

'Sally always calls me "the schoolmarm of our partnership" because I'm to one who makes her tidy everything at the end of the day. And sees that the Rotring pens are refilled . . . and stuff like that. Dare I ask what you are?'

Angela looked down at her dress and laughed, with a tinge of embarrassment. 'It seemed such a good idea, but it hasn't exactly worked out the way I thought. My inner self is all the *sounds* of my life, from which I make my living.'

Her dress was made of tier upon tier of flounces, each with what looked like a randomly torn bottom edge. 'But they're not random at all,' she explained. 'Each one is a sound wave. These ones up here' – she passed a hand down over the bodice – 'are pure tones of an octave. This one's middle C—'

'A good thing it's where it is and not a bit lower down, or Eric would make some comment about it, I'm sure! Middle C? Oh, never mind. What are the lower ones, around the dress – they just look ragged?'

'They're all based on traces of sounds I recorded around the Dower House. This one's Alex's Bentley ticking over . . . and rooks in the bluebell wood . . . and the milk float delivering, the bottles clanking in the crate . . . and, oh, yes – this is Felix snoring, which he wouldn't believe until I recorded it.'

'Yes, I can see how it might have seemed a wonderful idea on paper!'

Angela grinned ruefully. 'Well, don't say any more about it.

I'm stuck with it now and so I'll just go through with it. Can I sneak one of these egg and caviar things? They're scrumptious.'

'As many as you want. Rationing and Willard do not coexist in the same universe, so there's plenty more.' She eyed her friend shrewdly. 'And why should I keep an eye on Felix today? It's too early for the seven-year itch, surely?'

'Well . . . don't let this go any further, but I had to talk him out of choosing an ss officer as his inner self!'

'What? Herre Gud!'

'I know. You could have knocked me down with a feather.'

'But why *that*? Of all things!'

Angela let out an explosive sigh. 'He . . . how did he explain it? It was so . . . such *Kvatsch*! He said he became so numbed in the KL that he could watch the guards beat another prisoner to death and feel absolutely nothing – not even relief that they hadn't picked on him. And he said it dawned on him that that sort of indifference was *exactly* what the guards must have felt. They didn't even seem to take pleasure in what they did. They, too, had no obvious feelings. So then he wondered how big a gulf really existed between him and them, and—'

'Oh, my God! Poor man!'

'I know. I know. He said that, with just a little nudge in the opposite direction when he was seventeen . . . eighteen . . . he could have been one of the guards himself. So he thinks that sort of potential must be still inside him somewhere.'

'But it's . . . *Kvatsch*, like you say.' She raised both hands in a gesture of exasperation. 'Seven years . . . and still . . . all that damage.'

Angela nodded. 'A different seven-year itch!'

'So what *is* his inner self now? What did you persuade him . . .?'

'A voyager. Ahazuerus, the Wandering Jew? The Flying Dutchman? Pilgrim? Some sort of wayfaring man, compelled never to rest while there are new discoveries to be made.'

'Well, well, well!' Marianne was impressed. 'Your idea?'

She shook her head. 'Eric's. I couldn't think of anything to shake Felix out of . . . well, it would have been a disaster.'

Marianne handed her a cheese-and-anchovy *smörgås*. 'D'you think these are OK? I thought the cheese on its own was a bit bland.' She chuckled. 'You know what Adam's inner self is – apparently?'

'What? Yeah, it tastes fine.'

'Sally told me. A Welsh Baptist preacher! He's wearing his old demob suit with the flies sewn together. And the trouser pockets. And he threatens to preach against anybody caught doing things they shouldn't in secret corners.'

Angela laughed. 'He's got a nerve! I wonder how many others will choose an inner self that is the exact opposite of their outer self?'

'Well, Nicole is coming as a *man*! Which is about as far as one could get from her *outer* self, I'd say.'

'Why? A man! Good Lord.'

'I suppose because there's no famous *woman* castaway on a desert island.'

'And what's so special about a desert island?' Angela asked.

'She says the attractions . . . it's all come about since they saw *The Admirable Crichton*. She says the attractions of a desert island occur to her a hundred times a day. I think it's a public hint to Tony, because they haven't had a real holiday for two years.'

'So what's *his* inner self? We should cover these – the flies are beginning to notice.'

They stacked the completed trays and threw a cheesecloth over them before returning to the final assortment.

'Tony's inner self?' Angela reminded Marianne.

'*Woman* Friday, of course! Willard says that when the officers put on a show for the other ranks, back in the days of AMGOT, Tony always strapped a pair of half-coconuts to his chest and put on a grass skirt and did a hula-hula dance. He says Tony was quite sexy but I'll believe that when I see it.' She lifted the tray. 'Hold up the cloth and I'll add this to the stack.'

A minute or so later there was a scream from the bathroom, where Angela had gone for a pee. Marianne came running, only to find her fully clothed in all her flounces, staring down at the long drive. 'What – or who – is *that*?' she asked.

Deep in the shadow of the limes that flanked the drive as it neared the house walked . . . a *skeleton*!

Marianne ran to fetch their binoculars. 'My God, it's Hilary!' she murmured, and then laughed. 'No one can be more literal than Hilary when she puts her mind to it.'

She passed the binoculars to Angela, who saw that it was, indeed, Hilary Lanyon, and now that she had emerged into the early afternoon sun, it was obvious why she had appeared to be a mere skeleton back there in the deep shade of the trees: she was dressed from head to toe in black: black sweater, black slacks, black socks, black gym shoes – onto which she had painted the bones of a skeleton – a complete front view on her front, including the front of her arms, and (as they saw when she turned to shout at Terence and the children to catch up) a complete rear view on her back, again including her arms. Her hair had been scooped up inside what, from this distance, looked like half an ostrich eggshell or a giant half ping-pong ball and she had Leichnered the elements of a skull upon her face.

'Trust her!' Angela murmured. 'What *is* one's inner self if it is not one's own skeleton, after all! I wonder what Terence has chosen for *his* inner self?'

Her question was answered almost at once, when Terence, leading Maynard and Diana and pushing six-month-old Karl in his pram, emerged from the shade of the trees. By parental edict, the children – almost all of whom wanted to come in last year's personae as Victorian waifs and strays – were dressed like the rest of The Tribe as members of those other tribes, the Lost Boys and the Faeries of *Peter Pan and Wendy*. Terence himself was dressed as . . .

'Some kind of eighteenth-century gentleman,' Marianne said in a puzzled tone.

'Adam Smith – isn't it obvious?' Terence told Willard. 'Who the hell are you?'

Willard took off his hat, a high-crown affair in the shape of a church spire. 'Crocketed finials,' he said, pointing out a few. 'Isn't it obvious?'

'Not to me.'

'The Houses of Parliament? This monogram?' He indicated the sandwich-board that adorned him, front and back, bearing an elaborate Gothick monogram of the letters:

AWNP

'Still no?' He replaced his hat.

'Still no, I'm afraid, old chap.'

'Augustus Welby Northmore Pugin! Really! The ignorance of some people high in government these days is appalling. Pugin provided the setting in which you guys make all those disastrous policy decisions.'

The hula-hula girl leaned forward and said in confidential tones, 'Between you, me, and the gatepost, man, Willard is as likely to develop crocketed finials on any of his buildings as I am likely to express milk from these coconuts.'

'Don't they scratch?' Terence asked.

'They do a bit. I'm going to the workshop when we've got this stall put up. Sand them down a bit more.'

'Sandpaper on breasts!' Willard shuddered and turned on Terence. 'And as for you – invoking the Great Adam Smith – have you no shame? You guys have even got the *Tories* thinking that nationalization is the only panacea for all ills.'

'You know what they say,' Terence answered lightly. 'If you laid all the economists in the world end-to-end, they'd still point in all directions. But if you want to be serious, only a fool would recommend a market-driven free-for-all these days – even to the Tories. You never travelled on troopships in the war, did you? British troopships.'

'Why?'

'Because below decks they were closer to hell than anything you ever heard a hellfire preacher describe. That's where British socialism finally took root and flourished among the hoi polloi who put crosses on ballot papers. Look – if I hold that for you, poor Tony can go and sandpaper his tits and you can knock a hole in the lawn. As I was saying – it's a British pandemic that has to run its course . . . burn itself out. Then Adam Smith will have his day once again. I'm keeping him good and warm, don't worry.'

'And meanwhile you'll go on pointing in all directions!'

'Oh, no! I point to the horrors that lie in the depths of the Marxist abyss – you have no idea how close to its edge some of them are.'

'There's Bruno,' Eric said a short while later. 'He managed to find his way, then.'

'To the man who found his way through Blake's poetry,' Faith remarked as they went to greet him, 'finding the Dower House would be a piece of cake. Especially as he's come by taxi. Bruno! You're very welcome.'

'Bruno!' Eric added, 'I suppose you got the invitation too late to devise an inner-self outfit?'

'But I am *wearing* my inner self!' Bronowski's eyes twinkled. 'In full view! I'm surprised that you of all people, Brandon, fail to spot it. I usually wear it inside, appropriately enough.' He touched the fountain pen clipped in his breast pocket.

'Your inner self is a *fountain pen*?' Eric asked.

That twinkle again. 'Pierrot must be a very *literal* character – as well as being a literary one. My inner self is the *ink inside my fountain pen*, of course. But I wasn't going to ruin a good suit to make that clear to the more slow-witted guests at your party.'

'Just ink?' Eric asked.

'Ah! But what may it *become*, you see? A word? A sketch? A blot? An incommensurable number?'

Faith turned on Eric. 'You really ought to know better by now. Come on, Bruno – let's see what treats Marianne and Nicole have for us this year.'

'Talking of treats,' Bronowski said as they crossed the lawns, making for the back of the house, 'you two missed a cornucopia after last Wednesday's meeting of the editorial board. Huxley started talking to James Fisher about the depletion of the human genetic pool because educated people are having smaller families than the *Lumpenproletariat* – not that he used those terms, exactly, but that's what he meant.'

'He's bent my ear on that theme a couple of times,' Eric said. 'He's trying to devise some sort of eugenics programme that doesn't awaken Nazi echoes. I'm going to suggest he should practice first on making water which doesn't feel wet.'

'James is broadly sympathetic, of course. It always amuses me how these old aristocrats of the intellect – once they get past their own procreative years – start devising schemes to curtail the potency of others.'

'Did you contribute a few pearls?' Faith asked.

'I pointed out that genius parents tended to have less-bright offspring while the sons and daughters of morons have higher IQs than their parents. It's a well-known statistical phenomenon called Regression to the Mean. But biologists seem to think they're excused mathematics.'

'It ought to be called *Progression* for morons,' Eric remarked, 'and *Regression* for geniuses.'

'Pay no attention to him, Bruno,' Faith advised. 'He's just miffed that he didn't spot your inner self at once. I, of course, saw it the moment you stepped out of the taxi and I realized straight away that you had only worked it out as you came up the Long Drive.'

'Did you paint the bones on the clothes yourself?' Sally asked; she was not so much her inner self as her earlier self – back in military uniform, in fact, in 'full mess undress' with the crown and three pips of a brigadier on her shoulders.

'Me? Paint like this?' Hilary craned her neck to admire, once again, the extremely lifelike skeleton that adorned her all-black outfit. 'Have a heart!' She tugged at her sleeve to straighten out the ulna and radius bones. 'Debbie did it.'

'Really?' Sally was suddenly showing a more-than-casual interest. 'Did you give her any reference?'

'Who to? I mean, what for? I wasn't *employing* her.'

'No, I mean reference material.'

'Ah. No, she didn't need any. She won some anatomy prize at the Slade – not that you'd know it from her paintings, mind. She showed me one. It's all paint dribbled down from the top of the canvas. Not a single line that's actually drawn.'

'And yet she can paint bones as realistically as this, just from memory!'

'Why this sudden interest, Sally?'

'Oh . . . well, not for myself personally, but last time I was at Enfield I heard they were looking for a medical illustrator. She'd probably think it beneath her dignity but it's a living wage – ten quid a week and meals while on duty. Would you tell her? Or would it be beneath the dignity of a brigadier?' She cocked an ear. 'That sounds like Rachel crying.'

Sally leaned toward the sound. 'Yes, that's my Rachel. It doesn't sound important.'

'And which part of the house do you live in, young lady?' the distinguished-looking old man asked.

'I don't,' Betty said. 'Not any more. We used to live in the oldest part – those windows up there – but then Mummy and

Daddy moved to Dormer Green. That one was my bedroom.' Her eyes lingered there.

'Ah! Now I *know* you don't live here. All the Dower House children seem to call their parents by their Christian names.'

'Well, it's no good standing crying in the garden and shouting "Mummy!" because there are nine mothers here and they'll all think there's only a one-in-nine chance it's them so you could howl until the cows come home.'

'You sound as if you wish you still lived here.'

'I do. And so does Charley. But Daddy says renting a house is a mug's game when you can pay the same money and end up owning it but Eric says that we probably don't own enough of our own house yet and when we do we'll pay Schedule A tax which is the same as rent so there's no difference.'

'Goodness gracious! The things you children know these days! What do you want to be when you grow up?'

'An architect like Sally and Marianne and come back here and live up there again in our flat. They could be very old by then and might be grateful for someone younger.'

He sat down beside her on the old car chassis, without – Betty noticed – bothering about the rust. She approved of him for that. 'D'you think being an architect is fun? I'm a journalist, you know, but I've had a lot of dealings with architects down the years. Did you go to the Festival of Britain?'

'Yes! I'll say! It was fun.'

'Well, I was the director for all that. I dealt with all those architects – but "fun" is not the first word that springs—'

'Did you meet Willard there?' She bit her lower lip, grinned, shrugged her shoulders, and added in a near whisper: 'He designed all the toilets there!'

The old man chuckled. 'I know. I was there when we offered him the contract. He was going to turn it down until he heard the size of the fee. But he's not my only connection with this place, you know. There's Faith Bullen-ffitch and Eric Brandon and—'

'Eric tells us funny stories when we walk to school and back.'

'I'm sure he does. D'you see that jolly man talking to that other man with a huge wig and silk britches?'

'That's Mister Fogel. He comes to every midsummer party. Faith works for him.'

'And so does Felix Breit. And Eric. And me, too, in a way. The jolly-looking man and I are advisors on all the books they publish. So I think you're quite right, young lady, to want to come back and live here. This house is a sort of powerhouse – you know about powerhouses where they generate electricity? Well, this old Dower House is like a powerhouse where they generate ideas. Keep in touch with it, eh? I must go now but I have really enjoyed our little talk. I didn't ask your name? I'm Gerald. Gerald Barry.'

'Betty Ferguson.'

Smiling self-consciously, they shook hands.

'The bestest tree! The bestest tree!' Sam and Hannah cried. 'Freddy's never been in the bestest tree.'

'Is that true, Freddy?' Felix bent low over him and peered deep into the little boy's eyes. Startled, he jerked his thumb from his mouth and shook his head slowly.

'Cat got your tongue?' Felix asked.

'He only talks scribble,' Hannah said impatiently.

'All the time,' Sam added. 'Come on!'

'All right. But you'll have to be very quiet when we get near the bestest tree because if he's asleep, I'm not going to wake him up – poor old fellow. He's soooo tired these days.' He laid his wide-brimmed hat and wanderer's staff aside, took Freddy on his shoulders, and gave a hand each to the other two.

Their mother ran to join them as they threaded their way through the creaking wrought-iron clapper gate, one at a time. 'Have they pestered you into doing this again?' she said. 'I'm so sorry. You two really are awful.'

Her accent surprised Felix – 'for two reasons,' as Bruno was wont to say: first, that it had modulated so far up the social scale since 1947; and second, that his own ear was now fine-tuned enough to notice it. 'I like your costume,' he said, trying not to stare too pointedly at the generous display of bosom . . . trying to focus instead on the outsize knitting needles and what looked like the start of a tricolor scarf. '*Une tricoteuse, peut être?*'

'*Mais oui!*' She laughed. 'I'd love to have heard the thud of all those precious royal heads falling in the basket. But then, I always was something of an idealist.'

'Freddy's never not been in the bestest tree,' Sam explained, tugging at her urgently.

'Ah!' Felix said. 'So we'll put just him inside it on his own this time, eh? You two have been there so often you must be bored to tears by now.'

'No!' they shrilled in unison.

They drew close to their goal. Felix held up a hand, put a finger to his lips, and leaned forward, listening toward the tree. After a while he assumed a deeply sorrowful, apologetic, sympathetic sort of face and whispered, 'Oh, children dear – I'm so sorry. He's managed to get off to sleep at last. We mustn't disturb him. It wouldn't be fair. He—'

'No!' the two elder ones cried in disappointment but he frowned and shushed them angrily, whispering fiercely, 'Do have a bit of sympathy! We'll tiptoe away and come back in an hour. Perhaps he'll be awake again by then.'

As they dragged their feet back the way they had come, Felix turned toward the tree and gave out the groan he always used for the tree's voice.

'Hurray! Hurray!' The three children barged past him and ran up to the tree. Hannah put her arms around its ancient trunk – or, actually, around about a fifth of its ancient trunk – and said, 'Thank you, Bestest Tree. We'll be very quick and then you can go back to sleep.'

Sam, now nine, was half-scornful, half-envious that, at seven, she could still hold this game in the shadowlands of her belief. And Freddy, Felix noticed, was watching his brother intently and copying every fleeting emotion in his face. 'Up you go!' He lifted them inside the tree, one by one, starting with Sam.

Then he went round the side, near the hole through which he projected his voice, and waited. And waited. May stood a little way off, leaning against the fence, watching him.

'Bestest Tree?' Sam ventured uncertainly.

Felix gave a little groan.

'How are you today?' Hannah asked. 'It's midsummer.'

'I'm soooo ooooold,' Felix moaned.

'Don't you like midsummer?' Sam asked.

'I've already lived through four hundred and seventy-two midsummers,' Felix wheezed. 'I can't get excited about one more. What's good about them, anyway?'

'Party! Party!'

'What's the bestest bit of the party?'

'The maypole!' the two elder children cried together. 'Betty and class seven are doing a maypole dance.'

Freddy began to cry – and it was a cry of fear, not of boredom.

'Oh, dear!' Felix groaned as May sprang forward to rescue her little boy. 'The sound of children crying . . . [yawn] . . . always makes me . . . [yawn] . . . so . . . [snore].'

When Freddy, who was lifted out first, of course, saw Felix leaning against the tree and speaking the last of his speech, he stopped crying and burst into laughter. All the same, he showed no inclination to return to the hollow heart of the tree.

'That sounds like the music for the maypole,' he told them when they were all out. 'You'd best cut along if you don't want to miss it.'

He and May set off at a more leisurely pace in their anarchic wake. To his surprise, she took his arm and slowed him even more. 'That was well done,' she murmured. He thought she meant his game with the children until she added, 'Getting rid of them so smartly.'

Was she aware she was rubbing her breast against his arm? He turned to look at her and was dismayed to see a tear rolling down her cheek. 'Oh . . . May . . .' he mumbled.

'Stupid!' She shook her head crossly and the tears fell away. 'I'm going to miss this place.'

'What d'you mean?'

'And I'm going to miss you, dear Felix, more than all the others.'

'You're going away?'

She nodded and sniffed back a noseful of tears. 'I don't want to. But Arthur's been offered a very good position with the BBC in Plymouth. We can't really say no. He's sorry to leave here, too, of course, but he's also got the satisfaction of this new job. I suppose I ought to feel more . . . I should be happy for him . . . but all I can think of is losing the Dower House and all our friends here.' The tears flowed again before she added, 'And you! I think you're a marvellous man and Angela and Pippin and Andrew are so lucky.'

'Well . . .! Um . . .' An unwelcome erection was starting to hamper his gait; in trousers it would have been safely confined but in the flowing, Bedouin-style sheet of The Wanderer, the horizontal waggle was embarrassingly obvious.

Fortunately, they had reached the narrow clapper-gate stile by now, so he was able to disengage and push her ahead. But . . . too late. As her arm fell to her side, her hand snaked back and closed gently round the tip of that awkward protrusion. Just for a second. Then, as he negotiated the stile, she let go, smiled at him over her shoulder, and said, '*À toute à l'heure,* eh? The cellar – round midnight.'

'One of the many mysteries connected with Blake,' Bronowski was saying to Chris as they edged their way over the big lawn toward the bonfire, 'is that, for an artist who rose so high in esteem not too long after his death, and who is still highly regarded today – indeed, today more than ever – he is not actually very good!'

'Didn't he sneer at the idea of drawing from nature?' Chris asked. 'There was something about if an artist couldn't see things more clearly in his mind's eye than in nature, he might as well pack it in.'

'He certainly said something very like that. But that was where he let himself down, you see. Brandon! Join us – we're discussing Blake-the-artist not Blake-the-poet.'

'Excellent!' Eric grinned. 'Could we sort-of-accidentally drift over near Willard? He says he greatly admires Blake but it's clear he has no idea what a fearful communist old Billy was.'

'We *were* being serious,' Chris informed him.

'Oops! Sorry. There's an excellent book on Blake, by the way – *A Man Without a Mask*. Have you read it? In my view (despite a lamentable confusion between defining and non-defining relative pronouns), it's the last word on Blake between now and the end of time. So anything I might contribute would be a poor distillation of that. Let's just listen and learn, because, dear Chris, we stand here in the shadow of its author.'

Bronowski stared at him evenly – an awkward long time – before murmuring, '*Timeo Danaos et dona ferentes!* I was about to say that Blake's inner eye – ha! The eye of *his inner self*! How appropriate to this day! It let him down constantly. His poetry called for Titans and mighty-muscled gods but his inner eye served up nothing more than some half-remembered hackwork

he did for *Grant's Cyclopedia* – engravings after Michelangelo
and Praxiteles and unknown Roman sculptors. He remembers
engraving a biceps by Michelangelo but he has no understanding
of the form and tension of a living muscle. So he gives us a
. . . a stocking stuffed with rolled-up tissue.'

'I was always afraid to say things like that at the Slade,' Chris
said. 'But it's the truth. I've seen better drawings in tattoo
parlours. Me, I'd go for Sam Palmer any day. Back in May when
the blossom was out, one night when the moon was full, I
walked all night round the bridle paths, up round Queen Hoo
. . . Bramfield . . . Tattle Hill . . . Thieves Lane to Hertingfordbury
. . . then back through Panshanger and all up the Maran valley
– just me and the owls – and it was like strolling through one
giant Sam Palmer all the way. I tell you – this is the most beautiful country anywhere.'

'But, on the other hand, Blake's poetry . . .?' Eric prompted.

'Ah!' Bronowski was off again, with an impish smile at Eric.
'No question. He was, indeed, one of the greatest poets in the
English language. In any language. To me it raises interesting
questions about the validity of the many arrangements by which
the arts are governed today. If Blake's genius as a poet was so
blind to his failings as a visual artist, how can we expect these
hybrid committees – one painter, one novelist, one orchestral
conductor, one theatre director, and so forth – to make fruitful
decisions about the state's patronage of all the arts? I don't yet
know where the solution lies, but—'

'The answer's clear,' Eric cut in. 'Ban all state patronage. If
any politician dares suggest throwing a penny of public money
at a living artist, hound him out of office. But give a hundred
per cent tax write-off to all private patrons.'

'Ah . . . gotta go. Sorry,' Chris cut in. 'I see Debbie . . . er
. . .' A vague gesture added nothing to the vagueness of his
words.

Bronowski fixed Eric with an accusing stare. 'I suspect you've
been reading Wyndham Lewis, eh, Brandon? *Time and Western
Man?*'

Eric conceded with a dip of his head. 'Or *Spice and West End
Women,* as Joyce renamed it. That was a right old ding-dong.
Funnily enough, I called at Lewis's house last month, in
Kensington Church Street. I wanted to offer to read to him a

couple of hours a week, because he's almost completely blind, you know. But there are two old harridans there who guard him like their own personal crown jewels. They just shooshed me off the threshold. Wouldn't let me near him.'

'How would you prevent the Duchamp or Dada effect?' Bronowski asked.

'Why prevent it? If Lady Docker wants to spend a small fortune on some artist who picks up a second-hand lavatory bowl and sells it to her as a piece of art for ten-thousand quid and she gets a ten-thousand-quid tax break, people would boo and hiss at her in the street.'

'With you to lead them!'

'Who else! And she'd soon stop doing it. But these anonymous back-room committees that hand out *hundreds* of thousands of taxpayers' money to artworks every bit as daft – they get away with it because no one knows who they are.'

'So the patrons would go for *safe* choices, eh? Before the war, Bristol City Council spent six thousand pounds on a safe choice – a history painting that showed John Cabot, a son of Bristol, embarking for Newfoundland. It is so bad that they dare not now exhibit it. Before the war they could have bought a Cézanne for the same money. I think that even the hybrid committee I mentioned would have chosen the Cézanne.'

'Food for thought, Bruno!' Eric gave his arm a squeeze. 'As always!'

'So tell me about this Dower House community of yours . . . this capitalist kibbutz, as Fogel calls it.'

Debbie passed her home-rolled to Chris, who took a deep drag, inhaled ecstatically, and passed it back. 'So what d'you think?' she asked.

'It's *commercial*,' he said.

'I know, but there's commercial and commercial. And there's the baby to think of.'

'You're not going to have a baby, pet. It's just . . . you'll see.' Last time he said 'hysterical' she had hysterics.

'I had a look at Bateman Artists in Soho but I couldn't work there. Now that *is* commercial art. They showed me the artwork for a car ad – shiny car, happy family, dog, stockbroker-Tudor house in the country, strong sunshine – and every one of those components had been done by a different artist. So-called. There was even one man – "our skiagrapher," they called him – who drew the outlines of all the shadows for the others to follow. He told me I'd be mad to work there. Either be mad or go mad, he said. I'd die from the inside outwards.' She took another drag and passed it to him again. 'But medical illustrator in a proper hospital – that would be *something.*'

Faith, who was passing at the time, paused. 'Did you say medical illustrator?'

Debbie explained.

So did Faith. 'We're doing dummies for a book on human anatomy at this very moment. For laymen, not doctors. We've got some artwork from a man who did the illustrations in the latest *Gray's Anatomy*. They're good, of course, but there's something airless and sterile about them. And he charges a small fortune. Would you like to try out – no promises, no strings?'

For reply, Debbie thrust the remaining half of her cigarette between Chris's lips and ran back into the house to fetch her anatomy sketchbook – and her anatomy prize certificate.

'Is that what I think it is?' Faith asked Chris.

He took another deep drag and passed it to her, crying, 'Whee!' He assumed an intentionally stupid grin and made his eyes vanish upward in their sockets.

'Is that your little farm down beyond the old pigsties?'

He became serious again at once. 'For God's sake!'

'You're all right. Nobody knows what it looks like, growing.'

'Except you, apparently.'

She pulled the corners of her lips into an imitation smile.

He looked right and left. 'Willard thought they were a different variety of comfrey when he saw them. I said, "Yeah, but obviously non-invasive." Anyway, it's well outside the walled garden, which is all he bothers about, really.'

Debbie returned with her treasures.

Faith flipped through the sketchbook, then trawled it more carefully, then called out: 'Wolf! Come and look – I think we've struck gold!'

Chris passed the butt back to Debbie for the last drag but she waved it away. He guessed that, mentally, she was already moving all her gear into a little bedsit in Camden Town or the Finchley Road, where she could say, 'Hampstead, actually.'

And, indeed, he could hardly wait for the day. As with all redheads her skin held a particular aroma – an enticing blend of cinnamon and honey but a thousand times more aphrodisiac, and it was driving him mad to have her around the flat and yet *not* have her.

Coming from double-British-summertime midnight into the gloom of the boiler room, Felix still had to pause to let his eyes adapt to the true dark down there. It was a moment or two before he could even see the outlines of the far door, which led into the cross-passage and the coal bunkers. He was here to tell May – in the nicest possible way – that it was no go. He didn't actually have the words yet, not quite, but they would come to him. He was sure of that. His erection had come and gone a dozen times over the past few hours but he wasn't going to let *that* rule his better judgement.

He was still hunting for words, the right words, when he heard someone approaching in the cross-passage. He was now dark adapted enough to skip across the room to the boiler without stumbling over the intervening litter. He was already opening the firedoor when the passage door was opened by . . . Adam!

Adam carrying a blanket.

'Felix!' he said jovially.

'I think this could do with a bit of stoking. Ah, there's the poker.' It sounded so fake but Adam was too bent on misdirections of his own to notice. 'Found this lying in the passage out there,' he said, arranging the blanket precisely where Felix had placed it earlier (and in a less determined frame of mind, of course). More, he was laying it down with, presumably, the same side showing and with one corner cocked up over the arm of the prototype chair. Felix, of course, hadn't noticed these details when he first threw it there – but Adam, the true professional, had. 'Well, on with the motley, then!' And off he went, dry-soaping his hands and whistling *The Rich Maharajah of Maggadore* (who, in the words of the song, *never learned how to do-oo the rumba*).

As the echoes died away, May drifted ghostlike into the boiler room. When she saw Felix she halted, just inside the door. 'I thought he was *you*,' she said, 'until it was too late. I'm sorry.'

Felix shut the firedoor and flipped the turnbuckle. 'I can't cope with this,' he told her.

'Give us a hug before you go?'

He shuffled awkwardly to her and she fell into his arms. The true conversation occurred between their bodies; that is, his erection did not revive and she sensed it and he knew she sensed it and so they parted on a wave of . . . mere warmth.

'It's really very good of you,' Bruno said.

'Oh . . . we couldn't let one of the choice and master spirits of this age doss down among hoi polloi,' Eric assured him. 'Besides, your earlier remark − that our little capitalist kibbutz could be a portent of the future for all − has nagged at me ever since. You see, I don't think we're nearly capitalist enough.'

'But that is *precisely* why this community may foreshadow the future. For two reasons—'

'No! Hear me out . . . please.'

'Why are you laughing − or trying not to?'

'Oh!' Eric lifted both hands in resignation. 'We have a joke at Manutius that at the end of your honeymoon you said to your wife, "I enjoyed that, my darling . . . for two reasons" . . . Anyway! Let me start by revealing that our rent here − our total rent for all eight families and five acres of garden − is just five-hundred-odd per *year*! It's even more ludicrous than the ludicrously subsidized rents they enjoy in Russia. And even though we divide it roughly in proportion to what would be the market value of each apartment, the rents only vary between seventy-odd at the most and twenty nine at the lowest − per year, remember. If we were out there in the real world, *each* of us would be paying at least five hundred a year for something much pokier than *this*! You could actually fit a council house inside this one room. So we all feel pretty equal.'

'But?'

'Yes − *but*! But one of these years the gravel company will have to face the fact that, having secured the right to tear the guts out of the old Panshanger estate, they are never, ever going to be allowed to extend their gravel pits to this side of the main road. When that penny drops, the second will follow − that the Dower House is worth far more to us than it ever will be to them. Between thirty and forty thou', I'd guess. And, of course, we'd snap it up!'

'Sitting tenants!'

'Exactly.'

Bruno chuckled. 'But that, of itself, won't turn you all into rabid capitalists!'

'What? When *my* apartment has a precise commercial value to *me*? And those bastards in the next-door apartment go on neglecting their bit the way we *all* benignly neglect the place now? Dragging down the value of mine? And of everyone else's? There will be divisions among us deep enough to lose a herd of elephants in. We will be as fissiparous as the most bourgeois street in upper-class suburbia. *But* . . .' Eric held up a magician's finger. 'There's more! Stir into that mix some twenty . . . twenty-five children! What people here haven't grasped yet is that the *children* make this community – not us. The Tribe, we call them. At the moment there are twenty-three of them – including three who moved away to the village. But ten years from now there'll be about twenty-nine . . . thirty. And a few years after that, they'll start flying the coop. The young of all species are – as you well know – nidifugous, and ours will be no exception. And as they go, they will take some of their spirit with them, leaving us, the founders as mere husks. Yes!' He leaned back with a contented sigh, swirling the brandy round and round in his balloon.

'You can be sure of this?' Bruno asked before turning to Isabella, who had sighed and kept her eyes on the ceiling throughout her husband's diatribe. 'What do you say?'

'I say he's talking utter nonsense,' she replied. 'But that's true almost all the time.'

Eric smiled. 'When they asked Groucho Marx what happened to Zeppo, he said they kept him on the payroll and showed him every script and if he laughed at a joke, they cut it out.' He waved a hand toward Isabella. 'Every family has one. So it's certain, you see.'

He imbibed the brandy by sniffing its fumes.

He leaned back and closed his eyes in ecstasy.

'The future of the Dower House Community,' he said, 'is – inevitably – fissiparous and nidifugous.'

nidifugous: flying from the nest as soon as capable of living independently.

fissiparous: divisive, tending to break into parts or factions.

Is Eric right to make this prophecy? Or was Faith closer to the mark when she told the Rowhanis in Istanbul that Eric only ever sees half of any truth – and always misses its essence?

You can follow the continuing fortunes of the Dower House community in the next volume: *Promises to Keep* – coming soon.

And if you're curious about the earlier history of this little powerhouse of a community – how Adam and Tony and (reluctantly) Willard, conceived the idea . . . how Willard almost lost Marianne . . . how Felix almost failed to join . . . how Faith became his mistress and then steered Angela his way . . . how Nicole would gladly have killed Marianne until . . . but no! The rest of that list, and much, much more, is lovingly detailed in the first of these Felix Breit novels: *The Dower House*.